Highest Praise for Gregg Olsen

The Girl in the Woods

"Frightening . . . A goose-bump read by a
very talented author. The characters are incredibly
real, causing each page to become a nail-biter, as
readers wonder who the killer could possibly be.
And as the last pages come to pass, the final revelation is truly unforgettable."
—*Suspense Magazine*

"Olsen weaves an intricate thriller that begins with a
missing girl and ends up in unexpected territory. The
characters of forensic pathologist Birdy Waterman
and her colleague Detective Kendall Stark are both
intriguing and compelling. The whodunit might be a
bit obvious, but the journey is still terrifying and the
writing is stellar. Readers will clamor for more stories
featuring Waterman and Stark."
—*RT Book Reviews,* **4 stars**

Fear Collector

"Thrills, chills, and absolute fear erupt in a story that
focuses on the evil Ted Bundy brought to society.
Readers will not see the twists and turns coming
and, even better, they'll get the shock of a lifetime.
This author has gone out of his way to make sure
this is a novel of true and utter fear!"
—*Suspense Magazine*

"Excellent, well written, fascinating . . . an engaging story that will captivate from the very start. Olsen has combined the power of fiction with the stark reality of fact. It's a book you'll not easily forget."
—**Kevin M. Sullivan, author of**
The Bundy Murders: A Comprehensive History

Closer Than Blood

"Olsen, a skilled true-crime writer and novelist, brings back Kitsap County sheriff's detective Kendall Stark in his fleet-footed novel *Closer Than Blood*."
—*The Seattle Times*

"A cat-and-mouse hunt for an individual who is motivated in equal parts by bloodlust and greed. . . . Olsen keeps his readers Velcroed to the edge of their seats from first page to last. . . . By far Olsen's best work to date."
—*Bookreporter.com*

Victim Six

"A rapid-fire page-turner."
—*The Seattle Times*

"Olsen knows how to write a terrifying story."
—*The Daily Vanguard*

"*Victim Six* is a bloody thriller with a nonstop, page-turning pace."
—*The Oregonian*

A Wicked Snow

"Real narrative drive, a great setup, a gruesome crime, fine characters."
—**Lee Child**

"A taut thriller."
—*Seattle Post-Intelligencer*

"Wickedly clever! A finely crafted, genuinely twisted tale of one mother's capacity for murder and one daughter's search for the truth."
—**Lisa Gardner**

"An irresistible page-turner."
—**Kevin O'Brien**

"Complex mystery, crackling authenticity . . . will keep fans of crime fiction hooked."
—*Publishers Weekly*

"Vivid, powerful, action-packed . . . a terrific, tense thriller that grips the reader."
—*Midwest Book Review*

"Tight plotting, nerve-wracking suspense, and a wonderful climax make this debut a winner."
—*Crimespree* **magazine**

"*A Wicked Snow*'s plot—about a CSI investigator who's repressed a horrific crime from her childhood until it comes back to haunt her—moves at a satisfyingly fast clip."
—*Seattle Times*

Books by GREGG OLSEN

FICTION

Water's Edge

Snow Creek

Lying Next to Me

The Weight
of Silence

The Last Thing
She Ever Did

The Sound of Rain

Just Try to Stop Me

Now That She's Gone

The Girl in the Woods

The Girl on the Run

The Boy
She Left Behind

Shocking True Story

Fear Collector

Betrayal

The Bone Box

Envy

Closer Than Blood

Victim Six

Heart of Ice

A Wicked Snow

A Cold Dark Place

NONFICTION

*If You Tell: A True Story of Murder, Family Secrets
and the Unbreakable Bond of Sisterhood*

*A Killing in Amish Country: Sex, Betrayal,
and a Cold-Blooded Murder*

*A Twisted Faith: A Minister's Obsession and
the Murder That Destroyed a Church*

*The Deep Dark: Disaster and Redemption
in America's Richest Silver Mine*

*Starvation Heights: A True Story of Murder and
Malice in the Woods of the Pacific Northwest*

*Cruel Deception: A Mother's Deadly Game,
a Prosecutor's Crusade for Justice*

*If Loving You Is Wrong: The Shocking True Story
of Mary Kay Letourneau*

*Abandoned Prayers: The Incredible True Story of Murder,
Obsession, and Amish Secrets*

*Bitter Almonds: The True Story of Mothers,
Daughters, and the Seattle Cyanide Murders*

*Bitch on Wheels: The True Story of Black Widow
Killer Sharon Nelson*

*If I Can't Have You: Susan Powell, Her Mysterious
Disappearance, and the Murder of Her Children*

A
WICKED
SNOW

GREGG
OLSEN

PINNACLE BOOKS
Kensington Publishing Corp.
www.kensingtonbooks.com

PINNACLE BOOKS are published by

Kensington Publishing Corp.
119 West 40th Street
New York, NY 10018

All Kensington titles, imprints, and distributed lines are available at special quantity discounts for bulk purchases for sales promotions, premiums, fund-raising, educational, or institutional use. Special book excerpts or customized printings can also be created to fit specific needs. For details, write or phone the office of the Kensington sales manager: Kensington Publishing Corp., 119 West 40th Street, New York, NY 10018, attn: Sales Department; phone 1-800-221-2647.

This book is a work of fiction. Names, characters, businesses, organizations, places, events, and incidents either are the product of the author's imagination or are used fictitiously. Any resemblance to actual persons, living or dead, events, or locales is entirely coincidental.

ISBN-13: 978-0-7860-4846-5
ISBN-10: 0-7860-4846-8

First printing: March 2007

12 11 10 9 8 7 6 5

Printed in the United States of America

Electronic edition:

ISBN-13: 978-0-7860-3658-5 (e-book)
ISBN-10: 0-7860-3658-3 (e-book)

For Susan and Michaela

On the Oregon farm she ran,
Claire Logan hatched a plan.
She told the men they'd better hurry,
"Come out West and we'll marry."
But just how many did she bury?
One, two, three, four . . .

—A jump-rope verse from the 1970s

Prologue

The girl remembered the snow and the evil that had come with it. She shuddered at the very idea of the velvety white shroud over a mountaintop—the drifts of cream around fence posts on the country lane of a Christmas card. For many, such images brought to mind the beauty of the winter season and the holidays that hang from a frosty bow. But not for her. It wasn't just the snow, of course. It was what came with it. Whenever she saw or felt the cold heart of winter, she thought of her mother.

A snow scene brought a thumping of her heart and the shadowy image of a woman in wine-colored coveralls and a navy-blue down-filled vest. Vapors formed a halo around the woman's head, though the girl knew the irony of the image. She knew it was her mother. And her mother was far from an angel in every way that could be imagined. The face, however, was blank in her memory. The girl was unsure what color eyes her mother had or if her nose was straight or slightly crooked like her own. She knew their coloring was the same, but nothing more. Nothing she could swear to. She had done a good job of trying to forget just what her mother looked like. She stopped wondering if, as she approached her mother's age, *she* looked like her. In her mind's eye, the girl's mother was bent over doing something in the snowy dark of a nighttime long ago. Pink bloomed on a white blanket. *What was it?* The girl allowed herself to try to peer into the space just beyond her mother's shoulder. She strained to see. She wanted to tap her, to get her attention. *Why are we doing this?* But no action, no words came. And then, the fleeting image evaporated like the smoke from a candle.

The girl would grow into a woman. She'd marry. She'd become a mother herself. Yet she'd hold everything inside. She'd tell no one. What happened could be squeezed from her brain only by the force of her considerable will. She alone could release it. Still, she took no chances. She'd live a life away from the snow that chilled her heart and brought tears to her eyes. She'd keep a house free of powdered sugar, white granular laundry detergent, and anything else that reminded her of the icy darkness that she fought so hard to forget. No snow globes from airport gift shops. No ski trips to Vail. Nothing to trip a memory from rearing its breathless visage and reminding her of what she knew she had to forget.

BEFORE IT PUT US ON the map, we were a county known for tight-grained lumber and the finest run of Chinook that the Northwest had ever seen. Our schools were good; our roadways safe. But a decade after the incident, we're left with a reputation that belies our hearts and our way of life. For Spruce County, this has gone on too long. It is time to bury this story and move on. We urge a "no" vote on the annexation of the Logan property for a possible public park and memorial.

—Editorial, *Spruce County Lumberman,* ten years after

BOOK ONE
REUNION

CHAPTER ONE

The sun cut over the jagged edge of the San Gabriel Mountains. Sharp and bright, its rays hacked through the haze from the millions who crawled to work on the hot, gummy freeways of the Los Angeles basin fifty-five miles away. Magenta clouds of bougainvillea softened the chain-link fences corralling the cinder-block homes lining Cabrillo Avenue, the busiest street into Santa Louisa. As Hannah Griffin drove to work on a sunny August morning, a newsman's voice droned on about the date being the anniversary of President Nixon's resignation. Even at that hour, Hannah was not the first to pull into the parking lot of the Santa Louisa County Courthouse where she had worked in the crime investigations unit for the past five and a half years. She guided the burgundy Volvo wagon into a spot east of a stand of eucalyptus that ran along the median. *Messy trees, ugly trees*, she thought. But when the temperature hit the ninety-degree mark as had been warned by the weatherman, shade would make a difference before the day was over. Hannah craned her neck and reached for a cardboard shield her husband had bought her to prevent the dashboard from cracking in the heat. On one side was a pair of cartoon sunglasses with eyebrows arched over the lenses. On the other, foot-tall letters: *Call 911! Emergency!*

Santa Louisa County was an hour and a half northeast of Los Angeles. It was a world away from California's most imitated and chided city. Santa Louisa, the county and the town that shared the same name, was nothing but a Southern California footnote. Santa Louisa's biggest industry was agriculture. Flower seeds grew in a zigzag afghan that gave the monotony of the landscape a Crayola jolt with strawflowers and bachelor's buttons. A welcome sign into town invited tourists to have a BLOOMING GOOD TIME. Hannah, her husband, Ethan, and their daughter, Amber, made the pilgrimage to the flower fields every spring. Amber looked like her father—at least Hannah thought so as she studied her profile. Amber's nose was a slight ski jump, like Ethan's. Her blond hair was wavy, as was Ethan's. Whenever Hannah told Ethan their daughter resembled him, he'd exaggerate a cringing reaction. It was, Hannah knew, an act. In reality, Ethan was very handsome, and if Amber looked like him, she'd grow up to be a good-looking woman. That spring, as in the others, the couple took turns snapping photographs of their eight-year-old, up to her waist in yellow and blue.

"I promise this'll be the last year," Hannah lied as she framed Amber in one more gorgeous exposure. Then a quick second shot, too.

Of course, there will always be a next year. Hannah

had an old *Life* magazine she had kept for years . . . the reason why it has followed her for two decades was not important, not now. In the back of the magazine there was a photo spread of a little girl posed in her father's fireman's uniform. Boots nearly swallow her stubby limbs; the helmet, an awning over her face. But as the years pass, the little girl grows into the uniform. By the end of the series, a pretty young woman stands next to her mother and father, helmet askew, grin as wide as the pages allowed. Hannah liked that kind of continuum. She'd always wanted that for Amber because it had eluded her.

Before getting out of her car, Hannah caught her reflection in the mirror. Her eyes were puffy, and she rubbed them with her forefinger. In her early thirties, she knew that popping out of bed after four hours' sleep exacted a price. And yet with her dark blond hair streaked by the California sun, freckles across the bridge of her nose, and enormous brown eyes, she was lovely even on a bad day. Even so, she thanked Max Factor for cover-up stick as she walked across the lot. Ted Ripperton, CSI lead, met her by the door.

"You're here early," he said, a paper coffee cup in hand.

"No more than any other day this summer. Make that this year," she said. "Glad you came in early yourself. I'm going to see Joanne Garcia this morning."

"She expecting you?" Ripp asked, tilting his coffee awkwardly to suck the nipple-lid for the last drop.

"We talked last night," Hannah answered. "At least, she *listened*." She unloaded her briefcase and spread out the Garcia case file. The forty-four-year-old investigator's eyes darted around the room, more indicative of a person who couldn't focus on a damn thing than a man who didn't have the skills to do so. Hannah had gone to county attorney Bill Gilliand twice to register complaints about Ripp's work—two times more than she had ought to have. Both complaints had been made in her first two weeks of service. She felt so foolish. She didn't know Ted Ripperton's wife's maiden name was Gilliand. Geneva Ripperton had been born Geneva *Gilliand*. Ripp's job was a family favor.

"I'm between things," he said. "You want me to go out to Taco Trench with you?"

"Her home is in Valle los Reyes," Hannah said, without giving Ripp the satisfaction of a glare.

He shrugged. "Well, they should raze the whole damn place."

"Not everyone marries well or is handed a good job."

"Don't go there, Hannah."

"Or you'll tell?" She let a beat pass. "You know I'm only kidding," Hannah lied as she studied the photo on the top of the file once more. A little girl's eyes stared from a Polaroid. Mimi Garcia was five. She had sullen hazel eyes.

"We're leaving at nine thirty," she said, taking off an earring and reaching over to the phone. That was her signal to Ripp that he was to leave. Thankfully, he took the hint. Hannah watched him turn down the hall to the little room where coffee was brewed and lunches consumed by the lab staff and a few of the clerks who hadn't learned that in the various legal professions everything is about association. Of course, Ripp didn't care about that. He had a job for as long as voters kept his brother-in-law in office. And for as long as Geneva put up with him. Hannah knew it was only a matter of time and he'd be a school crossing guard on the west side of town. Maybe he'd even end up in Valle los Reyes? *That*, she thought, *would be so sweet.*

Hannah took a Dr Pepper from the vending machine, a bad habit she'd started when a case kept her coming into the lab in the wee hours before Lotta Latte on Cabrillo opened its drive-thru window for the morning commute. Her eyes scanned the break room's notice board. A rental cabin at Big Bear beckoned, but the idea of the mountains chilled her so much she shuddered. A flyer for a cat that had been homeless had met with success. It had "*Thank You, Katie Marino*," scrawled across it. Hannah smiled, flipped the top on her soda can, and shuffled off to her cramped office. She was beat, but resolute. The Garcia case was just the kind she loved to work. It would suck her in like a whirlpool until justice was done. She had some calls to make and reports to scrutinize—the benefit of being promoted into a supervisory job that no one else had really wanted.

Before taking her chair, Hannah saw a small box atop her heaping pile of incoming mail. It was addressed to her, but with a middle name that caused her pulse to jack-hammer.

HANNAH LOGAN GRIFFIN

She tore at the brown wrapper with a nail file she retrieved from a tidy desk drawer. *Logan. No one called her that. No one knew.* Carefully, but quickly, she turned back the sealed edges of the box. A musty odor and a glimpse of dark, nearly winy, color startled her so much, that the container slipped from her hands and fell to the floor.

For a second, she could not take her eyes off the carton. She averted her gaze only long enough to glance through the narrow glass window that ran the full length of her office door and provided a view of the county crime laboratory. *Please, no one come in.* In one rapid movement, she swiveled her chair and picked up the brown wrapper that had enclosed the contents for shipping. The address was written in permanent marker in an odd combination of printed letters and cursive script. There was no return address. On the backside of the brown paper, Hannah could see that the sender had simply cut apart a grocery bag to cover the box for mailing. Red ink spelled out *S-a-f-e-w*. For a second, she wondered how the box could have been delivered to her desk in the first place. It could be anything, from anyone. Even a bomb.

But the instant she saw it, she knew. The package was not a bomb. It was something far worse.

Hannah brushed wisps of dark blond hair from her forehead. The office was warm, though she could hear the air conditioner hum through the overhead ducts. As tears rained from her eyes, she fumbled for a tissue. She blotted and then studied the tissue as though the tears had been blood.

The postmark indicated the package had come from Los Angeles. *Jesus Christ, L.A. was only the second largest city in the country.* Anyone could have dumped it into a bin and walked off to a job, a bus station, LAX. She felt the burning warning of bile rise in her throat, telling her to fight the urge to vomit, swallow hard, or look for a trash receptacle. Extending the tip of her shoe, Hannah peeled back the rest of the tissue concealing the contents of the box. She did so gingerly, the way one might gently kick a dead rattlesnake to ensure that the venomous reptile was no longer a threat. A swatch of black and brown caught her eye. Her stomach knotted. Her first glance had not misled her. *Dear Jesus, sweet Jesus.*

Just then Ted Ripperton pushed open the door and burst in, with all the grace of the interloper he was and always would be. Blank-eyed and reeking of cigarette smoke, he was oblivious to her tears.

"Ready?" he asked.

Hannah had barely caught her breath. "Don't you knock?"

Ripp made a face. "Don't you act like a bitch," he said. "*Kidding*," he added as quickly as he could, evidently recalling the time he'd been turned into Human Resources for saying something inappropriate to a surly file clerk. *Surly* was his adjective. "I mean, you look upset."

It was true the color had drained from her face, but Hannah shook off his half-baked attempt at compassion and gave him some slack. That cobra basket on her floor had scared the hell out of her, and she didn't wish to discuss it with the likes of Ted Ripperton.

"Let's go. I'm fine and you're stupid," she said, letting a beat pass before she returned the favor: *"Kidding."*

She reached for her briefcase, hoping that Ripp hadn't noticed her slightly trembling hands.

Berto and Joanne Garcia's mobile home was set amid the squalor of human-inhabited aluminum loaf pans called a "trailer-made community" by the owner/operator of the ten-acre tract that had once been a birdhouse gourd farm. Because the plant had readily reseeded, most of the hot boxes that residents called home were festooned with the bulbous gourds cut with portholes for swallows and, for the luckier, purple martins. It was flat land—the bottom of a broad valley. It had, at most, seven or eight palm trees to bring up the vertical space. They were the spindly kind of palms, each collared with aluminum bands to stop rats from nesting in their fernlike crowns.

Ripperton lurched his two-year-old Town Car in front of Space 22. They knew Joanne was home alone; Berto was a guest of the county—in jail on suspicion of child abuse.

"I'll go in first," Hannah said, swinging the passenger door open and brushing against a Big Wheel tricycle bleached to pale amber by the Santa Louisa summer.

Ripp pulled out a smoke. "I'll sit tight and play radio roulette. Better not be long."

As if his advice mattered. The fact was she wouldn't be long regardless of Ripperton's demands. Hannah wanted to interview Mrs. Garcia about her daughter and husband, and she knew if Mrs. Garcia was indeed ready to talk, Ripperton would be called inside anyway. He was as good a witness as she had to ensure the woman couldn't back out of her story later. He provided the kind of pressure they'd need to take her into the courtroom.

A woman met Hannah at the door. She peered through the wire mesh of a tattered screen and introduced herself as Joanne Garcia. She was thirty years old, unemployed, a few months pregnant. Mascara clumped at the tips of her spiky eyelashes. She pressed her face close to the aluminum doorframe and warily regarded her visitor.

"Mrs. Garcia, I'm Hannah Griffin. I'm with the county, here to investigate your daughter's case."

"Oh, Miss Griffin," Garcia said, pausing before muttering something that went nowhere. Her eyes traced Hannah from head to toe, lingering on a jade silk blouse and creamy white linen skirt that was the well-dressed CSI's summer uniform. Not that it mattered. Inside the confines of the lab, Hannah was shrouded with a dingy lab coat anyway.

"I don't think I have anything to say to you," Garcia finally said.

Hannah inched closer. "That surprises me," she said. "Yesterday you told me you had a lot to say. I understand that this is very, very difficult. But you know," she paused, "you—more than anyone—can ensure that what happened to Mimi never happens again."

Joanne Garcia's tongue ran over cracked lips. "Yeah, but—"

"Don't you realize that you are running out of options here? You have no choice but to do the right thing. I think you know that. Can I come in?"

Joanne Garcia hesitated as if she didn't want to say much, but Hannah knew the woman in the trailer wanted to spill her guts. She knew it from all of the child rapes, the molestations, the neglect and abuse cases—the "chick cases," as the jealous in the lab called them to demean her work. Guys like Ripp figured no case was worth working on unless it was murder with special circumstances—the grislier the better. Throw in a few sexual elements and they'd be in CSI nirvana, stomping around the lab like sand-kicking macho men.

"You're letting all the air conditioning out of the house. Come inside for a minute," Joanne said, flinging the screen open with her foot pressing against the metal spring that kept it shut. Light fell on her features with a blast of white. "Then you'll have to go."

Joanne wore a halter top with black-and-white cows printed on it, blue jean shorts that were doing battle with her fleshy thighs. Hannah didn't doubt that the fabric— that odd kind of denim that looks too thin to be the real thing—and the woman's increasing girth would be fighting to the finish. She led Hannah into an overloaded family room separated from the entry by a turned-knob room divider resembling Early American furniture. A spider plant spilled variegated green-and-white foliage over the salmon-colored laminate countertop. A shiny yellow Tonka truck positioned on a shelf served as magazine holder. Old issues of *Dirt Biker* filled the back end of the toy.

"Sit here," Joanne said, pointing to a pillow-strewn sofa. "But only for a minute. Like I said, I don't have anything to say."

Photos in Plexiglas frames lined a shelf behind the fake log fireplace that served as the focal point of the small room. Hannah recognized the face of the little girl with corkscrew pigtails. All of the photos were of Mimi.

"She's a very pretty girl," Hannah said. "How is she?"

Joanne made a face. It was a hard, angry visage, and it made her look older than her years. "How *should* she be? You've taken her from her home! Her father is in jail!"

The words were familiar to Hannah. A few said them with more conviction than Joanne Garcia did that morning in her mobile home. Some recited the words as though they'd rehearsed them in front of a mirror and knew that practiced indignation and outrage were but a small and necessary step in the direction toward a defense of some kind.

"How in the hell should she be? Her daddy didn't do nothin' and you've taken her away, lady!"

"To save her life."

Joanne's face was now blood red. "Her life didn't need saving. It was an accident."

"I'm sorry, but I don't think so. Listen to me very carefully," Hannah said, fixing her eyes on Joanne's. "Woman to woman, mother to mother—I am a mother, too—your daughter's life is in danger. Your job is to protect her."

Joanne stood and spun around, grabbing a photograph of her daughter.

"You don't know me, my husband, or anything about us." She punched her empty fist into the air and held the photo to her bosom.

Hannah felt her stomach flutter slightly as though the woman was going to hit her. Instead, Joanne started to cry and held out a picture of the little girl that had brought Santa Louisa criminal investigators into her life.

"She is all I have. All *we* have! Don't do this to us. Do not ruin this family. People like you are always trying to judge people like us."

She set the picture back on the top shelf of the room divider.

"We're not trying to ruin anything. We're trying to help you and your daughter."

"Right. Like I'm going to believe anything you say," she said. "Get the fuck out of my house! Now!"

Hannah let the front door swing open on its squeaky spring and returned to the car. Her heels clacked on the cracked and patched sidewalk.

"Handled that one real smooth, Hannah," Ripp said. His words dripped with his own brand of malevolent sarcasm. "Maybe I could coach you sometime?"

Hannah didn't want Ripp to know that she'd been un-nerved by the encounter in the trailer. She didn't want him to know what was really on her mind, what she had boxed up in her trunk. *Eat shit.* She didn't say the words, but she thought them. And she smiled back at him once more.

"Glad I got out of bed today," she muttered.

The Santa Louisa County sheriff had been dispatched to Mucho Muchachos Daycare Center on the south end of Valle los Reyes the day before. An employee there had in-dicated a little girl had showed evidence of abuse. It was reported around noon, though the telltale signs of abuse had been evident at six in the morning. Mimi Garcia's bottom had been hemorrhaging; a bloom of crimson had spotted her panties. The little girl paid it no mind, but a caregiver—a girl of seventeen named Nadine Myers—had noticed the bleeding when she served her breakfast snack.

"Did someone hurt you?" asked Nadine, a high school dropout with a smile that begged for braces and hands scarred from filing ragged edges while working in her fa-ther's sheet metal shop.

Mimi shook her head as she picked out the shriveled black fruits in the raisin bran growing soft in a pink Tup-perware bowl. Two other kids, a boy and a girl, both four, argued over the sugar bowl, and Nadine went to settle the dispute with promises of a frosted Pop-Tart.

A couple of hours later, Nadine was up to her neck in acrid disposable diapers when she returned to Mimi. She sat on the floor, Indian-style, crying. When Nadine pulled her to her feet, she revealed a small smudge of congealed blood.

"We have a problem with Mimi," she called over the din of the TV.

Fifteen minutes later, a uniformed deputy and a Child Protective Services worker arrived, and Mimi Garcia was off to the Valley Medical Center. She was the possible victim of abuse, possibly sexual.

Hannah and Ripp arrived at the day care center just before 4 p.m. to talk with Nadine Myers, but the young woman was of little help. Her ignorance/evasiveness made Hannah angry, and after a few rounds of pointless responses, Hannah turned it around and beat her up with the questions. At least they wouldn't leave any marks.

"If you were so worried about her, *worried enough to ask*, why didn't you report it to someone?"

Nadine narrowed her eyes defensively. Dry skin creased her tight little mouth.

"Excuse me," she said. "But if you had to report every little problem that comes in the front door every morning multiplied by twenty-eight kids, you'd find you were reporting every bump and bruise."

"But this wasn't just a bump, Nadine," Hannah said.

Nadine bristled. "What do you expect me to be, a doctor? God, I don't even make as much money as two of my friends who work at McDonald's."

"That's all for now," Hannah said. "We'll be in touch."

The girl seemed surprised. "Do you want my number or something?"

"No, thanks," Hannah said as they turned to leave. "We know where to find you."

"Did someone say McDonald's?" Ripp asked. "I could use a burger about now. Maybe we could pull a drive-thru on our way back to the office?"

A drive by, maybe, Hannah thought, but said, "All right. If you must."

"Need to gas up, too."

Hannah shook her head. "Do you mind if we hold off on that? I have to get back. I can't stop everywhere and you, you know, you need that burger."

The truth was the smell of any petroleum product could send Hannah to near retching. The lawn mower had to be electric, because a more powerful gas one sent off fumes that made her ill even if Ethan did the work, or later, when they could afford it, a gardener. Vicks Vapo-Rub made her sick. Forget pumping fuel at a service station. Hannah loved Oregon more than any state because it was one of the few that didn't force people to fuel up their own cars; in fact, a state law prohibited anyone from self-service. This, like so many of her phobias, came from that terrible Christmas Eve.

When they suffered a power outage earlier in their marriage, Ethan produced a kerosene lantern and Hannah nearly went berserk. She caught herself before her rant went too far—first it was a safety issue, then she said it would be more romantic if they burned candles or just sat alone in the dark. Ethan took her to be in a romantic mood, but as they made love, the images of that night played in her mind. And though sex with her husband was the last thing on her mind, she was grateful for the diversion, but felt guilty that the moment held no more for her than a way to try to forget that night.

CHAPTER TWO

Her car still smelling of Ripp's fast-food binge, it was after seven o'clock when Hannah returned to 1422 Loma Linda Avenue, the single-story stucco home she shared with her husband and daughter. It was a pretty little place with a thicket of bird-of-paradise by the front windows, twin date palms on the property line, and a sandbox made of old oil-soaked railroad ties that had somehow morphed into a cat box in the backyard.

A ten-year veteran of the Santa Louisa County P.D., Ethan Griffin had parked his police cruiser in the driveway, leaving the garage open for his wife. Ethan was thoughtful that way. He was loading the dishwasher when she came inside. French fries and ketchup marked two plates. Ethan had brown eyes and black hair that had just started to fleck silver. His mustache ("part of the uniform," he joked) was a bit of a problem. It turned somewhat skunk striped the year before, and rather than shave it off or live with the indication that, at forty-two, he was growing older, he dyed it black with one of the so-gradual-no-one-will-detect products.

"I promise you," he told Hannah then, "I'm not running out to a gym or a tanning spa. I don't have a girlfriend, and I don't really care how I look. I could live with a little padding in the middle. It isn't any of that. I just want to compete."

Hannah smiled and warned Ethan not to let the concoction foaming above his lip drip onto the linens she kept folded by the sink.

"Stains like murder," she had told him.

The Griffins had lived in the house on Loma Linda since Hannah's first pregnancy, which, sadly, had ended in a miscarriage at a devastating twenty-one weeks. Amber, now eight, was conceived the year after her sister, Annie, had died. Despite their seemingly all-involving careers as a cop and a CSI, they made plenty of time for Amber. The little girl was never overindulged, but neither did she go without. Hannah was not among the growing group of mothers who sought to make her daughter into a "better me," but she did want her child to have the opportunities that had eluded her.

Amber was engrossed in a television program when Hannah swooped down and pecked her on the top of the head. In her mind, Hannah repeated a phrase as she always did, *"I'm sending all my love to you."* Amber murmured approval, but kept her eyes glued on the screen. A moment later, having heard his wife come in, Ethan emerged from the kitchen.

"Hungry?" he asked.

"Not really. Ripp made a stop at McDonald's. I'm still dealing with the fumes." She rolled her eyes.

Ethan thought his wife looked pale. "You okay?" he asked.

"Tough day, I guess."

Ethan had heard about the Garcia mess over the week-end. Hannah, as always, was obsessed about nailing someone—the mother, the father—for the abuse of a child. The Garcia case was the most recent in a long line of cases that consumed her. She was tired; her eyelids hooded, and her smile was plastered on. Ethan served her a slice of pizza and a glass of wine.

"I just need to unwind," she finally said. She wanted to tell her husband about the special delivery someone had made to her office, about the box she carried in her car trunk. But she couldn't. The time didn't seem right. Amber needed to be tucked in and there was a chapter of *Oz* to read.

It wasn't that Ethan Griffin with his kind and expressive brown eyes and massive, prickly haired shoulders wasn't a smart man. He *was*. He'd advanced several rungs up the lad-der at the sheriff's office, and although no longer a *wunder-kind* once he hit his fortieth birthday, he was still seen by many around the department as an up-and-comer. But what Hannah loved most about her husband had nothing to do with his ability as a cop, his intellect, or his wit at a social service fund-raiser. It was that above all, Ethan was a passionate man when it came to his family. His wife and his daughter were his world, the only world he needed. She admired Ethan for his total devotion. Some-times she was even jealous of her husband's capacity to be so devoted. She was always on the run.

In part, Hannah chose Ethan for her husband and the father of her children because she knew his family history was built on love and stability, things that despite the valiant efforts of her aunt and uncle, she had lacked for much of her growing years. Even so, though Ethan knew nearly everything about her life, there were still things she felt unable to share. Some things, she felt, were not to be disclosed. She did not view her refusal to tell him everything a betrayal or unjust secrecy. It was solely an issue of personal privacy. If things got difficult for her to deal with on the inside, she could always keep Ethan at bay by telling him that it was a case that was eating at her like a battery-acid drip. Now, following the receipt of the box in her office, Hannah found herself using such subterfuge. She was jittery and laconic whenever Ethan inquired about her frayed nerves.

Ethan saw that Hannah was preoccupied. But, he told himself, it was the Garcia case. He'd felt the brunt of such frustration over the years—be it the case of a seventeen-year-old slashed with a box cutter and raped in the back of a bookmobile. Or the time Hannah broke her seemingly ceaseless string of sex cases with the prosecution of a man who walked into a dry cleaner and forced two of the women facedown on the pressing machine while he robbed them at gunpoint. He knew that when a certain case came along, the kind in which an advocate was needed to work the details and press for justice, she'd be gone. She was the only one in Santa Louisa County who could do it.

"I know the Garcia thing is getting to you," he told her as they slid under the covers. "Amber knows it, too."

"I'm fine," Hannah said. She kissed him and snuggled in his arms. For a second, she no longer seemed unsettled. She even appeared to relax. Hannah was somewhat adept at hiding her feelings. It came with practice.

This time Ethan wasn't buying it completely. "You don't look fine. You look like you've been drained. I'm half expecting that you're going to keel over from stress or something."

Hannah forced a slight smile. "You're more likely to go into cardiac arrest than I. Twenty-to-one chances I'd say."

"I'm worried, that's all."

"I know. Me, too."

CHAPTER THREE

Hannah could no longer wait. She threw on her favorite white terry bathrobe and, without slippers on her feet, went down the hall. She flipped on the coffee pot, and went out to her Volvo. It was not the Garcia case that brought her from a warm bed with her husband, though the abused little girl weighed heavily on her mind. The contents of the car trunk had been gnawing at her like a mosquito bite that wouldn't go away despite the pink crust of calamine that had been dabbed on to soothe it. It was *there*. It was outside, and tossing and turning and avoiding it wouldn't do a damn thing about getting it out of her thoughts. Though she doubted anything could wipe it from her mind, she knew confrontation was the answer. She moved quietly across the garage, opened the driver's door, and flipped the lever that released the trunk latch. Her breathing quickened. Beneath a Pendleton wool blanket she kept in the event that she was ever stranded on a chilly night, she found the box loosely wrapped in the grocery sack. She held it close to her thumping heart and returned to the kitchen.

The box sat on the table in front of her, and just as she'd done when it was delivered to her office, she fell back in time; the memories began flickering by. Even to think it was to conjure the worst images a brain had ever captured in the gray and pink folds of its tissue.

It was black, very black. And cold. The temperature had dipped well below freezing, a heavy layer of talc-like snow had tucked in all but the largest of the Douglas firs that marched up the mountain from the little house in the valley. Ice daggers hung from the corners of a farmhouse. A wisp of smoke, then a raging storm of fumes spiraled into the sky, then downward to the shed and the pump house to the carport. God had said never to forget, never to forgive. In the window, two little boys cowered in fear . . . the images flashed like old 8-mm film. Scratches of light cut through the images and in time, tears ran down her face.

"Hannah!" Ethan rushed into the kitchen, grabbing a hand towel off the oven door handle. A river of brown was flowing from the Krups coffeemaker down the face of the lower cabinets. He dropped a towel to the tile floor and it turned from white to brown.

"You forgot to put the pot under the filter," he said, his words slowed as he noticed his wife hadn't turned around despite the commotion.

"What's that?" he asked, moving closer and looking over her shoulder at the box.

Hannah remained mute. Her eyes were fastened on what was in front of her.

"What is it?" he repeated.

"Shoes," she finally answered. She looked up at Ethan and then back down at the table. She'd been crying. Her eyes were puffy and red. "I think they are Erik's and Danny's."

Ethan was astonished by the sight of the scorched boys' shoes. "Shit," he said, because no other word came.

Erik and Danny Logan were Hannah's little brothers and they had been dead far longer than they had ever lived. Even though their lives had been short, they had made their marks in ways that history's footnotes often are constructed—through stories told by friends, family members, and in a handful of photographs that had survived. They'd become legend (a pop group from the UK called "The Dead Boys" had a string of hits in the late '70s). But because of who his wife was, Ethan also knew what kind of boys they had been. Erik was somewhat bookish for a little boy; Danny was more of a cutup. Though the boys were twins, they were not identical in appearance at all. Most people who discussed the twins' role in the tragedy assumed they had been identical boys when, in fact, they were fraternal. Erik was fair like his sister and Danny was somewhat swarthy and dark eyed. The boys had just turned six when they left this earth for what their Aunt Leanna would call "their great reward in heaven." Leftover angel-food birthday cake from their party was still in the refrigerator when their young lives literally went up in smoke.

Hannah's attention stayed on the small shoes: Buster Brown oxfords. One pair had survived the fire better than the other; its laces were intact and its leather still showed hints of the oxblood color that had once covered the surface with a mirror-like luster.

"Jesus, Hannah," Ethan said. "*Those* can't be the boys' actual shoes?" He set the coffee-soaked towel in the sink and slid next to her.

"I think they are," she said. She cradled the pair with the intact laces. Inside was a notation made in ballpoint pen. It read: "JB/12/25."

Ethan put his arm around her.

"I don't know for sure," she continued. "I never saw them except for the times when Erik and Danny wore them. They look like their shoes . . . and the . . ." Her words fell flat. "They could be."

"Where in the hell did they come from?"

"Someone sent them to me. At the office." Her words came slowly.

"Who sent them?" Ethan asked again, rephrasing the question for which he most wanted the answer.

Hannah shook her head. She didn't know who or why. She thought she'd call Veronica Paine, the prosecutor who'd guided her through the courtroom so many years ago. "I'll ask her," she said, her characteristic resolve finally kicking in. "I need to know if these are from the evidence vault and, if so, who took them and sent them to me."

Ethan noticed the *Life* magazine that held the photo spread that inspired their annual photo of Amber in the flower fields was open to the story about "the incident." There was a photograph of a burned-out farmhouse, the skeletal remains of a family's life stuck in the mud and scattered across the black-and-white images. Smoldering rafters and floor joists jutted from an earth that had been soaked with water and melted snow. The headline read:

HOLIDAY OF HORROR: OREGON MURDER FARM DIES A SMOLDER-ING DEATH. A second photo, inset into the two-page bleed of the burned building, depicted a volunteer fireman. Stuck on the butt of his axe was a little boy's shoe.

"I think that's one of Danny's shoes," Hannah said as she took the magazine and placed it on the top of the refrigerator, out of view.

Ethan put his arms around his wife's shoulders. She seemed so small and very frail. She didn't make a sound, but she sobbed.

"There's something else," Hannah said, finally, pulling away and reaching for her purse. She unzipped a side pocket. "I got this from the receptionist handling the phones during the lunch hour." She held out a slip of pale pink paper folded in half.

Ethan fixed his eyes on Hannah and unfolded it. Across the top were the familiar words: WHILE YOU WERE OUT. Underneath were the date, Hannah's name, and a box with "Called" checked. The message was only two words, but they were heart stopping.

Your mom.

CHAPTER FOUR

Despite her worries, unfounded as she knew they had to be, Hannah Griffin was about to find out that hell had frozen over. And that was a good thing.

Ted Ripperton hadn't done anything right since 1993. And most of the observers in the Santa Louisa County Courthouse who were *not* related to him readily conceded as much. Ripp, with his leathery tan face and eyes popping from white rings of flesh left by tanning goggles, had his head so far up his ass that he needed a snorkel to breathe. At least most thought so. Hannah kept her opinions to herself, but she never defended him when others complained about his work ethic (as lax as could be), his personality (boorish and cocksure), even the way he dressed (Hush Puppies with black socks, khakis, white shirt, and a navy suit coat). Ripp was tolerated because he had to be. But a few days into the Garcia investigation he surprised them all, including Hannah. He stopped her in the hall on her way to the cluttered warren of cubicles and minuscule offices that were supposed to support the functions of the DA's office, but really kept people apart like eggs in too-tight cartons.

He held up a manila folder. "Did you know Mimi Garcia had a little brother?" he asked. Coffee rings on the folder and powder from a bakery donut on his navy sleeves indicated what he'd had for breakfast.

Hannah didn't know what he was talking about. Police interviews hadn't disclosed anything about a son. Her brown eyes fixed on the white goggle-rimmed eyes of the county's best, worst, and *only* full-time gumshoe.

"Here it is," he said. Ripperton handed over the file slowly as though he was passing it on to a co-conspirator. He looked around. "And that's not all. He's dead."

"Dead?"

"Yeah. Died of SIDS two and half years ago over in Landon. I found mention of it—I mean found mention of the *kid*—when I ran a DMV search on Berto Garcia. Came back that'd he'd been stopped for speeding and was cited for not having his son in a car seat."

"His son?" Hannah fanned the pages and set her purse on the floor. "Jesus," she said, "Joanne never said a word about a son." Her mind flashed to the Tonka truck on the room divider. Too new to be Berto's childhood relic; not played with enough to belong to Mimi. The toy, she thought, must have been the little boy's.

"Nope," Ripperton said, a smug smile now in place. He'd found something good and he knew it. "I guess she had reason to keep her mouth shut on that."

Of course she did. Hannah Griffin had worked another case at the beginning of her career with similar facts. A child had been beaten up and hospitalized with a broken collarbone. X-rays revealed a previous fracture of the tibia that had healed long before, despite the fact that it hadn't been set properly. The child survived, but further and long-overdue investigation by Hannah and her paralegal indicated he hadn't been the first to suffer in the household. It turned out that the child's older brother died three years before. Parents told friends and family members their son had died of SIDS. The hospital had been told the boy fell from a tree fort while playing in his backyard. No one—not the police, not the caseworker assigned to the family—bothered to check out the family's residence. They lived on a treeless lot. There was no fort. Besides, what parent would allow a three-year-old to play in a fort off the ground in the first place? Furthermore, a SIDS case involving a three-year-old?

The little boy's body was exhumed; charges were filed, and six months later, both parents were on paid vacations as guests of the California Department of Corrections.

Hannah sighed and read the report Ripp had given her. The little boy's name was Enrique Garcia.

"The mother says her son turned blue and she was unable to revive him. Father was at home and made the call for emergency aid. Both parents reported that such an incident had never occurred previously . . ."

Hannah felt her arms draw closer to her own body. More than anything in her job she hated the prospect of an exhumation. Plowing the earth for the remains of the dead made the bile rise into her throat.

"I'll get Judge Newell to issue the order," she said stiffly. "We're going to exhume Mimi Garcia's little brother."

By the end of the afternoon, Judge Bernice Newell lived up to her reputation as the DA's best friend in the judiciary. Judge Newell almost never turned down a request for a warrant. It was true she dotted the i's and crossed the t's, and could seldom be faulted. Lawyers for the defense despised her. She was hardly impartial. She had a statue of Lady Justice on her desk. Super-glued across its eyes were reading glasses instead of a blindfold. It was kitschy and jokey, but it spoke volumes.

Hannah Griffin didn't notice her as she left for the day. But a woman waited in the lobby of the Santa Louisa courthouse drinking a cup of black tea from a paper cup. She pushed her long, dark hair behind her ears and tapped her pointed shoes in time with the Muzak undulating over the marble floors. *A Helen Reddy song*, she thought. *Maybe Cher*? She smelled of White Shoulders perfume and spearmint gum. When Hannah walked by, the woman smiled and raised a hand as if to wave. But the friendliness of the gesture was not returned.

Hannah, of course, had no idea who she was. She had no idea of the hope the woman had for her. The hope that she'd bring her close to the one she'd loved and lost.

The next day before work, Hannah dropped Amber off at school, as she did nearly every morning at half past eight. She handed Amber a tissue from her purse as she drove.

"You missed a spot," Hannah said.

Amber had worked the entire evening on an oil pastel of a lioness and her cub; smudges of rust and tan colored the bottoms of her palms. Hannah handed her a Wet-Nap left from a drive-in chicken place. She kissed her daughter good-bye as she pulled up to the bus turnaround. A school crossing guard opened the passenger door to let the girl out.

"I love you," Hannah said with a warm smile.

In a habit she picked up from her mother, the eight-year-old rolled her eyes, more for the benefit of the crossing guard than any real statement of her affection for her mom.

"Love you, too," she said.

As she watched Amber run off, her pastel drawing fluttering in the morning breeze, Hannah felt satisfied about her daughter in a way that she knew she had missed for herself. She was safe, without fear, and she was loved. Later that afternoon, like all the others, Ethan would take a late lunch break from the precinct and pick up their daughter for dance class.

And Hannah Griffin, lab coat over her linen suit, would do what she hated more than just about anything in the world. She was going to peer inside the dead body of a child.

CHAPTER FIVE

The exhumation at Green Lawn Rest Memorial Park in nearby Landon was delayed from two to three that afternoon because another family was burying their grandfather six plots down from two-year-old Enrique Garcia's grave. Hannah arrived ten minutes late and parked by the chapel. The memorial park was a ten-acre emerald patch in the middle of an industrial compound adjacent to a ticky-tacky apartment complex that had sprung up around it. It was an old-fashioned cemetery with headstones that rose from the ground, instead of being flush mounted in that style the penny-pinching owners of such places prefer for easy mowing. A gentle breeze blew through the rows of granite markers. Crows called from the phone lines strung from the road to the apartments abutting the west side of the patch of green.

By the time Hannah joined the others gathered around the backhoe, Joanne Garcia had arrived. She bolted from her VW bug and ran toward the group of police officers, lawyers, and cemetery personnel. She didn't even take the keys from the ignition or shut the car door.

"You'll rot in hell for this," she yelled at a cop blocking her from the grave site. Her veins popped as expletives convulsed into tears.

"Why would she want to be here?" muttered Ripperton. "Why would any mother want to see her kid after he'd been planted for a couple of years?"

"Ripp, you've got to be kidding. Haven't you done this job long enough to know?" Hannah shot him a chilly look. "Because she's his mother."

Ripperton said nothing more. He smoked and kept his hand on his pager, as if holding it would make someone call and he could leave. There were a lot of things that could be said about Ted Ripperton. Strong-stomached, however, was not among them.

A yellow backhoe gently scooted a headstone affixed with Enrique Garcia's name and a faded photograph of a sweet, but somewhat sullen, little boy. Hannah stood close to the wound in the lawn as the wheelbarrow-sized claw peeled off the sod. A few feet down, the big machine backed away, and a couple of cops felt the top of the cement liner with their shovels. A half hour later, the tiny casket was chained and strapped in preparation for its removal from the hole.

"I want video," Hannah said, "every step of the way." An officer with an overly eager-to-please manner framed the scene with the camera lens as he ambled closer to the slash of soil.

"As long as I have juice in the battery, you'll have your video," he said.

The casket had been flocked with a pattern of daisies, but groundwater or runoff from the sprinklers had weakened the glue. Sheets of fabric hung like a little curtain around the grimy edges. The box dripped fluid as it hung in the air for ten minutes. The county arranged for a hearse to take Enrique Garcia's remains to the coroner's office in Santa Louisa, but it never showed. Instead, after scrambling about, a cemetery pickup truck was loaded with the box holding the boy's body. Hannah nodded to Ripp and walked to her car. A police escort blared sirens and flashed blue lights, and two hours after they arrived at the cemetery, they were gone.

Joanne Garcia yelled from the other side of the parking lot as Hannah got into her car. Her blue eyes flashed hatred and her mouth spewed vulgarities that had been absent from her exceedingly coarse vocabulary when they met at her mobile home. Joanne also looked older; her blond hair seemed white, almost gray.

"You have no fuckin' right to do this!" Joanne yelled. "You have no idea what you are doing!"

Hannah felt a jolt of adrenaline and looked over at the red-faced woman with the battered daughter in foster care and the dead son just plucked from the earth like a turnip.

"We have every right to do so. The judge's order says so. You're making this more difficult than it has to be—and it's damn difficult."

"How would you like to have your baby pulled from his rest with God? You don't know how this feels!"

Hannah shook her head. "But I do," she said quietly, more to herself than to Joanne as she clicked the shoulder harness of her seat belt. In a few moments, she turned to look, maybe even to say something, but the woman with the dead baby was out of view.

"I really do," she said once more inside her head.

An exhumation and the scientific, the *clinical*, procedures that follow it are nothing short of ghoulish. No one with a heart could say otherwise. The very idea of waking the dead with the scrape of a shovel is a revolting affair. No matter if it is part of one's job. No matter whether it is clinical. Ripperton made an excuse, and Hannah stood alone with medical examiner Lina Kent as she and her assistant, an Asian man with the singsong name of Ron Fong, went about the business that was Enrique Garcia. Halogen lights blasted the boy's little figure, a mummified body with sunken eyes and reptilian lips, drawn tightly in a peculiar smile. Body fluids had stained the shiny polyester fabric that had cushioned his lifeless frame. While M.E. Kent recorded each observation into a shoulder microphone, Fong, chomping on a mouthful of peppermints, snapped photographs with a Polaroid camera. Images spat out of the camera.

"Looking at the original autopsy report I see no mention of the crescent-shaped contusion on the subject's right forearm. . . . Ron, take a close-up, please."

The M.E., a sixty-ish woman with snowy hair and dimestore bifocals on a chain around her corrugated neck, stepped aside while Fong reloaded the camera and took three shots in rapid succession. Dr. Kent was so nonchalant about her request for the close-up that Hannah nearly missed its importance. She looked through the report. Nothing had been written about a crescent-shaped mark.

"What is it?" Hannah asked.

"Hard to say for sure," the M.E. said slowly. "But I'd be willing to bet a cup of coffee that it's a bite mark."

"There's no mention of any bite trauma," Hannah said, flipping through reports and stepping closer to the little body stretched and pinned out like a butterfly on a corkboard.

Dr. Kent looked at the clock with the red sweep second hand. They'd been picking apart Enrique's remains for two hours—longer than they thought they'd need, given the fact that he'd been autopsied before.

"So there's no mention of bite trauma," she said, repeating Hannah's remarks. "That's not really surprising. Dean Wallen was about the worst pathologist that ever made a Y incision on a cadaver." She tossed her latex gloves into an empty stainless-steel drum marked for hazardous waste. "Cases like this make me wonder how many more we'll have to dig up and review. Whenever something like this happens it invites more prisoners with half-good lawyers to call the evidence into question. I've done seven of these and I don't want to do any more."

"Retirement is next year," Fong reminded her.

"Six months," she said, pausing and adding with a smile, "and twelve days. Give me a calculator and I'll give you the hours and minutes."

While the M.E. and her young assistant refocused on the work at hand, Hannah stared at the body. She hadn't noticed it before in the blinding light of late summer's day, but the child's skin was covered with the milky white of mold spores that resembled baby powder, or a light dusting of snow. She felt a chill deep inside. The eyes had sunken into their sockets, but other than that he was remarkably preserved. Though the image was oddly sweet in its own peculiarly horrific way, Hannah felt her stomach churn. *The baby was a beautiful boy*, she thought. Beautiful, and stiff, like some waxy doll no one wanted anymore. Beads of sweat collected at her temples, though the room was kept on the cool side. Rather than touch her hands to her face, she turned her head to her shoulders and wiped the perspiration. And though the stench of death hung in the air, it wasn't the smell but the sight before her that gave her pause. It was familiar in its own cruel way.

Back in her office later that day, Dr. Kent phoned Hannah. Enrique Garcia had not only been bitten and bruised, but evidence found in his lung tissue indicated he had most likely drowned.

"Drowned?" Hannah asked.

"Yes. A wetting agent, some kind of soap residue, was present in the tox report."

"Soap?"

Dr. Kent paused a moment. "I'd say Mr. Bubble, if I had to guess without a full analysis. I've seen it before."

With her husband asleep, making the kind of muffled snores that had never irritated her until that night, Hannah grabbed her pillow and dragged her tired body to the sofa. *Couldn't sleep. So tired.* It ran around her head like a pinball in one of those old-school arcade machines Amber liked to play. The mantel clock chimed at one. She knew that in an hour the numbers would increase. There would be no sleep, only the wait for the chimes. She took the clock from above the fireplace and carried it to the kitchen, sliding the pocket door as she returned to the couch. *There*, she thought, *at least that will silence the clock.* She pulled a knit throw around her shoulders and slumped against the arm of the camelback. She scrunched up in a ball as the tears began to fall. She remembered the smoke, and like the flash of a camera an image of cedar boughs and piles of gilded pinecones came to her. She pressed her palms into her eyes to stop the images. And for a second, it worked. But when the images resumed, it was the box in the Safeway bag that came to her mind. She remembered unfolding the brown paper and lifting the lid to peer inside. She hadn't touched the contents, but had stared at two pairs of little shoes that nestled in the folds of tissue and packing peanuts.

She turned on the television. In a half hour she was able, somehow, to escape her memories. She heard the toilet flush and her husband's footsteps come down the hall. He turned on the light.

"Honey, are you all right?" Ethan stood over her in his Jockey shorts and T-shirt. His whisker-stubbled face was awash with concern.

"Can't sleep, that's all," she said quickly.

"Headache?" Ethan turned on the lamp, running past the brightest wattage back to the lowest light.

"A little," she said, flinching as the light took over the room. Her face was red and blotchy and her eyes puffy from her tears. She turned her head away, but it was too late.

Ethan moved closer. "Hannah, you've been crying." His words were full of concern. "What is it, honey? Is it Garcia?"

Hannah wanted to speak, but she couldn't. She felt a strange tightness in her throat that prevented her from saying anything. The thought of her speechlessness nearly caused her to smile, in that odd way people sometimes do when they are frightened or unsure, but her lips did not move. Ethan put his arms around her. He smelled of sleep, and his warm skin was comforting.

"Please talk to me," he said quietly as he held her.

"I can't," she finally answered. "Sometimes I feel as if I'm falling down some dark hole, deeper and deeper. I don't want to go, but I can feel myself being sucked in. Taken back to Rock Point and my family's tree farm." Tears started to fall again and she buried her face in his chest. "I feel so out of it. So alone."

"But you're not alone," he said tenderly. "You have us."

Her gaze shifted from her hands to her husband's face. His eyes glistened with emotion. "Sometimes I don't know what I have, Ethan. Sometimes I don't know who I am and where I've been—" She put her fingertips to his mouth to stifle him from speaking. "Before you say anything," she said, "I'll admit it sounds completely crazy and it could be, but it is the truth. So much has been said about my life, or my mother's, that I don't know what's real."

"None of that matters. You know what does."

With that, he took her by the hand and led her down the hall to Amber's room. He said nothing. He didn't have to. He didn't even point to emphasize the connection. Hannah knew it. The two slipped back under the covers of their antique pineapple-post bed and held each other close and kissed. As the early-morning sun crawled over the saw tooth of the mountains, Ethan and Hannah made love, and for at least a little while, she set aside what haunted her.

* * *

The glow of their closeness, their much-needed love-making, was shattered the next morning at the breakfast table. As Ethan ate a bagel that had seen better days, Hannah poured milk into a cereal bowl as their daughter dropped a bomb.

"I met a lady that knows your mommy," Amber said.

Hannah felt the blood drain from her face. She steadied herself and looked at Ethan. He, too, sat in stunned silence. Milk splashed on the floor, spraying the dark wood white. Hannah stared at it for a milli-second, then grabbed a paper towel. She thought she was going to vomit.

"You did?" Ethan asked. His tone was calm, but as a cop he was a pretty good actor when he needed to be. "What do you mean? You know that Mommy's mother is in heaven." He hated the euphemism, but at Amber's age it would be harder to explain that Grandma was in hell, or at least he *hoped* she was.

Hannah set the milk carton on the table, unspooled some paper towels, and spoke. "Tell us what happened. Was it at school?"

Amber knew her parents were upset, and a flicker of fear came over her face. Not because she knew exactly why she should be afraid, but empathy nevertheless set in. Something was wrong and she didn't know what, exactly, she had done. She didn't get in a car with some man with a sack of candy.

"We just talked. I didn't do anything."

"Honey," Hannah said. "No one's mad. Sorry. Just interested in learning more about the lady."

Amber looked satisfied. "Outside. Yesterday. The lady was walking her dog and came over when I was sidewalk-chalking with Maddie. She came over, we petted her dog, and she said she knew Mommy, and Mommy's mother. She said, you and Grandma were 'peas in a pod.' She was nice."

Hannah's stomach turned once more. She leaped to cruel conclusions, none of which she could voice or needed to voice at that moment. Ethan patted her arm and dismissed what Amber had just said.

"Must have been a mistake," he said. "Mommy never really knew her mother. Aunt Leanna raised her. You know that, Amber. Right?"

"Uh-huh," she said, clearly confused.

Hannah's memory loss wasn't a soap opera case of amnesia, the kind that is brought back with a bump on the head by the evil twin sister. It certainly wasn't the result of Alzheimer's or some other disease that steals the mind of the happy and sad times that make memories worth visiting. It had been a studied effort. One that she had accomplished on her own. Hannah never talked about anything from those days, especially once the nightmare became real. She shuttered the pictures in her mind so handily that when she needed to recall the face of her mother there was nothing there. A shadowy form. A face devoid of features. Not even a voice.

And now her little girl had forced her hand. She *needed* to remember.

"What did the lady look like, honey?"

"Just a lady. She was old, maybe forty or seventy."

Amber's ability to pinpoint age needed work.

"That's a big gap," Hannah said softly. "Did she have gray hair?"

She shook her head. "It was dark, but it didn't match her face."

Hannah looked at Amber quizzically; her daughter was untouched by the past and she wanted it to stay that way.

"Match her face?"

"I don't know. She had a grandma face, but *mom* hair."

Amber slid from the table to scurry for her backpack.

"Don't even think it," Ethan said.

Hannah pretended not to be bothered. "She must have heard wrong, because this isn't happening."

CHAPTER SIX

Amber had a loose tooth and Hannah was unable to take her eyes off it. She watched her daughter work the tiny tooth with her tongue at the dinner table and wiggle it with her fingertip in the car. It swung like a little white tombstone. When it finally fell and Amber ran to her, Amber held her hand out as if she were presenting the gift of all gifts. Most children think so. Most mothers agree.

But not Hannah Griffin.

"Those go under the pillow, honey. Better do it fast. You never know when the Tooth Fairy will show up."

"Sure I do. She comes at night. Don't you want to see my tooth?" Amber kept her hand outstretched.

"No, not now. You know how I feel. It will never be more beautiful than when it was in your mouth. You know, Mommy loved it most when it was part of your smile."

Amber smiled proudly, the empty space in her grin a black trap door.

"Go put it under your pillow, baby."

And so she did.

Ethan thought that for someone who had worked with the grisliest of evidence, had talked to the vilest of criminals, and had examined the most intimate areas of the human body with a microscope, a kid's tooth wouldn't or *couldn't* repulse.

"I can't play the Tooth Fairy," she said flatly. "Not now, not ever. And you know that. I have a thing about it. A phobia for which there's no name."

"Odontophobia," Ethan shot back, his dark brown eyes sparkling with the satisfaction of coming up with the perfect word. He smiled. He had trumped his wife, and that always felt good.

Hannah knew what he was doing and suppressed a smile.

"That's the *fear* of teeth. I'm just disgusted by teeth that have been excised from the human body."

"So you've said, but Jesus. It's just a tooth."

"Yeah, but they creep me out."

"Just a tooth. Don't you want to fetch it from under her pillow and leave a dollar tonight?"

Hannah refused. "I can't explain it. But nothing makes my stomach turn more than the idea—not even the sight of one—but the idea of a little piece of human enamel with a tail of bloody pulp."

"Just a little baby tooth."

"Just a *no*. You do it."

* * *

Veronica Paine was sixty-seven and retired from a long career on the bench, serving her last four years as a Supreme Court Justice in Salem, Oregon. She had expected to be carried out of the temple of justice on a stretcher as a very old lady, so consumed with being a part of the judiciary was she. But when breast cancer struck at age sixty-one and a radical mastectomy was the course of treatment, Paine decided that puttering around in her lilac and fern garden, and visiting with her seven grandchildren were too precious to miss. Besides, she told colleagues, she didn't have a taste for the legal profession anymore.

"Too political," she said. "I liked it better when I *thought* it was about right and wrong and not about how much money either side had."

She was watching the *Today* show and working the *New York Times* crossword puzzle when her phone rang. It was just after 8 a.m.

"Mrs. Paine?" The caller's tone was cautious. "*Judge* Paine?"

"Who's calling?" she demanded. Her voice had a kind of harsh, gravelly timbre that was intimidating, especially to defense lawyers. Judge Paine was not tentative in her words; she never had to be. She commanded a conversation just as she had once held dominion in her courtroom before a small lump took away her breast and her career and, with its own twist of irony, gave her back her life.

"Judge . . ." Again hesitation came from the voice. "This is Hannah Griffin."

Hannah knew her last name wouldn't bring any particular recognition. How could it? Before the retired judge could respond with irritation or confusion, she jumped back in with, "I used to be Hannah Logan."

There was a quiet gasp followed by silence, then a deep, husky-sounding breath.

"Is this a joke?" Paine asked.

"I wish. But this is very real."

"Our Hannah Logan? Claire's daughter?"

"Yes," she said.

"I don't believe it."

"I wish I wasn't, but I am."

A flood of questions followed and Hannah informed her that she was a criminal investigator, married to a wonderful man—a police officer. She told her about her daughter, Amber, and even about the baby she had lost. She was glad she had years of background to share. She was grateful because each detail kept her from the purpose of the call. She talked about her life in California and how she had never returned to Rock Point or Spruce County.

"Never saw a reason to," she said.

Judge Paine understood. She told Hannah she had hoped her life had turned out well.

"We all wished the best for you," she said. "We've— *I've*—thought of you often. It has been what? Eighteen, nineteen years?"

"Twenty this December," Hannah said. "We're coming up on twenty."

After a few more minutes of small talk about their lives, Rock Point, the fact that the younger woman had followed in the footsteps of the woman she had telephoned out of the blue that morning, Hannah explained she had something important to ask.

"What is it, dear?"

"I couldn't think of anyone else to call," Hannah said. "I need some help and I thought of you." She explained about the package she had received and what was inside. Judge Paine was stunned into silence, then anger hit. The very idea of someone picking at a scar healed so long ago was such a cruel prank.

"What is wrong with this world these days?" she asked. "Why on earth do some people feel compelled to engage in this kind of nonsensical harassment?"

"I don't know and that doesn't concern me right now. Two things do. Who sent the shoes to me and how did they get them? They look like the ones you might have used in court. They look very genuine."

Paine processed the information and remained resolute. "They can't be. That evidence is in a vault. No one can get in there . . . we bought the vault because of your—your *mother's*—case," she said. "You know, souvenir hunters and other ghouls who think they can make some money by selling stuff to the tabloids or some Japanese collector of criminal memorabilia."

"I guess," Hannah said, realizing for the first time there could be someone out there collecting artifacts from her mother's case. "They appear to be Erik's and Danny's," Hannah said, referring to the shoes. "They have your identification number written inside—in one shoe of both pairs. State's Exhibit Number 25."

Paine hated being wrong, and it was a good thing that she seldom was. "I can't imagine who would take something like that from the vault," she said, feeling for a cigarette and her silver-plated lighter, etched with her name and LAWYER OF THE YEAR. She rolled the flint-striking gear against the callused edge of her right thumb. The flame came and she drew on a cigarette, talking all the while.

"This breach of security is very troubling," she added.

"I'm concerned," Hannah said, "not so much because the evidence vault was violated, but that someone could find me after all these years. I thought I'd faded off the radar screen for good."

"I'll go down to the courthouse myself if I have to. I'll get to the bottom of this."

Hannah thanked the judge and gave her her office telephone number.

"Unfortunately, it isn't a direct line," she said. "Please don't tell anyone we spoke. If you miss me, don't leave a message, other than that you've called."

It felt very strange, very unsettling, to hear Veronica Paine say her mother's name. After all the notoriety, all the *infamy*, that had attached to her mother, the name *Claire Logan* seldom came from Hannah's own lips. It was curious and she knew it. God knew that *Claire Logan* had been a Jeopardy answer and a Trivial Pursuit question more than a time or two. Yet it was peculiar to hear "Claire Logan" uttered by someone who actually *knew* her. Hannah had certainly heard her mother's name mentioned countless times, but when others had spoken of her, she'd seemed a figment, a bedtime story, and a *ghost* story.

Most who knew Hannah assumed that she'd been orphaned as a little girl, which was only partially true. Her father had indeed died when she was in grade school. Her mother? That was the subject of great debate. Hannah wasn't quite sure.

Not an hour later, Hannah's phone rang. It was Judge Paine, and she sounded slightly unhinged.

"Hannah," she said, "I'm terribly sorry. This is very, very bad. I truly am at a loss for what has happened."

"Just what has happened?"

Paine chose her words carefully. "It turns out the evidence vault has indeed been compromised. Can you imagine that? It appears that some things are, in fact, missing." She sighed heavily, and air escaped her lungs like a balloon stuck with a railroad spike. "I really don't know what to say. This is very upsetting."

"What else is missing? And," Hannah said, before allowing a response, "who could have done this?"

Judge Paine admitted—*hated* to admit—she had no idea. No one she spoke to had a clue. The evidence review log, volume no. 4, was still in pristine condition. The Logan file hadn't been looked at for more than eighteen months when a criminology student from the University of Oregon came to review it for a term paper. The retired judge was insistent that the college student couldn't have taken the shoes.

"This girl was very nice. Very smart. She interviewed me and several other 'old timers'—even sent me a copy of the paper she wrote. Because of the sensitivity . . ." the judge continued, searching for words and drawing on a cigarette, "the magnitude of your mother's case, I think you should get the authorities involved. At least talk to *somebody*."

When she hung up, Hannah did so knowing that there was only one person to call, an FBI agent named Jeff Bauer.

CHAPTER SEVEN

Jeff Bauer used to think about the Claire Logan case every day. Every night, too. It was like a leaky faucet dripping incessantly in the night down some hallway laid out with razor blades and broken glass; he could do nothing but just keep coming after the irritating and omnipresent noise. *Got to shut it off.* Thoughts of the woman simply couldn't be extricated from his mind. They became a part of his every routine, from shaving in the morning (the white peaks of Gillette shaving foam sometimes reminded him of the snow banks) to eating an English muffin for breakfast (he'd had one that first morning on the case), it had always been there. For a time, whatever he did, wherever he went, Claire Logan was a kind of permanent memory tattoo. For a time, he marked his success on how many days had elapsed that he *hadn't* thought of her. After ten years, his personal best for staving off thoughts of Logan was a mere nine days. After nearly twenty years, a month or two would pass before she came to mind. The relationship (some thought "obsession" was a more accurate description) with a woman whom he'd never met had cost him, too. Though he disputed it, his fixation on the Logan case had helped ruin two marriages.

Some two-plus decades after Claire Logan became a part of his life, Special Agent Bauer was back in the Portland field office of the FBI following a five-year stint in Anchorage, Alaska. In Anchorage, the handsome six-footer with a rangy physique and ice-blue eyes had been the case agent in charge of a sting operation that resulted in the arrest of forty-four men and women who had smuggled stolen artwork and other antiquities from Russia to the United States. Most of the arrested were baggage handlers and ticket agents, though two had been top pilots with a major U.S. airline. It was a great assignment—the second best, he told reporters when he made the rounds, of his career. He threw himself into it with utter devotion. He earned a commendation from the Justice Department and a divorce petition from his second wife.

Two events had come together within a week of each other that brought forth a torrent of memories. The first was a brief letter and a notice sent by officials at the Oregon Bureau of Prisons and Rehabilitation Facilities and the state's star prisoner. The second was a phone call.

The notice was for a parole hearing for Marcus Wheaton, the sole individual convicted in the Logan tragedy. The hearing would be a formality and would end with the former handyman's release. He'd earned more good time than any man in the history of the state, but because of his crime—and its notoriety—he'd been passed by a dozen times. State law would not permit incarceration a single day beyond his twenty-year sentence.

Bauer wouldn't have bothered much with the notice if a message from Wheaton himself hadn't accompanied it.

Dear Mr. Bauer:

Soon the state will set me free. My lawyer tells me there is no possibility that I can be held beyond my sentence, despite the debate raging in Salem. I plan on disappearing and living the rest of my days away from the spectacle that has become my existence here in prison. Before I can do that, I need to exorcise the ghosts of the past. Maybe you do, too. I know things. I do.

In our Savior's arms,
Marcus James Wheaton

The debate to which Wheaton had referred was a hastily crafted resolution that a legislator from southern Oregon had pushed before colleagues and media at the state capitol earlier in the year. The representative was a known publicity seeker, a woman who piously harangued against violent crime and was swept into office three terms prior as "a mom who cares." Fading into the crowd of lawmakers was not to her liking and every once in a while she climbed back onto her soapbox. She had sought the spotlight by attempting to bar Wheaton from release by applying present-day sentencing standards for his crime. No one thought it would go anywhere, and in the end, it didn't. Justice, no matter how unfairly administered, cannot easily be rewritten.

At five minutes past nine, Bauer set down his coffee and reached to stop the ringing of the phone on his desk.

"Bauer here," he said.

"Special Agent Jeff Bauer?" The husky voice of a woman was somewhat familiar.

"You're talking to him," he said.

"I wasn't sure I'd be able to reach you so early. This goes under the heading of what I guess we used to call a blast from the past, Agent Bauer. This is Veronica Paine. We need to talk."

"*Judge* Paine?" He asked, though he knew there could be only one—the one he'd once called "Veronica Paine-in-the-ass."

"Retired, thankfully," she answered, letting a touch of levity break the tenseness of her voice. They extended a few pleasantries, though no mention was made of the investigation and trial that had given them their connection for life. Paine told the federal cop that she'd followed his career and congratulated him on the sting in Alaska. He returned a similar favor by telling her how happy he had been when she'd been appointed to the bench.

Paine told Bauer that her husband had died following an afternoon of pruning the apple trees they'd espaliered along a fence. They had been blessed with two daughters, both of whom were living in southern California. Bauer shared nothing of a personal nature. He didn't really have anything to say. His marriages had gone belly-up and neither of his wives had given him any children. At divorce time, buddies at the Bureau had told him he was lucky to be without the burden of child support payments. He went along with their congratulations, but deep down, he was as sorry as a man could be.

Then it was the judge's turn once more. She told him of the call from Hannah Griffin.

"Hannah?" he asked. "*Our* Hannah?"

"Yes," she said, "Claire Logan's daughter. *Our* Hannah."

She went on to tell him Hannah had been the recipient of some evidence that had been stolen from the Spruce County property vault.

"Her brothers' shoes," she said. "Exhibit Number 25."

Bauer tilted his head toward the phone and held his chin with his free hand. He sank into his chair like a melted chocolate. "Jesus," he said, "why would anyone want to do something like that?"

"Because people are basically fuckheads," Paine answered. The coarseness of her language seemed appropriate; though he'd never heard a woman, a judge of all people, say the term *fuckhead*.

"Speaking of which," Bauer said, "Marcus Wheaton's getting out of prison soon."

Paine let out a loud sigh. "So I heard. I doubt it, but anything's possible these days."

"I got a note from him. Says he's willing to talk. He wants to tell us what we've always wanted to know. Or so he says."

Paine lit a cigarette. Bauer could hear her suck the smoke deep into her lungs.

"He's had plenty of time to think of a story. I wouldn't bank on him saying much, other than he loved Claire and blah, blah, blah . . . she done him wrong, like some crying-in-your-beer country song."

"I guess so," Bauer said. "But I'm going anyhow. I still like Willie Nelson. By the way, did Hannah say if there was a note?"

"She didn't. And I didn't ask. Should have, I know. I was just so startled to hear from her and so angry that someone would dredge up the past and shove it on her doorstep in such a cruel, outlandish way."

"Like a fuckhead," he said.

"You got that right."

Paine declined Bauer's request for Hannah's contact information.

"She's started a new life and she can contact you if she wants to," she said. "I know that you can find her if you wanted, anyway. But don't. Stay away from your databases. Let her come to you."

The house on Loma Linda should have been quiet at that hour. It should have been still as the warm summer night. At 2 a.m., the sprinklers hissed outside in the backyard, kicked on by a timer that ensured the Korean grass would never scorch to brown. Amber's guppy tank sent a pool of light across the hall. Aunt Leanna's Seth Thomas ticked the hours like a bomb. Ethan snored softly, oblivious to Hannah's unhinged torment. She pressed her face against a pillow, trying to suppress the recollections that were coming after her in a nightmare that had been absent for years. It was no use. She shivered. It was cold. Even awake, she could still see the nightmare. The woman in the coveralls was there. The woman—a nearly gauzy figure, though Hannah knew it was her mother—wore coveralls that were not blue. They were wine colored, she had long thought as the ephemeral memory took shape. She bent closer to the figure she saw in her mind's eye. The fabric was blue, mottled with splashes of red, a color that her brain had blurred and processed and whirled into a reddish hue. Hannah knew why it was that color and the realization nearly stopped her heart. As if she could control the memory, she focused on the vest. It had been slashed somehow and was leaking bits of white fluff, floating above her mother's head, mixing with a light snowfall.

A voice called out. It was a harsh, but controlled whisper. It came from the faceless woman in the coveralls.

"Now that you're here, Hannah, you might as well be helpful. Get a shovel."

The girl of Hannah's memory did as she had been taught. She obeyed the strident command without hesitation. Mechanically, she spun around, ran across the snow, and returned from the potting barn. Her fingers froze around the staff of a shovel. She stepped closer to her mother, noticing for the first time that they were standing in front of an open trench.

"Are you going to help me? Start filling it in."

In her jagged memory, Hannah tried to see what was in the trench, dirt falling from the shovel onto something in the dark of a deep hole. Something gleamed. As dirt fell, the movement sent light to brass buttons. But it was more than that. The figure in the hole stirred slightly.

The man in the hole was still alive, maybe barely so. But his chest heaved. Hannah could not see his face. Her mother had already covered it in a white powder.

"Hurry up," she said, her tone decidedly impatient. Not unnerved at what they were doing. Just annoyed that Hannah wasn't doing what needed to be done.

"I have a mess to clean up tonight and three pies to bake in the morning."

The red of blood oozed and bloomed against the snow.

Hannah broke down and cried into her pillow. She had *helped* her mother. She had done so without question. But that wasn't the worst of it. And deep down, she was sure that God would never forgive her for what she had done.

Hannah sat up with a start. The nightmare was bad enough, but it wasn't what woke her. A pair of headlights glowed from behind the blinds, splintering the light like a moonlit picket fence. She could barely breathe. Just as she was about to rouse Ethan, the lights dimmed slightly as the driver pressed the accelerator and drove off into the California night.

CHAPTER EIGHT

From a grimy window that needed a dousing of sudsy water and a squeegee, Hannah watched the sun shine against the backlit trees on the eastern side of the parking lot. Had the car she'd seen outside her window been a terrible dream? Had she only heard what her mind wanted to tease her with? Her eyes were slightly puffy and underscored by the dark circles of a sleepless night. She'd looked better; much better, and she knew it. She could hear a puffed-up, self-satisfied Ted Ripperton in the hallway talking about the Garcia case and how he was going to "nail that bitch for killing her son." She shut her door and went to her desk. In front of her were photographs of tragedy and love. Pictures of Enrique Garcia taken at the autopsy were blurry Polaroids of the unspeakable tragedy of abuse and possible murder of a child; framed snapshots of Ethan and Amber occupied another corner. Her husband and daughter smiled in a way she doubted Enrique or his sister, Mimi, could have ever experienced—carefree, *worry-free*. Her husband and daughter wore smiles that indicated they had been enveloped in uncompromising love.

At a few minutes before 10 a.m., Hannah answered Paine's call from Spruce County.

"Oh," was all she could manage when the former prosecutor confirmed that the shoes more than likely were genuine.

"I'm sorry," Judge Paine said. "And I'm worried."

"It's some prank, isn't it?" Hannah asked.

The judge didn't know. "It well could be, but I think it would be foolish to treat it as such. Hannah," she said haltingly, "I contacted Jeff Bauer. I didn't tell him where you are. But I told him I'd tell you where he is."

"Portland," Hannah said.

"Why, yes. How did you know?"

"I read it somewhere," Hannah said. She didn't want to say that she'd tracked Bauer's career for years. She'd never let go of him because he'd done so much for her. "How is he?" she asked.

"Fine, I suppose," Paine said. "He's concerned. He wants to help. I think you should call him. Here's the number."

Hannah pretended to take it down; on the "B" page of her address book, where she'd written it years ago. Just in case. Paine promised to do a little more digging at Spruce County, but she was unsure how much she could really find out.

"It's been a while since I've busted heads over there. You don't know it when you're building them, but reputations fade, my dear," she said somewhat ruefully. "My name used to invoke the fear of God, or at least a few hours in the cooler for contempt. Now, I can't even get the cleaning lady to do my refrigerator once a week."

"My mother's name still holds a lot of power," Hannah muttered before she thanked Paine and said good-bye.

Hannah considered calling Ethan to let him know what the judge had said, but she knew he'd want her to "take the ball and run the rest of the way." Ethan was the type to use a sports metaphor for nearly every occasion. Instead, she dialed the Portland field office of the FBI and asked for Special Agent Bauer. Her stomach twisted and she pressed her hand against her abdomen to stifle the pangs of anxiety. She pulled off an earring and pressed the phone against her ear. After a minute that ticked like an hour, a somewhat familiar voice got on the line. While Bauer's voice had deepened with age, his manner was still compassionate. For an instant, Hannah let herself feel safe.

"Hannah, is it really you? Are you okay?" he asked.

"Yes, Mr. Bauer. It's me." Hannah shifted in her office chair. "Once again, it's me, a little angry and a little bewildered." She kept her confident tone; at least she imagined that she kept it. So many thoughts were racing through her, it was very difficult. She didn't want Bauer to think she was weak, not when he'd done so much to ensure that she'd be strong. And safe.

"It has been a long time," he said. "You're never outside of my thoughts. I hope you know that."

"I try to forget, but if I succeeded, I'd forget the good that came of this. Most of that good came from you."

Bauer didn't know what to say. He'd been an FBI agent for more than twenty-two years and he'd never been touched so deeply.

They talked a bit more. She told him that she was a

CSI, was married, and had a daughter. She had worked hard, despite a media machine hungry for every detail, to remain out of the spotlight. Her life was her own and she wasn't about to be plucked from obscurity by someone playing games with her past.

"My husband's a cop," she said. "No shrink needs to tell me why, but that's what he was when I fell in love with him."

Bauer asked about the shoes, and Hannah described their condition, the grocery bag packaging, and how it came to be delivered to her. She also indicated she'd saved the packaging.

"In case you want to test it for DNA," she said.

When Bauer dug for her thoughts on why the shoes had been sent to her, Hannah drew a blank. She couldn't imagine what possessed someone to do such a thing, nor could she figure out how she could have been found in the first place. Her name had vanished from the pages of newspapers and magazines at least a dozen years ago.

"I've made my life a disappearing act," she said.

"Only one person's done it better," he said, an obvious reference to her mother. Hannah let the remark pass, knowing the two of them shared more than a history. They both believed that Claire Logan, the female boogey man, the woman whose name had been used by parents threatening their children when they didn't take out the garbage or pull all the weeds from the garden, was alive. She was out there somewhere. Maybe she was frightened that one day she'd be discovered. Maybe not. Maybe she didn't give a flying fuck about anyone, even now.

"Anything else but the package of shoes? Anything out of the ordinary happening down there?" Bauer asked.

"I'm not sure," Hannah said, hesitating slightly. "I didn't

tell Judge Paine. I haven't told anyone. Not even my husband. But I have received a number of hang-up calls over the past month. Maybe a half dozen or so. I started keeping a log in my date book."

"Anything said? Anything to indicate any calls were associated with your mother's case?"

Silence fell for a moment. "Only one got through. The receptionist gave me a message memo that a call came from my mother. It was out of the blue. Just like that. *Your mother called.* I didn't say anything at the time because . . ." her voice went quiet once more. "Because," she took in a breath, "I didn't know *how* to explain why I was alarmed my mother had called. I thought, at first, that it was a mistake."

"I see. What of the hang-ups? At the office? At home?"

"Both—which is the troubling part. Our home number is unlisted. When I tried to trace the call back by using the redial function, the operator said that the call was 'out of area.' There have been a few cases of my own, including one I'm working now, in which people weren't happy with me. But those calls are local and are stopped easily."

She was thinking of Joanne Garcia. Joanne had called four times with epithets and threats since the investigation into her son's death and daughter's abuse had begun. She had even promised to make sure that Hannah didn't "dig up anyone else's baby." A visit from Ripp indicating that obstruction of justice charges could be filed against her had put the brakes on Garcia's campaign for revenge.

"Hannah?" Bauer's voice cut in. "You still there?"

Snapped back into the conversation, she apologized. She said she'd been distracted by someone outside her office.

"I'll send an agent from the L.A. office to get the package," he said.

"Fine. I'll be here most of the day. But Mr. Bauer—"

"Jeff," he cut in.

"Okay, though it sounds peculiar, *Jeff*, be discreet. Outside of Ethan no one knows I'm Claire Logan's daughter. I intend to keep it that way. For good."

"Understood," he said, "but I think you should know something from this end. I heard from Marcus Wheaton not long ago."

The name was a shockwave of its own, bringing back memories that Hannah held tightly within.

"Not that it is connected to the shoes," Bauer said, "but I'm going to Cutter's Landing on Friday to see Wheaton."

There was a long silence. Bauer waited until Hannah spoke. "What does Marcus want?" Her tone was ice.

"I'm not sure. You know that Oregon can't hold him much longer. His time is about up. His health isn't great, and the state has no cause to keep him beyond his original sentencing—no matter what you've read."

"Oh," Hannah lied, "I'd forgotten that it was coming up. I haven't thought about Marcus for a long time."

It was another deceit. It was the kind of lie she had told herself. She thought about Marcus all the time, but she felt comfort in her thoughts. He was in prison. She knew where he was. He'd tried to contact her after the trial. His mother phoned her Aunt Leanna once in Misery Bay on Oregon's southern coast, urging her to bring Hannah to the prison to see the man who'd once loved her mother. Leanna refused.

"How often do you think about *her*?" Bauer asked,

meaning Hannah's mother, of course. There was no other *her*.

"The only time she doesn't come to mind is when I'm deep into my work," Hannah said, her voice catching a little. "It sounds pathetic, I'm sure, but I'm always a little too grateful for a really heinous case."

"It takes something real ugly to chase it from your mind," Bauer said. He felt sorry for her. "There's a lot to chase."

"You know," she said, her hands trembling, "the peculiar thing is that I've read *Twenty in a Row* so often that sometimes I'm not sure what I remember and what others wrote. Sometimes I think some memories that I hold to be true are just planted."

Bauer had a copy of the book on his bookcase. He instinctively glanced in its direction at its mention, its worn binding showing its age. "*Twenty,*" as aficionados of the case called it, was the first book on the Logan case and considered by most to be the best.

"One day," Bauer said before they said their good-byes, "we'll know what really happened."

"Maybe so," Hannah said, wishing she didn't care anymore. "I hope so."

The hours flew by, though later, Hannah would plead with Ethan that she didn't even know what had preoccupied her to such a degree. It was not like her. Not at all. She was, she knew, a mother before anything else. A little after five, Hannah looked at her watch and jumped from her chair. In that instant she remembered how she had promised Ethan, who was busy with an inane ethics meeting, that she'd pick up Amber. *How could she be late?* She raced toward the after-school care offices, but by the time she arrived, they were closed. A janitor who spoke no English, at least that he admitted to, shrugged when she mentioned her daughter's name. Ten minutes later, she was in the driveway of their house on Loma Linda. Ethan's car was not out front, and her heart sank even lower.

Where was Amber?

"Honey!" she called out, but no one responded. "Amber, honey! Where are you?"

Hannah was frantic by then. She ran through the house, swinging open doors and pulling the covers from her daughter's unmade bed. She fell to her knees and peered under the bed.

"Let's not play the hiding game!" she called out. "If we are, then I give up. Come out."

She knew that was a ridiculous hope. They hadn't played that game for months, maybe longer than a year.

For any parent, the moment when a child is thought to be missing is the longest moment of a lifetime. Guilt, shame, fear, and hope converge in a stunning force that squeezes the breath from a person's lungs, male or female. *Catch a breath. Take a second. She's here. She's with her father. She's at Maddie's.*

Hannah dialed Maddie's house, and Elena Jackson answered, her voice annoyingly chirpy, given the circumstances.

"Hi, Hannah. How are *you*? Saw your name in the paper about that terrible case you're working."

"Oh yes," she answered, glad for the chance to calm her voice. "Is Amber over there?"

"No. Is everything all right?"

"I'm sure she's with her dad. Sorry. Got home late. A million things on my mind and I forgot to call Ethan."

She thought of the woman walking her dog. Maybe she'd come by again. Maybe this time, she took Amber from the day care. Setting the phone down, Hannah noticed the red eye of the answering machine blinking at her. She pushed the button.

"Four new messages," the auto voice intoned.

There were three hang ups, each one ratcheting her fear to a new level.

Not more. Not her?

Hannah felt the warm flow of tears down her cheeks as she strained to hear. The last call was Ethan's voice. In the background she could hear the sounds of a public place, the clatter of dishes. Maybe music.

"Hannah," he said, with an irritated tone that she barely knew, "I'm trying to be understanding. But this is too much. You have too much on your mind. Or something. Amber's with me. We're getting something to eat. You know if I'd have left our daughter waiting alone, you'd have filed for divorce. Pull yourself together."

Ethan was right, of course. He almost always was. At that moment, she hated him for his cool head. She was floundering; a big messy mix of worry and fear had consumed her and held her hostage. There is a moment of truth for everyone, and Hannah knew hers had been squandered long ago. But knowing this only made her sick to her stomach at what she'd done—what she had somehow allowed to happen. She'd heard Ethan talk about family members, mothers mostly, who'd done nothing to save their children from unspeakable horrors of men with damp, sticky fingers, probing under the covers. She'd

seen cases of her own come through the lab—the frag-
ments of lives interrupted before they'd begun. Hannah
had a sixth sense about cases like that. The Rorschach of
bloodstains on a sheet. The minute tear in a child's under-
pants. A man's pubic hair under a murder victim's broken
nail. Each spoke to her in a loud and menacing voice.
They told her the words she hadn't heeded when she
could have.

Stop it. Only you can save them.

CHAPTER NINE

Hannah sat up and stared into the darkness. Ethan rolled away, as though moving to allow her space to get in and out of bed. But she sat there, still. Her breathing so labored, so slow, she could see her nightgown rise and fall like a malevolent tide. In her sudden lurch to awakening, the memories she had sought to hold deep inside flooded her consciousness. There was no escaping them. As the foggy memory of the worst of days came into sharper focus, the words played in her head like the backbeat to a song that refused to die. She turned to Ethan, afraid she was saying them in a voice loud enough to be heard.

I should have killed her myself, she thought. *I should have killed her when I had the chance.*

A partial memory played . . .

* * *

It was about half an hour before midnight when an unexpected noise outside converged with the chill of a snowy December night and woke Hannah. She was only a thirteen-year-old girl then, but even so, she held a kind of strength within her that kept her both caregiver to her brothers and unwitting confidant to a mother she had ceased really trusting. But that night, more than ever, something was wrong. Certainly, she could feel and taste Christmas. Yes, there was the anticipation of a morning of surprises. All of it. But whatever spell the season had held in years past was annihilated by voices outside. It was her mother and Marcus Wheaton. Their declarations and murmurs overlapped, and it took Hannah a minute or two to grasp what they were saying.

She heard her mother first. It sounded as if she was calling out from across the snowy driveway in front of the wreath maker's shed.

"Get moving! We have about ten minutes, and as you know, ten minutes is barely a breath of time to do anything right. If you can't do it, I'll take care of the boys myself."

Marcus said something, but Hannah was unsure what it was.

Then her mother called out. "Pull yourself together. Jesus! Act like a man."

Hannah strained to hear. Although the words were incongruous with the holiday, she allowed herself to think that they were arguing over the assembly of gifts or something. Maybe for the boys? A pair of bikes? She got up and quietly crept to the window.

She knew, despite his job as her mother's so-called handyman, Marcus Wheaton wasn't mechanically inclined.

Then Wheaton called out, but his voice remained lower and therefore harder to decipher. Snow was falling and the wind sent a breeze that snapped the Santa banners that were hanging in the yard. Molly, the Logans' black Lab, barked. There was commotion out there, but the two figures in the yard were maintaining some kind of control. This wasn't, thankfully, a knock-down, drag-out fight like they'd engaged in in the past. Hannah peeled aside a window shade to get a better view. Light seeped into the room, and she rubbed her eyes. She stared down from her window to the odd and snowy scene.

Vapors of white puffed from Marcus Wheaton's mouth. She'd tease him tomorrow about being a dragon or something. She waited to see bikes or whatever wheeled across the white yard, but nothing happened. Her mother was nowhere in sight, and Wheaton disappeared. Whatever they were doing was over. Whatever they'd been up to had to be some kind of Christmas surprise for her brothers. Hannah crawled back in bed, pulled the covers up to her neck, and fell asleep.

And Hannah, now grown, a mother herself, still couldn't let the rest of the story play in her mind. She finally fell asleep. It was after two.

The next day was filled with paperwork for Hannah, though interrupted more than occasionally with thoughts of Jeff Bauer. Hannah examined documents she hoped would prove that little Enrique Garcia had been murdered by his violence-prone father, Berto. Each line needed to be examined. Tedious, to be sure, but necessary. It was difficult and slow going, with eyes bloodshot from lack of sleep. A visit from Ripperton didn't make it any easier. He sauntered into her office like he owned the place. There was boldness in his manner, more exaggerated than usual. It was obvious that he was still proud of his investigative work on the Garcia case. Hannah noticed that the white circles around his eyes were pronounced. He had been tanning again.

"Ted, this isn't a good time," she said a little too harshly when he asked if they could go over the Garcia interview report.

"Someone," he said somewhat snidely, "got up on the wrong side of the bed this morning." Next, he paused and dropped a nugget of information that made her nearly jump from her chair.

"Now Joanne Garcia says Mimi killed her brother," he said.

Hannah was stunned. "What?"

"I know you heard me, but I'll say it again. Mimi Garcia is the one who drowned the baby. Joanne says that she and Berto covered it up to spare the girl from living with such a horrendous deed."

Hannah set down her paperwork. "That's complete bullshit."

"I wish. I just got off the phone with her so-called lawyer—Deke Meyer. They want to work out a deal so that Mimi can be spared any emotional trauma."

If it hadn't been so serious, Hannah would have laughed out loud. Ripp had a lot of nerve casting aspersions on anyone. He was, she was sure, the world's worst at what he did. Deke Meyer was merely in the bottom ten percentile of his profession.

"Joanne Garcia is the biggest idiot or bitch. Maybe

both. We're going to put her away for a long, long time. This is complete bullshit," she repeated, raising her voice. "Using a little girl to bail them out—unbelievable!"

"I'm just the messenger," Ripp said, faking a cringe while he dropped another file on her desk before exiting, "remember?"

Alone once more, Hannah felt the color drain from her face. The Garcias were not going to get away with what she was sure was the most outrageous defense a parent could fabricate. It disgusted her. Despite what she'd heard, she still couldn't concentrate. She tried Deke Meyer's office, but his secretary (his fourth wife, Sheila) said he was out "running errands or something." Her mind was preoccupied, and she couldn't focus on anything other than the conversation with the FBI agent. At 11:30, she looked at her watch and called Ethan. When he answered his phone, she told him about her conversation with Bauer.

"He's going to see Marcus on Friday," she said.

Ethan knew his wife better than anyone. He knew what she was going to say next and was already exasperated by her, so he said it out loud.

"You're thinking of going up there, aren't you?"

"I am," she answered, her words surprising her a little. "I guess I am."

"Hannah, haven't you been through enough?" he asked. "Haven't we all? Remember when you told me— promised *us*—that Orlando would be the last time you went chasing after your mother? I hate to say it. I hate to *think* it, but you've got to pull yourself in and stop this before we go through this over and over."

"This isn't about her," she said, stiffening in her chair. "Someone out there knows who I am. Don't you get it?

This could ruin our lives." Her voice started to crack. "It could destroy everything."

Ethan was in a no-win situation, and he knew it. "You've made up your mind. I already know that. Let's talk about it tonight," he said. His voice was uncharacteristically flat. *There was no talking about it.* The absence of emotion had more to do with resignation than lack of genuine concern. Ethan had stood by his wife as she chased the memories that haunted her. She'd pursued four Claire Logan sightings since their marriage. She'd gone after her mother when news agencies reported appearances in Orlando, Pittsburgh, Tulsa, and Cabo San Lucas. And though Ethan knew this time could be like all the others—a literal dead end—it appeared a bit more promising. The shoes were either a prank or a taunt. He wondered if Claire Logan herself had sent them.

Hannah had already packed and Amber was reading at the kitchen table by the time Ethan came home that evening. She'd told her boss, DA Bill Gilliand, that she needed a couple days off for personal reasons. And she'd be back in the lab on Monday. After some characteristic browbeating—mostly for show—he acquiesced. Gilliand considered Hannah among the brightest and the most dedicated of the county employees—lawyers *and* lab rats—in his office. He did not know her family background, even though there had been a hundred times when she wanted to talk to him about it. There were times when she wanted to talk to *anyone* besides Ethan about it. But outside of her aunt and uncle and a cousin in Georgia, no one knew. Until, of course, an unknown someone had sent the package.

Hannah also double-checked the refrigerator to make sure Ethan would find something to eat, though she expected he'd take their daughter out to California Pizza Kitchen or another of the little girl's favorite places. The last thing she did was to call a message in to Jeff Bauer. She knew he'd be at the office and he'd given her his home number. Voice mail picked up.

"Jeff, this is Hannah Griffin. I'll meet you at Cutter's Landing in the prison parking lot at nine thirty tomorrow morning. I'm leaving as soon as I hang up, and I won't have my cell with me. See you there. I want to see Marcus Wheaton, too. Bye."

When she hung up, she turned to find Ethan standing beside her. He knew what Hannah was going to say, so he spoke first.

"You're going to see Wheaton. Do you want me to go with you? We could get a sitter."

"No," she said. She couldn't do that to Amber. "I'll be all right."

Amber rushed to her mother and wrapped her arms around her.

"I'll see you and Daddy on Saturday. I promise. Cross my heart and hope to die." She made the motion across her breast.

"Be careful, babe," Ethan said without looking at her.

"You know I will," she said.

Amber hugged her a second time. "Love you, Mommy," she said.

"Love you more."

It was around 8 p.m., and the sky was blush with an impending sunset when Hannah started north to Oregon. She planned to drive until midnight, hopefully reaching Janesville, a speck just on the south side of the California/Oregon border. There was a truck stop with a small motel and café there. Coffee would fuel her; thoughts of Marcus, her mother, and Bauer would keep her going. Hannah loved the solitude and the strobe of the golden, then dusky, scenery that flashed by the windshield. She made decent time and arrived at the motel at 12:45. She'd driven almost 330 miles in four and a half hours. A woman with bird legs and a uni-brow checked her in and gave her a room key.

"Free pastries in the morning," she said. "Just pay your bill and you can take some eats for the road."

Hannah opted to prepay and gave the woman her Visa card and was charged $55. She'd try to get four hours of sleep before heading out for Cutter's Landing and the penitentiary.

The last thing she thought of before drifting off to sleep were the faces of Mimi Garcia and her dead brother, Enrique. His was lifeless, chalky white. His sister's was full of fear.

I'll take care of you, she thought.

Then thoughts of Erik and Danny came to her mind, and she tried to force them back to the darkness of her memory. She started to cry. There was nothing she could do for them—not then, not now. Even so, the memories came. It was snowy. She was only thirteen.

"Hannah?"

Her eyes opened. Marcus Wheaton held his finger to his lips. His eyes were wild, and the sight of his mammoth frame hovering over her caused Hannah to cry out. She thought of how her mother and he'd been yelling out in the yard earlier. What time was it?

"Shhhhh. Don't say a word. Not an utterance. Hannah, you understand? You must keep calm and be still."

To make his point, he pressed the palm of his hand over Hannah's mouth.

Fear seized her entire body. He's going to mess with me, she thought. Mom warned me. He's going to touch me in a way that is wrong. She wriggled and bit his hand. Wheaton winced.

Not you, she thought. *Not you. Don't do this to me.*

"You don't understand," he said. "I'm here to help you."

Her eyes pooled, and she trembled. She had reason to, of course. Wheaton was an intimidating figure, swarthy and imposing. He was crouched over her bed like a monster of some kind. Big. Heavy. Smelly. Oddly so. Like gasoline or something.

"I won't harm you," he whispered. "Promise, no matter what, you won't say a word."

Hannah wanted his cold, fat fingers off her mouth. The smell from his hands was so overpowering she could barely breathe. She stared hard into his eyes; her own were awash with fear. They begged Marcus Wheaton to ease up, which is what he did.

"Listen to me carefully. Your mother is leaving tonight. She's going away. Far away. She's never coming back." He parceled his words in tiny batches as though he was acutely aware that the girl under her bedcovers would have a difficult time assimilating all that was going on around her.

Indeed, Hannah was paralyzed. She said nothing. She managed a nod of understanding. No words. Just the nod.

"I'm going with her," he went on. "You aren't. None

of you are." Wheaton's good eye glistened with tears. Was he crying? "This is hard. This is nothing you should ever have to hear, but your mother wants no part of any of you. She's not happy here and she's going away. I'm afraid this . . . is . . . is forever."

Hannah didn't believe him. "I want my mother," she said, holding her voice to a whisper.

"I know, but it isn't what she wants."

"But I'm her daughter."

He shook his head.

"She's not made to be a mother. You know that. She doesn't have it in her. Never has. She doesn't even look at you like she even knows you."

"She is my mother and she loves me."

"Hannah, you know that she really cares for nobody."

She hesitated. The unspoken had to be said.

"But you? Is that what you're saying? She only cares about you?"

"No. She probably doesn't want me, either. But I am damned to love her until she tosses me aside. You're too young to understand that sometimes things are bigger, stronger than what you know to be right."

"I don't want her to leave us."

"Hannah, you don't want her to stay. Trust me. You don't."

"You don't know how I feel. Where are my brothers?"

He shook his head. "Set that aside for now. Just for a moment. This is my chance to do something for you. I don't want anything to happen to you, Hannah. Bad things have been happening around here. I'm getting you out of here."

"What bad things?"

"You know what I'm talking about. You know about your mother. You've seen it for yourself. Remember the big jar?"

Hannah's eyes widened in the kind of full-out terror that comes with the realization that the mother who had rocked her as a baby, who had held her as a baby to her breast, was not really a mother. Not the mommy type. Hannah thought of the jar of bloody teeth she'd found when searching for ribbons above the wreath-fabricating bench. She thought the vessel held rusted screws or bolts. But it was lighter. She unscrewed the top and tilted the contents. It was a cache of blood-dried teeth her mother had put away like some grotesque souvenir.

Her mother asked her about it, after she noticed it had been disturbed.

"What were you doing in my things? I've asked you children to be mindful of what's mine and what's yours. My things are not toys—not to be played with. Don't you ever listen?"

"I wasn't playing with anything," Hannah had said. "I mean, I don't even know what you're talking about."

Claire shoved the jar in her face.

"This is what I'm talking about, and don't tell me again that you haven't seen this before."

"But I haven't." Lying was a necessity, and Hannah knew it. "What is it?"

Claire studied her daughter's face, but Hannah stayed cool, almost remote. The idea that her mother was some alien force was setting in, slowly, but it was coming.

"I almost believe you," Claire had said. Her eyes were ice. "But believing a practiced liar is a dangerous game."

"I'm not a liar."

"Don't make me laugh and don't make me mad. I've caught you before."

"I'm not lying. I don't know anything. Maybe someone else moved it?"

After she had said those words, Hannah would have done anything to retrieve them, reeling them in like a bed sheet knotted out a window for escape.

Claire smiled. She had caught the flutter of fear. It propelled her to push.

"Maybe Didi got into this. Like I've said a million times, she's always straightening things where we don't need it."

"I didn't see her here."

Hannah wasn't convincing, and she didn't really try to be. Later, she wished she'd been more careful in what she said and how she acted. She never saw Didi again after that day.

"Just what is that in that jar anyway?" Hannah hesitated. "Looks disgusting . . . like bloody teeth."

Claire laughed and spun the jar top and peered inside. "You watch too much TV. Just the bric-a-brac of buttons and sequins and pushpins . . . and some red paint."

But the odor was acrid and unmistakable. Hannah knew the smell of blood. She'd been there when her mother snapped the heads of chickens who no longer laid enough to justify the sack of scratch. She did it with a kind of flourish that indicated more enjoyment than resignation that the heads had to come off to kill the birds. She didn't even use a hatchet or a knife, but did it with her bare hands.

"Hands are easy to wash, and they don't rust," she said.

Hannah also knew the color of drying blood. It was a sienna tone on the edges, drying to a deep mahogany. What her mother had insisted was red paint could pass for the hue of blood.

Early the next morning the sky was indigo with stars popping from the darkness in a spray that looked like one of those fiber-optic bouquets that old ladies adore. Hannah Griffin was on the road, sans free pastry, by 4:15 a.m.

Just past the state line most of the conifers that had swathed the area had been reduced to a pillow fringe, as though one couldn't see beyond it to the stump-barnacled field of fireweed and blackberries. Alders, the first tree to arrive on the scene of deforestation, filled in like harried brush strokes where they could. Nothing about the landscape was particularly pretty, though Hannah had to admit the cool colors of green and blue were certainly pleasant on the eye, a change from the dusty palette of Santa Louisa County. She thought of Christmas trees and the evil, wicked snow that had ruined her life . . . and sent her to that place.

CHAPTER TEN

Eastern Oregon is nothing like the wet side—the western side—of the state. The mountains that divide Oregon into two distinct regions act as a barrier from the marine rainfall that keeps Portland and points south and west lush throughout most of the year. The eastern side is vast and dry—a landscape of craggy basalt formations and glacial moraines. Only through the lenses of a pair of sunglasses is it cool and green. But when irrigated, the soil produces the world's sweetest and most succulent fruits. Fruit stands clustered the roadside now and then, though most seemed abandoned or hopelessly unkempt. Where the ranch land crawled from one end of the horizon to the other was a dried basin, a crusty residue of earth and tumbleweeds. *Just add water.* Just keep driving. Just get the hell out of the east and run for the Pacific Ocean.

But Hannah was heading northeast, going away from the ocean. She was following the interstate to Cutter's Landing, so named for an old airstrip and not a body of water. It was three hours into the desert, a population injected into the dirt of Oregon's bleakest eastern territory. It was a place for losers. Cutter's Landing was a town of romance readers, ex-hookers, and do-gooders who lived in rundown frame houses and converted Quonset huts. The citizens were the women and the spawn of the killers and rapists who claimed 97337 as the zip code of the vile and depraved. Cutter's Landing was the home of Eastern Oregon's Correctional Facility for Men, and Hannah Griffin had a date with one of them.

A black-and-white sign with a flashing yellow light flew by the windshield: APPROACHING CORRECTIONAL FACILITY: DO NOT PICK UP HITCHHIKERS.

Hannah lowered the volume of the Spanish language radio station she had endured for the last hour of her journey to the center of nowhere. The bombastic host went soft . . . then away. And once more she was alone.

Oregon's largest prison was also its oldest, having been built brick by brick in the mid-1920s by the descendants of Chinese coolie laborers, whose blood, some said, never dried. In fact, eighteen men and two women died when a load of dynamite unexpectedly detonated as they prepared to blast a two-story-deep foundation out of a basalt basin that had been the remnant of a great lava flow. When the workers weren't blasting, they were hauling brick from the tracks of what would come to be known as Cutter's Landing when an airstrip was laid on top of the dusty landscape. Some considered the work barely short of slavery.

The towering bricks of the prison cast a foreboding

image on the craggy hillside. Four turrets sprang from the main building like razor wire–encrusted dragonheads. No trees grew around the site. The basalt formation on which the prison had been erected was a sterile stone dish the size of six football fields. The penitentiary housed upward of 400 men, though there had been more residing there in the recent past. When it was built, it had been designed to hold no more than 250.

Hannah followed little yellow signs to the parking lot adjacent to what some idiot bureaucrat had dubbed the "Visitors' Comfort Area." She wasn't sure if it sounded more like a bathroom or a motel. As she pulled her Volvo closer, she passed row after row of dust-covered old cars. Many of the cars' windows had the greasy fingerprints of children run amok. A few had tattered yellow ribbons tied to their antennae. It was sad, but clear: the ex-hookers and the do-gooders who populated Cutter's Landing had arrived in droves to see their men, to meet in the run-down visitors' area to play cards or maybe even sneak a little sex.

Hannah parked next to a boat of a car that had "government-issue" stamped all over it. A man, one of the two she'd come to see, was leaning against the driver's door, talking on a cell phone. His profile was familiar, and the sight of him brought a nervous smile to her lips. It was Jeff Bauer. Hannah turned off the ignition and reached for her right shoe. She was glad the drive was over, but she loathed the final destination.

Jeff Bauer had arrived at the prison parking lot an hour earlier. He'd actually stayed at the Landing Motel, thinking that getting a night's sleep before meeting with Wheaton might not be a bad idea. But it had not been a restful night. At about 3:30 that morning, he called the manager and told the twenty-three-year-old wisenheimer to get his ass out of bed to quiet the rumble that was going on in the room next to his. Pounding on the door, smacking the walls, and yelling hadn't stifled the noise. Up all night and smelling of bong water and pepperoni, the smart-ass told Bauer to fuck off. Bauer informed the manager he was a federal agent. Two minutes later, the party was over and silence returned.

Dressed in a gray chalk-striped suit, a white shirt, and solid red silk tie, he looked every bit the man he was. His hair had a few small glints of silver, and pale streaks highlighted the deepening fissures on his face. Whether deep in thought or wincing in pain when wrestling a suspect to the ground, Bauer had a habit of scrunching his face. He joked that it was his "concerned" look. In reality, that was exactly what it was.

He was older, Hannah could see, but then again, so was she.

He flipped off the phone and turned around, and for the first time in years, their eyes met.

"Hannah? Is that you?" he said. His smile was warm and familiar.

"Agent Bauer?"

"I got your message," he said, moving toward her. "I thought of calling you to tell you to forget it, but if you're anything like you were twenty years ago, you were packed by the time you called."

"I was," she said.

"You look great. I mean, considering the long ride across the shittiest landscape this side of Oklahoma."

"You look well, too." She retrieved her purse from the backseat and did a quick glance to ensure all the doors were locked. "And you're right. The drive was long, dusty, and boring."

"This won't be boring," he said, squinting at the sun as he sized her up. She was grown, beautiful. Her hair flashed golden in the sun.

"You think Marcus sent the package to me," she said.

"You must, too. Otherwise you wouldn't be here." He paused. "I'd like you to read his note," he said. He reached into his pocket and handed her a folded letter.

She took it and read:

"Before I can do that, I need to exorcise the ghosts of the past. Maybe you do, too. I know things. I do."

"Is he talking about *her*?"

"Ghosts of the past? Honestly, Hannah, I don't know. I've wanted to see this nutcase for twenty years. I've wanted to slam him to the ground and hold a gun to his fat head to get him to tell me what he really knows." He motioned at a small bus coming toward them. "Maybe he will tell us something that we've all wanted to know for a very long time."

"I know that. And as much as I want to see him, I almost can't bear to do it," she said.

"Understood," he answered. "I can only imagine."

"Imagine is a good word. I've *imagined* talking to him over the years. I've *imagined* shaking him and pleading with him to tell me where she is . . . if he knows," she added softly.

Bauer moved closer and offered his hand. It was a kind of awkward attempt at reassurance. Hannah wasn't sure if he wanted to hold her hand, shake it, or carry her purse.

"I know I'll get through it," she said. "I've done all right. I've got a life, but I still want some answers."

Bauer nodded. "This is the time," he added. "I feel it."

The bus parked, and the pair followed a stream of prison groupies, wives, mothers, and fathers into a modular building that functioned as the processing center for visitors. After five minutes of what amounted to nothing more than rubber-stamp processing, they were on yet another small bus alone, headed for the warden's entrance on the eastern wall. There, Warden Thomas's information officer would take them to a private visitation room.

The minibus bounced over a speed bump and lurched forward.

"This thing needs new shocks," Bauer said.

"And a new driver," Hannah added.

There was no argument there. The kid at the wheel reeked of Brut and attitude. He was hell-bent on showing his two passengers just how fast he could get from point A to point B. Luck, for the time being, had likely spared him from the fate of being on the other side of the walls. Driving like he did, he was sure to end up in jail, or prison. Maybe he wouldn't mind. At least he knew his way around Cutter's Landing.

Inside the walls, a behemoth of a man was about to have the rare visitor—two, no less. He's been alone so long, not completely by choice, of course. Liz Wheaton had tried to visit her son, but he'd refused to see her. She sent at least one letter or card a month—some newsy, others full of bile—all doused in White Shoulders. Marcus Wheaton also refused to answer any, save for one letter he had sent his first week in Cutter's Landing. Liz Wheaton saved the single note and carried it in her purse.

I love Claire. She loves me. No one is perfect, but you should know that better than anyone. She and I will be together. And as long as you don't accept that, then you're nothing to me.

CHAPTER ELEVEN

Miriam Thomas, the warden's wife, had done all she could to make her husband's office as homey as possible. Family photos in beautiful polished brass frames adorned one wall and a painting of Haystack Rock, a favorite of Oregon seascape artists, occupied another. Miriam had frequently told her husband of almost thirty years that just because he worked in a prison, it didn't mean his office had to look like a *cell*. Warden Rex Thomas, tough as he was, and as tough as he had to be considering his line of work, gave in to his wife and let her do her thing. The sole item he rarely put out was the pink Depression-glass candy dish that she picked up at a flea market in Roseburg. A candy dish didn't feel quite right to Thomas. Didn't fit the image. Besides, he didn't like the sugar-free hard candies Miriam had supplied in the first place. Even so, whenever she came to the prison to see her husband's environment, to make sure he made the best of it, he took the pink dish from the bottom drawer and set it out for her to see.

"I'd better get you more candy, dear," she'd say.

"Already have it on my list, Mir."

When the Portland FBI field agent and the CSI from California were escorted into his office, the warden had just finished reviewing the meal plans for the prison cafeteria for the month of November.

"Gonna be pressed turkey for Thanksgiving," he said with a wink, putting the sloppily typed menu aside. "It is every year. No surprise there, I'd say."

"And they say prisons aren't tough enough," Bauer said.

After exchanging introductions and innocuous pleasantries in a place where there are undoubtedly few, Warden Thomas outlined the rules for seeing the convicted arsonist Marcus Wheaton.

"The man hasn't had a visitor in some time, and while we might have relaxed the rules some years ago, for him we have not. You'll be in a visiting cell, with a guard stationed in the corner. We don't consider the prisoner to be violent, but considering why he's here, we just don't take any chances."

"Will he be restrained?" Hannah asked.

"Not that there is a need to, but frankly, he's put on so much weight that we don't have shackles or leg irons that fit him."

They signed the necessary disclaimers, the kind of legal scapegoat documents that every state and federal penitentiary puts before anyone dubbed a "slight risk contact visit."

"Corrections Officer Madsen will take you to him."

Gregg Olsen

The warden nodded at a young man with Elvis sideburns who had just appeared in the hallway.

Hannah and Bauer walked toward Madsen standing by the door.

"Any reason why he called for us now?" Hannah asked the warden. "I mean, anything I don't know?" She shot a look at Bauer.

"Don't look at me," he said.

The warden shook his head. "Your guess is as good as mine. His poor health? Lonely? Hell, maybe for a little drama? Who knows? But he's opened the door and, I'd guess, this is your chance. Maybe he'll finally answer that question you've always wanted to ask him."

With Jeff Bauer by her side, Hannah Griffin stared hard as she entered the small, seemingly airless room. There he was. *He must weigh 325 pounds.* He was honeydew-round in the face; his fingers were bloated rows of frankfurters with grille marks left by a fire long ago. He wore Day-Glo orange coveralls that could have doubled as a hunter's tent, so much fabric had been used. At first, nothing about him looked the same. She searched the man seated in front of her, hands clasped on the empty table, for any recognition that he was the man he said he was. He looked much younger than a man in his sixties.

An extra hundred pounds or so sure fills in the wrinkles, Hannah thought to herself. When she took her seat, she noticed his left eye didn't track.

It was Marcus Wheaton. It had to be. Wheaton had a glass eye thanks to a beer bottle shoved in his face during a bar brawl when he was twenty-one. It was so odd. The dead, lifeless eye always begged more attention than its mobile partner. Whenever Wheaton spoke, eyes would light upon the glass eye. It almost seemed as though the live eye would turn slightly to look at what it was that everyone focused on.

In seconds it started coming back. Hannah remembered how Marcus used to take the brown eye out to scare her and her little brothers. He'd pop it out and boom across the house that he was a cartoon superhero reject called "Mar-clops." He was "half man, all evil."

"I would know you anywhere," he said.

Hannah took a seat next to Bauer with Wheaton across the table. His pudding features were ashen. His hair was almost white, and his fingernails were long and paper thin; dark crescents marked each cuticle.

"Glad that you've come to see me," he said. He leaned forward and whispered to the guard that he needed a drink of water.

"I have wanted to see you for some time," she said.

The guard delivered a paper cup and stood, hovering like a blue uniformed wasp, until the last sip had been drained from the container. The cup was removed as if some how, some way, it could pose a danger to the inmate or his guests.

Wheaton cleared his throat. "Is that so? I can't recall a message from you in the past ten years."

"In the past ten years I've tried to forget."

"And forgive, I hope," he said.

Hannah bristled, though she tried to hide it. "How do you forgive a permanent nightmare?"

The fat man nodded very slowly. A sad mask slipped over his bulbous features. "How do you forget a broken heart? I don't deny that I set the fire, but I didn't kill anybody. In a way, I'm one of your mom's victims, too."

Bauer let out a breath of exasperation. "We get it. Today, everyone is a victim of something. Yes, we know. Now, why don't you just cut the crap," he said, his voice rising with each word. "And tell us what you've summoned us to hear?"

Wheaton fiddled with the valve on an oxygen tank that Hannah noticed for the first time. A thin tube ran to his left nostril.

"Special Agent Bauer, the past two decades have been good to you. Not so to me, I'm afraid. I'm morbidly obese. I have emphysema, and I don't have much time. Time is all I used to have. I used to count the days here. I stopped counting because it only made freedom seem more impossible." He paused and then a smile broke out over his face. "It's funny to think that after all these years, I'd be sitting in prison and you'd be wearing the same light blue dress shirt."

Bauer ignored the feeble dig.

"If you called us for a sympathy sob session, you misdialed, Wheaton."

"Call me Marcus," he said. "That's what they called me when I was a person. When I could walk free. Like you and others we know."

Hannah spoke, tentatively. "Like my mother."

The eye fixed on her. "Could be. But then we've just started our visit. Wouldn't want it to end so soon. The last visitor I had came at least ten years ago. A nun from Pittsburgh took the Greyhound out here to this godforsaken piece of shit country to see me. They let her stay four minutes."

"I saw it on the news," Hannah said. "She seemed a little obsessed."

"Yes, I understand she was interviewed by Diane Sawyer, too."

"Sorry, didn't catch that," Bauer said.

Wheaton looked at the FBI agent, then back at Hannah. "Neither did I. They took the television away from me after the riots of seventy-nine. That was a time. A terrible time when I didn't know if I'd be ground into dog food or raped by some big guy with a baseball bat. But, you know, I digress."

Bauer found it impossible to contain his irritation. "Why don't you tell us why we're here," he said.

The eye blinked once more. "Did I read you have a daughter, Hannah?"

Hannah didn't want to discuss any of that with Wheaton. "I'm not here—"

He cut her off. "—to talk about your personal life? I guess not. But I read in the Sunday *Oregonian* that you are the mother of a little girl. How nice. How is the husband? Still married to the fellow?"

Hannah put her palms on the table and started to get up from the yellow oak chairs. Her fine features went pink. "I'm leaving," she said. She didn't want to let on that she'd never been featured in the *Oregonian*. *Where did Wheaton come up with that?*

Wheaton shook his head, and the room vibrated slightly. "No. You're not. Because I will tell you what you need to know."

"About my mother?"

"Yes."

"Is she alive?"

He held his lips together and looked around the room. Finally, like air escaping a bicycle tire, he spoke.

"She is. I'm sure of it."

Hannah felt woozy, and Bauer instinctively leaned closer to her.

"You all right?" he asked.

"I'm fine," she said. She always knew her mother had not fallen from the face of the earth, but to hear someone who might know something actually say so was hard to take. Marcus Wheaton could be lying, of course, and Hannah knew that. But there were many things that people could call Wheaton. A liar wasn't one of them.

She thought about the shoes and how they came to her office. "Did you send them?"

"No, I did not." Wheaton's tone was indignant, and both Bauer and Hannah thought he was either sincere or a practiced liar.

"Do you know who did?" Hannah asked.

Wheaton pondered her question. "I'm not at liberty."

Not at liberty—Hannah and Bauer thought the word choice was strange.

"My mother," she pressed on, "did my mother send them to me somehow?"

Another man stood outside the door, and Madsen let him in. He said he was a doctor, and Wheaton had to be removed to the infirmary for medication relating to his emphysema.

The diagnosis seemed off to Hannah. Symptoms, at least overt physical ones, didn't seem to match Wheaton's physical embodiment. He was a two-ton load. Most suffering from the disease were staggering skeletons, hooked up to a tank that followed them everywhere like a precious little dachshund. She asked Madsen about Wheaton as they walked down the corridor to the warden's sanctuary.

"Just how sick is he?"

"Emphysema, cancer, the flu . . . you name it, he's had it all since I've been here," Madsen said. "No telling what he'd *suffered* from before my five years started here. He's what we call an infirmary moth. They bitch and moan about illness just to get out of their cells. I don't much blame them. The infirmary has the only window in the cellblock . . . the only source of natural light. But for God's sake, *emphysema?* Jesus . . . he'd be better off claiming something like high blood pressure."

"Cholesterol poisoning," Bauer jumped in, trying to make a lighter moment while holding the door open for Hannah.

"The donut disease," she said, unable to even manage a smile.

Madsen said they'd be having lunch in the warden's private dining room. It would be only the two of them. The warden had a crown that needed replacing, and he'd driven down to the Landing to see the dentist—though the prison had its own dentist, one who found a little too much joy in his work. Madsen led the pair into a cubbyhole of a room with a massive oak table.

"Not everyone gets this treatment. I've been in here only a dozen times in ten years," Madsen said.

A ceramic bowl of blown-glass fruit commanded the center of the table. Miriam Thomas had left her homey touch. Lunch was surprisingly elegant, consisting of salmon with dill (from the prison's pea patch), spears of late-season asparagus, and a pretty decent Waldorf salad.

"Wheaton's always more cheerful after eating," Madsen said, exiting the dining room. "Especially happy after a double serving of chili-mac."

"That's fine," Bauer said. "Feed the behemoth. We've got catching up to do."

"That's one way to put it. More like opening old wounds, I'd say," Hannah said. She tried to manage an ironic smile.

BOOK TWO
ASHES

If Hannah Logan had shared any happy times with her mother, they must have been the warm evenings of Oregon's all-too-brief summer. Just after 9 p.m., Claire Logan would summon her daughter, and they'd sit on a log that had been split lengthwise and shaped as a bench to watch their moonflowers unfurl. Her father had created the bench with a chainsaw, during the off-season the year he thought he could sell "Lumber Jack Furniture." But each evening, against a stump of a tree that had burned into a stubby snag, mother and daughter would sit and watch the flowers come to life. The white moonflowers, grown from seeds purchased from Burpee's catalog, had always been Claire's favorite. Their almost magical opening was a cherished reminder of her youth in Oregon. Hannah was equally enthralled. In front of their eyes, milky white tubes would twist and open into trumpets. From closed tight to open and swirling in fifteen minutes.

And while the pirouetting imagery was lovely, later, when she revisited those moments, Hannah could see that her mother was a bitter woman. She was a schemer, more than a dreamer.

"Hannah," she said, "don't let a man get in the way of your dreams. Don't let anyone tell you that you can't be what your heart tells you."

"Yes, Mother."

"Remember my words. Carve them on my head-stone with acid when I'm gone. I don't care. As long as you remember."

Hannah nodded, then nuzzled her mother and smiled at the laughter of her brothers as they played in their upstairs bedroom.

"I remember when Hannah told me about the moon-flowers," childhood friend Michelle Masour *later told a magazine reporter. "Her mother was weird, but she did have some good qualities. Hannah loved her mother. She never saw any of this stuff coming. Not at all."*

—From *Twenty in a Row: The Claire Logan Murders*, by Marcella Hoffman

CHAPTER TWELVE

Patty Masour knew the scanner codes better than anyone in Rock Point, Oregon. She was the part-time dispatcher at the Spruce County Sheriff's Department, a job she shared with her sister, Sandy. The code sputtering over the scanner next to her davenport meant trouble, big trouble. *Multiple homicide in the woods of the county.* She turned off her TV and told her husband she felt uneasy about what she had half heard crackle, and she dialed her sister.

"County Sheriff. Merry Christmas and hello," a woman's voice answered. Her voice was flat, her words sounded as though they were read from a card, not words from the heart.

"Sandy?"

"Yes, Patty? Oh dear," she said when recognition came. "Have you heard? They're hauling bodies out of the Logan family's tree farm. I haven't had time to call you; things have been off the meter over here for the past two and a half hours!"

"Logan?" Patty's heart sank. She knew the family. Everyone in Rock Point did. The Logan place had been their destination just ten days before when she and her children went to get their tree, a perfect, pyramidal-shaped Noble fir.

"Claire and her two little boys are missing. It's *real* bad out there. I mean *real* bad! Place is burning to the ground and the girl . . ."

"Hannah?"

"Yeah, she's the *only* survivor we know about."

Patty's knees weakened, and she slid into the soft folds of her velveteen davenport. "Michelle goes to school with Hannah," she said. Michelle was her daughter, thirteen. Patty hung on every word while her sister went on about the investigation under way. She remembered how Claire's daughter had rung up the sale for the Christmas tree in the little kiosk set up outside of the wreath shed. She was a pretty girl, big brown eyes with thick, ash-blond hair, held in a ponytail. Michelle and Hannah had been in the same second- and fourth-grade classes. They were best friends back then. By seventh grade, though, they'd stopped seeing each other outside of the classroom. Michelle told her mother that Hannah was no longer much fun to be around. Patty thought it might have had to do with what was going on at home with the girl's mother.

"They're taking Hannah to the hospital for an exam, then back here," Sandy went on. "You got any clothes that might fit her?"

"Yes," Patty answered. "Hannah and Michelle are about the same size."

"Well, she hadn't barely a stitch on when they found her. She was wearing her nightgown and socks. Soaking wet, too. The poor thing was out in the snow when they found her."

Patty mumbled something about Christmas being ruined, hung up, and spun around for her car keys. She hurried to her daughter's bedroom in search of something for the Logan girl to wear. The room was a mess, and she couldn't find anything clean. She thought of the Christmas tree and rifled for a package under its fragrant boughs. Ten minutes later, she was at the hospital with a pair of Michelle's blue sailor-style jeans, brand new panties, socks pulled from under the tree, and a bright red Rock Point Bobcats sweatshirt still warm from the dryer. Patty handed the clothing to a duty nurse, explaining they were for the Logan girl.

"Where's her mother?" Patty asked.

The nurse shrugged. "Haven't a clue. Seems like she ought to be here, considering what her daughter's been through."

"Can I do anything?" Patty asked.

"Not that I can think of," the nurse said. She stuffed the clothing into a plastic hospital garment bag and zipped it up. "Police are going to talk to her. The FBI's even been called."

"Oh dear," Patty said. "I wonder what's going on."

Entering his mid-twenties, Jeff Bauer was the kind of federal cop that more senior special agents labeled a "greenhorn" or some other antiquated term left from the

days of Eliot Ness, or at the very least, before color television. It only meant he was young and, even he had to
admit when the occasion called for it, brash. He had graduated with honors from Stanford University with a degree in criminology and psychology. It wasn't family
money that got him to Palo Alto, either, but a widowed
mother who typed indexes and rewrote obits for the Boise
Statesman and who had the good sense to push her only
son into applying for every scholarship she could find. Instead of pursuing a doctorate in psychology as he had
once pondered, Bauer enrolled in the FBI Academy in
Virginia, where he graduated a respectable thirty-fifth in
his class. He had a sandy thatch of hair, clear blue eyes,
and the chiseled features that were a gift of genetics, still
crisp from youth. He was on the slender, though not
slight, side, with a stomach that stayed above his belt and
a waistband that didn't roll. Women noticed him. That
alone denied him a kind of welcome among the jaded,
craggy-faced, scotch-and-water-gutted agents with thirty
years of fieldwork. His first assignment had been in Portland. It was a small office with eighteen agents and five
clerical staff. The Federal Building in downtown Portland
was undergoing renovations when the new kid arrived for
his first work assignment. He shared his cubbyhole office
with a U.S. Marshall Service agent who, thankfully, was
never around.

It was barely 5:30, Christmas morning, when Bauer got
up, emptied his bladder, and shuffled to the kitchen. He re-
suscitated an English muffin by sprinkling water on it and
running it through the toaster. Bauer pulled the metal ring
from the top of a pop can, hooked the tab onto a long
chain he had made, and sloshed Dr Pepper into the back
of his throat. Warm, sweet. *Not too bad.* He didn't wait

for coffee to brew. He turned on the radio to listen to Christmas tunes. Karen Carpenter's butterscotch alto filled the room, and for a blissful, melancholy moment he relaxed, closed his eyes, and conjured images of Christmas at home in Harper, an Idaho paper mill town just outside of Boise. He knew that in a few hours, his sisters would be converging on their mother's house with presents and a ham the size and weight of a bowling ball. Boise was only an hour from Portland by air, but that Christmas morning Bauer had holiday duty. He was low man on the totem pole.

A few minutes before six, the phone rang and his sleepy eyes popped open. It was the dispatcher calling. The man's voice was devoid of humanity or warmth. No Christmas cheer there.

"You'll need to get down to Spruce County," the dispatcher said. "Big to-do down there. Big snow dumping down that way, too."

The reason for the call was some sort of criminal activity, of course, not a weather report. And Bauer was summoned not because he was the most suited for the job, but because he had no family and the bureau director thought he'd be able to "hold down the fort" for a few days. Holding it down, as the agent in charge put it, was hardly a solo job. A handful of agents on a skeleton crew made sure the holidays went better for those with kids, wives, dogs, gerbils, and the other trappings of real life, than those with giant microwave ovens. The dispatcher, a guy named Walter with a Polish last name that no one could pronounce, let alone *spell*, said that an enormous fire on a Christmas tree farm had resulted in several deaths, most likely members of a family.

"That's a case for local law enforcement," Bauer said.

He glanced out the window at the Willamette River, a silver strand with a shoreline dotted with boat hulls. In the glow of the streetlights and the light of an awakening morning on the riverside path below his window, a man and a small boy rode by. Shiny new wheels sparkled in the light.

"Yeah," the dispatcher said. "You'd think so, but not after what a volunteer fireman found."

The little boy outside fell down and the father ran to pick him up.

"And what was that?" Bauer asked.

"The skeletal remains of a man in a uniform found in a grave near the barn."

"Uniform?"

"A Marine lieutenant's."

Bauer set aside his poor excuse for an English muffin.

"Still there?" the voice asked.

"Yeah. Do they know who the guy is?"

"Not yet, but there's more. A lot more, I guess. After the fireman called his buddies over, they found another grave. And another after that. The weirdest thing is that all—presuming there are no others—have been related in some way to the military. A few had some form of identification, and they have been confirmed as missing for some time. A long time. *Years*. One guy on the list has been AWOL, they thought, for almost seven years."

"What the hell?" Bauer said. "What do you mean *presuming* there are *no others*?"

"They're up to six. You better get down there. Infrared has already identified four other hot spots. Could be dead animals, of course. Hell, it could be a compost pile rotting under the heavy layer of snow. Who knows? It's a damn massacre in Rock Point, Spruce County."

"Got it," Bauer said, jotting down the phone number of the local sheriff, Bob Howe.

"It gets better. Get this, it's a goddamn Christmas-tree farm."

"Great," Bauer said. "I mean, how appropriate."

"Hey, Bauer," the dispatcher said, "some of the bodies are disfigured pretty bad. Better take some Rolaids with you if you got a nervous stomach for that kind of thing."

"Ah, thanks," he said.

Bauer threw some clothes into a duffel bag, wishing he'd done the laundry earlier in the week as he'd planned. He yanked the blinds closed and grabbed another Dr Pepper. Rock Point was more than three hours away. He walked to his car and felt the icy fingers of a chill in the air. It looked like snow.

CHAPTER THIRTEEN

Rock Point, Oregon, lay under a heavy coating of coarse, granular snow of the type that experienced kids insist make the best, the most *lethal* snowballs. Twinkly lights cobwebbed naked tree limbs flanking the Kiwanis Club's WELCOME TO ROCK POINT sign, and a three-quarter-inch plywood Santa and his reindeer were parked atop what locals considered the center of the town, the old Wigwam Discount Store. And on the way through town were row after row of single-story wood-framed homes, built for mill workers and their families in the '20s. Most were perfectly maintained, with yards of lawn and rhododendrons snuggled under curtained windows. It was Christmas, and those converging there would never forget that particular place, that day, the terrible occurrence that brought them together. Northerly wind gusts shot spiny darts into Jeff Bauer's handsome face as he stepped from his car and made his way across the Rock Point High School parking lot. It was the home of the Bobcats, and necessity made it the heart, albeit, a broken one, of the community.

He'd been told before leaving Portland to go straight to the high school, which was the staging area for the recovery effort.

Ordinarily—though it was unlikely such a word could be used in conjunction with what was happening in Rock Point—Ressler's Chapel of Flowers had the county contract to serve as the area's morgue, but a horrendous traffic accident four days earlier had filled its pair of refrigerator units with a mother, father, and their two children. Only one time before had there been a need for an additional refrigerator, and in that case, another traffic accident, the mortician's old Kenmore chest freezer was emptied. He lined it with black plastic used to block weeds from growing in the flowerbed, and set it on its warmest "cold" setting. When word got out that multiple bodies were being recovered from a Christmas tree farm outside of town, a decision was made that Ressler's Chapel of Flowers wasn't going to do.

Rock Point High's gymnasium was the only building sizable enough for what police were saying would be needed, given the early reports from the Christmas tree farm. The remains of holiday banners touting the HOLLY DAZE DANCE hung forlornly on dank, masking tape–marked cinderblock walls. GO BOBCATS! and WE'VE GOT SPIRIT! YES WE DO! rested in a heap on the gleaming, blond, wooden floor. A trophy case filled with plaques and faded ribbons commanded a space next to the gym's entrance.

More than three dozen people congregated in the gym—and some of those were dead.

Bauer introduced himself to the Spruce County coroner, a bald man with an egg-shaped head and marshmallow middle. His name was Bertram Wilder. Dr. Wilder apologized for his damp hands as they greeted each other.

"Just washed up," he said.

Bauer surreptitiously wiped his hands on the back of his trousers and looked just beyond the doctor. He counted the row of midnight blue body bags elevated from the floor on army-issued cots.

"Eight?" he asked.

The egghead nodded. "Not counting Claire Logan and her kids."

"How many kids?" he asked.

"Two boys."

"Jesus. What about Mr. Logan? Where's he?"

"An old case of mine," the coroner said flatly. "Mr. Logan has been dead for years."

"Is everyone else accounted for?"

"As far as we know. But we don't know who else is planted out there. If we keep digging, maybe we'll find some more."

Bauer followed the coroner over to the first row of bodies and knelt down as though a closer proximity would provide additional clarity. Thick black plastic had been arranged to protect the floor from any seepage. The coroner pulled on the zipper and the cocoon split open. A sharp odor shot forth, like steam from a putrid, foil-wrapped baked potato. Bauer turned away for a split second to catch his breath before turning his attention back to the corpse.

Dr. Wilder's expressionless face twitched a smile.

"The smell could be worse," he said. "Ten or twenty times worse if it weren't for the quicklime." He opened the body bag more fully and the stench that was nearly intolerable intensified. "Yeah, lime eats the flesh like a flame melts candle wax. Whoever put the bodies in the ground packed them in large quantities of lime first. *Wrapped* them in the stuff."

The odor was so intense, it seemed more a solid than a gas to Bauer, pushing into his windpipe like a plug. It nearly choked him. He let out a hacking cough and found his voice, "I don't follow you. What do you mean?"

The doctor smiled his weird grin and examined a pair of rubber gloves for tears by holding them up to the row of fluorescent lights suspended by cables over the basketball floor. He snapped them on and opened the bag farther, pulling the zipper past the sternum and nearly to the crotch. A piece of metal of some importance caught the light and glinted a golden tone through the murky stench that wafted from fabric and flesh. Bauer bent closer. It appeared that the dead man was wearing some kind of a military uniform and the uniform was intact. Filthy, thick with mud, and stiffened by dried bodily secretions, but the fabric was completely intact. Right down to the buttons, *brass ones,* Bauer thought to himself.

Dr. Wilder turned the flap of the jacket to reveal a yellow residue. "Lime. See that there." He pointed with a gloved finger. "Whoever put the bodies in the ground packed them with lime on the *inside* of their clothes."

"Why would anyone do that?" Bauer had heard of quicklime being used to dispose of bodies, but not in that manner. Usually the bodies were dredged in lime like drumsticks in flour for Sunday dinner, then buried. Of course, the young agent had heard of the technique—the Nazis used it in Poland during World War II—but the smell and the sight of the putrid corpse made him lose his train of thought. *Derailed it.*

"I wondered about that, too. Then it came to me. Out here it rains half the year. Our soil is lime-poor because it's leeched right out of the dirt by the rain. By packing the bodies with lime on the inside of their clothes, the killer kept the lime right where it would do some good."

Bauer listened intently. "Wouldn't it leech out anyway?" he asked.

"In time . . . Special Agent . . ."

"Bauer," he said.

"In time, Agent Bauer, but not nearly as rapidly. By keeping the lime next to the corpse, it eats away at the flesh ten times faster. At least. Who's to say, really? It is only an estimate. Not every vile and disgusting thing known to man has been cataloged and measured. But the quicklime and the water and the enzymes present in the human body turn the corpse into a slurry. It's like a churning, a Waring blender of—for lack of a better word—*gunk.*"

Ignoring signs posted over the doorway, Dr. Wilder lit up a cigarette and looked about the gym for a place to drop his match. When he found none, he let it land on the floor before rapidly grinding it out.

Bauer spoke up. "Are all the victims in uniform?"

"All, insofar as we can tell, are dressed in some kind of a military uniform. There's another similarity, or so it seems. While we can't be sure given their decomposed condition, most appear to be older gentlemen. I'd say fifties and sixties."

"Any I.D. made?"

Dr. Wilder drew a deep breath through his Camel and shook his head. The filterless end of the cigarette was wet and mashed from his clenched lips.

"That's the kicker. None of these guys have any teeth." The bald-headed doctor blew two channels of smoke out of his nose and watched warily for the agent's response.

Bauer's face remained stone. "No teeth?"

"Yes, it appears whoever murdered these fellows knew how to work a sledge hammer or something of the sort. I've never seen anything like it, except maybe in cases in which a face is bashed in by a steering wheel in the course of a head-on. But not deliberate. Postmortem, I'm sure. It's strange. All of the corpses are missing their smiles." Wilder touched his lips and let out a short, peculiar laugh. It was the kind of embarrassed laugh someone makes when they know they've said the wrong thing.

A small group of uniformed county personnel swarmed the scene. They were worker ants and the bodies were their blue egg cases. Moving from one to another, officers took pictures and cataloged whatever seemed pertinent.

A young cop came up and offered a cup of coffee. Bauer happily took it. The stench had permeated everything, even his taste buds. The coffee was lousy, but at the same time it was the best he ever tasted. At least, Jeff Bauer needed something in his mouth and throat.

"You want to see the survivor?" the officer asked as Bauer gulped. "Hannah Logan, Claire Logan's *daughter*. She's thirteen or fourteen. They're processing her now and taking her to the Inn and Sheriff says you can see her there. It would be better for her, less threatening than the county building, I guess. Poor kid's really shaken up. Got no family, no place to stay."

It was only years later that Hannah Logan would piece together details of what happened in Rock Point that Christmas Eve night and the very early morning hours of Christmas Day. Some things were stored in memory, like smelly, moldy trinkets in a lead-lined box. She couldn't get to all of her memories, even if she had tried. In fact, she said little about what happened during the first hours, and not surprisingly, even less as the years went by. She remembered how a fireman had given her his coat back at the farm. She would flash on that image time and again as she surveyed that copy of *Life* magazine that featured similar photographs—along with the horror of that snowy night. She remembered how they took her to a small room at the department they called the "Victim Assistance Room" or the—in cop-speak buzzing around her— "VAR." She had a vague recollection that she looked terrible. A crust of blood on her hair had dried, leaving it matted to her head. She wore the Bobcats sweatshirt and jeans given by the sister of the sheriff's dispatcher. She sat with her arms folded, to conceal her budding breasts. No one had thought to bring her a bra.

VAR officer Sheila Wax was a wiry woman with a pack-a-day smoker's baritone and glasses that hung on a chain around her neck and moved to and fro as she walked, the bony plate of her chest rising and falling with each step. Part of her strategy for dealing with the shell-shocked victims of crime was called "whisking." She had to keep the victim's thought processes stirring from one idea to the next. Dwelling on a thought, on a task, could mean a breakdown. No one wanted to deal with the screams of someone falling apart, no matter how justified such a response might be. Those who said they didn't mind, that they wanted to be needed by the fragile and the cracked, were liars. Sheila Wax wasn't compassionless. She cared about doing a good job. But Wax also had a twenty-two-pound Tom turkey in the oven and a house full of relatives milling around a table that she still had to set. She handed Hannah a can of pop and a bag of chips.

"Want some Christmas cookies, hon? They have some Mexican wedding cakes and cherry bars out there," she said, indicating the spread of holiday treats fanned out in front of the dispatcher's command center.

Hannah shook her head. Her lips were dry and her throat felt tightly constricted. Food was far from her mind. She couldn't think of anything but what she'd seen and heard that night. For the next three hours she sat in that little room, a radio playing Christmas songs and the noise of running feet and lowered voices passing by the doorway. The VAR lady brought her a pillow and a blanket, but she couldn't sleep. Every time she closed her eyes she could see what she wanted to forget.

"What about my brothers?" she asked.

"I'll let you know as soon as I hear something, hon," Wax repeated.

But Hannah was insistent. "I want to see my mom."

"Soon, I'm sure," Wax said. "Soon."

A two-inch, second-degree burn on her right forearm

was the only injury recorded by an ER doctor, who prescribed a mild topical painkiller and dressed her arm in gauze. He gave Hannah a Charms sucker—sour apple flavored, green in color. The smell of that candy, apple and sugar, made her sick. She clutched her stomach. It was an odor that she would always associate with the "incident." Green apple candy was one thing Hannah could avoid fairly easily. Escaping the fact that she was Claire Logan's daughter was another matter. Of course, she didn't know that then.

CHAPTER FOURTEEN

1986 Save Our History project,
Rock Point High School, transcript

DARWIN REYNOLDS: When I got there the fire was
 nipping at the treetops. It was a fucking—excuse
 me—a *freaking* explosion, fully engulfed. It was
 around 2 a.m. on Christmas morning. I'd rather
 have been in bed. But it was bad. Real bad. Right
 off the roof of the main house the flames shot like a
 cannon. I could feel the blast of heat from the back
 of the truck.

INTERVIEWER: Were you scared?

REYNOLDS: Scared? That's a dumb question. It was my
 job to put out the fire. None of us were scared.

INTERVIEWER: (*embarrassed*) Sorry. Was anything else
 burning besides the house?

REYNOLDS: Everything was on fire. When my squad
 got there, we were divided into three teams of two

each. Rick [White] and I went out to the house.
It was fully engulfed. We yelled for survivors.
Nothing. Sam [Collingsly] and Scott [Armstrong]
went to the barn and it was burning. Livestock
had already been set free. Matt [Jared] and
Myron [Tanner] covered the area by the wreath
maker's shed. That's where they found the
girl.

INTERVIEWER: Hannah Logan? That's where they found
her? Describe what you saw.

REYNOLDS: I saw Myron and a kid, a girl. She was in a
flannel nightgown that had been singed at the hemline. I don't know if it was burned, but it was dark
at the hemline. Could have been mud. She was
screaming about her brothers. Over and over she
was saying, "Danny and Erik, why? Why?"

INTERVIEWER: Did she ask about her mother?

REYNOLDS: Not a peep. She never said a word about
Claire Logan. I think she knew what her mother
had done. I think that little girl knew it. She was a
tough little thing, tough enough to keep her mouth
shut, you know. Hey, can I ask you for a favor?

INTERVIEWER: Okay.

REYNOLDS: Can you take the "fucking" out of this
interview? I don't want my kids to see me using
that kind of language. You know, sounds kind of
bad.

INTERVIEWER: No problem. Understood. What about
Marcus Wheaton? Did you know him?

REYNOLDS: Saw him in Rock Point a time or two. You
know those guys with tats that say *Born to Lose*?
That's what I thought about Wheaton. That was
him all the way, the dumb fuck. Hey, I said it again!

Marcus Wheaton's run of bad luck started the day he was born with a cleft palate to a mother who vomited at the sight of her baby instead of cuddling him in her arms. It didn't get better as he got older, reconstructive surgery notwithstanding. Liz Wheaton sold cosmetics and perfume at the downtown Portland Meier and Frank department store during the day and worked stag parties on the weekends until the dim light of a motel room could no longer hide her advancing age. Reeking of the mélange of scents that permeated her workplace, Liz Wheaton never met a fragrance she didn't try. Often, with a heavy hand. She was known by some of her after-hours customers as the "whore who smelled better than she looked."

Marcus had been the result of Liz's moonlighting. "The worst bonus I ever got," she occasionally groused to her girlfriends. Marcus never knew his father because Liz was never sure which guy it had been. When he was seven, Liz told her only son that his disfigurement was God's way of punishing her for her sins. By then, she'd given up the Saturday-night sex parties for Sunday church services at a suburban Assemblies of God.

When Marcus fled south to Rock Point, Liz followed her son, which was odd. After all, he was the baby she puked on, the one she'd have sucked into a sink had she not been raised Catholic. But Liz said she wanted to make up for all she had done. By then Marcus had forgiven her, though at thirty-one, he longed for another woman in his life. Marty and Claire Logan advertised for a helper on the tree farm, and Wheaton answered the ad. Wheaton needed to believe that despite his weight, the scar from his surgeries, and only one real eye, he could find a woman. It was too bad the woman was married.

The fire was one more bad moment in a man's life corroded with disaster. It was, he would say later, the end of the big fall that started the day he was born.

On Christmas Eve night, a pair of sheriff's deputies driving from Icicle Creek Farm found the mammoth handyman stooped over fixing a flat about a mile from the smoldering house. It wasn't a pretty sight. The twin crescents of his buttocks caught the beam of the headlights and bounced a spray of white light into the black air. A radio was on, and the tune coming from the cab was the jangling sounds of Brenda Lee's *Rockin' Around the Christmas Tree*. When he heard the sheriff's Ford approach, Wheaton stood tall, hiked up his Levi's, and waved the deputies past with his smoky-link fingers. A puff of moist, warm air hovered by his beefy face, like the steam venting from the nostrils of a dairy cow. Though he never looked directly at the cops, Wheaton shrugged, as if to say: *Under control. Got it handled. Yes, sir, it's just a flat tire*. Paired with an older cop with forearms the size of kayaks, the young deputy with hair that brushed over the tops of his ears reached for the microphone as they passed. He was pissed off because he'd been left out of the action at the Logan place, so he ran the pickup's plate numbers—just to see.

Marcus Wheaton's name and an outstanding traffic ticket from the previous summer turned up a little unexpected gold. His address was the same as Icicle Creek Farm's—the cops had heard the dispatcher give it out more times than a television ad for a lip-synching has-been's greatest hits. Each time it crackled over the wire reminded them that they weren't on the scene of the biggest story coming out of Rock Point in years. Maybe ever.

The older deputy with the white-sidewalls crew cut made his way over to the truck, and Wheaton straightened his hunched spine. He blinked his puffy eyes in the beam of the officer's flashlight.

"Step in front of the vehicle, please." The deputy shone his flashlight over Wheaton's face and traced his arms. *No gun, good.* "Slowly."

Sweat freckled Wheaton's brow. His jacket was torn at the sleeves, and it appeared the spare tire he had hoisted from the bed of the truck had blackened his chest with a large, greasy smear.

"Marcus Wheaton?" asked the other deputy.

"Yes, sir," he said, his voice raspy.

"You work for the Logans?"

He nodded. "For quite some time."

"You know the place is burning tonight."

"Yeah."

"Know anything about it?"

Wheaton's shoulders hunched and he sank into the ground. His eyes were fixed in an odd stare. He started muttering something about how tired he was and how he hadn't really known what had happened on the farm. Then, strangely, he looked to the ground and told the pair of deputies that he didn't know a damn thing about Icicle Creek Farm, the fire, or anything much at all. But his protestations were his undoing.

"I didn't do anything," he said. "I didn't kill anybody."

The deputies exchanged looks, and the one with the head that begged for a "Firestone" tattoo coughed out the order that they were taking Wheaton in for questioning. "You've got something to tell us," he said.

Then Wheaton turned his face and both cops lost their

breath. His ear and the flesh from his temple to his jawline was shiny red and black. His hair was singed from
the jaw line to the nape of his neck.

"Jesus, what the hell happened to you?" the older one
asked.

Wheaton's eyes evaded the cops. Finally, he answered,
"I got burned."

"Jesus," the cop said, "you need a doctor."

Inside of five minutes of the police request for medical
help, Marcus Wheaton was on his way to the hospital for
what appeared to be second-degree, possibly third-degree
burns.

While the sirens caterwauled into the darkness of a landscape with no streetlights on the way to Rock Point General
Hospital, no one had any inkling what was to be learned by
the light of day. No one, save for Wheaton, probably had
any idea that his world was about to be turned upside down.
Only he knew that once the newborn baby bathed in the
warm, wretched spew of his mother's vomit, he was
about to suffer the greatest indignity and betrayal of his
life.

Early Christmas afternoon, Jeff Bauer surveyed what
had once been Icicle Creek Farm. It was the initial of
what would be dozens of visits, but it would always hold
great power in his memory because it was the first time
he saw the destruction brought by unmitigated evil. It
was a large property, forty-five acres of Noble, Balsam,
and Douglas fir. Some were only two feet high, while others had gotten away from the owners and hit twenty-five.
A sign in front of a gorgeous Noble proclaimed: RESERVED

FOR THE PRESIDENT OF THE UNITED STATES OF AMERICA. The noise of men, heavy equipment, steel shovels hitting rock and brick, and the sizzle of water on ash wove a dense fabric of sound. Bauer looked on in complete amazement at the destruction of what had surely been a lovely place. Only the wreath maker's shed was completely unscathed. The house was gone. The building that had been used first as a chicken house, and later for storage, was partially burned. Bauer parked his car in a muddy patch in front of what had been the house but was now a smoldering grave. All that remained was a basketball hoop and a car with melted tires. On the orange hoop, someone had put up a wreath with pinecones and a red plastic bow. The car had a circle of wire affixed to the burned-out grille. It, too, had been festooned with a wreath. Drifting snow had melted and refroze, surrounding the enormous black holes where the various structures had collapsed into themselves.

Bauer had the gruesome responsibility of witnessing the recovery of more bodies. While it was not truly a federal case, it had the potential to be one—kidnapping was a possibility.

"They found the woman and two boys over there," a cop in a black raincoat and stocking cap announced. The fringe of curly red hair peeking out from under the cop's knit cap made him look like a circus clown. Bauer remembered him from the gymnasium. The deputy pointed inside the foundation walls; a cement rectangle stood starkly alone.

"Yeah, I heard," Bauer said. He regarded a backhoe a hundred yards away as it exhaled diesel and lurched forward, its yellow bucket dumping sodden earth in a heap.

"Found two more before lunch." The cop cleared a

wad of phlegm from his throat and spat. It smacked against the muddy, melted ground. "So far."

Bauer brushed past the redhead to get a better look. The coroner and two other men Bauer did not know by name, but whose county-issued ponchos indicated they were crime scene investigators, had planted themselves in the center of the house, amid the charred ruins. One held a high-powered lamp to illuminate the darkest shadows. A piano, its keys buckled like an old ivory necklace, was the focus of their attention.

"The woman's under the piano," Wilder said. "It appears her twin boys are next to her."

Bauer inched forward and broke into the conversation. "How the hell did that happen?"

"We're told the piano was upstairs," one of the investigators said, nodding solemnly in Bauer's direction. "Some kind of a music room, I guess. The floor must have given way before falling down here on the victims—who, thank God, were probably already dead. Murdered or maybe just overcome by the smoke and heat. Coroner will make that call."

On top of a charred floorboard mottled with ash and debris, the boys' small bodies were laid out next to each other. Bauer bent closer. Their ears had been burned off, making their heads look like knobs. One appeared to be face down. The condition of the other body, seemingly more incinerated, made it difficult to determine. A third investigator loaded a camera and focused his long lens. Bauer was so absorbed, so riveted by the horror of what was in the ruins of the Logan house, he didn't even notice the man with the camera until the flashbulbs strobed the scene.

Jesus, he thought. *A couple of kids. Twin boys . . . born together and died together. How often does that happen, anyway?*

While the FBI out-of-towner stood behind them, the two investigators in ponchos used a couple of two-by-fours to hoist up what remained of the piano. They wore heavy, leather gloves to protect their hands from the still-smoldering remnants of the blaze. Sparks mixed with the steam and smoke. As the pair heaved, piano wires snapped and vibrated through the rubble. Once it was shoved to the side, they all saw a larger body; a woman's pink garment, not completely destroyed by the fire, covered the torso like an impossibly cheerful death shroud.

"God!" one of the men gasped, and Bauer moved closer to get a better view.

The body flat on its back was headless.

"Where the fuck is her head?" said one of the cops holding the two-by-four.

"Maybe it burned off or something," one said.

"Heads have a lot more bone than flesh," yet another voice added. "Heads don't burn up and skulls don't roll away from a crime scene."

Bauer said nothing. He was mesmerized by the sight and didn't even turn to look at who had made the comment.

"Yeah," he finally muttered.

A Nikon flash unit flooded the three cinder corpses with light as the photographer took more pictures. When he completed a roll, he licked the adhesive tab that sealed it, put it in his pocket, and reloaded. By the end of the day, he'd logged more than 400 photographs. And because he felt he was onto something special, he shot a roll for himself, which he hid in his back pocket. In the event that a major national magazine became interested in this story, he'd want to be able to send them some photos. He noticed that a reporter for the *Spruce County Lumberman* had also arrived on the scene. He'd heard others were on the way. The ABC television affiliate from Portland was en route before lunch. By the afternoon all networks were on the scene, mostly from Portland and the station in Salem. A San Francisco "Eyewitness" news team had chartered a jet and touched down around 3:30 p.m.

The Associated Press reporter, a tight-lipped, aggressive young woman named Marcella Hoffman, staked her claim to the story. She slugged her copy: "Merry Murders and Happy Homicides." A photo that a friend from the Oregon Department of Motor Vehicles had gladly requisitioned for a fee ("pays for some of this year's Christmas") accompanied the article. It was a standard driver's license picture, but it was also the world's first glimpse of Claire Logan. Logan stared with an intensity not usually seen in a DMV photograph. She had shoulder-length hair with a slight wave. Her earrings were medium-size hoops. Her features were patrician and symmetrical. She was beautiful by anyone's measure.

By the end of that first day, the Logans' bodies were slid into body bags and delivered by ambulance to the high school gymnasium. There they joined thirteen others, making a total of sixteen victims discovered at Icicle Creek Farm. *Sixteen dead.* With the exception of the headless woman, all victims had been male. With the exception of Mrs. Logan and her two little boys, all had been adult men.

Queasy from what he'd seen, Bauer checked into a room at the Whispering Pines, drank club soda, and reached for the telephone. His first call was to Portland.

The FBI dispatch agent got on the line and told him that agents would be joining him in Rock Point, probably before nightfall.

"Hang tight, Bauer," he said. "It goes without saying that this is more than your garden-variety serial killer."

"I get that," he said. He drank some more club soda.

"Quantico wants a lid on this as much as possible. All the military guys who are victims down there make this not only peculiar, but a little more sensitive than a run-of-the-mill body dump."

Bauer didn't need a lecture. "I'm not talking to anyone," he said. "Mostly because I don't know what's going on yet. This is pretty grim down here."

"Right, Bauer. Now don't forget, the sheriff down there is in charge. At least we want to let him feel he is."

The second call Bauer made was to his mother in Idaho. He told her he was working a big case and she's "probably heard about it on the TV news." He also talked to one of his sisters and promised he'd try to break away from the investigation to get home before the holidays were over.

"But I doubt it," he said. "Tell mom that I love her. Looks like I'll be in Rock Point for a while. I doubt I'll ever see anything worse than this. No matter how long I live."

CHAPTER FIFTEEN

Around five o'clock, the temperature dropped again, and the snow that had been spitting at the ground throughout the day began to fall with a renewed fury—more than eight inches in less than an hour. The north-south interstate became a skating rink, and the Oregon State Police did double duty pulling holiday motorists from ditches and away from Jersey barriers. The other FBI agents en route to Rock Point didn't get any farther south than Willamette, an hour away. Despite the white-crowned mountains around them and their obvious love of the beauty of the frozen precipitation, Bauer knew Northwesterners just didn't do that well driving in snow.

Bauer smoked a cigarette and logged a couple hours writing the text for his 302s, the code used by the bureau for interview reports. He braved the weather for a drink and a sandwich at the coffee shop two doors down from his room at the Whispering Pines. It was, without a doubt, the worst Christmas of his life. He imagined all that he missed; his family gathered to celebrate into the evening. By 11 p.m., he tucked into bed in time to watch himself on the news. Sheriff Howe, with his gentle country-fried demeanor was the spokesperson, but Bauer was visible in several of the shots. He wondered if his mom was watching, too.

Bauer didn't know it then, however, but people across the country were riveted to the first broadcasts coming from snowy Oregon. The Logan farm was on its way to being the site of a story that would never be forgotten.

Just after 8 a.m. the day after Christmas, the phone rang in Bauer's room at the "remodeled-for-the-Bicentennial-year" Whispering Pines. It was Bob Howe, the Spruce County sheriff.

"I've got an update for you," Howe said, "a kind of a good news/bad news deal. Guess you ought to know all that's going on down there. Found four more bodies overnight."

Bauer was stunned. "Four?"

"Yeah. We're up to twenty. A few more and we'll top Corona down in Yuba City."

Bauer instantly recalled how a few years before a California migrant labor contractor named Juan Vallejo Corona was convicted of killing twenty-five Mexican migrant workers in what had been the nation's greatest mass killing in history.

"It isn't a contest, sheriff," Bauer said, quickly adding a laugh because he didn't want to offend his only ally. "If it is, it isn't the kind we want to win, right?"

"Guess so. Anyway, two have been preliminary I.D.'d based on their effects. Kind of weird. Turns out two had their wallets tucked inside their breast pockets. Smashed their teeth, yet the perp left their wallets. What a dope. One guy's retired navy from Virginia; other's retired army from one of the Dakotas. We're working on the other two."

"Can I get the names?"

"Yeah," Howe said. "I'll have some stuff for you at the office. Come by any time."

"Thanks. I'll do just that."

"Now, if the fact that we've got a lead on identifying a couple of them is the good news, I do have some bad news, too."

"Yeah?"

Howe went quiet for a moment. "This is big," he said, his voice missing its jovial tone. "We sorta screwed up. Claire Logan's sister made arrangements to have her sister's remains sent to the funeral home, and our guys let the body go."

The young FBI agent's face turned red. "Jesus, Sheriff, we haven't even processed the body. Get it back."

Howe sighed. "I'd like to, but I'm afraid we're a little too late."

"Get a court order. The body is evidence."

"The body," the sheriff said in a very quiet, very embarrassed voice, "is gone." His words trailed off into near whisper.

Bauer got on his feet. "What do you mean, gone?" he asked.

"Cremated. The sister had the body cremated. We're talking Urn City. I told you we screwed up."

Bauer couldn't contain his outrage, though he surely

made an effort to do so. He spat out his words: "Jesus Christ! That's a fuck-up, big time! The body hasn't been identified, hasn't been processed for prints or trace. We didn't even have a head!"

Howe was surprised that this nice kid from Idaho would even raise his voice. It wasn't his fault that incompetence ran through the ranks of law enforcement in Spruce County. "I know," he said. "I know. You think you're telling me something I don't know? You think we're a bunch of loser locals, one step from being a rent-a-cop at some discount store? We made a mistake and my guys are real sorry."

Bauer bit his tongue. He knew the answer to his next question, but asked anyway.

"I don't suppose anyone took any tissue samples?"

Sheriff Howe continued to sputter in palpable embarrassment. "Sorry," he muttered. "None taken."

Bauer looked for a smoke. "There is a problem here, you know. We've got a body—rather we *had* a body—without a head and no real way to identify her."

"It's Claire Logan," Sheriff Howe said.

"How can you be so sure?"

"Her daughter Hannah said so. She looked at our Polaroids and I.D.'d her mother. Said, 'that's my mom.' Said it was her mom's pink bathrobe. No doubt about it. Said she and her brothers got it for her for Christmas. They each opened a gift Christmas Eve."

To blow up at the sheriff would only make matters worse. Bauer said nothing more.

"I'd like to talk to her, okay?" he asked.

"She's staying with her aunt, nice lady from the coast. They're checked in at the Rock Point Inn. The kid's pretty messed up. Lost everything and everyone. Her mom, her brothers, her dad years ago . . . she's an orphan. Got to be rough."

"And you showed her that photo of her headless mother?"

"Look, Bauer, we might be yokels out here, but we're not cruel. We masked off that part of the photo. All she saw was the torso. She doesn't know about her mom's head being missing. Give us some credit, okay?"

The two-tone myrtle-wood decor of the Rock Point Inn lobby was the hotel's signature feature and had been since the place was built in 1949. The lumber was harvested and milled in the town of Molten on the central Oregon coast. It was a rare wood, prized for its swirling grain and combination of light and dark. The wood was sold in tourist shops as boxes, tabletops, and lamp bases. No one who saw the lobby of the Rock Point Inn with its floor-to-ceiling myrtle wood would ever forget it.

Bauer asked for Sheila Wax, the victims' assistance officer who was assigned to the Logan girl, apparently the sole survivor of her entire family. Wax showed up, coughed a hello, and ushered him into a secluded area near the lobby bar. Over her coat-rack shoulders, he could see the figure of a slight girl, bent over. *Maybe reading a book?* He wasn't sure.

"Her aunt is over at Ressler's making funeral arrangements. You know her brothers are dead, too."

Bauer suppressed a grimace and nodded as pleasantly as he could. *Of course*, he thought, *the aunt was at Ressler's mortuary. She's the one who ordered her sister's remains cremated.*

"How's the girl holding up?" he asked.

"I'd say, not too bad considering all she's been through. Really, if you ask me—and you did—she's holding it together like a little trouper," Wax said, then shrugged. "But God knows what she's really thinking. She *seems* okay."

She led him away from the lobby to a seating area with two couches and an overstuffed ottoman. A young girl sat quietly with her back facing them.

"Hannah, this is Jeff Bauer. He's with the FBI. He's here to help figure out what happened at your tree farm."

She turned around, and the first thing that Bauer noticed was her brown eyes, enormous and so very sad. Though she wasn't particularly thin for her age, she looked small. Her frame had been gulped up by a Bobcats sweatshirt.

"Okay," she said. Her braces caught the light. "I'll do what I can, but I don't think I can help that much. I mean, I really don't know what happened for sure."

Bauer sat down, knowing it was not the first time this ground would be trod, and with the ongoing discoveries at Icicle Creek Farm it would not be the last. He'd never interviewed a child before; in all, he'd barely conducted two dozen 302s since he'd been assigned in Portland, and all of those were adults investigated for racketeering and money laundering.

"I know this is a very bad time, Hannah. I don't want to add to your grief, but Mrs. Wax is correct. I'm here to help."

Hannah studied the FBI man's face. The muscles in her throat constricted so tightly, she felt as if she'd suffocate. She needed help, and she wanted to believe that the man with the sparkly blue eyes and messy sandy hair that hung over his forehead was the one to give it to her.

"Okay," she said, moving her eyes downcast and tucking her small hands into her lap.

"Good. First of all," he said, "I want to tell you that I'm very sorry about what happened to your family. I am so very, very sorry."

He touched her shoulder very gently and Hannah shuddered slightly. Her eyes welled up and she started to cry. Bauer didn't know what to do next. *What's appropriate?* He stood there, his hand on her shoulder, for a few moments and watched Hannah wrestle for composure. He felt sorrow, deep gut-wrenching sadness. But more than anything, a twinge of shame, too. He felt badly that his job called upon him to add to her misery by probing for information at the worst moment in her young life.

"Can you tell me what happened?" he asked gently.

Hannah drew her knees up to her chest. "I was asleep," she said. "I heard some yelling coming from outside. I sleep with my window open a little. Even in winter. It was my mother yelling at Marcus."

"That would be Marcus Wheaton," Bauer confirmed.

She nodded. "Right. Marcus worked on the farm, but he was also a friend of my mom's. Mine, too. He lived in a trailer my mom brought in so he'd have a place to stay. He worked for us as a handyman and tree cutter."

"What was your mom yelling?" Bauer asked.

Hannah pondered the question for a moment. "I couldn't make out the words at first; I hadn't woken up all the way. I went to my window and I saw them by the wreath shed. Marcus was carrying the big gun we use to flock the trees. We call it the sno-gun. He had the tank, too."

"What time was it?" Bauer asked. "Do you know?"

"I looked at the clock when I got up. It was 11:40," she

said. Bauer noticed that she seemed proud that she could be so precise.

"That's a great help," he said. "What happened next?"

"I don't really know. I went back to bed and a half hour later I woke up a second time. Smoke was coming into my room. I opened the door and it was so black and dark and thick. I didn't know what to do. I called out for my mom—her room is next to mine. But she didn't say anything. I went back to the door, opened it, and crawled on my hands and knees. The floor felt cold."

The pace of her story accelerated. It was as if Hannah Logan wanted to get the whole tale out between a single pair of breaths. She was a runaway train. Inhale . . . tell the world what happened . . . exhale. "The floor was wet. I couldn't see what it was, but I could smell it. I put my hands to my face in the dark and I could smell it." Tears fell down her cheeks.

"What? Smelled *what*? The smoke?"

Hannah shook her head rapidly. "No," she answered. "Well, yes, I smelled the smoke. But when I held my hands to my face . . . I smelled the snow."

"Snow?" Bauer scratched his head. He didn't get it.

Hannah nodded. "Not *real* snow. I smelled the snow stuff we use on the trees. Marcus had sprayed the snow all down the hallway, down the stairs . . . the house was covered inside with snow."

Bauer was utterly perplexed. The image of a house with floors and furniture coated in fake snow just didn't compute. "Why would anyone do that? That stuff is flame retardant."

"No. No," she said, starting to cry. "Mom used the old stuff. We had a shed full of it. Got it half price because it wasn't any good. You see, it wasn't safe. It burned up."

Sheila Wax caught Bauer's eye. The VAR woman was beside herself with alarm. The girl had gotten herself out of the house and to safety when she obviously wasn't supposed to. Wax knew it and so did Bauer: she'd been left to die.

"I went to my brothers' room," Hannah continued, crying harder, "and I tried to get in. I couldn't. The door was stuck. I called for Erik and Danny. But they didn't answer. I called for my mom again, but she didn't hear me."

Between sobs, the kind of deep, guttural cries that break the listener's heart, she told the FBI agent she didn't see anything that night but a burning house, barn, sheds, even their car.

"I never saw anyone until the firemen came. I never saw my mom, my brothers, or Marcus. Everyone was gone. Everything was burning." Hannah stared down at her lap and went quiet.

"I think she's had enough," Sheila Wax interrupted. "Maybe a break now?"

Bauer agreed, but he had one more question ricocheting around his mind. He took a deep breath and mulled it over for a moment. He wanted to know what Hannah could tell him about the other bodies police were finding planted around Icicle Creek Farm like a human crop.

"Hannah," he said very gently, "we discovered something else at the farm. Something very, very bad."

Her eyes fixed on Bauer, but she said nothing.

"Others may have died there, too. Besides your mother and brothers."

He used the word "may" to soften the incontrovertible facts.

"Who?" she asked.

"We were hoping you could tell us. It appears that some men, some army guys, were found dead." Again he chose words that he hoped would lessen her fear, soften the blow, and yet help in the investigation.

But Hannah became agitated and stood up. Sheila Wax glared at Bauer and moved closer, as if to brace the girl from falling.

"I don't know," she said, crying loudly. "I really don't know. Anything. Anything more."

The interview was over and Bauer knew it.

Later that night at the Whispering Pines, over a cold beer, a greasy tuna-melt, and an impossibly limp kosher dill spear, Bauer flipped through a folder Sheriff Howe had left at the hotel's front desk. He felt rotten. He'd made a young girl cry. *Real nice.* Among the papers were the names of the first non-Logan victims to be partially identified by Spruce County authorities. One was a man from Deer Lake, Idaho. Bauer called the Portland office.

"I grew up near there," he said. "That one's mine."

CHAPTER SIXTEEN

Federal law enforcement agents from across the country were yanked from their holiday gatherings by phone calls from overstuffed-with-turkey field office chiefs. Jeff Bauer, as it turned out, was not the *only* lowest man on the totem pole. There were others, too. The flight to Deer Lake was white-knuckled from its liftoff from the small airport just north of Rock Point to the icy, slag-rimmed Idaho mining enclave about an hour from Boise, the city of potatoes and Mormons. Bauer didn't much care for flying to begin with, but for crying out loud, he could envision nothing worse than a ride on one of those twin prop planes he felt were more suited to crop dusting than passenger service. The gate agent at Mountain Air laughed when Bauer asked for a window seat.

"*Every* seat's a window seat on this one," the sheepish agent said.

Bauer flipped through the airline's complimentary newsletter—it wasn't even a real *magazine*—as the plane bounced around over the mountains, making the kind of noise that reminded him of a bowling alley, knocking pins and rolling balls in the gutter. He was en route to see the sister of the first identified victim, an army retiree named Cyrus Crowe. The file, like Crowe's body when unearthed on the farm, was almost skeletal. Like several others—though not all—Crowe's teeth had been extracted with a blunt object, probably a hammer. The forensics guys on the scene in Rock Point recalled a case in Cleveland in the 1960s where a serial killer had done the same thing to a half-dozen victims to avoid detection. And it worked in that case. None of the Cleveland victims, street whores and runaways, were ever claimed. No dental charts were produced, and because the victims were never named, neither was their killer. But Crowe was identified because of a distinctive eagle tattoo that had been preserved as though it were a scrap of tanned hide. A Missing Persons data bank in Washington, D.C., had a description of the tattoo among its vast files of the missing but not forgotten. Crowe had been sixty years old, had served twenty-five years in the army, retiring as a staff sergeant. He'd been married, but sadly his wife—pregnant with his only child—died in an auto accident in 1962. He had one surviving relative, a sister named Barbara Layton. She reported her brother missing when he didn't show up for Thanksgiving at her home in Deer Lake, November 1972. It had been more than four years since Crowe's disappearance. According to the report, the sister gave up looking after three years.

Bauer parked the rental car, a maroon Pacer with a tree-shaped air freshener hanging from the mirror, in front of the white-gabled house that had been converted to the duplex that had been Barbara Layton's home for the past decade. A hand-lettered sign pitched next to the mailbox fringed with icicles indicated the other unit was available for rent.

Barbara Layton came to the door in a cloud of smoke. A cigarette hung from her lip; deep pink lipstick crept into the fissures around her mouth. She looked older than her years—late fifties, according to the FBI file. Bauer introduced himself, and the woman with the nicotine-ravaged voice extended her arm and motioned him inside. A wood stove sent out a blast of dry heat that nearly knocked him to the braided rug–scattered floor. She offered coffee and Bauer accepted.

"He never got over DeAnn's death," Barbara said. "And, of course, the baby, too."

DeAnn had been the name tattooed with the image of a red rose with a broken and bleeding stem on his forearm.

"I'm sorry about your brother," Bauer said, acknowledging the death of the man before asking questions that would form the backbone of his investigation. He launched into a few rudimentary facts and emphasized that the case was only beginning and more, hopefully *much* more, would be known later. She said she understood and told the handsome young man that she would be grateful for any information he came across.

"I want to know what happened to him. I want to know if the man, the handyman they arrested out there in Oregon, did it. I expect he did. And I want an answer. For my brother. He was decent and deserves that much."

"All victims deserve nothing less," he said. As Bauer brought out a tablet of paper and a silver Cross pen, his eyes fastened on a photo atop a creaky table crowded with spider plants and cloudy jars of rooting cuttings. The framed photo pictured a man in an army uniform.

"Mr. Crowe?" he asked, nodding in the direction of the photograph in the chrome frame.

"Yes, that's my brother . . ." Her voice fell to a near whisper. "I knew he was dead. I've known for a long time. Even so, this is very, very hard." Her eyes watered.

Bauer would later say that was the only time the woman would express anything that resembled emotion. It was fleeting, but unmistakable. While she stirred heaping spoons of freeze-dried coffee into earthenware mugs, she told Bauer that while she had loved her brother, the truth was they had not remained particularly close. He left Idaho for the military and never really looked back.

"Oh, after he retired," she said bitterly, "he said he'd come back here and live. I'm alone, you know. My husband ran out on the kids and me thirty years ago. Talk about a real jerk. The kids live on the coast now. No one wants to stick around Deer Lake."

"That must be rough," Bauer said, steering the woman back to her brother's life. "I'm sorry about your brother. Your . . . loss."

Barbara dropped powdered creamer into her cup. "You know, I'm kind of glad that he's dead," she said.

Bauer looked at her, but said nothing. *He didn't know what to say.*

"I realize it sounds a bit harsh," she said, "and I don't mean for it to be that way. It's just that with him being dead, I know that he's not coming back to Deer Lake. I know that I don't have to wait. He was never really happy after he lost DeAnn anyway."

Bauer pretended to understand, though he couldn't

quite grasp it. He'd rather have hope than finality, if indeed it meant the death of a loved one.

The dead man's sister lit another cigarette and told Bauer that she had no firsthand knowledge of who Claire Logan and Marcus Wheaton were or why her brother would have landed in Oregon in the first place. She only knew what she had seen on television. As a way of appeasing the young man who had traveled so far, she offered him a box of her brother's belongings.

"I have some of his papers if you want to go through them; you're welcome to take them with you. Just send them back when you're done."

She held out a shoebox, and Bauer took it.

"Special Agent Bauer," Layton said, holding the door open, "is it true that they found a dozen dead bodies out there in Oregon?"

"Twenty, ma'am, counting the dead woman and the two boys."

"Were the others, the seventeen, were they all army? That's what I heard. That's what everyone is saying."

Bauer shook his head. "Not all. I'm not really supposed to say. The investigation has just started." Her eyes were so pained that he found it hard to refuse her simple request. "Not all army," he said, "some are Marines. Even a couple of navy guys."

"What does that mean?" she asked. "I mean, I wonder why?"

"We don't know. Not yet."

Special agents in six other states conducted interviews similar to Bauer's chat with Barbara Layton. It turned out that Cyrus Crowe and the others unearthed at the Logan farm shared a number of similarities beyond their pursuit of a military career. All had been single and lonely. All but four had been sixty or older when they disappeared. All had few close relatives to report them missing, though in actuality most had been reported missing by someone. In some cases, there had been more than one report made.

One agent made the trek to rural Liberty, Mississippi, and talked to a woman who had filed a report with the Jackson police two years before. She was convinced her friend—a man who raised pigeons and cut her lawn with a riding mower—had met foul play on a trip out to Seattle or somewhere *out there*.

"But nothin' was done. I called three times! The cops only do so much before they give up," she said. "After a while I gave up. Someone else cuts my grass and I let his pigeons go. Thought he'd be real mad at me for that. But I guess not."

A retired Marine from Pittsburgh named Conrad "Connie" Patterson was also a loner. Connie was discovered missing when his Chinese pugs, Ding and Sing, weren't collected as promised. The dog kennel owner reported it because he had to bathe the pugs a second time—four days after the owner didn't show up.

"I still have Ding and Sing," the kennel owner said. "Nice dogs. Nice guy, too."

An army officer from Weed, California, was the oldest at seventy-three. He had a thirty-year career in the military before opening a secondhand store in the small northern California town. Business hadn't been great, and when the man turned the grimy cardboard sign over to CLOSED never to flip it back, no one cared but the landlord.

The agent who was dispatched from San Francisco to Weed filed a brief report: "No contacts made. No one knows anything about the victim."

Darrin Hoadley left behind two daughters when he disappeared. The women, both in their late twenties, couldn't stop crying when the agent, a woman, came calling three days after Christmas.

"We knew something like this would happen," the elder of the daughters muttered. "He wouldn't have left us for good . . . not without a reason."

"How could this happen?" the other said, a blonde with violet eye shadow and an overbite.

The special agent, a seasoned veteran from the Salt Lake City field office named Donna Andrews, pulled some tissue from her purse.

"We're doing our best to get to the bottom of it," Andrews soothed.

"You'd better," the older sister said, her anger barely contained and ever close to seeping to the surface. "I want someone to pay for this! Our father was a good man. For Christ's sake, he was a man of God!"

The three talked for two hours in a room the female agent had rented at a motel, though she had no intention of staying overnight. Both sisters were married to staunch Mormons and didn't want to talk about the investigation in their homes.

As in the case with the others, it appeared that Chaplain Hoadley was like the others—single. His wife had divorced him when she could no longer take the months apart when he was at sea. The girls were ten and seven at the time and saw their father only occasionally over the first few years following the divorce. Even so, somehow they managed to remain close.

"I have no idea why he'd go there," the younger sister said of her father's trip to Oregon. "He didn't like the rain. He used to tell us he had enough of water from being on the Pacific all those years. He was stationed in San Diego."

The women didn't know if he had any friends in Oregon, but they suspected he probably did.

"He never knew a stranger. The men on the ship loved my dad. He was booked for fourteen weddings when he retired."

"Did he know Marcus Wheaton? Claire Logan?"

The older of the two wrinkled her brow. "I read about them in the paper today," she said. "But, no, he did not know them that we ever heard."

"Even though he didn't say that he was leaving town," the other said, finally speaking up. "There is one thing that we always wondered about."

"What's that?"

"He sold his condo two months before he disappeared. We don't know what happened with that money . . . and what about his pension? The navy wouldn't tell us a thing about it, but I got the impression that he was still getting his checks. For the longest time I thought he was alive."

"How much money did he have?" the agent asked. "I mean, was your father wealthy?"

"Not really. He spent most of his money on photography equipment. He bought two Nikons and a Hasselblad in one year. But the money from the condo was probably greater than two hundred thousand dollars. It had a view of the Hotel del Coronado. He loved that red peaked roof. My dad thought it looked like a circus tent. And it did. He was like that sometimes. He liked the circus."

* * *

It was the box, or more accurately its contents, Barbara Layton had given Bauer in Deer Lake that gave the case an entirely new and, some would say, disturbing focus. It was true that Bauer gave the contents a cursory review before scrunching his six-foot frame into a seat on the flight to Portland and had fully intended to pore over the entire contents. But the bumpy ride and the queasiness in his stomach forced him to set everything aside. Upchucking into the box, he suspected, would be extremely poor form. It wasn't until he got back to his apartment in Portland that he made a pivotal discovery.

The apartment building manager was lurking in the parking lot in the way he always did—giving young girls the creeps and making awkward conversation necessary from those who caught his eye. Bauer slung his bag over his shoulder and locked his car. And since conversation couldn't be completely avoided, he told the lurking manager that he'd likely be "in and out" over the next few weeks.

The man nodded, his eyes hinting for more information in the transparently pathetic way frequently employed by bad actors and the very lonely.

"On assignment," he said, though he felt like a jerk after the words slipped off his tongue. It sounded so . . . so . . . *Mr. Big.*

"The Rock Point slaughter?" asked the tiny man with bug eyes and slicked back hair, a style that made him amphibian or vaguely reptilian. His ever-present olive-colored turtleneck didn't lessen the image.

Bauer brushed past him. "Can't say," he answered, wishing he hadn't even opened his mouth. "Sorry."

In his apartment, Bauer fished out an Elton John cassette from his collection, *Madman Across the Water*, stuck it in the machine, and put up his feet and went to work. What he had wasn't evidence, per se, but the personal effects given to him by what had been a missing, now a *dead*, man's sister. He was not, Bauer was sure, compromising any investigation. Instead, he was giving himself a head start on a case that he was sure would be the biggest of his career.

Inside the box with the foxed edges were photocopies of Social Security documents, discharge papers, medical history (including test results indicating the presence of prostate cancer), a passport, and several news clippings. There were no financial papers. This omission was surprising and he made a note to follow up on that. Barbara Layton had said her brother had closed his bank account before leaving San Diego. It was the sole thing about which she was utterly convinced.

A news article folded accordion-style before being placed in an envelope fluttered to the floor. It had been cut from a newspaper called something-*Guard*. Bauer thought the first word might be *Honor*, but he had never heard of it. An advertisement on the reverse side provided fodder for his thesis. It indicated it was a newspaper or magazine aimed at military retirees. Who else, Bauer wondered, would want a mock cover of *Life* magazine with their picture inserted and "VJ Day Hero!" emblazoned on the cover. A headline in block letters read GREAT FOR THE GRANDKIDS. The article was not trimmed in its entirety, so Bauer focused on the other side that appeared to be a portion of a classified ad section. Further inspection showed five notices circled in the skipping ink of a dying blue ballpoint pen. The marked section contained personal "Meet a Mate" ads from women. One advertisement stood out from all the others:

Searching for a Silver Eagle. Come soar with me on wings of friendship . . . and more. I am 42 years old and own my own business. I'm told I'm attractive and I've kept my figure. You'll have to be the judge. Yes, I have three children, but they are young and well behaved. I have a beautiful farm in the woods of the Great Northwest and am looking for the right man to share it with. I have everything . . . but You? Write Ms. W, P.O. Box 111, Rock Point, Oregon.

It was the address that made Bauer sit up and slide his feet under him as if he was going to jump up, which in a split-second, he did. It also drained the blood from his face. Bauer went for the phone and made two calls, the first to Derek Saunders, the Special Agent in charge of the Portland field office. Saunders wasn't in, but his secretary took down a message. The next call was to the Spruce County Sheriff's office in Rock Point. The discourse was brief. The sheriff said he was heading out for a smoke break.

"You need to find out who had Box Triple One—111—at the Rock Point post office," Bauer said, his eager-beaver voice as evident as it had ever been in his entire life. He caught himself and slowed down before adding, "I'm on my way down there."

"No prob," the sheriff said. "Don't get your panties bunched up and I'll get what you need."

Bauer made a quick trip to the bathroom, picked up his

bag, slung it over his shoulder, and left Elton to finish his songs alone.

The postmistress at Rock Point was a wiry woman with a one-color-all-over curly brunette helmet, which hugged her head as if it were a midget octopus. She also had the surly attitude that most agreed came with the inky territory. Della Holm had been working at the "new" post office for nine years. Before that, she worked a dozen years at what had once been billed as the "Smallest Post Office West of the Rockies" in the back of the Mullins Hardware Emporium in downtown Rock Point. But that was over when a bureaucrat who had never set foot outside the Washington Beltway decided Rock Point needed a new post office. *A new facility*—was how the memo referred to the place. *Facility.* It was such an iceberg way of talking about something as important as a post office. A post office, Della knew, was the heartbeat of any town—no matter its size. Della hated the new building, a modular structure with indoor-outdoor carpeting and a butcher block counter because "it looks like a bureaucrat's idea of cost savings for white-trash America." Della was bitter because she had no longer had a claim to fame; she no longer could boast at the annual regional postmasters' conference in Portland that her station was the smallest, biggest, busiest, prettiest. *Nothing.* She was now in charge of a post office that resembled an RV, and, she readily admitted to anyone who asked, it hurt her.

"I've given my life to the government and I get this?" she would ruminate over and over. "Who ever heard of such an incredibly stupid idea as a carpeted meter work area? *Those idiots!*"

She pinned up a drawing of Uncle Sam holding a mail-bag with the words SIZE MATTERS! She pretended it was a gift from a disgruntled customer who sympathized with her plight, and she didn't have the heart to take the darn thing down.

On December 28, Della Holm was busy hating the world and fiddling with the Pitney Bowes label maker when Sheriff Bob Howe and the pleasant-looking out-of-towner, a young FBI agent named Jeff Bauer, arrived. She didn't protest when the sheriff inquired about the holder of Box 111. She could have asked for a warrant. She could have said a flat-out "no" and told the cops to beat feet. The information was confidential. "Our patrons have a right—*are guaranteed the right*—to privacy," she had read in the manual when she first started her so-called career. That was in the days when she was young enough to still believe the government gave a hoot about her tiny post office and doing things the right way. Instead, tired of hand stamping half the stuff that came through the slot in the counter, pissed off because her pension wasn't going to be enough, Della brushed her creatures-of-the-deep hair from her eyes and told the sheriff what he wanted to know.

"Claire Logan," she said, "rented that box for years. Icicle Creek Farm has a separate box, though. This one's for her 'personal' mail. All addressed to Ms. Logan. Ms. Shoot, who is she fooling? She's a *Mrs.*! Husband was a nice guy, Marty Logan."

"Lot of mail for Ms. Logan? Her private box?" Bauer asked, ignoring the commentary.

Della Holm looked at the young man, for what probably was the first time, and nodded an acknowledgment. He was about the same age as her own son, a history teacher at Rock Point High. If his appearance hadn't been so pleasant and his manner so earnest she'd have likely been a bigger bitch.

"That's what I thought I said. Though to be fair, her mail came in fits and starts," she said. "Sometimes she'd get four pieces in a day. Sometimes she'd come in and bitch when I didn't have any for her. Like it was my fault or something. The woman was a piece of work."

Bauer nodded. He expected that Claire Logan was many things; a piece of work was at the top of the list.

"Not that I paid too much attention, and I never read any of it for sure—a violation of USPS codes. But I did notice that the mail came in cycle-like. At the end of each month."

"Thank you, Mrs. Holm. By chance is there any mail in her box?"

Her response was lightning quick. "No," she said.

"Would you please check?"

"No need to check. She doesn't have a box anymore. Closed out both on Monday."

"Closed them?"

"That's what I said."

Bauer was extremely interested in the timing. Claire Logan gave up her post office boxes two days before the fire, two days before her purported death. Sheriff Howe didn't seem quite so interested. He shifted his weight from one foot to the other and let out a sigh.

"Did she say why?"

"Yes, she did. She said she was going traveling after the holidays. Didn't say where and I didn't ask. I'm not the nosey type."

She slammed another stamp on a parcel and muttered

something about how people never put enough postage on anything.

"Got what you need?" Howe asked Bauer, jamming his hand in his pocket in search of his car keys. "Wife's got French dip makings for lunch, leftovers from our Christmas prime rib, and I want to get home." He patted his round belly as if it were a baby that needed feeding. Bauer just smiled. And like a petulant child left out of a conversation, Della pounded the rubber of a "hand-cancel" stamp against a manila envelope addressed to someone in Eugene.

"I've got work to do," she said. "Short week, you know."

Bauer had one more question. "Did she leave a forwarding address?" he asked.

Holm kept her head down and slammed her rubber stamp with rapid, machine gun–like emphasis.

"Nope," she said. "Good riddance, I say. I always had to hassle her about paying for her box."

The days following the fire were both seamless and numbing for Hannah. Like the small globe calendar that sat on her father's highboy dresser before her mother put it away in a sock drawer, each day just rolled by, clink-clink, to the next. Leanna came from the coast to take care of her, but Hannah didn't know her aunt that well. Claire didn't have much room in her life for her sister. In fact, Hannah had only met her mother's sister one other time—when she was almost five. Leanna and her new husband, Rod, came to visit one Sunday afternoon, but they argued with her mother and father and left in a tearful huff. Her mother never talked about Leanna after that visit.

Hannah stayed in her motel room bed, curled in a ball. She felt numb, like when she and Erik and Danny used to play in the paraffin vat their mother used for sealing the ends of Western cedar branches used for garlands. With the hot wax coating their fingertips, they would tap against the big wood worktable, but couldn't feel a thing. Leanna gave her a candy cane and Hannah sucked on it for three days. Her mouth was so dry, so cottony, she was sure it was because she had cried so many tears. She was dried up.

She imagined that the fire hadn't happened at all. She and Danny and Erik were on vacation. The boys were at a motel and their mother and father were in an adjacent room watching television or putting quarters into the Magic Fingers machine. In a moment, they'd be pounding on the wall telling all of them to go to sleep. *"Right this minute!"*

CHAPTER SEVENTEEN

As the third day of the investigation drew to a close, Spruce County resembled a law enforcement convention with more uniforms and mustaches swarming the place than had ever been seen there. Oregon State Police, Spruce County Sheriff's deputies, reserve officers from neighboring Cascade County, and of course, the agents from the FBI vied for parking spaces, restaurant tables, and hotel rooms with members of the media. And though he was probably the youngest of the lot, Jeff Bauer had the kind of amiable ("Let me work with you") presence that made him a natural focal point. His good looks didn't hurt either. When the camera went to him, it captured the image of a young man who knew what he was talking about even when he wasn't supposed to say something. Such a performance meant a lot to the higher-ups back in

Portland and even more so to the big guys in Washington,
D.C. In fact, not saying anything at all while appearing to
answer a question was an enviable skill, one others seldom achieved. Some cops could talk; and some couldn't
without making room in their mouths for a foot. Sometimes two.

Bauer wasn't the special agent in charge of the Rock
Point case, though he felt he should have been. That honor
and responsibility fell on the slightly stooped shoulders
of a nearly retired agent named Sam Ross. Ross was named
agent in charge of LOMURS as the bureau tagged it—for
Logan Murders. It was an exciting case to most everyone
but Ross, who was burned out and bored and more than
ready to move on. He'd been in the bureau twenty-five
years and didn't give one whit about going out in a blaze of
glory on January 18, his retirement day. He kept a pocket
calculator and counted down the days and hours toward his
gold Seiko watch, his retirement home on Loon Lake west
of Spokane, and his none-too-great government pension.
Ross met up with Bauer after the interview with the postmistress. They shook hands and Ross went to lunch. They
met a second time at the motel, where the older man simply hung around and stayed on the phone with agents at
the Portland field office. When it came time to talk with
Marcus Wheaton, Ross pretended to be interested.

"Important interview," he said of the Wheaton interrogation. "Key, I'd say. Why don't you handle it?"

The offer caught Bauer off guard. "You want me to
take the lead on it?"

"That's what I said. Got a hearing problem?"

"No. I can do it."

"Good. I'm not really sure if we have any jurisdiction

here anyway. Seems this is shaking out like a county case. But we're here. Might as well work through this."

Inside, Bauer disregarded Ross's comments. This was *his* case now. He notified Sheriff Howe.

"We want to talk to Wheaton."

"He lawyered up a couple of hours ago. Brinker's the name. A good guy, but court-appointed and you know what they say."

"You get what you pay for?" Bauer said.

"You got that right." Howe chuckled as though he'd heard the remark for the first time.

Forty-five minutes later, Bauer and Ross signed in to see Marcus Wheaton at the Spruce County jail. It was a nice jail, as those places go. Surprisingly modern, given it was more than twenty-five years old. It had been built during the then-governor's push to make sure prisons and jails in Oregon were humane. There were six cells at Spruce County Corrections and Justice Center. Five were outfitted for men and ran the length of the building. A sixth was segregated from the others—a toilet with a beige tiled enclosure was its primary distinction. The men's commodes—the other five—were stainless steel and planted in the open where anyone using them could be observed at all times. The women's cell had been used infrequently. In fact, the last time it had an occupant was when a transvestite from Colorado got in a fistfight with a local fry cook outside the Crazy Eight, a downtown Rock Point bar. A *straight* bar. A guidebook to the gay Northwest apparently contained an embarrassing error.

In late December, a couple of drunks and a kid serving

out the last days of a pot possession conviction occupied the first three cells. Ostensibly for security measures, though Sheriff Howe later conceded it was because they wanted to keep an eye on Wheaton at all times, the handyman with the gas can was kept in the women's cell, which was adjacent to the sheriff's office.

The FBI agents followed Sheriff Howe into the interview room where Wheaton sat in a turquoise, plastic-molded chair and stared at the table as if the white-and-gold splattered surface held some keen interest. The room looked more like a kitchenette than any "justice center." Wheaton was not handcuffed. When he looked up, it was with a single eye.

"As I've said, I didn't kill nobody," he said.

"Right. Tell that to Erik and Danny's sister," Ross said.

Ross wanted to show the greenhorn how it was done, but also to get the damn thing going as quickly as possible. The sooner they were done, the sooner they'd be able to leave and return to Portland. Even so, Bauer was impressed. He didn't know Ross even knew the twin boys' names. He didn't think Ross had paid a bit of attention to any of it.

Ross must have sensed that Bauer was impressed, because in an instant, the older FBI man decided to do a little grandstanding to show the new kid how it was done.

"How's it feel to kill a couple of little kids? A bunch of old men . . . and a woman?"

Wheaton shook his head. "You, mister, don't know what you're talking about."

"We know enough," Ross retorted. "Enough to have you swinging from the gallows in Cutter's Landing by Easter."

The big man stopped himself from bubbling over,

though his anxiousness covered his bulbous face. "Where's Brinker?" he asked.

"He's coming. Be here any minute." Sheriff Howe drained the last of his Pepsi. "You keep talking, Marcus."

"You and Mrs. Logan had a little thing going? Usually it is the employee who gets fucked by the boss. Funny, you really turned the tables on her, didn't you?"

Bauer wasn't sure where it was going, but Wheaton made it crystal clear.

"I don't want to talk to you," he said, looking at Sam Ross with his good eye. "I'll talk to *him*." He pointed to Bauer.

Ross shrugged. "Fine," he said. He didn't care at all and didn't even bother pretending that he did. "You talk with Agent Bauer and I'll get a head start on my beauty sleep."

After Ross departed for the hotel, Wheaton cleared the phlegm in his throat and spoke softly. Bauer had to strain to hear each word. He noticed the gauze wrapping over his ear wept some fluid.

"I just want you to know. I would never hurt those boys. I'd never hurt Claire. Never in a billion years."

"If you didn't, then who?"

"I'm not saying anything about anyone else. I'm just telling you about me. And I'm telling you that I wouldn't, *couldn't*, hurt Erik and Danny." The big man blinked back a tear from his good eye.

"Then who? If not you? I mean, did Claire kill her boys?" Bauer asked. It was a question that had never been asked out loud. But it had been brewing in Bauer's mind since the conversation with Della Holm at the Rock Point post office.

Wheaton sat mute.

"Listen to me very carefully, Marcus. You might be a decent guy mixed up with a bad woman. You wouldn't be the first. Prisons are full of men who did something stupid for the love of the wrong woman."

"I don't follow you," the singed handyman said. His face was expressionless.

"Okay. I'll be direct. You were screwed by Claire Logan," Bauer said. "The corpse found beside Erik and Danny was not their mother's. Are you following me now? If you didn't put the body there to help Claire fake her death, then I'd say you were tricked just like everyone else."

"What are you talking about? Claire is dead. She just has to be . . ."

"Don't think so . . ."

Travis Brinker, decked out in a three-piece navy blue suit and a spanking new black leather briefcase, burst into the room. "This interview is over," he said.

"Too bad," Sheriff Howe deadpanned. "We're just getting started."

Bauer nodded. "Yeah, Marcus Wheaton wants to tell us something. We're ready to listen, too."

"This is over," Brinker said as Wheaton looked on. "Right *now*."

CHAPTER EIGHTEEN

The homicide and arson investigators didn't have it easy—even when they knew Claire Logan had probably advertised for her victims in a military newspaper. They needed to know more than just how, who, and when. The "why" would be helpful, too. But the crime scene was vast and the number of victims was unlike anything anyone had ever seen. Only a cop who had worked an apartment fire in Detroit that killed thirty-one had even the remotest point of personal reference. The Logan house and outbuildings had, for the most part, been reduced to ash. The fire that ignited as children across the world dreamed of Santa and presents had burned so hot that no pour patterns survived the inferno. Investigators picked through the rubble in search of clues. Shards of metal and the coils of several mattresses survived, as did the burned-out remnants of the kitchen—a stove, a refrigerator, the ghostly web of a hanging rack for pots and pans. Jeff Bauer observed the police criminalists as they carefully bagged the charred remains of Claire Logan's house. It was tedious, mundane work and, with the snow against the blackened debris, oddly reminiscent of the old black-and-whites shot at some early twentieth-century disaster like the 1906 earthquake in San Francisco.

From the burned deadfall of Claire Logan's house, one investigator recovered the blackened and burned figure of what appeared to be an infant. Horror seized him and he called for the others to help while he gingerly cleared away the debris and rubble that nestled the baby's blackened body. Then he saw the baby's black face peer from a hole in the debris, its small mouth appearing to cry out in a scream that no one could hear. The crime scene investigator started to laugh—a soft, then loud rolling laugh, the kind meant to get attention.

"It's a doll," he said. "It's just a goddamn kid's baby doll!"

And it was. A swarm of men in yellow slickers gathered to laugh, too. The kind of laughter that firemen know, and police officers, and EMTs, and even reporters with strong stomachs and the crime beat: the laughter of relief.

The investigator later told a newsman, "After all that we found out there in the fire and out in the earth, I started to expect the worst. What's another dead baby to this nightmare? Makes my heart sick, those little boys died there."

Scraps of wood, including a doorframe, the piano, and the floorboards that were pinned under the piano, were sent back East for examination. While the murder of the boys, the woman, and the men found in the ground at the

Logan farm were the focus of the growing investigation, the arson was also of critical importance. Speculation ran through town that Claire Logan and Marcus Wheaton had been in on the blaze together. It seemed from statements he made that he protected her, might have even loved her. Della Holm, the postmistress, beat that drum to her customers as they came to the post office to send back gifts that hadn't suited them. Others gossiped, too. As Bauer and others continued digging—literally and figuratively—they learned more details about the woman and her connection to the one-eyed, son-of-a-bitch slob who was locked up at the jail.

One woman called Bauer at the Whispering Pines Motel and told him the story of the time Claire gave her a ride home from work. She did not want to give her name.

"I needed a job and Claire gave me one. I twisted cedar garland for most of October through December and I was good at it. She said my garland was flawless. She was nice to me. One night when my car wouldn't start, Claire offered to give me a ride home. Her husband was dead by then. Just after we got onto the highway we hit a deer. I remember the jolt and how the doe lurched to the side of the road. The deer was still alive and making this awful noise, kind of a gurgling sound. Anyway, Claire turned off the car and reached over me to the glove box and grabbed a hunting knife. I saw a gun in the glove box. You know that little light? Well I could see the gun very plainly. Anyway, she got outside and grabbed the deer's head like she was going to hug the poor thing, then took that knife and slit its throat. She started screaming and I was freaking out. I didn't blame her. But you know why she was screaming? The deer sprayed blood on her jacket. She was mad at the deer. And I said, 'Claire, why didn't you just shoot it? You got a gun.' And she turns to me and kind of smiles a weird smile. 'I was pretending it was my husband and I wanted to feel him die.' Then she laughs and I started laughing. I don't even know why I'm laughing, except for the fact that she is. I thought it was pretty cold killing that deer the way she did. A bullet through the head would have been quicker."

Bauer wrote his thoughts in a report he knew he'd probably never officially file. He wasn't a forensic psychiatrist; he was a federal cop and his job was to catch a killer, not profile one. Even so, he kept a notebook of observations that he hoped would help him find young Hannah's mother:

> *Claire Logan is a classic loner. Her pleasant façade masks a bitter and angry woman. No one is good enough; no one is worth anything. Her ambitions and desires take precedence over all others and their needs and wants. She has no close friends. Her only living family member appears to be a younger sister. Her first husband died in an accident, and there was some suspicion of Claire's possible involvement. None was proven. She was—is—a very controlling woman. With the exception of Marcus Wheaton, she's never been able to retain an employee longer than a single Christmas season. Those who knew her insist that she was brilliant, abrasive, and full of grandiosity when it came to her business and her lifestyle.*

A week after the remnants of the Logan house were flown in a commercial aircraft's cargo hold to the labs at Quantico, word came back to Bauer and the others working the case that an accelerant had, in fact, been used to burn down the house. Significant traces of acetone were found on the doorframe and floorboards. The piano, however, was clean. This puzzled Bauer at first, until he remembered the original location of the piano—the *second* floor. Bauer felt a chill. The brave little girl had been the final intended victim.

The volunteer fire department's pump truck had arrived eleven minutes after the call—a remarkable, an *incredible*, response for a rural area, but the two-story farmhouse was already a blazing shell when the team arrived. They said it looked like the sun had crash-landed on Icicle Creek Farm. As the steam rose from the spray of their hoses, they knew little property and no people could have survived such an intense fire. Oddly, like a blackened monument, it was the piano that stood alone in the center of the debris. And as the days passed, that monolithic burned-out instrument commanded the most attention. The piano was of considerable interest because the bodies of the two boys and the headless woman had been sandwiched between it and the floor.

Further chemical microscopic analysis revealed an abundance of cellulose and mica particles found in the area under the piano. At first it was thought to be packing material, but a sharp-witted chemist put two and two together—the chemicals *and* the business of the tree farm. The acetone and the cellulose were two components of Christmas-tree flocking material. The cellulose provided the puffy white bulk of the spray and the mica added silvery sparkles that some revelers found especially festive. Hannah Logan had told investigators that she had seen Wheaton with the sno-gun that night . . . and as she felt around in the smoke, she touched a coating of spray flocking on the hallway and the stairs. Bauer theorized that Wheaton used the flocking to increase the speed of the fire. Traces of kerosene were also identified.

A photo lineup showing Marcus Wheaton's one-eyed mug among five others (his lawyer would argue that the lineup was unfair because each of the other men had two eyes) got a positive identification from a salesman for Cascade Floral, Inc., a Portland wholesaler. Beyond mums and roses for the floral trade, the company specialized in supplies for Northwest tree growers. Among their product lines were various brands of cellulose and rayon flocking. When the FBI agent showed up to ask about the various products they sold, the counter salesgirl tried to sell him on buying rayon over cellulose.

"Half the price, twice the markup," she said, assuming he was there to place an order for his own farm and tree lot. "It fluffs nicely. Looks very real."

The agent explained that he wasn't a grower in search of flocking, but an FBI agent looking for answers. He didn't say which crime. But the girl seemed to know. She pressed the "call" button of the intercom mounted next to her telephone and summoned her manager. A minute later, a short butterball of a man emerged from his corner office and confirmed that Icicle Creek Farm was a customer.

"Not a big customer, but steady," he said. "Paid on time and always took the two percent cash discount. Could use more like Icicle Creek."

It took the manager all of ten seconds to identify Wheaton.

"His is a face you'd never forget," he said, using the eraser end of a pencil to indicate the Icicle Creek Farm's handyman.

* * *

Several days into the LOMURS investigation, the first of what would eventually become scores of Claire Logan "sightings" made the broadcast airwaves. Sheriff Howe and Bauer were drinking coffee when a deputy came in and told them to turn on the old TV that sat on a shelf above departmental service awards and certificates for community involvement.

"Quick! She's on the tube. Flip on channel six!"

"Who?" the sheriff asked.

"Claire Logan!" the deputy replied, pushing past the round table with the morning's paper and an overloaded ashtray. He turned the knob and rolled the dial to Channel Six. An attractive female reporter in a tan raincoat and a robin's-egg-blue scarf stood in slushy snowfall gripping a microphone and pointing to a strip mall twenty yards behind her. Despite the frigid air, her hands were bare. Her showy lacquered talons couldn't be contained in gloves.

". . . police responded after a Salem woman reportedly spotted Logan at this washateria just west of the university . . ."

Bauer and Howe were flabbergasted. Both wondered what the Salem police thought they were doing talking to the media. Why hadn't they bothered to notify the Spruce County authorities, not to mention the FBI?

"What the hell?" Howe said. Anger showed on his face. Even his ears were dipped in red. He slammed his fist on the table with such force that a weaker man would have yelped. "Get that cocksucker Reid on the line," he barked at the deputy. "RIGHT NOW!"

The deputy spun around and went for the phone.

Chuck Reid was the police chief for Salem, Oregon's capital, a jurisdiction that was big on pulling over boozed-up legislators, busting hookers on the stroll, and cleaning up the vices that appear to go hand in hand with government work. Violent crime wasn't a part of the mix. Not usually. And criminals the likes of Claire Logan were never caught in places like Salem. Just didn't happen.

The TV reporter asked a woman of about thirty what she had seen. The woman held a baby with curly brown hair to her shoulder and rocked back and forth as she spoke.

"It was her, all right," she said. "I saw her picture on the news and the next thing I knew she was standing in line with me waiting for the change girl at the Laundromat. It was Claire Logan . . . I'm sure of it."

As the reporter interjected little pieces of the story, the number of the dead, the missing money, and the fact that what was purported to be Claire's body had been destroyed, the deputy hurried back into the room.

"Got Chief Reid on the line." The deputy's eyes bulged. "Says he's sorry. And sounds like he means it."

Bauer watched as Sheriff Bob Howe let the police chief of Salem have it with both barrels. His Andy Griffith demeanor vanished in an instant, and for a split second it looked as if he were going to tear the roof off the jail. But Bauer thought it was justified—every word Sheriff Howe uttered Bauer could have easily echoed.

"We've got a major investigation here, Reid. I know sure as hell you've been reading the papers and watching television news. We've got bodies stacked up in our gymnasium, for crying out loud. And you guys do this without so much as a phone call? What the hell are you doing . . . grabbing a bit of glory for yourselves?!"

After half a minute's tirade, complete with spittle foaming the corners of his mouth, the sheriff grew quiet and appeared to listen to Reid. Another minute passed and he ended the dialogue. "Talk to you later," he said. His tone was congenial, without being apologetic. His ears were no longer red.

"It wasn't Claire Logan the woman saw doing her laundry. It was a local gal with the friends to prove it. The alias wasn't an alias, after all. She left her goddamn wallet at home. That idiot from Channel Six pushed a story out there when she already knew better."

"Not the first time that's happened," Bauer muttered. Despite allowing the woman's body from under the piano to be cremated, he liked Sheriff Howe.

Later, a ticket taker reported seeing Claire Logan at a bus station in Portland; a jealous woman reported her husband's mistress was Claire; and a woman from Rock Point was sure she saw Claire at the Fred Meyer on Colfax Avenue. If the woman from Rock Point got away with murder, she didn't go unnoticed. At least it seemed that way.

Was she dead or not? Had she engineered the most astonishing disappearance in criminal history? The FBI broke tradition, and for the first time since Clyde Barrow's love and partner in crime, Bonnie Parker, and a San Francisco antiwar protester/fire bomber named Colleen Deming, a woman's name was added to the FBI's Most Wanted List.

Della Holm, the Rock Point postmistress, hung the poster all over the tiny post office.

"Local girl makes good," she said to customers.

CHAPTER NINETEEN

A woman who appeared to be at least fifty, certainly old enough to know that her bird legs and paunchy tummy didn't qualify her to wear the short skirt she had on, approached the front desk of the Whispering Pines Motel. Never mind that the ensemble was ludicrous for Oregon in the winter (and probably, given the conservative nature of that part of the state, wrong in any season). She lugged a purse the size of an overnight bag. She knew who she was looking for; she'd seen the fellow on the news the night before. The young FBI agent from Portland was standing there checking his messages. She'd come in person to deliver hers.

"Mr. Bauer?" she asked.

Bauer felt a chill down his spine as he turned around to face Marcus Wheaton's mother, Liz. Her voice had a husky, steeped in bourbon, quality. He, too, had heard her on the news the night before.

"Liz Wheaton," she said, extending her hand. "I got the message that you wanted to see me about my son. So here I am. And you know what I want to tell you?" She steamrolled ahead. "I want to tell you what you need to know to get this whole damn thing over with."

Bauer shook her hand. It was as cold as a crab claw. "Hello, Mrs. Wheaton," he said, "I'm glad to see you. Is this a good time to talk?"

The motel manager looked on. His eyes bulged. "I wouldn't be here if it wasn't. Actually," she added, "it is not a good time. But here I am. I am a mother and that's why I'm here. Mr. Bauer, my son might be a lot of things—fat, stupid, lazy, ugly. *Whatever*. But he is not— and hear me loudly and clearly—a murderer."

"I see," Bauer said. "Let's sit down." He motioned to a corner by the pop machine and the day-old Danishes left over from the free continental breakfast.

"Let's not and just say we did." Her voice was harder-edged in person than on TV when she was whining about her son being railroaded. "I want you to know that Marcus is a good boy, a decent young man. If he were killing those men and had killed those two little boys, I'd have known about it. I am his mother, for Christ's sake. I know my son! He could never hide anything like that from me."

The manager pretended to read the day's paper while he listened to every word. Bauer longed for a private room with a stenographer and a yellow pad.

"Mrs. Wheaton," Bauer said, "supposing you tell me what your son had to do with the fire and the murders. He was there, you know."

"Of course he was there." Her voice was rising and her pumps were digging into the Berber carpet like cat claws. "He worked for that bitch-on-wheels, Claire Logan. And like I told you, he was stupid. He was in love with her. Get it? She was the woman of his dreams. Don't ask me why. Don't even try to explain it. I told him over and over that she was just using him. 'Go to town and get this! Harvest twenty-five more trees before lunch. Clean the goat barn!' She had him on a string ten feet long!"

"I see. He was in love with her?"

Mrs. Wheaton set her suitcase-size handbag on a chair and stooped to fish through it for a lipstick. Sample-size containers of all kinds spilled out. She scooped them up, grabbed the shade she wanted, and started applying it to her thin lips, going over the edge to make them fuller. All the while talking.

"Mesmerized is more like it. Claire Logan mesmerized him. And for what? She's knocking off all these old guys for their money, life insurance, I bet, and what is he getting? Nothing. He's getting screwed. She screwed him big time. She left my boy and flew the coop."

"How do you know that? I mean how do you know she's not dead?"

"Listen, I know. I know because I've met Claire a time or two. Been out to the place. Met the kids. Poor Erik and Danny. I feel bad about the kids, I really do. I have a soft spot in my heart for kids," she said.

I bet you do, Bauer thought. *Real good with kids, aren't you.* "What do you mean? What about Claire Logan makes you think she's not dead?"

Liz Wheaton hoisted her purse from the chair seat. "Because she's as cold as a witch's tit in a brass bra. She's like some reptile. All Claire cares about is money. She'd do anything for money. *Trust me*. I know the type."

With that she turned around and walked out the door.

Three doors down from the mortuary was the main local branch of the Oregon State Bank. A phone call made by Bauer that afternoon had secured an appointment with Darwin Graves, the bank manager. Graves was a pleasant fellow with a moon face speckled with acne scars. He smelled of Clearasil and Head & Shoulders shampoo. He wore a brown knit tie and a plaid shirt, rolled up to the elbows.

"I can't give you any records," Graves said, ushering Bauer into his office.

Bauer was nonplussed. It was part of the game. "I understand," he said. "I'll get a subpoena here tomorrow."

"All I can do is confirm whether she had an account here or not."

"She," of course, was Claire Logan.

"That will be fine."

Graves flipped through a manila folder. If it was meant to telegraph that he had more to say about Claire Logan and her accounts at Oregon State, then it worked like a charm.

"She doesn't," the bank manager said.

"Did she ever have an account here?"

"Not now, but ever? At any time?"

"Yes, that's what I mean."

"She did." Graves looked down at the folder. "Not now, not *anymore*, but she did."

"When? When did she close it?"

Again a slight stall. "Recently," he said.

"How recently?"

"I don't want to say. I could probably get in trouble for this. You know, without the subpoena, the banking ethics guys will get on me. We have rules, you know."

"I know," Bauer said, though he sometimes hated the rules. He understood the reason for them. "This is a major investigation. Your help could turn out to be vital to solving this crime."

Graves' face went white. "I'll tell you that she no longer has an account here. Hasn't had one since she closed it on December twenty-third. All of her money is gone. Cleaned out."

"Was the amount substantial?" Bauer asked.

"I'm really not going to say anything more. I can think of two hundred thousand reasons not to." He nodded in the direction of the door, satisfied with his own cleverness. "You have a nice day and good luck on the case. Claire's kids were very well behaved. So sorry to hear about her boys. Very, very nice little boys. Hope the girl will come out of this all right."

As the pair walked toward the door, Graves leaned over to whisper in Bauer's ear.

"She's got an account at First Oregon, too. On Cherry Street next to the Marcie's Silver Spoon. Ben Rafferty is the manager. Don't tell him I sent you."

An hour later, Rafferty, a dolt with half the intellect of his banking colleague Graves, outlined the same story to Bauer. Claire Logan had cleaned out her account on the same day. Her account totaled more than $220,000.

"She was in a hurry when she came in. We didn't have

much time to chat, but she said she was going to invest in her farm," he said. "Too bad it burned down. Kind of ironic, if you ask me."

"That's one way of looking at it," Bauer said. "Thanks for your help."

"No problem," Rafferty said. "You want the stuff she left in her box? I know the rules, but you're making me feel like she's never coming back."

"I don't know that," Bauer said. "But what stuff?"

"Some paperwork," he said, walking over to the vault to retrieve the contents of another of Claire Logan's safe deposit boxes. "If you're looking for an escape plan, you're out of luck. I'll get it for you."

A moment later, Rafferty appeared with an oversized envelope. It was curled in a U-shape from being held in the narrow box.

Bauer opened the envelope and pulled out some papers. It took only a moment to realize what they were.

Jesus, he thought. *What am I supposed to do with this*?

Later that day, Bauer dropped the packet off with Veronica Paine. She was at her office; a ceramic tree fitted with twinkling lights sat on a small table between two visitors' chairs. The room was cool. The heat had been kept off for the holidays.

"This belongs with you, I'd say," Bauer said. "Doesn't apply to anything I'm doing. And I doubt the sheriff should have it."

"I'm intrigued," she said. She smiled and took the packet. She put on her stylish readers and scanned the documents, pulling one after another and placing them face down on her office desk. She looked up at Bauer. Her face went from quizzical to concerned.

"I'm glad that you brought this to me. I'm taking this to Judge Wells. This is going to be sealed."

The greatest disappointment of the Logan case happened so slowly that no one recognized it until it enveloped them like a dense fog, quiet and omnipresent. Law enforcement had discovered three obvious murder victims in the house, and seventeen bodies in various states of decomposition planted in two areas of the property. An extensive search employing a backhoe and infrared analysis turned up no other lime-stewed corpses or rotting hotspots. *Twenty dead.* The problem with the case was that the autopsies of the two boys showed they had been poisoned with sodium cyanide and were dead *before* the fire consumed so much of their flesh. The fire, probably started by Marcus Wheaton, had not killed them. While he theoretically could be charged with their murder, it was a poor case. Nothing could connect him with poisoning the boys. For a time, Spruce County prosecutor Veronica Paine thought she'd try, but she knew only too well that a loss would mean that the victims of Oregon's worst mass murder or serial homicide (the debate raged for a decade, *which was it?*) would go without retribution.

After talking with Liz Wheaton, Bauer came to accept the possibility that her son had been duped by a very clever, if not diabolical, woman. Not that torching a house with the bodies of two little kids and some woman wasn't a horrendous deed, but Bauer doubted whether the hefty, one-eyed man was really a killer. An accomplice, maybe, but a killer? After all, Bauer reasoned, the bodies started disappearing before Wheaton came to work for

Claire Logan. Several years before. Since autopsies revealed that the missing military men had been poisoned with cyanide in the same manner as Erik and Danny Logan, it was clear that it could not be proven that Wheaton had a hand in the murders. Coupled with the fact that the only living witness, Hannah Logan, never saw Wheaton do anything other than spread the flocking. It was only an arson case.

Almost one month into the investigation, Paine telephoned Bauer at the Portland field office. He'd been back for a couple of weeks. Pending the outcome of further lab analysis from Washington, he fully expected to head back to Rock Point at some point, though it was not a federal case. There was no joy in Ms. Paine's voice. She sounded tired and drained of emotion.

"We can't make the murder charges stick," she said. "We can't connect Wheaton to the murders—not to the extent it would take to nail him."

Bauer knew it was coming. Deep down, he'd known all along. The person behind the murders was exceedingly clever. "Brilliant" was the word he thought of first, but he didn't want to waste an accolade on Claire Logan.

"I figured as much," he said. His tone was calm and meant for the Rock Point lawyer to understand that it was resignation, not disappointment, he was registering. He added, "You had a lousy hand from the beginning."

"We did. We *all* did," she said. "The arson will stick and we'll put him away for a long time. And," she paused, "if we ever find out if Claire Logan is alive—and where she is—we can probably use Wheaton against her. He might be agreeable after a few years in Cutter's Landing."

"Yeah," Bauer said, "especially if we can show how

his girlfriend, his soul mate, is living the high life with all that money."

An Associated Press story written by the barracuda reporter Marcella Hoffman broke the news two days later. The *Lumberman* ran the wire service piece because its own reporter couldn't get an interview with Veronica Paine. Editors headlined the story: MURDER CHARGES DROPPED, WHEATON WILL BE TRIED FOR ARSON

A sidebar described the continuing mystery of the headless woman and the growing belief that Claire Logan had killed her two sons and seventeen men before faking her own death by decapitating some hapless woman. Though all but three of the men would eventually be identified, the headless woman, "Number 20," as she became known by just about everybody, remained a mystery. *She belonged to someone*, Bauer thought, hoping that her mother, husband, boyfriend, sister, or someone would come forward and claim her. Didn't she deserve to be more than a stand-in for the infamous Claire Logan? Oddly, it was her unshakable anonymity that gave Number 20 such notoriety. The woman's gruesome plight was turned into a wildly popular catchphrase. "Drop a Twenty" meant "Lose your head; go crazy."

But more than anything, people speculated about where Claire Logan had run off to.

One woman, a cashier at Wigwam, a discount store, mused that she was sure Claire Logan had taken all her money and gone to Mexico. "She's down there, I'll bet you. It makes me sick to think she's down there laughing at all of this. Hope she chokes on her money."

A man who worked as a guard at the Stoneway paper mill disagreed. He was certain that Marcus Wheaton had killed his employer, probably in a fit of jealousy over one of his competitors for her affection. The disappearance story was "complete and utter bullpucky."

"She's dead. I'm convinced that headless body was *hers*. Wheaton gave her what she deserved. I'd have done the same thing."

CHAPTER TWENTY

On the southernmost edge of the windswept Oregon coast, just north of the California border, Misery Bay was a pit bull's bite out of the rocky coastline. It was all craggy cliffs and tumbled driftwood bisected by Fishfry Creek, which raged during the winter and trickled in the summer months. Misery Bay was far enough from Oregon's congested I-5 corridor that it had escaped the influx of country wannabes who insisted on living in half-million-dollar homes with satellite television and hot tubs. Those soft-bellied crybabies from Seattle, Portland, and even the San Francisco Bay Area were not welcome in Misery Bay. They were seen as whiners who covered their cars at night with parachute-silk blankets and yet had the gall to complain about the high prices of video rentals and nonfat milk at the mom-and-pop establishments that make up the majority of the businesses on Ore-

gon's salty side. One Misery Bay local had even put out an
unwelcome mat: DON'T CALIFORNICATE OREGON! Although
the town seemed somewhat isolated, Misery Bay was ac-
cessible by car, sea, or air (it had an airport with three
weekly flights to Oakland and Portland).

And yet, Misery Bay was far enough off the beaten
track that when The Nightmare was over, it was the perfect place to send Hannah Logan. It was the ideal landing
spot for Hannah to start over, fade into obscurity, and,
God-willing, begin a normal life. The fact that Hannah
had relatives living there was in a way almost incidental.
One of the caseworkers from Spruce County had even
suggested that it might not be prudent to have the girl
raised by anyone associated with the family.

*"What transpired at the Rock Point residence will fol-
low this child for the rest of her life,"* the social worker, a
childless woman of forty who raised West Highland terri-
ers, wrote in a purple-ink fountain pen. *"Constant re-
minders in the way of continuing family contact with
relatives who don't support the investigation and its find-
ings might prove detrimental to our efforts to assist in a
complete and full recovery. These family members seem
to want to care for the girl, but it is doubtful that they are
equipped to do so."*

But Leanna and Rod Schumacher were above re-
proach and there was nothing anyone could do about it.
Investigators hammered at the couple to see if they had
any knowledge of Claire's whereabouts, but they held
firm. It was easy to do so. They didn't have a clue where
she was, and if they did, neither had any qualms about
what they'd do to her with their bare hands. Nine visits by
social workers and a representative of a victims' rights group
resulted in the decision by a Spruce County Juvenile Court

judge that Misery Bay and the Schumacher home would be suitable after all. The social worker gave the family much-deserved Brownie points for keeping their silence throughout the run of their niece's ordeal. Not once was there a word of comment from Misery Bay. Not a single utterance of support or condemnation for Claire Logan was made by the Schumachers. *Nothing.*

Aunt Leanna was a strawberry blonde with large hands and freckled skin, both physical attributes causing her great embarrassment. Leanna was five years younger than her only sister, Claire. She was a teacher, married to Rod, the owner and operator of Misery Bay's first Speedy Mart, a wood- and glass-block box with a Slush Puppy dispenser and a pair of pinball machines. The Schumachers had no children. When circumstances called for them to step in and raise Hannah, they did so with the kind of assurance that comes from attending church, teaching school, and running a small business. The Schumachers had no choice. Their adult lives had been built on doing the right thing.

Besides her hands, the first thing Hannah noticed about her Aunt Leanna was that she perpetually smelled of citrus. Lemons to be exact. At first, Hannah assumed it was an air freshener or the scent of a particular brand of furniture polish that lingered on her aunt's clothing. Her first night in Misery Bay, she learned otherwise. From a chair in the master bedroom where she lingered before bedtime, Hannah watched Leanna Schumacher rub fresh-cut lemons on her face and arms. It was a ritual Leanna performed, she explained, every night before she went to bed. She had done so, she told her young niece, for the past ten years.

"It reduces the spots," she said with a laugh. Her woodpecker laugh rat-a-tatted throughout the porcelain confines of the master bathroom. After she split the lemons in half on a cutting board that she stowed under the sink, she let the juice run into a cup. Next, she emptied the juice into a spritz bottle and sprayed the sour mist all over her arms. She twisted the squeezed lemon halves on the knobs of her elbows. Last, she closed her eyes and misted her face.

"You're lucky you don't have to resort to this," she said, patting off the excess. "You have your daddy's skin," she said.

"I guess so," Hannah said, watching in awe at such a beauty regimen. "I guess I'm lucky about something."

Their eyes met in the mirror. Leanna's mouth went from a lemon pucker to a frown. "I'm glad you're here," she said. "Your uncle Rod and I wanted a child of our own for so long and now we have you. This was never the way we would have wanted to have you, but we thank the Lord every day that He has chosen us to watch over you."

And in a minute, both began to weep. They held each other in the lemony bathroom and convulsed into spasms of tears. Each time Hannah cried harder, Leanna let loose with her own anguish.

"In time, I do believe things will get better," Leanna said softly.

Hannah wiped her eyes with the back of her hand. Her eyes were red, and spots mottled her complexion. "I wish I was dead," she said.

Leanna put her big hands around the girl's still-shaking shoulders and caressed her. "Oh everyone does a time or two in their lives. Even *me*. But we get by. Someday, I'm certain, that will pass," she said, her composure complete. "It may not be for a while, but I know someday you'll be all right."

Hannah wasn't ready to accept that. "I do wish I was dead," she said. "If I was dead then I wouldn't have to think about any of this again."

Leanna held her niece more snuggly. "Don't be so dramatic, dear. Give yourself time. Lots of time. If you don't—*we* don't—put it out of our minds, even just a little, we'll never be able to do anything but relive it over and over."

"I don't want to relive it," Hannah said. "I want to forget it."

Leanna folded a face towel and set it on top of the toilet tank. "I want to forget it, too."

Hannah and Leanna were bound by the horror and unimaginable tragedy of what had transpired at Icicle Creek Farm. Leanna, of course, hadn't been out to the site until after it had been partially cleaned up, but she'd read everything she could get her hands on and had the stomach-turning sense about what her niece had seen and endured. Though there were many times when she could have brought the subject up, she didn't. She never asked Hannah a direct question, preferring to allow her niece to tell her in her own good time. But after weeks turned into years, it was apparent that there'd never be a good time to talk about it. And that, both figured independently of each other, was the way it should be.

For Hannah, it turned out, living in Misery Bay made it possible to live in obscurity. While the story was covered by all of the TV networks, the local stations in Portland and Salem rooted themselves in Spruce County, tilling the soil and turning every rock of the case for the evening news. TV reception was so poor in Misery Bay, people caught their news from the three stations in San Francisco that came in best. Obscurity hadn't been a concrete plan of the Schumachers, it just *happened*. And it wasn't that her aunt and uncle didn't do what they could to help Hannah Logan get on with her life. They did so very quietly and behind the scenes. Rod made sure that the driver for the periodical distributor made his store the first stop whenever any of the tabloids came out with a Claire Logan update.

When *People* magazine featured Claire's photo on the cover and the headline: WHERE IS SHE? Rod dipped into the petty cash drawer and bought every copy delivered for resale. He trashed all but one, which he and his wife read in their lemon-scented bedroom after Hannah went to bed. Then, like the other magazines and newspapers he collected, Rod encased the *People* in Saran wrap and put it in a trunk for the day when Hannah might want to know everything that had been written about her mother—right or wrong.

When Rod Schumacher had enrolled Hannah in school, he improperly prepared the paperwork and accidentally put his own surname for Hannah's. The office administrator, who knew the Schumachers from church, assumed that Hannah was the daughter of Rod's brother, whom she had heard had died with his wife in a car crash in Seattle. No one bothered to correct her. Hannah Logan became Hannah Schumacher.

In the beginning, at least to the other students who were clueless about her circumstances, she was sullen, a zombie, shy, a weirdo from some unknown place back East. But in time she made friends and even joined the school volleyball team. It wasn't that Hannah didn't think about her mother, her brothers, her father, her life before Misery Bay; she just knew that by keeping busy, by *acting* normal, she'd be able to *be* normal.

But Aunt Leanna noticed that night after night, Hannah was up reading, studying, writing. *Doing something.* She worried that her niece was not getting enough sleep.

"You need to get some rest," she said after 11 p.m. one evening when she saw the light still on.

Hannah looked up from her Oregon history book. "Test tomorrow," she answered. "Just a few more minutes and I'll turn off the light."

"All right. Just tonight."

"Aunt Leanna," Hannah said, "it works better for me to just drift off thinking about something that really matters to me. When I do that, I'm sure it sounds stupid, but I can almost pick my dreams. I pretend that my mind is a TV and I can turn the channels of my thoughts to something that will keep me from thinking about any of what happened to my brothers or my mom. I'm always turning the channels."

"That's a great idea," Leanna said. "I'll have to try that, too. But with my luck I'll end up only getting commercials."

Both laughed and it felt good.

Misery Bay, Hannah would later tell her husband, Ethan, probably explained how she'd survived the first months after the fire. While the rest of the world felt sorry for her, the people of Misery Bay never gave what happened in Rock Point much thought. As isolated as they were in their windswept coastal location, as busy as they were with the real concerns of their own lives, they just didn't seem to care much about the story that was preoccupying the rest of the country.

For the most part, Hannah suffered in silence while the adults who watched over her did the best they could. She had several counselors, a guardian ad litem, a court-appointed social worker, and the Rock Point chapter of the Jaycees, who quietly collected money for her college education (by the time she was ready for college, their donations with interest totaled $71,000).

As her time on the witness stand approached, all associated with the case knew Claire Logan's daughter was the key. If she could deliver testimony as compelling as she had when she made her first police and FBI statements, Marcus Wheaton was not going to leave Spruce County a free man.

Hannah knew that. "It's up to me," she told Bauer one afternoon in late February, two months after the fire when the special agent came out to see the Schumachers. The four of them—Rod, Leanna, Hannah, and Bauer—sat around the maple kitchen table that faced the ocean. Sideways rain splattered the windows, and Leanna rolled up a towel to catch the drips that seeped onto the window ledge.

"Not completely. There is other evidence tying him to the fire. Mrs. Paine has other witnesses," Bauer said.

Leanna spoke up. "But they aren't enough to send Marcus to prison," she said.

"They could be," Bauer said as he consumed the last swallow of coffee.

Hannah looked up from her cocoa.

"But the other witnesses aren't enough, not all by themselves," she said, a slight quaver in her voice. "I mean, without *me* they aren't going to convict Marcus. Am I right?"

Leanna reached over and held her niece's hand while Uncle Rod looked on with concern.

Bauer leaned forward from the other side of the table. "Yes, Hannah, I guess they couldn't convict. I wish that your testimony wasn't needed. Sometimes we have to do things that we don't want to do."

"I've told her that, I have," Leanna said, still holding Hannah's hand. "I've also told her that by telling the truth, Hannah will be able to put some of this behind her. Not all, but some."

"True. But even so, I suspect it will take a long, long time." Even after saying that, Bauer felt compelled to offer her an out. "As I expect the court psychologist has told you," he said, "you don't have to do this."

"I know."

"And you know, it isn't really about your mother. This is about something you can do, for yourself, for your brothers."

Hannah looked away. "You have said that before. So have Uncle Rod and Aunt Leanna. But I know better. Mom's not here, but whatever she *did* is the reason we are here. She's the reason Marcus did what he did."

Although a well-meaning psychologist without a clue about adolescents had suggested "putting things on paper helps with the healing process," the fact was, long before the tragedy, Hannah had kept a diary. She had written her thoughts in a padded vinyl book she kept under her bed. That diary had been lost in the chaos that had consumed

Icicle Creek Farm, the FBI with their German shepherds in search of flesh and bone, and the media with their rabid hunger for any tidbit of news. The fire had devoured all the belongings that would have linked Hannah with her past.

As a matter of course—growing up, changing tastes—the diaries evolved. Some had locks; others did not. Two were written on steno pads. In time, she graduated to yellow legal pads. Aunt Leanna always assumed her niece was writing notes for composition class, so firm was her commitment to the endeavor of writing. Hannah wrote notes upon notes.

Each entry began with the same three words: *Today I remember*.

Today I remember—Something gnaws at me as if to tell me that I had been told to go to the supply shed where the ribbons and shears were stored. I was told to go there and get something. Wire? Ribbons? A tool? I remember walking across the snowy path that the boys and dogs and I had made from the house to the shed. The spot in front of the door was muddy and trampled. Icy footprints marred the surface of the landing like the plaza in front of Grauman's Chinese Theatre in L.A. where Mom and Dad took us for vacation the year before he died.

When she wrote those words she was in a lock-hold battle with herself and her memories of what had happened on that particular Christmas. She remembered it had snowed heavily. From late afternoon to early evening, white nestled against the green of the trees outside. In her mind's eye, Hannah could rerun the images. She watched as the white came after her like a million moths drawn to the light of the wreath maker's shed.

Hannah kept her diary in the top drawer of the 1930s blond-wood nightstand that had been the sole survivor of her aunt and uncle's first matching bedroom set. Before bed, Hannah pulled a Bic pen from the drawer and began to write. First impressions she knew were important. Her mother had said those very words many times before one of her "visitors" came to the farm.

> *It almost scares me, this open sky over the ocean. In the woods, we had the cover of the trees. When it rained we could still stay dry. My brothers and I—I can't even write their names yet—we used to make forts out of fir boughs and sword ferns, and no matter how much it rained, we stayed dry. Here there is no place to hide. No place to run for cover. I look out at the ocean and I just want to put an umbrella up and stare at my feet. I don't know why. I don't know why the water and the sky scare me. I wonder if it is because here at the ocean there is no place to hide.*

She closed the entry with a row of W's, waves for the ocean. Underneath the waterline she carefully sketched the figure of a small girl, her arms waving through the Ws. From her mouth was a bubble with the words: *"Help! Can't swim!"*

Bauer made several trips to Misery Bay before the trial—on the Spruce County Superior Court docket for the spring. He was drawn to her not only because his job demanded that he stay in touch, but Hannah had endured a terrible tragedy and he'd been there to pick up the pieces. They had bonded. One night he, Rod, Leanna, and Hannah played Monopoly until nearly 1 a.m. It was an evening of pizza, Dr Pepper, and kidding around—an evening without tears, guilt, or the specter of Claire Logan looming over them. For the first time, Bauer saw that Hannah was going to be all right. There was a chance that she'd not only survive her mother, but be able to move on.

"The way you laugh," Hannah said, her eyes hooded from the late hour, "reminds me of my dad."

"That's nice," Bauer said, touched by the remark, but a little embarrassed. Leanna watched him carefully and made a slight smile in his direction.

"It's late," she said. "Time for bed."

"My dad was a wonderful man," Hannah continued. "My dad didn't deserve my mother."

"You got that right," Uncle Rod said, finally weighing in on Claire Logan.

CHAPTER TWENTY-ONE

It would be charitable of anyone to say that the Spruce County Courthouse resembled an oversized hatbox as it squatted on Second and Lewis Avenues in downtown Rock Point, Oregon. It was such an intrinsically ugly edifice. It was a round, postmodern structure with tiled horizontal stripes and rows of windows the size of those found on a Boeing 727. For two weeks, it was to be the home of the Wheaton arson trial. Cars filled the parking lot hours before the first day of the trial—an occurrence not seen since the 1952 trial of a dentist who had drowned his mistress in Lake Joy and weighted her body with brick-filled potato sacks. She was discovered when her left arm tore from its socket and floated to the shore. A sportsman found the wayward limb. Her inscribed wristwatch was still attached to her wrist: I'LL LOVE YOU FOR ETERNITY.

The bricks retrieved with the rest of the body had been the tooth doc's undoing. The bricks were the remainders of a special order he had used on a two-tiered outdoor barbecue pit built for his backyard. His wife had read the first article on the case that mentioned the yellow bricks and turned her two-timing husband in. The "Yellow Brick Murder," as it became known, attracted immense press coverage.

But of course, in the world of media vultures that was to come, that level of coverage was dust bunnies. Claire Logan had put Spruce County on the map when she vanished and left twenty bodies on her Christmas tree farm. She had been transformed into an anti-folk hero. In the months since she pulled off the biggest Houdini in criminal history, Claire Logan had become a superstar of the infamous kind. And though she was not going on trial that warm spring day—Marcus Wheaton was—it was still all about her. And as far as most observers could tell, Wheaton was as close as anyone was going to get to Claire Logan.

Spruce County prosecutor Veronica Paine and defense attorney Travis Brinker narrowed the potential jurors from a field of fifty to twelve. Among those sitting on the jury were a high-school biology teacher, a convenience store clerk, an office secretary, a mill manager from Stoneway Paper, and a mill hand. A few smiled at the sight of the mill worker, a strikingly handsome man of twenty-five, and the manager, a cello-shaped fellow with a wisp of smoke-gray hair: Stoneway had just completed a drawn-out labor dispute in February that left both sides pointing the finger. The very idea that representatives from both sides would work together on anything was almost ludicrous. But that's what they were to do. Seven women and five men were sworn to listen to the evidence and dispatch justice in the biggest crime to hit Spruce County in more than two decades.

As grotesque as the whole affair was and as close to the action as they were, no one in Rock Point really knew any of the victims. In its own bizarre way, that fact allowed them to give their stories, tell their tales, pose for pictures, and shake their heads for the TV cameras. As one high school student told the reporter from the *Today* show, "Nothing much ever happens around here, so this is kind of fun. Sad, but fun at the same time."

A single, hunched-over figure had come to watch the trial with the hope that Marcus Wheaton would leave Spruce County a free man. No one paid any attention to the woman in the long woolen skirt, though the day was too warm for such attire. She was in her fifties, with thin, gray hair, the color and texture of bread mold. Her breath smelled of cherry Lifesavers. Obviously the recipient of some kind of reverse makeover, Liz Wheaton, now looking older than her years, kept her head down when she entered the back of the courtroom. In her wallet, she carried grade-school photos of her only son, a man now accused of torching a farm house and setting off the chain of events that shocked the world. She stared at a little photograph of her boy. His eyes had gazed sweetly at the lens. Both eyes. He had not been transformed by tragedy into a one-eyed terror. He was thin, sweet, and, in short, an all-American boy.

"But, sir," she had said in her only interview, a phoner with a reporter from Omaha who had found her in her old Craftsman-style house in Portland, "my son couldn't have killed all those people. I raised him right. He wasn't a bad boy. *Never*. I think it was that Logan woman who caused this whole affair. If they ever find her, they'll have the real demon of this sorry occurrence."

The first glimpse of a defendant always brings a reaction. In the case of Marcus Wheaton, it was a muffled gasp from a courtroom. He had put on a few pounds. One reporter thought he might weigh upward of 250. He wore a dark blue suit with wide lapels and a bias-striped tie that most likely had been a loaner. Liz Wheaton stayed focused on her son as if she were sitting alone on a pinnacle and staring down a long tube. No one else was there to judge her for loving him. She didn't care what anyone thought.

Wheaton lumbered to the defense table, wrists red from the too-tight cuffs that had been removed by the bailiff just before the jury walked in. From their seats, none of the twelve could see what everyone else could. The defendant was wearing leg shackles.

A yellow pad, a cup of water, a pencil, and an empty manila folder were on the table. Wheaton would never touch any of those objects. Not that day, and never as the trial progressed. For the most part, as he had during voir dire, he stared straight ahead with little discernable emotion. Once in a while he looked out of the courtroom toward the tiny airplane-like window panels.

"Maybe he's looking for Claire," one woman mused as she put away her crossword puzzle and fumbled for change for the vending machines during the morning break.

"Yeah, maybe he's hoping she'll show up," her trial-watching companion said. "He loved her, you know, and my sister knows someone who briefly worked with him at Icicle Creek Farm, and he said the guy's been in love with Mrs. Logan for years. Do anything for her."

"Well he shouldn't have done this!"

"Guess so."

Defense attorney Travis Brinker was a young man, no more than twenty-six. His face had the kind of roundness associated with a fat person, though he was trim and physically fit. His skin was silky smooth with no evidence that decent whiskers could sprout from its glistening surface. But that didn't stop the strawberry-blond Brinker—a wispy caterpillar rested under his ski jump nose. He was sweet and nervous. Pitted against Veronica Paine, the young man clearly had his work cut out for him.

Many thought Paine fit her name. The defense lawyers around the cavernous halls of the Spruce County Courthouse called her Veronica *Paine-in-the-ass*. The moniker wasn't original, but it suited her just fine. She was no-nonsense and abrupt and she never gave the other side one bit of wiggle room. Paine was not unattractive by any means. Her hair was a glossy and thick mass of chestnut twisted up onto her head in a tight bun. She wore suits that flattered her figure. Her blouses almost always ruffled about her neck.

Paine shoved her evidence cart past the spectators as if she were bringing the mountain to Muhammad.

A woman nudged her friend to look up from her crossword a second time.

"She's a damn sight prettier in person than she is on the TV," she said approvingly.

"Why doesn't someone help her with the cart? God, that cart must weight two hundred pounds."

"She's one of those women who don't want any help at all."

"Maybe the men around here don't know how to treat a lady, lawyer or not."

Paine overheard the spectators and offered a slight smile in response. As she turned her head to regard the defense table and the defendant, her smile instantly retreated. Wheaton smiled in turn, but Paine turned away.

Veronica Paine's opening argument detailed the case against Wheaton. While she ran down each item of evidence, she jabbed a finger in the air in the direction of the defendant. Though everyone knew this was not a murder trial, Paine made sure all were aware of the charred bodies that were discovered in the ashy remnants of the farmhouse. She told the jurors Marcus Wheaton might not be a murderer.

"Not as far as we know," she said slowly and deliberately. "We don't know who killed those people. What we do know is that Marcus Wheaton was so in love with Claire Logan that he proceeded to cover up a horrendous crime to prove his undying devotion for her."

Wheaton glanced over his shoulder toward his mother's gaze. She smiled back.

"The evidence will show through receipts from Cascade Supply and Hardware that the defendant bought two gallons of kerosene oil of the kind used to fuel hurricane lamps. A witness from Cascade Floral, Inc. will tell you that the defendant routinely purchased flocking material used at Icicle Creek Farm . . . *and* used by the defendant to accelerate the fire."

A juror, number seven, nodded in affirmation.

"The evidence will show that the fuel and cellulose splattered on the defendant when he was setting the blaze. Lab analysis will prove this beyond any doubt."

Travis Brinker started to stand as if to object, his trousers sticking to the back of his thighs. Instead, he stayed put. Some wondered why he didn't object if only to stymie Paine's rhythm.

"What's more, we have an eyewitness. Not just any witness, mind you, but the daughter of Claire Logan. Hannah Logan will take the stand and tell you what happened that night and what she saw in the days and months leading up to the catastrophic fire."

She reviewed her notes for the flicker of a second.

"You will learn what was going on in that house, and yes, what went on between the defendant and Claire Logan as best as can be recalled by a young girl."

Paine warned the jury Hannah Logan might seem confused and overwrought with grief.

"This is to be expected," she said. "This is not an indication of anything other than a young girl torn apart by a terrible family tragedy."

Almost an hour had passed, and still she went on.

"A word about the deaths at Icicle Creek Farm," Paine said, her voice serious. "By stipulation, the defense, prosecution, and the judge have all agreed to acknowledge that a number of people died there. More than one and less than twenty-five. Though some will be mentioned by name during this trial, others will not. This is not a murder trial. This trial is about arson, a devastating criminal act in itself. In no way should any member of the jury construe that the defendant is responsible for the deaths of anyone."

With that, Paine took her seat. She looked satisfied; a quick read of the spectators' faces indicated she'd made her point.

Travis Brinker took a breath and placed his hand on Wheaton's bulky shoulder. A gentle smile broke across his face. If he had meant the gesture to indicate warmth and regard for his client, it did not. One woman among the spectators rolled her eyes. (*"I wish the jury could have seen the distance the two maintained when they were not in the courtroom,"* the woman later told a TV reporter.)

Brinker emphasized that the case was a circumstantial one. Not only that, the defendant was a victim, too. A victim of love.

"Let's get this out of the way right now," Brinker said. "We won't deny that Marcus was in love with Mrs. Logan. We won't deny he was there the night of the terrible blaze. He was. She was. But he was trying to put the fire out. This man is a hero, for goodness' sake. Not a criminal. Not an arsonist. We could say that Claire Logan was the arsonist. It would be easy for us to point the finger. Many lawyers would do that. But we can't in this case. We really don't know—and we cannot determine in this court—if she's alive or dead. If we say she's alive, then they"—Brinker looked at the prosecution's table—"they'll say she's dead."

Brinker's assistant, a woman with wire-rimmed glasses, looked astonished. She telegraphed her thoughts across the courtroom: *You're going too far!*

He continued anyway.

"Yes, you'll hear from witnesses who will recount much of what went on around the Logan place over the years," he said. "But again, so what? Who among us couldn't be painted with a sticky black brush by those who chose to? Who among us, indeed?

"Now, let's go to the evidence. Yes, he did purchase the fuel for the lanterns. Ladies and gentlemen, that was Marcus Wheaton's job. He also bought the faulty flocking because he had been instructed to do so! By whom? His boss, of course. The woman he loved, Claire Logan."

Brinker stepped to the oak rail that segregated the jurors from the rest of the courtroom.

"Listen carefully to the little girl. *Listen to Hannah Logan,*" he said. "We do not suggest she is a liar. No, not at all. But she is a girl born into a life of tragedy. She is fragile and weary. She is also mistaken. Hannah Logan has been pushed and prodded by the prosecution and by federal agents into—"

Paine was on her feet. "Objection, malicious and misleading!" Her face was red and her eyes were fixed in a glare. "There is no testimony to support such remarks."

"This is argument, counsel," Brinker said.

Judge Wells overruled the prosecutor and she shook her head in exaggerated disgust.

"I'll allow this kind of latitude for opening remarks," Judge Wells said, "but you've pressed the issue close to the line. Any more and we'll shut this down for the day to see what evidence you can produce to back up your remarks."

Fifteen minutes later, Brinker wrapped up and thanked the jury for their attention.

Veronica Paine was a methodical prosecutor. She was not given to grandstanding or punching the air of the courtroom with raw emotion. There would be time for that later. Just after ten in the morning, a handsome young man took a seat within the confines of the oak-paneled witness box. It was Myron Tanner, the volunteer fireman who was one of the first on the scene the night of the fire. At six-foot-seven, Myron was a giant. He had strong hands and a dazzling white smile. And more than anything, he deserved a name that suited his sheer physical presence better than Myron.

He told the court how he had happened to hear about the fire on his police scanner as he drove home from a party. Though he was off duty as a fireman, he turned around and drove over to the Logan farm. As coincidence would have it, Tanner had purchased last year's Christmas tree there—a six-foot Scotch pine that filled the front room of his rented mobile home. Tanner had seen nothing peculiar the week before. And he certainly had not expected what he'd find that snowy night.

"Tell the jury," Paine said, "what you saw when you first arrived."

Tanner turned to the jury box and tilted his head. He'd obviously testified in court before. "Oh, it was awful," he said. "There were smoke and flames everywhere. I got there a minute or so behind the truck with the squad. The house was completely engulfed. The barn where they stored a bunch of their stuff was pretty far gone, too. I've never seen anything like it. Never."

"Did there come a time that you saw a person or persons on the property?" Paine asked.

"Yes, ma'am, I did."

"Please tell the jury," she instructed.

"Well," the giant in the box continued, "I parked and ran over to the house, you know, to see if anyone needed help or whatnot. It was hot. Hotter than any fire I'd ever seen in my life. When I came around the corner on the southwest side of the place, I saw him."

"Him?"

"Yes," he said. "The defendant. I saw the defendant, Marcus Wheaton."

"The defendant?"

"Objection. He's already said so," Travis Brinker said, standing. "Asked and answered." Brinker's client was impassive. Some wondered if Wheaton had any other expressions at all. His good eye was as blank as a sprayed and wiped chalkboard. Judge Wells sustained the objection and prodded Paine to move on.

"What, if anything, was the defendant doing?" she asked.

"He was throwing things in his truck and gunning it out of there."

Over the next six days, Paine called her witnesses as though she was creating one of those construction-paper chains; each person was linked to the one before him or her and all led back to Wheaton. The manager from the Portland floral supplier who had sold the flocking material; the FBI chemist who identified the traces found on Wheaton and the charred piano; the firemen and the sheriff's personnel who had recovered the evidence of arson; the deputies who picked up Wheaton the night of the blaze; and others. Link after link, a connection was made. Point A was Wheaton and point B was the fire.

And then there were the exhibits. The crashed piano had been reconstructed by a team of scientists and carpenters in an FBI lab in Virginia. Its appearance brought gasps when brought into Judge Wells's courtroom. Blackened keys, wires spraying forth like a broken box spring. It had been marked with small white-and-red self-adhesive tags with letters and numbers indicating where evidence had been logged. Its broken and missing keys looked like a hillbilly's malicious grin.

But nothing matched the final piece of evidence, which had been argued over by the lawyers for weeks. Brinker thought that State's Exhibit No. 25 was exceedingly prejudicial. Paine argued that she wasn't bringing the exhibit for any other reason than the lab analysis, which recovered cellulose fibers that matched what had been vacuumed from Wheaton's clothes.

Two pairs of boy's shoes that had burned and melted were entered into evidence as State's Exhibit No. 25. She called upon Jeff Bauer to identify the Buster Browns as being among the items removed from the arson site. Bauer, dressed in a fashionable gray chalk-stripe suit and black wingtips, looked handsome and confident. He spoke in a clear, decisive voice.

"Yes," he said, "these are the shoes that I recovered from Icicle Creek Farm."

"How can you be sure?"

He poked his forefinger into the interior of a shoe. Triangular pieces the size of a dime had been snipped from the leather for the lab.

"I can see my initials and the date," he said, pointing to inside one of the shoes. "Right *here*."

Nothing was admitted about who specifically had worn the shoes. It wasn't necessary. Those familiar with the case, which included just about everyone with a TV or newspaper delivery, knew that they had belonged to Danny and Erik Logan. Everyone knew that the boys had been incinerated and only the piano's shield-like form had protected their shoes from complete annihilation.

The same chemist who had authenticated the lab work

on the piano returned to the witness box to go over the microscopic and chemical analysis of the shoes. Traces of a fake snow product were found on both pairs.

"We determined the brand—Mighty White," he said. "It was recalled two years ago because of its extremely flammable nature. It had been the suspected source of fires in fourteen states. Four deaths, only, thank God."

If the shoes were bullets aimed at the jury's hearts, they scored a direct hit. One woman, Juror Five, let a tear roll down her cheek.

Paine had one more witness. It was the girl who had lost everything: her mother, her brothers, and her home.

"Call Hannah Logan!" she said.

CHAPTER TWENTY-TWO

No one could have ever accused Leanna Schumacher of being frivolous. She and her husband, Rod, had lived quiet, steady, *background* kind of lives on the Oregon coast. But as the date of Hannah's day in court came nearer, Leanna was oddly focused on appearances. She insisted Hannah wear a dress for the trial and took her to the only halfway decent ladies' dress shop in Misery Bay, Marcia's Fine Things, to buy one. Hannah hadn't worn a dress since her brothers' memorial service in early January. Dresses weren't practical at Icicle Creek Farm.

"Can't I wear jeans?" she asked.

"I know this isn't fun," Leanna said, "but it's important you look your best; folks will be watching. Even though we've got no say in how people think, they'll be judging you."

On the morning of March 30, everything seemed to be speeding around Hannah like the faces on the other side of a carousel. Aunt Leanna had placed a tan-and-light-blue Gunne Sax dress on the motel room bed. She took a few minutes to smooth out the fabric with her long, slender, and very freckled fingers.

"You'll look just beautiful in this," she said. "The color will pick up the lovely hue of your eyes."

Hannah had forgotten what color her eyes were, and the fabric's subtle mix of blue and brown did little to clue her in. She hadn't looked at her own face for weeks. She hated to see her eyes staring back at her from the silvery field of a mirror.

"I think I'll look stupid, Auntie," was all she could come up with, though she put the dress on. They watched television while they got ready to meet their escort to the courthouse. Leanna called Rod at the Speedy Mart, and the two talked while she waited for hot curlers to warm. She burbled something about how Hannah seemed to be holding up "despite the pain of the hour." She whispered an I-love-you and disappeared into the little foyer in front of the hotel bathroom.

"Hannah," Leanna called out from the noise of the hairdryer, "you'll be just fine, honey. I know it. You're from tough stock."

Hannah flopped on the bed and stared up at the ceiling, and the world around her spun. Little bits of silvery glitter clung into the dried cottage cheese surface. She started counting the glints of glitter, regarding each as a star in the Milky Way. She wondered what it would be like to be anywhere else just then. She had a duty, and she'd been told so nearly from the day she had been rescued from the farm. Ten minutes later, the pair was headed for the door. Aunt Leanna put the plastic MAID SERVICE PLEASE hanger on the doorknob and pressed the steel door shut.

"Hungry?" she asked as she slipped her room key into her purse.

Hannah shook her head. "I don't think so."

"You have to eat. You have to put some fuel in that tummy of yours."

Hannah put her hand on her stomach. "I'm gonna barf," she said. Her pale skin color backed up her words.

"That doesn't surprise me one iota," Leanna said. "If you don't eat, you won't feel better. You need something to settle your stomach."

The Rock Point Inn coffee shop was crowded, though it might have been less so if the area roped off with a PARDON OUR MESS, WE'RE PREPARING TO SERVE YOU BETTER! sign had been in use. Smoke hung in the air mixing with morning scents of frying bacon, perked coffee, and Listerine.

Jeff Bauer waved Leanna and Hannah to a booth in the back. He looked tired, his blue eyes puffy from lack of sleep, his hair askew. While the federal government was not prosecuting the case, they were there to help nevertheless. The men murdered at the Christmas tree farm had been the victims of interstate robbery, and some speculated, kidnapping. Pending the outcome of the Wheaton case, there was always the possibility of filing federal charges.

The star witness in both circumstances was Claire Logan's daughter, a girl with the budding breasts dressed in a brand-new Gunne Sax dress.

They ordered big breakfasts, not because they were particularly hungry, but to shut up the waitress who persisted on recounting every special the establishment offered. Toast and coffee for the adults, cereal for Hannah, would have sufficed. Hannah put down her fork. Her eggs stared at her with unblinking yolks and weepy, clear edges.

"I'm sorry to put you through this," Bauer said.

"We all are," Aunt Leanna said. She reached over and patted Hannah's hand, but it brought no real response.

"Can I go back to the room and wait there?" Hannah asked, pushing back from the table.

"No," Bauer said, "you'll have to wait with the bailiff in a special witness room they've put together for you."

"Can Aunt Leanna come?"

"Sure, she can. Since she's not a witness and she's your guardian."

Bauer searched his pants pocket for his money clip, left money on the table, and picked up the receipt. When he looked up, everything had changed. Hannah started to shake and cry. Leanna reached her arms around her niece and held her as they walked past the cashier. She held tight.

Hold on and the hurt will move from you to me, my love, she thought.

She ushered the girl off to the side of the elevator near a shimmering grouping of potted dracaenas.

"It'll be okay, honey," she said softly.

Hannah buried her face into the soft folds of her aunt's shoulder. Bauer looked on awkwardly. He reached over and touched Hannah's hand. It would be all right, he said once more.

"Just tell them what you know," he said. "No one is going to hurt you. You're gonna be fine."

Though he clearly meant well, his words fell flat. Hannah kept her face pressed into the fabric of her aunt's new dress. Tears left wet marks on the white of the dress collar.

"I'm not afraid of testifying . . . I am ready for that, I am. I'm just wondering if what they are saying is true." Her eyes had welled up once more. Pools of tears crested against her lower lashes.

"What is that, dear?" Aunt Leanna said. "Tell me."

"Maybe Mom might come."

Leanna gave her niece another hug. "Not likely. You have no reason to worry about her." Leanna and Bauer had read the same reports in some of the fringe media that cruelly and outlandishly suggested Claire Logan would return to Spruce County.

From behind Hannah's back, Leanna shot Bauer a harsh look.

"It'll be all right," she said once more. "I don't think Claire will be here. Don't pay attention to anything you hear or see in the papers or on television. You know better than that." She sat Hannah in a chair and motioned to the special agent to follow her to the other side of the room.

"What's with the cold stare?" he asked.

Leanna kept her voice low. "Honestly, Mr. Bauer, don't you get it? She *wants* to see Claire. She *loves* her still. She's still a girl and she doesn't know how deep her mom was in this whole nightmare. You have your theories. I have mine. I don't know just how bad my sister was, but I do believe she's responsible for what happened out at her place. She *had* to be. But to that little girl, she's a mother who's missing."

"Or dead."

"I doubt that with my heart and soul. She'd never let anyone get the best of her."

"So you've said."

"Yes, I have. I can think she's a bitch, a killer, and a child abuser. I can think she's about the worst thing God ever put on this earth . . . I can think she's the kind of mistake that only the devil can spawn. But really, none of that matters. Not to Hannah. To Hannah, Claire is only one thing, neither good nor bad."

"And that is?"

"Her mother."

Bauer nodded. He knew Leanna was right. Just then, Hannah emerged from the restroom, her eyes red, but her face brave and full of resolve. It was obvious that she had splashed water on her face; damp tendrils of her hair clung to her forehead. She had pulled herself together. She was going to get through this. She even managed a smile.

"Let's go to the waiting room," she said.

By the end of the morning, Hannah Logan had told her story. It was the only time she'd ever do so publicly.

Hours away in Portland, a half-dozen field agents drank artificially sweetened, boiled coffee and passed around a sheet of paper. They smoked and laughed and talked about the trial as though it was a Trail Blazer's basketball game. The little scrap of paper was a "T" chart. On one side was the word "Fry," on the other, "Cry." The words were a younger agent's idea of clever. "Frying" was never an option in the Wheaton case. Not at that time, anyway. Agents indicated with their initials what they thought the girl would do. If she wept and appeared indecisive, Marcus Wheaton would get off. If she held firm, he'd fry.

Or at least be sent to prison.

While the men in Portland were betting on the outcome of a trial in which they had no real involvement,
Wheaton's defense attorney was walking the tightrope
between doing a good job for his client and beating up a
little girl. Hannah Logan's statements to the police had
troubled Travis Brinker. Not for what she had disclosed
to investigators, but for what she hadn't. At no point in
her dealings with the police had she indisputably pointed
the complete blame of the fire on the handyman.

Brinker asked Wheaton to go through Hannah's statements one more time. Was there anything, he posed, that
could be disputed?

"Gently disregarded," Brinker reminded his doughy
client. "This is a bit dicey, you know. After all, her
mother is missing, her brothers are dead, and she is basically an orphan."

"You have reminded me about that already," the prisoner said.

"And I will continue to do so. She is not the enemy,
Marcus. She is their *ammunition*. If she can paint you in
some degrees of sympathy, it will go a long way toward
absolving you of some of the more sinister aspects of this
particular crime."

"You said it again."

"What's that?"

"The phrase. That annoying phrase . . . this *particular*
crime."

"So I did. Sorry. Now, take a look at her statement to
Bauer. Let's see if anything is a bit more clear."

"*. . . I liked Mr. Wheaton. We all did. We trusted him.*"
Both men scanned the document.

"*. . . that night I went to the wreath shed after dinner*

and Mr. Wheaton was there working on something. We talked for a while. I put the ribbons back in the storage cupboard and went back inside the house."

The pages flipped at the same time. Both looked up, made eye contact, and went back to their reading:

"Yes, I did see a kerosene can in the shed. I even asked about it."

"She never asked about that," he said.

Brinker underlined the statement. *"Never,"* he wrote.

"I saw my mom kissing Mr. Wheaton one time. It was last year around Halloween, I think."

"Halloween? Are you sure?"

"I know it was Halloween," she said, *"because we'd be getting ready for Christmas season. Decorations had to be put up. Halloween was always the beginning of our busy time."*

In reality, Hannah had told the Halloween story so many times, she didn't know if it was a genuine event or a memory that she had planted in her own mind through frequent recitation. As she grew older, the blend of hearsay, fiction, and reality was hard to break down into its purest elements. How does someone decipher the truth from what is stirred into their mind by television, radio, books, TV, newspapers? Hannah Logan tried. Very hard, she did.

She recalled it had been a Friday night and she had stayed up to watch *Midnight Special* because Leif Garrett was performing. She loved Leif Garrett. *What girl didn't?* She had fallen asleep on the sofa when she awoke to the sound of voices in the kitchen. It sounded like her mother was laughing. It was so good to hear her laughter. When Hannah's father was alive, her mother seldom laughed.

After his death, she never did. A sleepy smile came to Hannah's lips that night, and she got up to say good night before going upstairs to her own bed.

"I felt so stupid," Hannah told Bauer later. "I wish I had knocked. I mean, my mother could have visitors. She could have a boyfriend. My daddy was dead. My mom worked hard and she deserved some happiness. She didn't want to be alone and she said so several times. But I didn't expect it to be *him*. Marcus Wheaton had his arms around her. She had her back to me. Marcus put on this really fake smile and said something like 'Look what we have here, Claire.' My mom turned around, pushed him away real fast, and almost as quickly went to me and slapped me kind of hard. Then she said in a mean voice, a voice I can still hear, 'Why don't you knock, Hannah?' I told her I was sorry, but she wouldn't have any of it. She wouldn't accept my apology. I didn't do anything wrong. It was the *kitchen*. Who knocks before going in the kitchen?"

And so, on the eighth day of the Wheaton arson trial, Veronica Paine and the People of Spruce County rested. Hannah and her brothers' shoes had said it all. The defense put on a meager handful of character witnesses, but even Liz Wheaton couldn't save her son, though she cried like a rainstorm and told the jury that her son was the victim of an evil woman.

"He was," she said between sobs, "a really good boy. Deserved a lot better than Claire Logan."

It took the jury less than three hours to bring back a verdict—and two of those hours were occupied with buckets of Kentucky Fried Chicken and the usual sides.

The *Lumberman* managing editor acted like an editor

for the first time in his life. He held the front page of the next day's paper to carry the headline that told the world that Wheaton was going away for a long time: FIREBUG GUILTY! WHEATON GETS 20 YEARS BUT QUESTIONS STILL UNANSWERED.

Wheaton, wrapped in shackles and wearing XXXL coveralls the screaming orange color of a hunter's cap, was shipped off to the prison at Cutter's Landing, and everyone else went home. Leanna Schumacher took Hannah back to Misery Bay. Bauer returned to Portland. Veronica Paine celebrated her win with her husband at their beach house in Cannon Beach on the Oregon coast. And though the years would pass, the people touched by what happened at Icicle Creek Farm would forever remain connected. They would not be able to forget what happened because Claire Logan could not be forgotten by anyone. She was the nightmare that didn't go away even when the lights went on.

Bauer continued to work the case on the limited time allowed by the FBI. He clipped whatever he read about it and continued to run Logan's Social Security number to see if she was living somewhere under a new name. She likely masterminded the murder of twenty, and the idea that she was using any of her old I.D. was the longest shot of many.

Bauer made a couple of trips to Rock Point, and he always went to the site of the fire. He felt sorry for Jim and Dina Campbell, the Portland couple who bought the Logan place from the bank a year after the trial. They were in their late thirties, refugees from the city with dreams of creating an income in the country. Jim had been a personnel manager for a frozen food company in Beaverton; Dina, a driver's license examiner for the Department of Motor Vehicles. Their dead end brought them to Rock Point. Their finances brought them to Icicle Creek Farm. It was, Jim told his wife, too good a deal to pass up. They could overlook the tragedy and notoriety and build a new house and start over. Their dream was not out of line, but their hope that things would be restful was lost. By the time the Campbells had assumed ownership (paying only the balance owed and not market value), the Logan story had passed into a near mythical state of infamy.

The landowner next door cleared a two-hundred-foot-wide strip along the fence line and stuck up a sign advertising the place as a campground for RVs. For power, he went cheap and ran extension wires from the house to the pads. Water was provided through a garden hose. And, as if further proof was needed to affirm the bad taste of those with beer-can hats and crocheted toilet tissue covers, the RV crowd came. When a newspaper ran a story on the campground with a "front row seat to the nation's most grisly mystery," all slots—twenty in a row—were perpetually filled through the spring, summer, and fall. Only winter brought a reprieve.

Campsite No. 21 was cordoned off with a yellow plastic rope. A sign made out of a routed piece of cedar proclaimed the place permanently reserved.

"In case Mrs. Logan comes back," the park owner said. "She's gonna need a place to stay."

CHAPTER TWENTY-THREE

Outside his window, summer weather flirted with Port-land, Oregon. Lilac blooms were faded and turning brown, and grass everywhere needed a good shearing. It was a half year after the Logan farm burned to the ground. Downtown in the offices of the FBI, a voice cut through a tinny-sounding speakerphone and Special Agent Jeff Bauer set down his tepid cup of coffee, an oil slick of powdered creamer swirling inside. He leaned forward and strained to hear. The sound resonated like a cheap citizen's-band radio, and he shook his head for the thousandth time. *The federal government could afford a four-hundred-dollar hammer*, he thought, swallowing the last gulp of oily brew, *but Uncle Sam couldn't get the bucks together for decent communication equipment for the FBI.*

"Bauer, there's someone here to see you," a female

agent's voice cracked for the second time. It was Special Agent Bonnie Ingersol, a twenty-five-year-old with a master's degree in criminology, who begrudgingly filled in to work the phones during lunch when the "front-desk girl" was off to lunch with her boyfriend. The front-desk "girl" was fifty-six and more a grandmother than an ingénue. Ingersol hated the duty, but was too nice to fight it. Paying dues was part of the drill. Being pleasant was fine with her, as long as it wasn't forever. She was as shrewd as she was beautiful, with long dark brown hair and ice-blue eyes.

"Says her daughter's missing," Ingersol said. "Might have something to do with the Logan case."

"Huh?" Bauer responded, staring at the squawk box.

"The woman says her daughter worked for Claire Logan," Ingersol said. "She hasn't seen her in almost a year." She lifted her finger from the "talk" button and waited for Bauer to respond. "Are you there? Jeesh, Bauer, she thinks her daughter's Number 20."

This time Bauer muttered back into the box that he'd go out to the lobby to meet her. *Not again. Not another.* It was only a few months after Marcus Wheaton had been sent to run the license plate paint-drying tunnel at the penitentiary in Cutter's Landing. Liz Wheaton's calls to the FBI had stopped by then. She no longer threatened to picket the front steps of the Spruce County Courthouse with her claim that her son had been railroaded by a conspiracy of local and federal cops. All but one of the military men had been identified and their bones returned to the earth in family cemeteries across the nation. Only two mysteries remained. Was Claire Logan really gone? And, if she was, just whose body was under the piano?

Bauer smiled at the woman in the waiting room. Peggy Hjermstad was thirty-nine and very pretty. Her eyes were the color of Navajo turquoise, and her skin was thin, milky white, almost translucent. She stood in front of the FBI—FIDELITY, BRAVERY, AND INTEGRITY—plaque that was the sole adornment of the waiting area, wearing a faded batik skirt from an import store. Silver-and-peacock-feather earrings fluttered from her earlobes. Bauer introduced himself and offered her coffee.

Peggy Hjermstad grimaced. "Tea would be better," she said. "Herbal would be best. If you have it. Honey would be nice, too."

He smiled and led her to a waiting room while Bonnie Ingersol, a woman smarter than two-thirds of the men in the office, scuttled off to look for tea. Just as Ingersol turned the corner with tea bags flailing and an enamel hot pot to heat water, Peggy started talking. As she spoke, her arms moved and her silver charm bracelet tinkled like small wind chimes.

"You know I had an inkling, *a feeling*, about this for some time. When my daughter didn't call me on my birthday, well, that was the first clue she was in trouble of some kind. But I dismissed it from my mind."

Ingersol, thankfully relieved of her phone duty, took a seat next to Bauer. "When was that?" she asked.

"February 2nd. Groundhog's Day. Oh, I know the jokes, but that *is* my birthday. Serena didn't call and unless she was strung out on something, I just couldn't fathom *why*. It wasn't that we even had a falling out. Not really."

"Let's back up," Bauer said. "Tell me about your daughter."

She reeled in her sodden teabag like a miniature anchor, rolling the string around a red-and-white plastic stir stick.

"It's all here," Hjermstad said, rifling through her purse. "I made a flyer to post around town. Saw one up on the way over here. Still up. I know it should have made me sad to see it, but you know, I actually smiled. There are still decent people in this world. They left it up!"

Bauer and Ingersol reviewed the smudged flyer that had been folded so many times, it nearly split into quarters. Serena Moon Hjermstad was nineteen, five-foot-six, and 120 pounds, her hair was brown, and her eyes green.

"When the sun shines in her hair, she has—*had*—red highlights."

Hjermstad had come from her home on the Oregon coast to the FBI offices to discuss the possibility that her daughter was the headless corpse under the piano that had first been thought to be Claire Logan. In that case, the color of her eyes and her hair had little relevance; both agents thought it, but they didn't say so.

"Last time I heard from her," she went on, "she was hanging around a sandwich shop in Cutter—not far from Rock Point. Said she was going to get a job at a tree farm."

"Did she say it was Rock Point?" Ingersol asked.

She shook her head. "But she did say she could bike there. Rock Point is in biking distance from Cutter."

"Yes," Bauer answered, though he didn't want to be dismissive. By that time he'd talked to at least fifteen, maybe twenty, other mothers who thought their daughter might be the one pinned under the piano. He urged her to be specific. "You know, Mrs. Hjermstad, we have chased down a hundred or more tips from people who thought their daughter, sister, mother, cousin, neighbor, biology teacher . . . *someone* could be victim twenty."

Hjermstad put down her tea and faced Bauer.

"But I just feel it has to be her. She wouldn't drop off the face of the earth. She really did love her family. Didn't always see eye to eye, but she loved us. I just know it deep in my bones that she's gone. Her light has gone to heaven."

"Couldn't she have just gone off somewhere? Maybe met someone?" he asked.

Hjermstad wouldn't hear of it. Her body stiffened. "No, I don't think so. Serena had no reason to do that. We accepted all of her soul mates—every one of them," she said, forcing a smile as she realized the irony of her words. "She'd have no reason to run off and leave us to worry."

Bauer could tell she was beginning to tear up. "How do you know she worked for Logan?" he asked.

"I don't know for sure, but she did send me a beautiful holiday swag. Spruce and balsam, I think. It was in a gift box from the Logan farm. I just know she had to have bought it because she worked there. Maybe had an employee discount? You're the FBI. Can't you find out if she worked there?"

"Wish we could, ma'am," Bauer said. "But there are no records left. Everything burned up. And there's no paper trail, either. Claire Logan didn't pay taxes for her employees. No record. Nothing."

Mrs. Hjermstad finished her tea and got up to leave. Her hands trembled slightly, and for the first time Bauer understood something that had eluded him in training: Peggy Hjermstad, like so many mothers, would rather know that her child was dead, and *where* she was, rather than not know anything at all. She didn't want her to be a Bundy girl, dumped like roadkill on some mountainside; bones scattered by animals and bleached by the filtered rays of a Pacific Northwest sun. Peggy had lived with that image every night when she closed her turquoise eyes to sleep. Sleep, she found in the months after Serena stopped calling, would never come easily until she had answers.

"I just want to know," she said. "You understand?"

"I'll let you know," he said, catching Ingersol's eye and corrected himself, "We'll let you know if we, if I, can tie her to the crime scene."

"Thanks. I just want to know that she's gone. Gone for sure."

With that, she pressed a slip of paper, the flyer she had folded like a Chinese fan, into Bauer's open hand.

"Call me if you find out anything. I mean *anything*."

He nodded once more.

"Mr. Bauer," she asked timidly, as though she was treading in a private area, "has Hannah Logan ever said who she thought was Number 20? I was thinking maybe she knows my daughter."

"I'm sorry. She believed the corpse was her mother's in the beginning. She couldn't even guess who it was if it"—he stopped and corrected himself—"if *she* was an imposter, a stand-in."

Ingersol offered to walk Hjermstad to the door.

"Thank you, dear. And thank you so much for the tea. It was delicious. How old are you? You look about my Serena's age . . ."

A moment later, Bauer cornered Ingersol to let off steam. Serena Hjermstad's mother would never get the final word that she needed because Spruce County had screwed up and the body was cremated before processing for forensics. There had been so much finger pointing, even an FBI agent couldn't pinpoint *who* exactly had made the blunder of all blunders when the headless body was cremated before autopsy.

"I'd like to have those fools in Spruce County face Mrs. Hjermstad and tell her that they are sorry for what they did, and if the body was her daughter's—and no one will really know for sure—well, sorry about that, too."

Ingersol noticed Bauer's face redden. His ears, the bridge of his nose, even his lips grew darker as his anger and frustration swelled.

"From what I heard," he said, "they don't own up to anything."

Bauer was mad as hell and knew that he and Peggy Hjermstad would both be cheated because of the incompetence of a couple of buffoons from a small town no one cared about until twenty people were found dead there.

"We're never really gonna know," he said bitterly, "if the victim is Serena, some other girl, or Claire Logan."

Ingersol disagreed. "We'll find out. It might take a while, but we'll get there. I have faith in us. You know, the whole concept that got us to the academy in the first place, good over evil?"

"Catching the bad guys and carrying the badge, I remember," he muttered. "I just think Claire Logan was a lot smarter than we imagined. Maybe even smarter than us."

"Smarter than you? Stop a second. I need to write that one down," Ingersol said.

CHAPTER TWENTY-FOUR

For everyone involved in the Logan case, back then and the years hence, there would be no concrete answers. Only lingering questions, spiraling mysteries, and leads made of mirages. If alive, Claire Logan was the cleverest of fugitives. She left no tracks. Not a single one. Not ever. The fall of 1980 brought cold weather and gales of wind to Misery Bay. It also brought reality home to Hannah Logan. As she sat staring at the newspaper, she found herself back in the journalism classroom at Misery Bay Senior High. She had been a junior then with ambitions of becoming a magazine editor, perhaps in New York. Anywhere, she had thought, anywhere, but Oregon. Far, far away.

A headline stopped her heart for just a moment: WOMAN ARRESTED IN MILWAUKEE, COULD IT BE CLAIRE LOGAN?

Hannah's eyes bulged. She looked around, self-conscious that others were staring at her. Could they see the flush on her face, the blood draining into a pool in her stomach? No one, it seemed, paid her any mind. The school paper's editor flirted with the photographer, a girl, about going into the darkroom to "see what develops." Hannah put her head down and read. The article described a food service worker who had been picked up for writing hot checks in several Wisconsin towns. She'd used the name *Claire Logan*—"the name of the notorious serial killer from Oregon"—on a phony bank account. The article went on further to describe the woman as dark-haired, about five-foot-five and 155 pounds. Hannah knew it was not her mother. This lady had *brown* eyes. As resourceful as Claire Logan had been in her life, dyeing her eyes was not something even she could do.

The periodic jolts brought by seeing her mother's name in print had a strange and unique rhythm. Like a rope swing caught in the crotch of a tree, the wind would come and drop it free to swing once more. The news accounts were like that. Every now and then the rope would fall from the sky and Hannah would be there to face her mother's name. She wasn't the only one who had to live that way, and she didn't feel sorry for herself because of that.

In her own way, Hannah shared a bond with many she had never met. There was the little girl who had been trapped in a Vermont storm drain and had been rescued by neighbors after a six-day ordeal. There was the boy from Pittsburgh who had escaped Dante Richards, the serial killer, and testified against him. And the four-year-old girl who had been the sole survivor of a 747 crash in

Bogotá in 1969. All of them were children of scandal or circumstance.

Because they made good copy, reporters would not leave them alone. The obligatory five-years-after stories turned into ten years after, then fifteen . . . all the while reopening sores with the hot and dirty knife of the media. None of the children of notorious events could be allowed the freedom to forget. Of course, Hannah knew well that forgetting was utter fantasy. Nothing so terrible can be forgotten. But all she wanted—all the others had wanted—was a chance to get on with their own lives. They deserved and hoped for a chance at being normal. But that was never to be, though in time the headlines would shrink, the interest would ebb. But it could not be completely disregarded. There was always the angle. *Always and forever.*

When the phone rang late at night or when the answering machine was a staccato recording of hang-up calls, Hannah felt certain it was a reporter. It almost had to be. They called to get the story. They called to see how she was. The woman who had written the book *Twenty in a Row* had been the worst offender. She had cast herself as an expert on the Claire Logan case. Marcella Hoffman had parlayed Hannah's family's tragedy into a livelihood, and for that, Hannah Griffin hated her. For that, if there was a choice between writers who would get to update the story—if, in fact, there was no stopping it—Hoffman would not be the one.

Hannah had seen Hoffman on a television morning show the week before the tenth anniversary of the nightmare. By that time she and her aunt called the author "Dog Face" or "DF." She was being asked the whereabouts of Claire's daughter—Hannah—as though she had some claim on her.

"Where her daughter, now twenty-three or twenty-four, has gone, I can't really say," Hoffman said.

"Can't say, or don't know?" the flashbulb-eyed interviewer probed, obviously annoyed at the evasiveness of the author.

"Let me put it this way," she said with supreme self-assuredness. "When Hannah Logan wants to come out and greet the world with her recollections of what happened in Rock Point, Oregon, it'll be in response to my request."

Hannah couldn't believe the puffed-up Hoffman's remarks. *Over your dead body,* she thought. *Add another number to your book title and make it* Twenty-*One* in a Row. *I will never talk to you.*

When Hannah finally broke down and purchased a copy of Hoffman's *Twenty in a Row,* she hid it from her aunt and uncle. She kept the paperback in the bottom drawer of the jewelry box they had given her for Christmas the year after it happened. *It.* She didn't even like to refer to what it was. But after *it* happened she had braved her way into a used bookstore to buy a copy. The saleswoman was a pretty, though somewhat pointy-nosed, woman nearly waist deep in romance novels that evidently another patron had brought in to sell or swap. She paid little attention to the pretty teenager who had come inside to browse.

Hannah found the book and gingerly removed it from the shelf. It had a slight musty smell, and the pages had swelled slightly as though the previous owner had brought the book to the bathtub. Hannah didn't even hold the book, but rather pinched a corner as though it would electrocute her. The words *Twenty in a Row* were written in an incongruous, delicate Roman lettering. Small drops of red blood clung to the letters' baseline. A photograph of what someone thought could pass for the Christmas tree farm was placed at a forty-five-degree angle; its edges ripped to roughness that implied great haste, ruin, or a designer's hackneyed sense of cleverness. It didn't look like their house, and that brought Hannah a small measure of comfort. As far as she knew, the only photos that remained of the Logan farm—pre-fire—were those taken by families who had visited the holiday wonderland, sat on Santa's lap, fed the "reindeer," and the like. None of those, at least none of what surfaced, showed the house beyond a few way-off-in-the-distance shots. The other photos of the house that were known to exist at one time belonged to the files of the Spruce County tax assessor. Those disappeared six months after Marcus Wheaton's trial. Souvenir hunters, probably.

"You like true-life mysteries, do you?" the bookseller said while the pretty teenager nudged the paperback on the counter.

Hannah said nothing at first. She fished through her front pocket for a five-dollar bill. "I guess so," she finally answered.

"I prefer Agatha Christie," the clerk offered as she rang up the sale. "I take great comfort, great personal assurance, in reading material that's not going to give me nightmares because it's true."

"My aunt's the same way," Hannah said. She had wanted the book so bad, for so long. It was a peculiar kind of desire, and she knew it. She was drawn to the book and repulsed by what it represented at the same time.

The woman counted out the change. "Four dollars and fifty cents back at you."

Hannah feigned a smile. It was a robotic response, one that she'd perfected after her world collapsed. At times she was an automaton. She used automatic response for Christmas, for birthdays, when babies were born. Whenever the moment called for a smile, when she had none to give. *But this?* This smile was part of a mask. Masks were necessary. She was certain it was a defense mechanism designed to save her from her past. But the book, the book brought back so much. It was strange. *Twenty in a Row* cost fifty cents. *Fifty cents?* Half a buck was all the tragedy was worth?

"Enjoy the book," the woman called out.

Hannah said nothing more as she slipped past the fetid stack of paperbacks waiting to be shelved and hurried to the bus stop. She wondered if she'd ever be able to read the book or if she had even really wanted to. A trash can five steps from where the bus door swung open caught her eye. She felt herself loosen her grip on the book. It was slipping from her fingers. And, she almost threw it away. But she didn't. She'd have to read it. How could she not? In some small way, she knew it was *her* story. She flipped through the book and the word "cyanide" leapt off a page:

CLAIRE LOGAN STOOD at the counter of Elements, Inc., a chemical supply company in the industrial area just outside of Eugene. Her hair was up, her lips painted a dark red, and her eyes flashed intelligence and authority. Her perfume was jasmine.

"I have gigantic mole problems," she said without a trace of irony. "Big ones. And I want to take every goddamn one of them out. They are ruining my garden."

The young man at the counter turned down his cassette player and Elton John's voice went to a whisper.

"We can recommend some pesticides for that. Rid-it-Fast is a good one."

Claire shook her head. "That won't do," she said, putting her purse down on the counter and pulling out her checkbook. "I want a pound of sodium cyanide."

The young man made a face. "That's enough to kill every mole in Spruce County," he said. "You sure you need that much? I mean, there are other ways, to kill 'em, you know."

"Look," she said, her demeanor suddenly shifting to extreme irritation. "I've tried everything. I've poured gas on them. I've flooded their burrows with the garden hose. I've even driven spikes through their velveteen bodies. I want something that will kill them fast, once and for all."

The young man nodded. He felt uneasy, but he didn't say so. "Okay, I guess. Though I think you're overreacting."

She pointed to the sign hanging behind him.

ELEMENTS, INC., THE HOMETOWN CHEMICAL COMPANY.
WE'RE HERE FOR YOU

She no longer smiled. "If you're here for me as your sign proclaims, then you'll tell me how much a pound of the poison will cost me?"

The young man took out a records book and thought that the woman was a complete bitch.

"Name?" he asked.

"Mrs. Logan. Claire Logan."

"You know, Mrs. Logan, you really need to be careful with this stuff. Even the slightest bit can kill a man in about five minutes. Suffocates him at the cellular level."

"Thanks, but I know what I'm doing." She got out her checkbook. "Five minutes, you say?"

BOOK THREE
MOTHER

CLAIRE: Nothing more needs to be said here, Marcus. Am I making myself clear or am I just talking to hear the sound of my own voice?

MARCUS: You are something else. You're knocking off these old geezers and acting like I'm doing something wrong because I don't do things *fast* enough for you?

CLAIRE: Listen, my dear. Let's get one thing straight. I'm doing all the work. This is my deal. You are helping me because I *allow* you to.

MARCUS: (*angry*) *Allow* me to? You ungrateful *wench*! [Writer Dante Martini had written "bitch" in his draft, but network censors changed it.]

CLAIRE: (*her back to the camera, she drops her bathrobe*) Let's not argue. Draw me a bath. And come rub my shoulders. You can bury the guy from Idaho in the morning.

MARCUS: What about the kids? They might overhear us.

CLAIRE: Don't worry about them. Hannah is over at Michelle's and the boys are zonked out on Dimetapp. They love the grape flavor.

—From the script for the February 1978 *ABC Movie of the Week*, "Twenty in a Row," starring Kate Jackson as Claire Logan

CHAPTER TWENTY-FIVE

The salmon served in Warden Thomas's dining room was a little dry, which was odd because it was poached in very good white wine with scallions and should have been moist. But the Waldorf salad was exactly as Hannah Griffin preferred it, light on the mayonnaise dressing, with large pieces of walnuts and grapes among sweet-tart apples. She wondered fleetingly if a serial killer or some notorious rapist had been the chef, but she dismissed the thought because she knew no inmates could wield a knife at the prison, at least not official cutlery in the kitchen.

Polite conversation filled the first few minutes as Hannah and FBI agent Jeff Bauer worked past the awkwardness and the bizarre circumstances of their reunion. They had time to kill after their interview with Wheaton had been cut short by the prisoner's meal-time requirements.

The break was welcome. Bauer could see that Hannah was a grown woman now, beautiful and intelligent. She was a mother. A wife. And she had sought a career in law enforcement as a CSI.

No surprise there, he thought. *Any psych student could have pegged that choice.*

Bauer was older, wiser, maybe even a little jaded by the years. But Hannah saw him as he had been to her that terrible day, twenty years before: a hero. He'd kept himself in good shape, and though he was in his forties, his features were still taut and his jawline crisp. Jeff Bauer still appeared as he did when they met in the Rock Point Inn almost two decades before.

Hannah speared a bite of salad. "I knew we'd see each other again one day," she said.

"I thought so, too." Bauer smiled. "I tried to keep tabs on you, best I could. You know, without getting in the way of you living a life." His demeanor changed and the smile disappeared. He had meant to mention Leanna sooner. "I'm sorry about your aunt. I heard she passed on a while back."

"It's been five years," Hannah said. She put down her fork and on her lap, she folded her napkin in an accordion fold. She was nervous. "Aunt Leanna was diagnosed with ovarian cancer in March and was dead before Memorial Day. Not much can be done for the disease, no matter what they say."

"I'm sorry," he repeated. "Your uncle?"

"Uncle Rod's doing all right. Still running the store. Still missing the only woman he ever loved. We're close. He loves Amber."

Bauer looked interested. "That's your little girl?"

"Yes," she said. Hannah reached for her purse, but, of

course, it wasn't there. It was with the guards at the visitors' screening room. No purses, wallets, nothing could be brought inside. She'd show a picture later. They talked a while longer about her family life with Ethan and Amber. Bauer was a good listener, and in a way, Hannah felt as though he needed to hear every bit of what had happened to her over the years. She knew his own personal life had been a disaster—and he had grown up with everything going for him. Loving family, an excellent education, good job, great personality, but all of that added up to nothing. No wife, nor any children.

Hannah, who had lived under the insidious shadow of a murderous mother, seemingly inexplicably, had achieved everything.

In a stream of consciousness rambling that only served to heighten her own nervousness, Hannah told Bauer about her life as a crime scene investigator and her love for gardening. She talked about the drive up from California and how she hadn't eaten anything all day. She'd skipped the free pastry at the motel in Janesville. And as she talked, so rapid and seemingly without the need for air, only one disclosure surprised the FBI agent.

"I don't mention this to anyone, of course," Hannah said, "but Ethan and I don't use a real tree at Christmastime." She stopped and studied Bauer's handsome face. "It appears to be the only residual aspect of what happened that remains with me to this day. The weirdest part is that I love trees. I love the woods. But I can't have a fir or pine in the house."

"Few could blame you for that," Bauer said, gently interjecting a word into the nearly one-sided conversation. "A lot of us never thought about Christmas in the same way after that day."

Hannah sipped her water. "We didn't even have a tree at all until Amber was three," she said. "Some things you have to do for your children."

"I wouldn't know about that, but I can imagine. You know, I guess, that I never had children."

She nodded. "So I gathered."

And so the conversation went, catching up, touching on the points of two lives that had once intersected, and were now reunited. After a while—after Madsen brought in coffee and a plate of cookies piled like a pyramid—they turned their talk to the reason she had come to Cutter's Landing from Santa Louisa, and he from Portland.

"Warden's wife made them." Madsen indicated the chocolate chip cookies. "Instead of 'Tollhouse' she calls them 'jailhouse' cookies." He rolled his eyes before turning to leave.

"They look delicious," Hannah said. "Tell her thank you. We never knew prison could be so—"

"Civilized," Bauer broke in.

"Hospitable," Hannah corrected.

Madsen nodded without turning around. He called over his shoulder as the door shut behind him. "About half an hour and I can take you back to see Wheaton. Warden said so."

"He looks terrible," Hannah said of Wheaton after Madsen disappeared. "I'd seen him on that TV interview a few years back, and he wasn't nearly so heavy."

The show to which she was referring was a prime-time special hosted by one of the morning news anchors, a blonde with a clipped nose and reshaped brows. The show breathlessly promised an inside look at America's most infamous criminals. The Wheaton interview had been one of the hyped bits. It was broadcast seven or eight years ago.

The Wheaton interview was a complete joke. All he talked about was some acrylic paintings he was creating on small oval-shaped stones. Each was the image of a curled-up sleeping cat.

"I saw that," Bauer said. "The last few years haven't been so terrific for Wheaton, that's for sure." He was referring to the inmate's hideous girth and the clear tubing that ran from his oxygen tank to his nose, a plastic lifeline that kept him somewhat mobile.

"He knows where she is," she said. "I know it. You know it. And he knows we are all members of the club that still gives a whit. The information is ours for the taking," she said, reaching for a second cookie, then stopping herself as her gut did another somersault.

"The fact of the matter is, Hannah, that Wheaton is on his last legs and he's looking to jerk a few chains before he goes. I've seen this before. 'Come on gather near my deathbed and I'll tell you who took the money and where they put it.' Except it never comes. Nothing ever comes. All they want is someone to talk to because their family flushed them down the toilet."

Hannah didn't feel that way.

"He's going to talk," she said. "He has to."

Madsen returned to the dining room. By now his visits to the room with food, coffee, cookies, and a half smile made him seem more a waiter than a prison employee. He told the pair that Wheaton had been returned to the visiting cell and they were free to see him again.

"If you want to finish your coffee, I'll tell him it'll be a while." Madsen actually smiled. "Joking, of course."

*　*　*

Marcus Wheaton sat behind the scarred wooden table, his hands folded over his ample, nearly breast-like chest, and his battered oxygen tank at the ready.

"How was the salmon?" he asked as Bauer and Hannah entered the room.

Hannah didn't want to know how he knew the menu. She didn't want to think he might have had a hand in making the meal. She was already queasy.

"Fine," she said.

Wheaton looked surprised. "Looked a bit dry to me," he said.

"We're not here to talk about prison cuisine," Bauer said, a little annoyed. "We came to talk about Claire."

"I'm sure," Wheaton shot back, fixing his good eye completely on Bauer. "But I've invited you here and I'll tell you what I want you to know. Claire"—he stopped and looked deep into Hannah's eyes—"your *mother* is only part of it."

Hannah felt a wave of nausea and bolstered herself by pressing her knees under the table, with such force she nearly levitated it.

"Fine. Start talking, Wheaton," Bauer instructed. "Or we'll leave."

Wheaton's face bubbled with mock indignation. "Then go."

Hannah wanted no part of leaving, not then, so she spoke up. "We're not going anywhere, Marcus," she said. "You want to tell us something, so please do."

Wheaton leaned back in what Hannah noticed for the first time was an office chair reinforced with steel. He seemed satisfied that he had their rapt attention. "First things first," the big man said. "I don't really care if you believe me or not. I'm going to die soon anyway," he said, regarding his oxygen tank. "I've wished my own death for twenty fucking years here, and now, the wish is about to come true. A little late, though. I'd have rather died inside. Prayed for it. *But no such luck.* I'm just alive enough to be booted out of here to make my mother's life miserable. Sweet, isn't it?"

No one said anything. The big Buddha was talking like there was no tomorrow.

"I did not kill any of those men. I did not kill your brothers." He fixed his eye on Hannah. She pressed her hands into her abdomen to quell the uneasiness. "You know this, don't you, Hannah?"

"I don't know what I know. I was a child then."

Bauer instinctively reached over to her, but she refused his gesture. Whatever comfort Hannah needed, she'd find it within herself. Leanna had taught her that. When you have no one, you find you *need* no one.

"And, though this seems to mean very little to anyone out there, I did not murder the girl, the one the media calls 'Number 20.'" His tone was indignant, as if he had nothing to do with any aspect of the crime. "It sickens me that she's nothing more than a number. It has for a long time. Long as I've acknowledged that she's got a name. She was a sweet kid named Serena. I don't recall her last name."

"Hjermstad. *Serena Hjermstad* was her name," Bauer said. His mind flashed to his visit with Peggy Hjermstad not long after the murders were discovered and how she had wanted to believe that her daughter had been killed at Icicle Creek Farm. Killed anywhere. Anything to stop the cruel hope that looped inside her that her daughter was out *there*. The woman's peacock earrings came to his mind. And so did the drawn-to-the-point-of-breaking faces that had belonged to the other dozen or so mothers who had made what must have been the most wrenching drive of their lives—to the Portland offices of the FBI. All sought the same thing: to find closure to the mysteries of their own daughters' disappearances.

"I don't know any Serena Hjermstad." Hannah searched her memory. "I don't know her."

Wheaton disagreed. "But you do. You called her by another name, Didi, I believe."

"That was not her," Hannah said, her voice slightly wavering. *Going to hold it together,* she thought. "Didi left weeks before the fire. She was gone. I know that. I remember my mother telling me that Didi had to get back to Seattle or Portland. I think she left for Thanksgiving." Hannah's voice quavered slightly before she found her reserves and bucked up. "She could not have been Number 20."

Wheaton didn't acknowledge Hannah's comment. He simply barreled on. He stopped only to drink water, more than a quart by Bauer's estimate. He talked about Serena and how Claire had hired her late in the season before the fire. According to Wheaton, Serena/Didi worked in the wreath shed with four other women from Rock Point. He described her as a cute, but unreliable, young woman who came to work late wrapped in a veil of rose-scented perfume applied in the morning to obscure pot smoke from the night before. She was angry at her mother for not understanding that her life was her own.

"I'm not living for anyone but me," she had told Wheaton one evening when she hitched a ride back to the Johnny Appleseed Motel where she was staying just outside of Rock Point. "I've had my parents tell me what to do and I've had a dumb-shit boyfriend run me like a clock. Forget that. I want to figure out my own way," she had said.

Wheaton said he liked the young woman.

"She was nice to me, friendly-like," he said. "She was pretty, too. A little ditzy, but you couldn't have asked for a nicer girl. Too bad what happened."

"Can we get on with this?" It was Bauer. He followed his question with a loud sigh. He wasn't as annoyed as he sounded—in fact, he was fascinated—he just wanted to keep Wheaton on track. If they had to hear every little thing, all of his thoughts and feelings, then, by God, it ought to be done at a decent clip.

Wheaton glowered. "I don't like to be rushed," he said. "You know you are only here because of my good nature and sense of fair play."

"Fine. Can we move on? Please?"

"Don't pressure me. I don't like to be pushed, either."

Bauer disregarded the comment and Wheaton gulped down more water. He went on to say that Claire came across Serena/Didi in the back of the supply building adjacent to the wreath maker's shed. It was two days before Thanksgiving, 1976.

"Didi was freaking out. She had found the jar of teeth," Wheaton said, stopping not for dramatic reasons, but because the idea of it repulsed him even two decades later. The teeth to which he was referring belonged to the seventeen men Claire Logan had smashed with a carpenter's hammer.

"She smashed them out herself, trust me on that. I had nothing to do with any of it. Claire told me that her biggest fear was that one day, long after she was gone, someone would dig up one of the victims and identify him by dental records."

Hannah put her fingers to her mouth. It was an unconscious gesture of horror for the cadavers that had been brutalized by the force of her mother's hammer.

"Jesus Christ," she said softly.

"I didn't do anything but cover up for your mother." He blinked his good eye.

"What happened to Didi?" she asked, staring back at Wheaton.

"She erased her. Like I've said, I wasn't there and I didn't see it. But from what she told me, Claire swung at her with a chainsaw. *It wasn't on*," he said, as though that were somehow beyond possibility. "She bashed Didi so hard she damn near cut off her head. When she told me what she'd done she used the old saying, you know the one where kids pick dandelions and flick off the flower tops? *Mama had a baby and the head popped off*? That's what she said. I thought it was funny back then," he said, showing for the first time an indication of remorse.

Now Bauer's face was pale. Even Madsen who had lingered on the other side of the room looked ill. Hannah steadied herself while Wheaton continued, oddly smiling as he recounted the details of his story.

When Claire had first told Wheaton about what had happened, he said that he assumed she'd want help with the burial. But when he went out to the supply building, there was no body. Not a drop of blood could be seen anywhere. The place was cleaner than a hospital room.

Hannah remembered the supply building; it came to her as though she was standing inside it in a dream. It was in perfect order. Her mother was fanatical about having a place for everything . . . "and keeping everything in its place." In her mind, she searched the rows of spools of grosgrain and French ribbons, the floral tape, the wire in various gauges. There was shelving to the ceiling in that drafty little room, and yes, a row of jars at the very top.

Wheaton licked his lips and went on. He was a steam engine now. A big, Day-Glo orange, stinking steam engine with chili-mac dried at the crusty corners of his mouth, and there was no stopping him.

"She told me she took care of Didi all by herself. You know what? I admired her for that. I thought, *what a wonderful woman.* She'd have been leader of the pack with the survivors of the Donner Party. Claire was the kind of woman who could shoot, skin, and cook a bear and make love to you on the fur rug she tanned herself—all in the same day. That's what I thought then."

Wheaton said he knew nothing more about Number 20 until the night of the fire.

"I helped set the fire that night. Yeah, I did pretty much everything the Spruce County prosecutor said I did. But I didn't kill anyone. After the fire Claire was going to meet me at the five-way stop."

Hannah knew that location. Two miles from the farm there was the only other sign of civilization—the convergence of two logging roads and the highway. Locals knew it as "the five-way."

"She told me that she loved me," he said, and saying those words brought a wave of emotion. His good eye seemed to water. "She said, 'no matter what happens, Marcus, we'll be together. You've proven your love and I've proven mine.' No one was supposed to die," he said.

Wheaton cleared his throat. It was followed by a loud hack. Hannah thought he was fighting back emotion, but she wasn't sure. Bauer urged him to continue.

"When I left that night, when I took my lighter and started the fuse just as we'd planned, there was no one in the house. No one—not Danny and Erik, not *you*, Hannah. I swear to *God*. And I do believe in God. Always have. I found out about them *after* the sheriff's deputies picked me up."

The steamroller was in overdrive. Hannah and Bauer pushed back and listened. Neither said a word.

"And I was so happy," Wheaton said. "I know it sounds so stupid now, but I was. I was so grateful for two things. That you," the good eye went straight to Hannah, "were spared and that your mother had vanished."

Hannah said nothing. She couldn't think of anything to say. She had no air in her lungs.

"But the body?" Bauer asked. "The body of the woman—how do you know that it wasn't Claire's for sure?"

"Because she's too smart. She fucked you. Me. Her kids. The men she slaughtered. She fucked us all. I know now that Didi's body had been kept in the freezer and brought out like a roast for the night of the fire."

"You saw her there?" Bauer asked.

"Two days after she whacked the girl's head off, she told me she hit a deer and butchered it herself. Very Claire. I saw the meat in the freezer. It was the biggest hindquarter I ever saw, all wrapped in white paper. 'It was a buck,' Claire said to me. 'Rack the size of a Vega hatchback, eight points.'"

But when Wheaton looked at the Icicle Creek Farm truck he could find no evidence that Claire hit anything, let alone a Kong-size buck. No hair, nor any blood. He rubbed his big hands over the front fenders and stared at them. Clean as could be.

"I can put two and two together," Wheaton told his visitors. "And you probably could have, too, if the funeral home hadn't cremated poor Didi's body—I mean, *torso*. I know Claire. I know what she's capable of. She kept that body in the freezer until she needed it. She planned it. She planned everything to get away. She planned making the world believe that she'd died. She'd have her money. Her new life. I was supposed to be part of her future. I wanted to be. I'd have done anything for her."

As Wheaton reached for the water, Madsen stood from his seat in the corner and acknowledged another of the warden's assistants. The sergeant in the visitors' processing station had asked the other officer to get a message to Hannah Griffin.

"Your pager's been going off every five minutes," he said. "Got to be urgent. You want to use a phone?"

Still stunned into silence by what Wheaton had told her, Hannah could not speak. She wanted to get the hell out of there. She was back in the waters of Misery Bay with a line of W's rolling to her neckline. She was drowning.

"Okay," she said. She needed the relief. She needed the break.

Wheaton did, too.

"Time for his meds, anyway," Madsen said. "Make your call."

Bauer reached over and this time Hannah took his hand. She was trembling. In a flash, the moment when everything changed had come back. Time stood still, and a million pieces of her shattered memory came to her. It all flooded back, a torrent of images. It was that Christmas Eve night in her bedroom—the beginning of the end.

Marcus Wheaton was nearly manic, which was unlike his lumbering, big-guy persona.

"We need to get you out of here, Hannah, now!"

"What's happening? You're scaring me."

"You ought to be scared. I am. But I'm gonna get you out of here."

She noticed the red metal can for the first time.

"What's that?"

"Don't ask. Just keep your mouth still. Let's go."

He grabbed her hand and pulled her toward the bedroom door, leaving a trail of what smelled like kerosene or gas behind.

"What are you doing?" Hannah asked.

"The same thing you're about to do. What you're being told to do."

Wheaton swung open the door and tucked his head around the corner. When he moved to the side, the scene came into view. It was white. There was white sprayed everywhere.

"What?" she asked, barely able to get the word out.

He yanked on her hand and pulled her into the hall, spreading kerosene like holy water on the walls, soaked in white. It was tree flocking, the texture of fake snow.

"If you don't come and come quietly, you'll die. We'll both die."

He pulled her past her mother's bedroom, past the boys' room. The doors were shut. With each step more kerosene hit the walls, the floor as it splashed against the ghostly spray of white.

"Where are Erik and Danny?"

Wheaton faced her dead-on. His face was stone.

"You don't want to know," he said. "Let's get you out of here."

"Where's Mom?"

"Say another word and we'll both die."

Wheaton led her down the stairs, past the Christmas tree, still lit and packed underneath with presents, but oddly and hastily sprayed with flocking. Hannah said nothing. She could barely breathe. Her feet were wet; her nightgown damp. Across the yard, to the potting shed; by then he was carrying her.

"Stay here," he said.

She managed a nod.

What was he doing? Where is everyone?

Wheaton, looking over his shoulder, ran toward the front door, still open and flooding the front yard with light. He tossed a match or lighter into the doorway and an enormous flash shot across the yard. Near blinding in its brightness, explosive in its suddenness.

Hannah opened her mouth to scream, but nothing but the empty white of her warm breath emerged. Not a real sound.

Say a word and you will die, he had told her.

Across the yard, the house burned and shot smoke into the leaden sky. Snow fell. Hannah retreated to the corner of the shed.

Wheaton returned a minute later, puffing and agitated. His eyes wild and full of the fear, maybe even for the first time the realization of what he'd done.

"They are all gone," he said. "Erik and Danny are gone. Your mother is gone. I didn't want it this way, you know me. You know how I feel about the boys. I got them dressed, ready to go, ready to get out of here. But she wouldn't have it. She wouldn't allow any of it."

Ribbons of tears streaked her face. Her fists clenched. It passed through her mind that she had to get past Marcus Wheaton, and that wasn't happening.

"I want to get them." Her voice was a whisper.

He held her, first to stop her from hurting him, then to comfort her.

"No, you don't," he said. "I'm going now, but know this forever: I never hurt the boys. I never hurt anyone. I could never hurt you."

"Why is this happening?"

"Because Didi's mother keeps calling." Wheaton disappeared around the corner of the shed. Hannah heard his truck start and rumble down the driveway. And from then on her life was no longer her own, not really.

CHAPTER TWENTY-SIX

In a small, seemingly airless room that amounted to nothing more than a closet adjacent to the prison warden's private dining room, Hannah Griffin dialed the telephone number that flashed on the tiny LED panel of her SatNet county-issued pager. It was Ted Ripperton's office extension at the Santa Louisa crime lab.

"Ted? Hannah here. What can't wait?"

"Where the hell are you?" he asked, ignoring her question. "Ethan said you went away for a couple days. You guys okay?"

Hannah didn't want to get personal with Ripp, and she didn't see how where she was at any given moment was any of his concern in the first place. As lousy an investigator as Hannah believed Ted Ripperton to be, she didn't want him asking any questions.

"It's personal and Ethan and I are fine. Furthermore,

you paged me," she snapped before adding, "a half dozen times."

"*Eighteen* times," he said. "Even called the phone company, er—telecommunications provider—to make sure your pager wasn't down. They did some sort of test and said your pager was operational. Said you weren't answering. And I thought you took the damn thing in the shower!"

"Very funny," Hannah said, her impatience amplified with another sigh. She felt her limbs for the first time in an hour. She realized she'd been numb from the interview with Wheaton. "What's so urgent?"

"Joanne Garcia's in critical condition in the ICU at Our Lady of Guadeloupe. Overdosed on Valium and tequila."

"Oh dear," Hannah said. "What happened?"

"Paramedics came out to her trailer house at ten this morning. The next-door neighbor who'd been keeping an eye on Garcia since we took Mimi into protective custody stopped by to see how she was faring. Garcia didn't answer the phone or the door. Her VW was in the driveway. The neighbor lady went inside and found Garcia on the sofa. TV going full-tilt boogie. Face blue. We've seen it before. This one was nice."

"Nice" was Ripp's way of categorizing suicides, as in nasty or nice. Nasty suicides were the man with a pistol in the mouth and brains sprayed on the television set or the teenage boy hanging from a rafter with underwear around his ankles and a *Penthouse* on the floor. Nice were the glue sniffers or pill poppers who died before their bodies rebelled with a gag reflex. Nasties were a mess, but they told the story with clarity and precision. Nice were clean, neat, and much harder to read.

"She leave a note?" Hannah asked.

"Not that we've found so far," Ripp answered.

"Do the docs think she'll make it?"

"Dunno. Hanging by a thread. I got a call into them for an update. Haven't heard from anyone for an hour. I know she's on life support. She's already lost the baby."

The baby. It had slipped Hannah's mind that Joanne Garcia, mother of Mimi and Enrique, was pregnant with her third child. She'd been through hell with her children; no one could deny it. Enrique was murdered, Mimi was in protective custody, and the baby was dead before it had been born. *Maybe the baby*, Hannah thought, *had been the lucky one.*

"There's something else," Ripp continued in his know-it-all voice that annoyed those who knew he didn't actually know much at all. "Some woman came to the lab today to talk with you. A reporter, I guess. From *Ladies' Home Journal* or something—I didn't get the name of the magazine. She said she wanted to talk to you for a profile she's writing about female crime scene investigators. She wants to interview me, too. Not as a female, of course, but as a man who works with one of the best."

"Not interested," Hannah said decisively, despite Ripp's attempt at sucking up. She had no intention of ever opening up that door. She never sought the spotlight, though she had had plenty of chances as Hannah Griffin, and a million times more as Hannah Logan, daughter of the woman who made the greatest escape in criminal history.

Hannah ended the conversation. "I'll be home tomorrow. Page me if you need me, but let's plan on talking late afternoon. And no interviews." She knew Ripp was an attention seeker of the highest order, so she added, "At least not now."

"But I want to," Ripp said, his voice a little whiny, like a kid being cheated out of a snow cone. "I know it's about you, but she wants to put me in the article, too."

"No. No interviews with anyone."

"I'm having lunch with her tomorrow. Got her business card right here. Very nice, embossed. *Freelance Writer*. Her name's Marcella Hoffman."

The name was like a bullet, and Hannah's heart tumbled down to her feet. Her head split into two, atom-smasher time. Hannah remained mute. A pair of glazed donut goggles stared at her from a greasy supermarket bakery box. On the open door, she could see the office was labeled PRESS ROOM.

"Wheaton's back," a voice called.

Hannah turned toward the voice; she sat still, frozen in worry. "I have to go now," she told Ripp. "I'll talk to you later."

"Who was on the phone? You look upset." It was Bauer. He stood in the doorway looking concerned. Hannah looked up and nodded. She was weary, and her eyes brimmed with tears. If she had been any closer to the edge, she would have been on the other side by now.

"Thanks," she said. "I'm glad I look the part. This day goes down in history as one of the most draining of my life. And I've had a few of those."

"That you have. Anything I can do?" Bauer asked, brightening his tone.

"No, I'm fine. It's just office stuff," she lied.

Hannah made no mention of the journalist or writer or trophy collector or whatever Hoffman could be termed. In reality, she didn't know what to think about Dog Face's sudden reappearance in her life. The timing was suspect. The shoes, the interview with Wheaton. All of it.

The pendulum was swinging back to the events of that terrible Christmas. What, if anything, did Hoffman want beyond the obvious, the all-important, exclusive interview for the update of the Logan case? How was it that she found her after all these years? Marcella *Fucking* Hoffman. Her features were chalk.

"I'll be fine," she said once more, steadying herself against the corner by the doorway. "I'm working a child abuse/murder case and it looks like Mom tried to kill herself."

"She a witness, key to the case?"

Hannah shrugged. "I'm not sure. We're still sorting it out."

Bauer backed off. He knew there would be time to talk later. They'd have to talk to decompress. Whether her pallid complexion had more to do with her phone call about her dead baby case or the business at hand with Wheaton, he couldn't be certain. They started down the corridor to the interrogation room. He searched his mind for some words to ease the transition back to what they were about to continue, when the door swung open and the one-eyed blob appeared in his seat behind the table.

"Wheaton, this is all very interesting, but you're twenty years too late to 'not confess' again. So you had nothing to do with the murders. *We know*. We've heard that before. I appreciate what you've said about Serena, and I'm sure her mother would like to lay her memory to rest. It has been difficult for the family."

"Difficult?" Wheaton turned away and looked at Hannah. "You have no goddamn idea. Try serving twenty years for torching someplace, while the real bad guy, in this case a woman, gets off scot-free."

Wheaton could have told Hannah and Bauer to get the

hell out of Cutter's Landing. This was *his* prison. But he didn't. He elected to continue.

"Your mother is alive. I'm sure of it," he said, still focused on Hannah sitting across from him.

Hannah felt the air sucked from her lungs, but she managed a response.

"No," she said. "I don't think so."

"Yes, I'm afraid she is," Wheaton said. He stared at Hannah, sizing her and tracing the lines of her face to see what reminded him of Claire. He thought her nose was very similar, even the shape of her eyebrows.

Bauer stepped in. "Where?"

"First I'll tell you how, then why and where. I'm absolutely certain of the why and the how, but the *where* is something you might have to do some actual work on."

Wheaton went on to restate how much he loved Claire, how he'd have done anything for her.

"Claire wanted me to pick her up at the five-way. But she didn't come. I waited. Five minutes turned into ten, ten to twenty. I could hear the sirens and see the glow of the inferno more than a mile away. I didn't see any footprints in the snow on the roadside. I thought something was wrong."

Wheaton took a drink, gulping loudly, before continuing.

"I mean, this was planned to the minute. I panicked and got back behind the wheel. When I pulled forward to find her, I ran over something and I felt it pierce the tire."

He said he got out and found a two-by-four with a row of nails running down the center like the spine of a dragon. He'd punctured only one tire, and that could be changed.

The recollection brought an odd look to Wheaton's

doughy face. Hannah couldn't make out his affect, though she wanted to desperately. *Was it regret? Anger?* The prisoner's good eye blinked rapidly. "She set me up. I didn't want to believe it." Wheaton looked down at the table again, searching for the words. "And I didn't for a long time. We had plans. She loved me. It sounds so pathetic, I know. Anyway, the cops came as I was fixing the tire and wondering how in the hell I was going to get out of there."

If Wheaton had hoped his story would bring sympathy from either Bauer or Hannah, he was mistaken. Maybe if he had said so a little earlier? Maybe if he had said so when it mattered? Wheaton fidgeted with the clear cord of his portable oxygen tank.

"I've had twenty fucking years to think about how stupid a man can be for the love of a woman. A fat man. A man with one eye. I mean, who was going to want me?"

As Hannah saw it, Wheaton's words were in defense of why he had stuck by the woman for so long.

"Where is she?" Hannah asked. "Where did she go?"

"Alaska," he answered. "Kodiak. If I know anything about your mother, she's up there. Running a fishing lodge on the southern end of the island. It was her dream. Rock Point wasn't remote enough. And God knew she had the money. Claire didn't want . . ." he stopped for a moment. "She didn't want nothing to hold her back. Not you or your brothers. And I guess, I mean, now I know, not even me."

Hannah had another question. There was one victim she had always wondered about.

"My father," she said. "Do you know? Was it an accident?"

"You know the answer," Wheaton answered, his voice

low and tired. "You've probably known it all along." He paused, once more evaluating what he'd say. He started wheezing and coughing, a fit that lasted almost a minute. But Wheaton waved his big, meaty hands, indicating he'd continue. "Your dad was in the way. Your dad was a road-block to your mom's desires. I think we all were. I mean I think she loved us for what she could get *from* us . . . and when we were used up, she didn't give a flying fuck."

There didn't seem to be anything more to say. Even so, Marcus Wheaton cleared the phlegm from his throat and spoke one more time.

"You know, Hannah. When I tell you you're nothing like your mother, I mean it."

Hannah muttered thanks, but nothing more.

She and Bauer walked almost in complete silence after saying good-bye to Madsen and leaving their best wishes for the warden. So frazzled by what she'd heard, Hannah almost forgot she'd left her purse—and car keys—in the visiting checkpoint. They walked to their cars. Dust swirled from exiting parents and wives, smudged windows catching the sun, low in the sky.

"Hannah," Bauer said, "I almost said, 'a penny for your thoughts' but you know that sounds so stupid . . . I want to know what you're thinking."

"I hate her," was all she could come up with. "I'm going home."

Bauer looked puzzled. "What did you expect?"

"I guess I hoped that he'd say she was dead. That, in fact, she was *Twenty*." Hannah inserted her key into the lock and opened her car door.

"Maybe he's lying. He's got plenty of reasons to put the blame on her."

She stared at Bauer and shook her head. "He loved her. He's bitter. I guess he's a lot like me."

"That's funny," Bauer said, and, looking at her, amended his words with, "as in *strange* funny."

Hannah let out an irritated sigh. "What's that?"

"Wheaton says you're nothing like your mother . . . and you think you're more like him, huh?"

Hannah shrugged. "I guess so. I'd rather not be like either one of them, if it's all the same to you."

Ethan Griffin was not, as he liked to say, "a happy camper." Still in his police uniform, Hannah's husband's blocky physique occupied the space like an overheated Kenmore as he stood in the kitchen in their home on Loma Linda Avenue. A *mad* Kenmore. He turned his head from Amber, who was busy moving her broccoli and a somewhat gray noodle casserole around her plate, and stepped away from the table. He held the phone firmly enough to break it in two. Hannah was on the line and she was about to get an earful, and as far as he could see, she deserved it. Freak-show mother or not.

"You left without saying much more than a word, and now you're not coming home," he said, doing his best to keep somewhat calm while his wife went off with some hot-shit FBI ghostbuster. "This is just perfect," he snapped, the sarcasm giving him some relief from his anger. "You don't know what you're messing with. And that idiot Ted Ripperton keeps calling looking for you. I've told him that you went to see a friend in the Bay Area."

"Thanks. I've already talked to him. He's been paging me all day."

"Amber and I want you home." Ethan softened when he saw that Amber was listening. "I'm worried about you." Ethan threw their daughter's name into his plea, knowing that a child's heart carries more weight than a husband's. In reality, he was more lonely and tired than angry.

"It's just for one more night," Hannah said, ignoring Ethan's brewing anger because there was no time to talk it out. "I'm not happy about it either," she said. "I'm going to stay in Cutter's Landing tonight, and I'll be home sometime late tomorrow. If I could leave right now, I'd do it. Believe me, I want out of here."

Ethan sighed, letting out an over-the-top noise that sounded like a leaking truck tire. The sound meant he loved her, but hated the situation. "I'll put your daughter on," Ethan's voice regained its characteristic understanding tone. He knew his anger had more to do with worry about her than any personal inconvenience.

Amber took the receiver and cooed into the phone. "Hi, Mommy!"

"Hello, darling. I miss you." Hannah realized that her words sounded flat, and she told herself keep the mood lighter.

"Miss you, too. Got a hundred on my spelling test," the little girl said, oblivious to her mother's somber tone. "I got extra credit, too."

"That's wonderful. I knew you could do it."

"I know. Daddy cooked tonight. I mean *you* cooked and Daddy reheated in the micro."

Hannah brightened for the first time during the conversation. "Good, I hope."

"I might have seconds," Amber lied. A lie she knew she

could get away with because her mother wasn't much of a cook and her father loved both of them so much that he would never spill the beans.

"Honey, I'll be home tomorrow. Give Daddy a big sloppy kiss for me."

Amber laughed. "Okay. Bye."

Ethan got his kiss and picked up the phone.

"This is very bad," Hannah said. Her voice broke a little. "This is very hard."

Seeing the exchange between mother and daughter, the sweetness of the little girl's lie, calmed him somewhat. "Are you all right? Sorry about being a jerk just now."

"I am, in fact, frightened as hell. I wish to God you were here. There is so much that needs sorting out."

Ethan was tense, but he didn't want to scare her anymore. She was hanging by a thread, and he knew it. "Can I help now, babe?" he asked. He pulled up a chair from the kitchen table and sat down. Amber continued to pick at her food. He'd heard worry in his wife's voice before, but not connected with anything associated with herself. Not directly. Nothing personal. When anxiety crept into Hannah's voice, it almost certainly was over a heavy caseload or the result of a desperate search for phantom evidence at the rebuttal phase or some other key point in a trial to prove a witness is lying.

"I don't know," she said, wanting to present what she had learned in that visiting room in a way that wouldn't worry Ethan. Instead, she just blurted it out.

"Wheaton says my mother is alive. And Marcella Hoffman is nosing around the lab asking questions and making a nuisance of herself. That's why Ripp was call-

ing so much. She wants an interview. She's got some pre-
text about women investigators, and thank God, Ripp is
too dense to figure anything out."

Ethan went blank. The name didn't quite track. "Who's
Marcella Hoffman?"

Silence fell for a second. "*Twenty in a Row.*"

"*Oh, that* Marcella Hoffman." When recognition
came, the name jolted like a radio in a bathtub. Ethan had
read the book before he met Hannah. He saw the TV
movie. "You're right," he said, his adrenaline pumping.
"This isn't good."

"Wheaton says my mother is alive. Thinks she's up in
Alaska somewhere. And you don't react to that?"

There was a short silence on the line.

"No, Hannah," Ethan finally said, "I didn't react because I've always thought she was out there somewhere.
I've always believed your mother got away with murder."

And for that I could kill her with my bare hands, he
thought, although he wisely didn't say the words.

"I don't know what to think," Hannah said, her voice
growing very quiet. "I need some time."

Across the Cascades in Spruce County where it all
began, Veronica Paine felt her stomach flutter and her
blood pressure rise. She paced over sumptuous Oriental
rugs that she and her husband had collected over the
years. She looked out the window at her garden. She
turned on the TV. But nothing could distract her from her
own thoughts. It had been long enough. She realized it
when she replayed the obvious anguish in Hannah Griffin's voice. Certainly, Hannah presented a brave face, but
for what? What had seemed like a good idea, the *right*

idea . . . the sanctity of the law, long ago, no longer felt as right to the former prosecutor and judge. She snuffed out a cigarette, let out the cat, and set the intruder alarm that her husband insisted they get the month before he died. Opening the front door was like a blast from a heater. No jacket was needed. She got into her red Chevy Blazer and started driving, heading in the direction of the Spruce County Courthouse.

She didn't know it, but a driver in a late-model car slipped behind her Blazer, staying just out of view.

CHAPTER TWENTY-SEVEN

Hannah Griffin stared into Jeff Bauer's eyes across a table in the Landing Zone, an incongruously cheery coffee shop with crisp white café curtains and a jukebox loaded with country music. It was in the heart of dusty Cutter's Landing, the town that survived only because it was home to a penitentiary. Marcus Wheaton's disclosure disturbed Hannah, but it also brought her a little relief. Although Wheaton revealed her mother could be somewhere in Alaska, possibly alive, Hannah didn't think about that just then. She kept her thoughts on her father.

She nodded to a waitress that more coffee was in order. Hannah turned away and stirred three spoonfuls of sugar into her coffee. A splash of cream from a dented, silver-lidded pitcher followed.

"Candy coffee, you have there," Bauer said.

A smile came to her face, but it was fleeting. She looked into the mug as though it held some answers.

"Let's go over it once more," he said. "If you think it will help?"

Hannah agreed. Her mind traveled back in time to Rock Point, where she was a grade-school girl with no upper front teeth and a bad haircut, given to her by her mother.

"It was late in the day," she began. "School would be out in an hour. . . . My mom came to school. My brothers were strapped in their car seats. They were quiet. Quieter than I'd ever seen Danny and Erik at that age. My mother's face was ashen. Flour highlighted the edges of the short-sleeved shirtdress she wore to keep cool that muggy day. 'Oh, Hannah, it's bad. So bad. He's gone, honey,' Mom said. 'Daddy's gone.'"

"Gone" was the word grown-ups used for "dead." It didn't fully dawn on Hannah until the car came to a stop. *Something hurt her.* Hannah didn't notice until her mother parked between the rutted and worn patch of grass in front of the house, but her hands had been clenched to the car-door handle all the way from school to home. It was a strange feeling, like her hand had been hammered into the chrome-plated lever. Like her hand was not her own. She turned her head to look at the door handle and hooked her fingers into the lever to command it to open.

Claire told her daughter how she and Marty had been working in the wreath maker's shed hoisting up a heavy part for a wood chipper. At one point, according to Claire, a grinder slipped down from its wall-mount harness and struck Marty squarely on the head, nearly splitting his skull in two. Claire struggled to stop the bleeding—blood splatter indicated as much—but it was to no avail. Marty didn't live long enough to see the volunteer paramedics when they arrived.

The Logans' yellow and white–painted house filled the car window. Sun splashed the green shutters and flowed over the cupola with the Santa Claus weathervane. The breeze of the day had been choppy, but Santa hadn't moved. Hannah stared into the nothingness beyond, the sky, the clouds. Then feeling was lost to a voice.

"Honey, we have to go inside."

The voice was her mother's. Soft, yet firm.

"Yes," Hannah said, once more turning to look at her frozen hand. "I'm coming."

Her mother's tears had dried; in fact, it later struck Hannah how there hadn't been many tears from her mother. She clutched her schoolbooks, carried Danny, and walked to the front porch. Claire held Erik and cooed to him. Hannah's flooded eyes swept over the yard, toward the work shed, over the back pasture where Bonnie, the family's sole horse, grazed lazily under a bloom-bursting apricot tree.

"Mom," she said. "I want to see Dad."

Claire juggled her toddler son and held the screen door open with her foot, allowing Hannah to pass by. "Honey," she said, "he's at the funeral home already. We'll go tonight."

Hannah dropped her books on the bench by the door and let out a cry. She held her brother and sobbed into the top of his tousled head. Her mother patted her back and put her arms around her. Both shook as though their grief could not be contained. Yet only one of them wept.

The kitchen with its knothole-free birch cabinets and ten-foot-high ceiling gleamed as it always did. It was always spotless because Claire Logan insisted that it be as pristine as a doctor's examining room. There was never a coffee ring on the counter, nor a water spot on the long chrome neck of the faucet. The curtains were white muslin, not because they added a stylish country touch, but because they could be washed once a week and not show evidence of fading.

On the afternoon that Martin Logan met his maker, Claire Logan had been baking bread—something she did on occasion because, she told her daughter, it relaxed her. The kitchen smelled heavenly, yeasty and sweet. Four loaves, shining with a coating of melted butter, were positioned on racks next to the sink.

"I came as soon as I could," her mother had said.

But the bread, and the flour on her sleeve, spoke of less of a hurried—frenzied—exit.

We'd been out working all morning when it happened.

But bread takes time . . .

It was so terrible. . . . I tried to help him, but I couldn't. There was blood everywhere.

Claire, however, carried no trace of blood; only the white flour on her sleeves marked her clothing and hinted that the day had been spent doing something before her husband died.

"Mom, you've been baking," Hannah said, staring at the crusty loaves nestled on a blue-and-white-checked towel.

Claire turned away and ran the faucet.

"You want some? It's still warm. Some food might do you good."

Hannah said no and left for her bedroom. Her pace

quickened as she climbed the stairs. By the time she had reached the final riser she was in an all-out run, a race to the softness of her mattress—a place where she could hide and cry.

Through furnace vents that had always been a pipeline to the goings-on in the house, Hannah could hear her mother's voice. She used to climb on the vent and, on the rare days when she wore a dress, she used to spread open her hemline over the metal grate to capture the warm air as it was forced from the basement to the rest of the house. In less than ten seconds, her dress would fill like a hot-air balloon, billowing in its fullness and keeping her legs warm.

But that morning the vents were a conduit for sound. Hannah overheard her mother talking with two men. The pair were from the sheriff's office; at least Hannah supposed they were, based on their questions. They certainly weren't friends of her mother's. They *couldn't* be friends with the kind of harsh and impatient tone they exhibited. She imagined two men. A short, fat man with a throaty voice and a taller, thinner fellow who said little other than to comment on what the other fellow said.

"You got that right," he said. "That's my understanding, too."

The fat man was pushy and direct. "Mrs. Logan," he said, "we're just here to put the report to bed. No one is trying to do anything other than get this over and done with. This unpleasant stuff is just part of the rigmarole of the law. The fact is, the injuries don't quite mix with what you've told us about your husband's death."

There was a short pause.

"In what way? What are you talking about?"

"I think you know," the other's voice cut in. It was deeper and had some kind of accent. "Why don't you tell us what happened to your husband?"

The sink water ran for a second. Hannah figured that her mother was rinsing plates or something.

"I don't know a thing about it," she said. "Are you accusing me of something here, deputy?"

"Did I say I was?"

"You've implied as much."

"Look, ma'am, please listen to me carefully. All I'm saying is that your husband's injury indicates he had been hit in front and back of the skull. *Both front and back.* Now how could that have happened?"

Again, the sink water ran.

"I'm not a cop," Claire said. "And I don't know what causes what. But if you are suggesting for one second that I know anything more than I've told you, you're as fucked up as your boss."

The F-word. It sent a decisive shock wave. Hannah had never heard her mother utter it in her entire life. Her mother didn't talk that way. Hannah found herself praying to God for her mother's soul. The F-word wasn't her mother's choice of language, not even in hammer-on-the-finger anger.

"I'll ask you to leave now."

"We want to talk with you again."

"Fine. Then call Marv Nelson's law office. Now get out."

"There's no need to be hostile, ma'am."

"Hostile is walking into a woman's house and so much as telling her you think she kissed off her old man. That's the very definition of hostile."

Hannah made her way down the stairs one hand over the other on the rail her father had crafted from a single piece of maple, cut not far from their farm. She stood in her nightgown, its flannel hem brushing against the landing. She wanted to tell the men to get out, just as her mother had. She wanted to scream at them for making her mother so upset. But she didn't. She didn't say a word. No one saw her standing there, so still and so quiet. No one turned to look in her direction when all three stomped out the front door.

A few minutes later, Claire came back inside.

"How long you been up, honey?" she asked, seeing her daughter. Her voice was sweet. *Sweeter than usual.*

"Are they gone?" she asked.

Claire looked surprised. "Yes, dear. They're gone."

"For good?"

"I think so. I don't think they'll ever be back."

And she was right.

Both Hannah and Bauer were exhausted by her disclosure. She, for what she had relived over coffee in the café, and he for the spinning wheels of a man who could do nothing to help the girl-turned-woman's realization of a dark truth, something she simply didn't want to believe.

"I'm talked out," she said. "I'm checking into the motel and going to bed."

"Want dinner?" he asked. He pointed to a placard on the table. "Pot roast is supposed to be their specialty."

"I can't eat." She feigned a smile. "I doubt I can sleep. I'll be up early and headed home at first light. Thanks for listening."

Bauer stood and embraced her. He felt her warm, limp body, and whispered in her ear.

"This isn't over, you know."

"I know," she said. "But someday it will be. I'll . . . we'll see to it."

Bauer let go and Hannah walked to the door. Her skirt was wrinkled and her blouse hung on her like it no longer fit. She didn't turn around. She didn't want him to see that she was crying.

The morning after he returned to Portland, Jeff Bauer made the call that Peggy Hjermstad had been expecting for two decades. Peggy was in her late fifties by then, remarried and living on her small farm in Tillamook, near the Pacific Ocean. She and her new husband raised dairy goats and had developed a successful line of goat cheeses.

She'd kept her last name and was listed in the phone book, in case her daughter ever came looking for her again. "Though I don't expect it," she'd say to friends or acquaintances inquiring about it.

Bauer hated making the call not only because it hurt like hell to tell a mother her daughter was likely deceased, but also because he only had the word of a convicted arsonist that she was the victim.

"Ms. Hjermstad?" he asked when a sweet voice answered the phone.

"Some call me that," she said warmly. "This is Peggy."

He told her who he was, and he could hear the rattling of bits of metal against the phone. It had to be her charm bracelet. He'd remembered that she wore it when she came to the FBI office so many years ago. Among the charms she pointed out during that visit was a silhouette of a girl's head with the name "Serena" engraved in curlicue lettering.

"I talked with Marcus Wheaton yesterday," Bauer said. "There's no easy way to say this. He identified your daughter as the female victim."

Peggy let out a small gasp, but quickly recomposed herself.

"Does he," she said, fumbling for words, "know where her head is? I mean, I know it doesn't matter. I know that she's gone. I've always known it. But I'd like to have her go to heaven in one piece."

"No. He didn't say."

"Why did he kill her?"

"Said he didn't. I don't know if he's a liar *and* an arsonist, but I believed him. He put the blame right on Claire Logan. Said your daughter went by the name 'Didi.'"

"Oh my," Peggy Hjermstad said, growing very quiet.

"I'm so sorry," Bauer said.

There was silence.

"Ms. Hjermstad? I mean, *Peggy.* You still on the line?"

"I'm here," she said. "The name caught me off guard, that's all. Didi was the name of Serena's poodle. A teacup. A pretty little apricot thing she loved to death. Wonder why she called herself that name?"

"I don't know, ma'am," Bauer said. "Some things we never know."

Peggy thanked the agent for calling. "I knew she was never coming home when she didn't call for my birthday or Christmas. Even so . . . it still hurts after all these years. Funny how it hurts. It almost seems like she's died all over again."

"I'm sorry," he said once more. "I'll let you know if anything else turns up, but this may be all we will ever know."

"No need. I know all I need to know. My darling girl is gone forever."

CHAPTER TWENTY-EIGHT

It was easy to get the assignment. Jeff Bauer had lived in Anchorage for five years when he worked the stolen Russian antiquities sting. He'd even been to Kodiak Island to fish with his teenage nephews one summer when his sister sent the boys up from Idaho. The idea that it was possible that Claire Logan had been right under his nose was more annoying than infuriating. Bauer wasn't completely sure that Wheaton was telling the truth or making a play for some attention before he was measured for a piano crate and converted into a worm smorgasbord. The supervising agent in Portland knew Bauer's history with LOMURS, as the case was still known in FBI-speak, and made it easy to procure a plane ticket and a hotel reservation in his name.

"Talk about a feather in your cap," the agent told him.

"You nail that bitch and it would be right up there with bringing in D. B. Cooper."

There was some truth to the remark. Cooper was the man who "skyjacked" a Northwest Airlines 727 in November 1971. With parachutes strapped on, Cooper jumped out of the plane at an altitude of 10,000 feet with $200,000 and was never heard from again. Some said he died. Others insisted he made his way to Margaritaville and was working on his tan. Though far less gruesome than Claire Logan, Cooper was in a weird way a male equivalent. Infamous and notorious, he had captured the public's imagination. A tavern hosted annual parties; there were many books and even a movie. Cooper was never found, which, like Logan, had kept alive the possibility that he'd gotten away with the crime.

Bauer caught the five-hour flight from Portland to Anchorage and a commuter flight to Kodiak, 250 miles south of Alaska's largest, and some alleged only "real" city. Although it was 10 p.m., it was still light out an hour later when he landed at the town with the same name as the island.

As pretty as it was with its gorgeous and grand expanses of green forests, meadows, and a navigator's nightmare of a craggy coastline, Kodiak had seen its share of hard times. Pretty, of course, doesn't account for much when money is hard to come by. Sagging motel rates were only one indicator that the island hadn't fully rebounded from the last downturn. There was work, but not enough workers for the kind of positions offered. Cannery jobs were advertised in every edition of the Kodiak paper. Times had changed. The scrappy folks who drank most of their days away before sobering up for the cash that came with a good Tanner crab or shrimp season were in dwindling supply. The money didn't flow as it once did. Even a decade before, a man could make as much dough in three months with shares from a decent salmon run as he could with a yearlong stint working a decent-paying job on the mainland.

Bauer picked up a rental car, loaded it with his luggage and fishing gear, and checked into a room at the Northern Lights Best Western Motor Inn. As a courtesy, he drove over to the Kodiak sheriff's office to say hello to the sheriff, Kim Stanton. An Aleut, Stanton was thirty-eight with almond eyes and the thickest, darkest hair imaginable. He'd been elected to the post twice and was considered one of the most competent public officials on the island. Bauer did not say *whom* he was there to find, nor did the pudgy officer on duty inquire. Bauer knew the drill—a kind of don't-volunteer-information protocol. Over the years, Bauer had learned much about local and federal law enforcement and how the two factions seldom forged a viable working relationship. Territory, he knew, mattered; getting something right wasn't as important, it seemed, as *who* got it.

"You know," the officer said, "we spend half our budget taking people back to the mainland for extradition to God-knows-where they came from. People think Alaska is the last good place to hide. Like we don't bother to catch them because we're too busy dog sledding or snow-mobiling."

"Or ice fishing," Bauer said, continuing the joke. He looked out the window at the dusky and nearly deserted street outside. A car slowly passed, then sped up, its tail-lights glowing red. "I'll let you go so you can skin a grizzly." He winked. "Be back when Sheriff Stanton's in. Thanks, deputy."

Letting the door swing closed behind him, Bauer walked across the street and ordered a BLT and fries to go from the coffee shop and returned to his room at the Northern Lights. It was 10:40 p.m. He had one more call to make, but given the hour he decided to put it off until the morning. *Maybe the afternoon. Just later,* he thought. He watched the tail end of the Anchorage news, though he paid little attention to what was being reported. His mind was fully occupied with Claire Logan. *Was she here?* Her Social Security number had long since been abandoned. After Leanna Schumacher died, surveillance was discontinued on her place in Misery Bay. Bauer never told Hannah about the wiretapping on the Schumachers' phone line in the event that Claire contacted her younger sister. It was never that the Feds didn't trust the Schumachers; they just had no other idea about whom Claire might call. The wiretaps were an insurance policy. But, of course, Claire never did call. They were discontinued several years after the murders, but the court order was always in place just in case.

And so Claire Logan remained a phantom. The only known photos of her were from her Bellingham High School yearbook. Sitting on the bed of his Kodiak motel room, Bauer studied the scan of Claire Berrenger's senior picture. Admittedly, it was black-and-white and that could account for some of his reaction. But, he thought, the woman looked so cold. In the photograph her eyes looked black—there was no differentiation between her pupils and her iris. Just two small puddles of blackness. He'd seen the photograph a million times before. An FBI artist had created a fast-forwarded image of what Claire Logan might look like in her sixties. Bauer didn't think much of the effort.

"She's not going to let nature take its course," he told his supervisor back in Portland before he left. "First of all, she has the money to have whatever she wants done as she got older. Secondly, she knows the whole fucking world knows her mug."

"Could be," the agent said.

"I know this woman," Bauer said. "She's a total control freak. She's been pinched and pulled tighter than a soap opera actress."

It was almost 11 p.m. when Bauer dialed Hannah's number at home. It was Ethan Griffin who answered. His voice was a little rough, a little sleepy sounding.

"Sorry this is so late," Bauer said, realizing the time difference between Alaska and the lower forty-eight. He identified himself and asked for Hannah. "It's about her mother."

"I hope my mother-in-law is dead," Ethan said.

"*Every* guy wishes that a time or two," Bauer said. But the joke fell flat.

"Right. It would be better off for everyone. Hannah and Amber, especially. Amber doesn't know anything about her grandmother, and I'd like to keep it that way."

"I'd probably feel the same way," Bauer said, "if she was my little girl."

"Trust me. You would," Ethan said.

"It's bound to come out. Hope you're prepared."

"Thanks for the advice," Ethan said. "But if you guys hadn't screwed up when this all went down in Rock Point, we wouldn't be talking about it now. Am I correct?"

"We did the best we could. You know that the law isn't perfect."

"Right," Ethan was annoyed. He was the law. He thought he could have done better if he'd have been handed such a case. "Nice talking with you. Here's Hannah."

She stared into her husband's eyes and took the phone. "You've already found her?" she asked Bauer, sounding slightly panicked.

"Not so fast. I just got here. I just wanted to let you know that it might take a while. Go about your business. I'll keep you in the loop, but it has to be unofficial. You understand?"

"Yes," she lied. How could she not be involved? If anyone in the world deserved to be "in the loop" it was she. She had waited a lifetime for the moment to arrive where everything she'd have ever wanted to know would spurt forth like a geyser. She hated Claire Logan the infamous murderess. But she loved her mother—or at least the good parts of her she could still remember.

"If you find her, there will be no hiding it from anyone, you know," Hannah said. "People—if you can call Marcella Hoffman that—are already sniffing around."

"I know. If we find her, it'll blow bigger than Mount St. Helens did in 1980," Bauer said before giving Hannah the phone number of the Northern Lights.

"Take care of yourself," he said.

"You, too," Hannah replied, laying the phone silently in its cradle.

Ethan was undressed and in bed, holding the covers open for his wife. Hannah refused his gesture and sat down on the edge of the mattress.

"That means you want to talk about it?" he asked.

Hannah looked at her husband. "I think I should tell Amber something," she said.

Ethan sat upright. "No," he said. "*We* agreed. She doesn't need to know anything about this. I don't want her living with this. It'll drive her crazy."

"I've lived with it," she muttered. "And I'm all right."

"Are you? I mean, Hannah, look at you." He held her by her shoulders, not really to shake her, but to snap her into some kind of awareness. "You haven't slept in days. You've lost weight. . . . You aren't the same person you were when you thought . . ." he stopped himself.

"*Thought* what?"

"Thought . . . she was probably dead."

"*Hoped.* I had *hoped* all these years that she was dead. And you need to know, I'm still hoping. But I've got Jeff Bauer, Marcus Wheaton, and that cretin Marcella Hoffman reminding me that Claire Logan lives. In one way or another. She lives. My mother won't die. Like Sissy Spacek's hand out of the grave grabbing at us all at the end of *Carrie*. My mother still lives."

She was crying now.

He tried to comfort her, but she seemed resistant to his touch. "You need to rest," he told her.

"No," she said. "I mean, yes, rest would help. But I can't sleep, because I keep thinking of her."

Ethan pulled her into bed and turned off the light. He held Hannah and felt ripples of grief pass through her body. She was a wreck.

"I love you, baby," he said.

"Love you."

In a half hour Ethan allowed himself to drift off. Hannah's eyes were wide open, staring at the clock as the digital numbers rolled from 2 to 3, then on to 4 a.m.

Each hour now meant something. Each hour, each tumble of the lighted drums emblazoned with boldface numbers, meant Hannah Logan Griffin was that much closer to resolution. Closer to truth. She tossed and turned for another hour, battering her pillow and twisting the coverlet. Strangely, when she finally fell asleep that night, it was moonflowers she thought about. The creamy white, swirling blossoms, twisted open in the magic of an early evening. She and her mother sat on the log and watched while her brothers played inside the big yellow house. In her sleep, Hannah smiled.

CHAPTER TWENTY-NINE

It would take some time. Computers could only do so much. In the decades-old case of Claire Logan, computers were useful only for eliminating potential suspects. All Bauer knew—and that was if Wheaton was telling the truth—was that Logan ran a fishing resort on Kodiak Island in Alaska. There were no Logans listed, of course. But there were dozens of resorts of the type that Marcus Wheaton had described.

"Close enough to whatever roads they have up there, because she didn't want to bother with seaplanes bringing guests in," Wheaton had said, huffing and puffing in the penitentiary's visiting cell. "She researched it. She did. Nice enough place that she'd be comfortable. Room for a dozen fishermen at any given time, because she wanted to make money."

The last remark almost brought a grin to Bauer's handsome face. Characteristic restraint, however, kept him from saying anything snide. But how did she plan on making her income? Fishing fees or murdering her guests?

Out of what turned out to be a hundred and fifty names, two-thirds were discounted right away because their lodges, resorts, and gear shops had been in operation far longer than twenty years. A cross-check of Alaska game and fishing licenses indicated as much—though Bauer knew that record keeping in Juneau, while improved since the advent of computers, wasn't the most reliable system.

That left around forty-five possible havens for Logan. Another series of checks indicated that about twenty of those could be discounted for reasons ranging from ethnicity and gender.

Claire Logan might be smart enough to make herself over, Bauer thought, *but she can't change her gender or turn herself into an Inuit.*

That left just twenty-five possibles, a more manageable but large number nonetheless. The FBI had gone through more possible Claire Logan expeditions than the higher-ups wanted to admit, so they'd send Bauer a backup only if an arrest appeared imminent. Bauer requested Bonnie Ingersol, the agent with whom he shared some of the first days of the investigation when they worked together in Portland in the late '70s. They had been quite close back then; even dated a few times, though nothing came of it. Neither one had the time for romance.

In the meantime, Bauer would have to pursue Claire Logan alone. He'd employ some old-fashioned nosing around, hopefully asking the right questions, as he trimmed the fat from the list. After four hours of phone calls, only one name remained on the list: *Louise Wallace.*

* * *

Louise Wallace lived in one of the prettiest houses on the island. It was a Victorian more suited to New England than Alaska, with twin turrets and a widow's walk that crossed the entire front side. Louise called it the front of the house, because it faced the choppy waters of Port Lion. The back side, as she termed it, faced the gravel road that ran up past the fishing cabins to the parking area adjacent to an enormous gazebo and fenced vegetable garden. The three-story house was painted seven colors, though the dominant hue was a creamy yellow that Louise called "shortbread." The main floor was an open plan with gorgeous wood floors and a two-story river-rock fireplace, the only concession Louise made to her late husband's desire for an Alaskan-style abode of rock, antlers, and peeled timbers. The furnishings were quite lovely. The majority were antiques the Wallaces had gathered throughout Alaska, though mostly from a trusted dealer on the outskirts of Anchorage.

An oak box lined with slippers of varying sizes sat next to the door and admonished visitors to take off their shoes before coming inside. WE WOOD APPRECIATE IT, read a little hand-lettered index card affixed to the box. The O's had been embellished into happy faces.

Bauer pulled his rental car to a shady spot near a rustic gazebo framed with silvery driftwood logs, choked with trumpet vines. The setting was gorgeous. Alaska's short growing season was short only in the number of days. In reality, the season was longer than points much further south, like Seattle or Portland. Eighteen hours of sunlight a day gave plants an extraordinary boost. Years ago, Bauer had been to the state fair in Palmer, not far from Anchorage, where "monster" vegetables vie for attention in one of the more popular gee-whiz exhibits. Three-foot zucchinis and cabbages with the astonishing girth of beach balls draw tourists from across the state to gawk in amazement. Bauer noticed that someone had been working in the Wallace garden that day. Sprinklers had been set to water the fluffy rows of vegetables and flowers that included everything from larkspur to delphinium to foxglove.

He heard sandpipers and gulls squawk from the surf below the house. The bell of a distant buoy clanged.

"Mrs. Wallace?" he called out as he knocked on the open door. No one responded. He called again and studied the splendor of leaded glass windows with maritime images inset into several panes.

"Yes? Can I help you?" The sweet face of an old woman appeared in the doorway. She was tall, somewhat thin, and had ashy blond hair streaked with gray. Gold-framed glasses didn't hide the fact that her blue eyes were the color of the cornflowers that stood high in the back of her garden border. Her lipstick was dark, a winy red that looked almost brown.

"Louise Wallace?" Bauer asked.

"Do I know you?" she said, brushing a wisp of silvery hair from her eyes. "Been out in the yard all morning. Must look like a fright."

"No ma'am. You don't know me. But I know you."

"You do? That's surprising to me, because I'm pretty good with faces. Names, not so much, but faces I never forget."

"We've never actually met," he said. "I know everything about you. I know your name is Claire Berrenger Logan and, more importantly, I know what you did in Spruce County twenty years ago."

It was a bluff and Bauer felt relief that he'd pulled it off, because he really wasn't that sure. She could be Claire Logan, but she didn't look exactly like the computer-aged model photo. Her chin was more angular, her nose a bit more pointed. He kept his face from betraying any emotion, though his chest pounded beneath his jacket. This was the bluff. The *big* bluff. The assumptive interview. If you tell the suspect you know they did something or are someone, you just might get lucky. Attitude, he knew, was everything.

"I'm sorry," Wallace said, peering over her glasses. "You must have me confused with someone else. My name is Louise. *Louise Wallace*. I don't know anyone by the name of Claire Morgan. Who are you?"

Nice touch, Bauer thought, *getting the name wrong.*

"Jeff Bauer, FBI," he said, presenting his I.D. badge and photo.

She took it and regarded it, then handed it back. "Oh my," she said. "I've never seen one of those in person. Very official and kind of pretty isn't it?" She didn't wait for a response. "I'm going to move the water again. Wish I had installed that drip system my husband had wanted. Would have saved me hours and hours of time. 'Course, lots of time in Alaska, anyway. Want some rhubarb?"

"No, thanks," Bauer said. "How long have you lived here?"

"Is this part of your official interview?" she asked with a wry smile.

He ignored her. "How long?"

"All right," she said. "I'll answer a few of your questions. I'll give you enough rhubarb for two pies. But you, Mr. Bauer, is it?"

He nodded, but said nothing.

"You will have to tell me who this Claire Morgan is and why you think I might know something about her. Is she in some kind of trouble?"

"I'd say so. Claire Logan murdered twenty people. Surely you've heard of her."

"Can't say that I have. We never got a satellite dish up here. My husband wanted one, but I kept saying no."

"The murders were discovered in Rock Point, Oregon. She killed nearly a score of lovelorn military men, plus her own two sons."

Holding a kitchen paring knife, Mrs. Wallace bent down and started cutting bright red stalks of rhubarb and arranging them in neat rows in the bottom of an antique vegetable basket.

"These will make a delicious pie," she said without looking up. "Does your wife bake?"

"No. Don't have a wife." Bauer felt a little foolish. This woman wasn't listening and she wasn't reacting to anything he had to say.

"As I was saying," he began again.

"As you were *accusing*," she said, still intent on her slicing. "Well, I've never had any children. And, I've never dated anyone from the military. I'm a Democrat."

"Mrs. Wallace," he said, stooping to face her directly. "Where were you living in the mid-70s?"

"This stalk is particularly suitable—thick and without all those nasty fibers."

Bauer was frustrated, and his tone couldn't conceal it. "Will you answer?"

Wallace stood up gripping the knife dripping, by then,

with the red juice of rhubarb. Her eyes were cold, glacial blue.

"I don't talk about that part of my life," she said harshly, the first shift in a demeanor that Bauer could only have described as sweet and kindly. "Not to anyone."

"You'll need to answer to me," he fired back. "I've waited two decades to find out what rock you've crawled under and your grandma-of-the-year act is as transparent as ice."

She bent back down and resumed slicing. She remained expressionless. "You, young man, are mistaken. Now, do you want the rhubarb or not?"

"I saw Marcus Wheaton last week," Bauer said. He stared at her, but nothing came from her in the way of a genuine reaction. Not even a flutter. "Saw him with your daughter, Hannah."

For a half second, Bauer thought he noticed a slight, very slight hesitation in the woman's cutting of glossy red stalks. Perhaps it was merely his hope that he could find something in her manner, demeanor, and cadence of her speech—*anything*—that could suggest she was not being truthful.

"I don't have any children," she said. "I've never had any children, sons, daughters, or any combination thereof. Mr. Wallace and I would have liked children and I suppose the fact that I couldn't have any is my cross to bear. Satisfied? Furthermore, I don't know anybody named Wheaton. Your accusations are very, very upsetting to me. I'm sure you didn't mean for them to be, and truly I'm sorry I can't help. I live my life being helpful to others."

With that she reached for her basket, turned abruptly, and started for the house, abandoning Bauer by the garden gate. There was no point in calling out to her to stop because Bauer really didn't know what to make of her. Louise Wallace was one of two things, a sweet old lady or a cold-blooded killer. He aimed to find out just which she was.

A half hour later and back in his room at the Northern Lights, Bauer used a handkerchief to carefully remove his photo I.D. badge from its protective leather and plastic sheath before sliding it into a glassine. It wasn't evidence per se. But he was treating it as such. Louise Wallace had held it as they stood in her garden. She had touched it after Bauer had made sure it was perfectly clean. He had only held it on its edge. He phoned Bonnie Ingersol at the Portland office. She was out, so he left a message for her to sit tight until he called her back in about an hour. Bauer got back behind the wheel and drove to the Kodiak airport where he put the small package on a plane that would connect with an Alaska Airlines flight to Portland. With a layover in Anchorage, and a connection in Seattle, Ingersol could pick it up by six the next morning. Bauer looked at his Seiko. In a few hours, he'd know the truth. He scratched his head and smiled. A beer seemed like a good idea right then.

CHAPTER THIRTY

The ladies of the First Methodist Church of Kodiak knew how to put on a wildly successful bake sale, no matter if the cause was directly related to the church or not. One time, the group of thirteen women raised almost a thousand dollars for Kodiak High's choral ensemble's trip to compete against school choir groups from Canada and the United States. (The Singing Grizzlies placed in the top ten and were greeted with a modest parade upon their return to the island, again courtesy of the ladies of First Methodist.) All but four were widows with grown children and scads of free time to devote to the cause—whatever it was at any given time.

Harriet Wilcox was in her late eighties, the oldest of the group. The oldest always admits her age as a badge of honor for living longest and still being able to keep up with the younger gals, in their sixties and seventies.

Marge Morrison, sixty-two, was the youngest and most active. Morrison was still working part-time at the local public utility as the secretary to the consumer services manager. She was an attractive woman with silvering hair that she wore in a low-slung ponytail held in place by a tortoiseshell barrette. Her only flaw was the fact that gum disease had taken her teeth and she wore a full set of dentures of which she was extremely self-conscious. Others of the group included a retired schoolteacher, Beth Tyson; Annie Potter, a crabber's widow, and Louise Wallace, the owner of a fishing resort.

In early September the ladies of First Methodist met at the church for their fall planning session. A Thanksgiving coat and blanket effort, a food drive for Christmas, and the annual cookie exchange were on the agenda for the next three months, and preparations were necessary. Marge Morrison arrived first. She was chairwoman for the fall events. Beth Tyson followed her inside. Beth took the minutes for the newsletter, *Divine Inspirations*. Beth propped open the doors, letting the breeze blow in from the Aleutians. September was Kodiak's second warmest month. Hitting a pleasant seventy degrees was possible, even with the summer wind blowing in from the north.

"Anyone hear from Sandy?" Morrison asked as she settled her considerable frame into a molded plastic chair. "Sandy called me last night. Her son's wife is ill. She flew to Anchorage this morning. Said she'd be gone for a week."

"Hope it isn't too serious," one said.

"No. Got the flu, a dreaded *summer* flu."

"That's just awful. Summer's short enough 'round here. Hate to be sick."

"You got that right."

"Anyone hear from Louise?"

When no one had, Morrison volunteered to make the call from the pastor's office phone.

"Be back in a jiff," she said cheerfully. "Go ahead and sample those peanut butter squares. Just out of the oven this morning."

Five minutes later, Morrison returned to the table.

"I couldn't reach her," she said. "She must be on her way. Let's get started."

Two hours later the women, full of lime Jell-O cake, peanut butter squares, and decaf coffee, adjourned their meeting. Still no Louise Wallace.

"It's not like her at all," Morrison said as she made her way to her car.

The voice was shaky, but it was familiar even under splintering layers of worry and fear. The words "accused" and "Federal Bureau of Investigation" floated above the others. Marge Morrison grabbed the remote control and turned down the volume of her soap opera, *General Hospital*.

"Louise, what did you say?"

Morrison heard her friend Louise Wallace speak, but nothing computed.

"I think I might need a lawyer," she repeated. "Something terrible has happened. A terrible mix-up."

"They think you are *who*?"

"I know it is ridiculous. But he—this FBI agent from Oregon—says he thinks I'm that horrible Claire what's-her-name. Claire *Logan*."

Morrison knew the name instantly. Most Americans over thirty did.

"That woman from Seattle who killed those men? What in the world?"

"Oregon or somewhere," Wallace corrected, her voice cracking. She was crying now. And Morrison had never heard her friend weep before—not even during the black days of her husband Hank's ordeal with inoperable colon cancer several summers before. "I think she lived down in Portland somewhere. *I can't believe this is happening.* I've never even been to Oregon."

"Of course not," Morrison said as she tried to process everything. "You've never been there."

Louise Wallace pulled herself together and gulped some air. "They don't care. He wouldn't listen. This could be bad. It has happened to others, you know. It doesn't matter what the truth is anymore. Remember that guy they blamed for *planting* a bomb at the Olympics in Atlanta just because he *found* it?"

"Dear Lord," Morrison muttered, "if our FBI can screw up so badly, no one is safe."

Morrison remained clear headed in any catastrophe, which was why she made such an excellent chairwoman for the First Methodist fund-raisers. If Louise Wallace needed support and counsel, she'd dialed the right number.

"Get your lawyer on the phone, dear," Morrison said. "Would you like me to come over?"

Louise said she didn't want to be a bother. But before she hung up, she stated the obvious. "I could use some company, a little moral support. I have to admit I'm a little scared."

"Of course you are. Who wouldn't be?" Morrison said, grabbing a blue-and-white down-filled jacket from the back of a kitchen chair. "I'm on my way."

* * *

Marge Morrison drove her two-year-old Dodge pickup like the proverbial bat out of hell. She didn't even slow down to wave to neighbors out washing their car or stop to tell them that a running hose was a waste of water. Morrison had known Louise Wallace for years. As she spun around the corner to the highway, she tried to calculate the number. *Was it a dozen years? More than that? Fifteen or twenty?* After a while, she knew, numbers no longer mattered. At some point, friends become family. In her heart, she'd known Louise forever. A half hour after she spoke to a rattled Louise on the phone, Morrison was driving up the long gravel driveway that led to the Wallace place. As it always did, the sight of the grand yellow house took her breath away. There was no place lovelier in all of Kodiak Island.

Wallace ran over to the pickup. It was obvious that she had been gardening because there were smudges of soil on her chambray blouse. A basket of baseball-size tomatoes and another of rhubarb sat on the steps of the gazebo.

"Oh, Marge!" she called out. "Thank you for coming. This is just terrible. Terrible."

Morrison got out of the cab and hugged Louise. "It'll be all right," she said. "Tell me what happened? What is this balderdash they are saying?"

"This agent from the FBI came today. *Right here.* Came here. And he asked me about those murders down in Oregon years ago. He said he thought I could be . . . no, he said he thought I was . . . *that* Claire Logan. I thought he was joking. But he wasn't, he kept saying it. Said he knew. *Knew* it. Can you believe it?"

Morrison was dumbfounded. While words of any real substance eluded her, she kept assuring her friend that things would be sorted out. When she noticed Louise shaking, she suggested they go inside.

"Chamomile," she said. "Let's figure out what to do over some tea. Chamomile will relax you. Dear, you must relax. You know this is no good for your heart."

Louise picked up the tomatoes and rhubarb, and the two went inside. Neither woman took off her shoes. Keeping Louise's prized wooden floors free from garden grit just didn't come to mind.

"I called my lawyer, like you said." Louise turned up the flame under the kettle. "He's not in. Out fishing until tomorrow."

"I'm sure you won't need him," Morrison said, though she didn't know why she offered such false assurance. The words just came out. "Now, tell me everything."

The tea kettle whistled to signal the water was hot, and Wallace loaded a tray with a teapot, cups, and lemon cookies. They retreated to a powder-blue settee that overlooked the waters of the Pacific through ten-foot-high windows. Wallace was upset—more upset than Morrison had ever seen her. She kept a tissue crumbled in a ball and when tears came, she dabbed at them.

"There is something about me that you don't know."

"Of course," Morrison said, "there are things we all keep private."

"Well, this is certainly that kind of thing. I've never talked about it. I don't particularly want all of Kodiak Island to know about it." She hedged, carefully considering her words. "But it might be necessary, you know, for it to come out."

Morrison was on the edge of her seat. She set her cup on a side table. She didn't think that her friend could possibly be Claire Logan. *Certainly not!* Up to an hour ago,

Morrison didn't think Louise could have a dark secret of any kind whatsoever.

"Better than twenty years ago," she began, "something terrible happened." Louise stood and looked out across the water. Her cup rattled in its saucer, and she turned to set it down. "I don't like talking about this, but you are my friend."

"Yes," Morrison said. "Of course. Always."

Wallace took another deep breath and steadied herself.

"All right," she said. "Twenty years ago, I had some problems—some terrible problems that the doctors couldn't help." She stopped again, took another breath, and searched the horizon.

"What kind of problems?"

"Depression caused by a tragic loss," Wallace answered. "There, I said it." She turned to face Marge. "I lost my boys in a car accident. A terrible, terrible crash. I never got over it."

Morrison felt tears come instantly to her eyes. "Oh, dear God, I had no idea," she said. The First Methodist ladies had always assumed Louise had never been blessed with children at all. She had no inkling there had once been two boys who had died in some automobile accident. Morrison reached out to Wallace and felt her trembling hands. Her eyes had flooded by then.

Tears now rolled down her cheeks and collected under her chin. "I needed help. I just couldn't do anything after the boys died. My husband couldn't help me. He tried. I know he did. But I wanted no part of anyone. Not after the accident. I pulled the curtains and stayed in bed for months. Sometimes, even now, when I look back I can barely remember that time. I feel as though I lost a whole year."

"Dear Lou, oh, my dear." Morrison felt her throat tighten over the thought of her friend's cruel ordeal. "I can't imagine."

"As much as I keep this inside—because I have to—there is something more that I haven't told you. Something very important. And even though I know that it is nothing to be ashamed about, I am. I know in my heart that I'm all right, now. Best as I can be . . ."

"You are wonderful," Morrison consoled. "You are very dear to all of us."

Wallace smiled a little and gripped the ball of tissue even tighter and ran it under her chin. "Marge, I was hospitalized after my little boys died in the crash. It was a mental hospital called Evergreen State just south of Seattle. I was there for six months, and it helped me. I did many, many strange things as I coped with my grief. Lithium was good, and though I hate to admit it, shock treatments probably helped me, too. I was able to come to terms with what happened when my sons died. I grew stronger. Stronger than ever."

While Morrison sat anguished and rapt, Louise Wallace sipped tea and told her friend that her husband left her during the hospitalization at Evergreen State. Few men could survive the loss of their sons. She could no longer face the world as she was.

"My doctor told me the best way to go out into the world—which I really didn't want to do—was to start over. All over. He said I was reborn. I took it literally. I changed my name and moved as far away from Seattle as I could."

"You came here to Kodiak," Morrison interjected.

"Not at first, but eventually. I worked in the canneries

for a short while, met Hank Wallace, and we fell in love. In a way, I was reborn," she said.

"A beautiful butterfly," Morrison said. "You are. And we love you."

Wallace walked around the settee to the tea cart and poured herself another cup. "So you see, there is a bit of a problem. Or there could be. There is no Louise Wallace, not really. I mean I am here with you, of course. But there are no records of any Louise Wallace."

Morrison refused to have any part of that kind of thinking. "You are our Louise—doesn't matter when you became *her*. That's who you are. Besides, you know what we've always said of Alaska."

She smiled and said, "A good place to hide."

"A good place to start over."

"Marge?" Louise asked as she turned to the window. "There is one more thing." Her voice started to crack on the last word.

Morrison stood. "Yes? What is it?"

"Marge, I was driving the car when I lost control. . . . I was the one driving. I was thrown from the car, but the boys were strapped in the car. There was an explosion and fire."

"I'm sorry," Morrison said. "I'm so sorry."

"Look, Marge, I don't think I can say this any more plainly. I think my past might be catching up with me. I won't allow it. I've been through too much already."

CHAPTER THIRTY-ONE

Our Lady of Guadeloupe Hospital was Catholic to its core, having been built on the ruins of the Santa Louisa Mission after the turn of the century—the *nineteenth* century. Framed in stately date palms, it was three stories high, a buttery-colored form of stucco walls capped with red Mexican tiles. A clock tower was lost in a relentless windstorm that cut through the region a couple of days after John F. Kennedy was gunned down in Dallas, an occurrence the faithful thought was God's way of grieving for the slain Catholic president.

Floor-to-ceiling stained-glass windows depicting Adam and Eve and Noah's Ark were the focal point of the lobby. Adjacent to the windows, a small brass plaque was placed at eye level: A GIFT OF THE WILLIAM GILLIAND FAMILY. It was under those windows that Hannah Griffin and Ted Ripperton conferred in the lobby a few days after Hannah returned from Cutter's Landing. They reviewed the police reports. One held their attention in particular: Berto Garcia's history of incarceration.

"This changes everything," Hannah said. "I've been doing this a while, and I'm seldom surprised, but really, this is the topper."

"I smell plea bargain," Ripp said, almost gleefully. "I like it when we don't have to do too much heavy lifting." Ripp playfully flexed a muscle, but Hannah wasn't amused.

"I don't like a child killer," she said. "Let's go talk to Joanne."

The Intensive Care Unit was up a flight of stairs on the third floor. Visitor elevators, a note taped over the call button indicated, were being refurbished. Nurses in cranberry scrubs and orderlies in smudged whites milled around by the nurses station. Silent portable fans blew cool air into the horseshoe-shaped group of desks, telephones, and computer terminals.

"We're here to see Mrs. Garcia," Hannah told a hefty woman basking in the manmade breeze. "County investigators," she continued, nodding at Ripp. She didn't use the word "crime scene" or "criminal investigator," because of the baggage the words invariably brought.

"Sunshine 4. You've got five minutes," the nurse said, indicating the fourth of the cluster rooms that provided the best in urgent care in Santa Louisa, which Hannah Griffin, and others, didn't think was much praise.

Joanne Garcia was under an octopus of clear hoses and white plastic tubing; a sky-blue sheet was pulled up to her neck. The bulge of her round, but empty, abdomen was still visible under the sheet. If only one thing in the world could be considered cruel, it was a woman who no longer had a baby inside her, but still looked pregnant. Stillborn. Given away for adoption. *Whatever*. Hannah couldn't help but be taken back to the moment when she lost Annie, but she removed it from her mind and stared down at Mrs. Garcia.

If Mrs. Garcia had meant to kill herself or if she had only sought to numb the pain of one dead child, a husband in the slammer, and a daughter in protective custody, she had gravely miscalculated. Hannah didn't tell the woman in the hospital bed that when she was released from Our Lady, she'd be arrested for the manslaughter of her unborn baby. Such cases were difficult to win, but worth it just to make a point.

Hannah's gaze met Joanne's puffy and jaundiced eyes. "I'm sorry about your loss," she said.

"Me, too," Ripp muttered awkwardly.

Garcia shifted her weight in the hospital bed and made a slight movement with her eyes, but said nothing. Then she closed her eyes tightly. Ripp retreated near the doorway. A nurse's aide with a cart of flowers scuttled by.

"You should be," Garcia finally croaked, her stare hard and cold in Hannah's direction. "You've made a mess of everything. You dug up my baby, my Ricky. And now you—" She cut herself off, before starting up again. "And now my baby, my new baby is gone. All of my children are taken from me."

"You know," Hannah said as gently as possible, "I did what was required of me, nothing more. I'm sorry for how it has turned out for you personally. But I didn't kill your unborn baby, *you* did."

Garcia winced and turned her head away, toward the window.

"My daughter Mimi had nothing to do with Ricky's—

Enrique's—death," she whispered, still not opening her eyes as tears rolled onto the thin, blue pillow that supported her head. "She never hurt anyone."

"Of course not. She was just a little girl. What happened?" Hannah did her best attempt at being and sounding sympathetic, but under the surface she could feel hatred rise.

Garcia's dark eyelids fluttered like two gray moths. "Berto can't stand the noise kids make. Any noise at all. Even when they laugh or giggle, like happy kids do. I try to keep the kids from him, but you can't always do that. They get into things, you know."

"Yes, I know. I'm a mother, too," Hannah said, though she sort of hated herself for using the fact that she had Amber in her work. She detested women like Mrs. Garcia. She was one of the horrible, eat-your-own-young breed. It seemed there were more of those women cropping up in Santa Louisa and beyond. Hannah admired the women who stood up for their children or themselves and left their abusers when there was still a chance. The women who shot abusive husbands in their backs or even the one who sliced off her no-good husband's penis as if it were a Ball Park frank deserved, she thought, a lighter sentence than California law allowed. But not Joanne Garcia.

Garcia looked past Hannah for a moment at Ripp, and then closed her eyes once more. "Berto was watching television and Ricky was playing in the kitchen with his toys. He wasn't even in the living room. Berto yelled at him a couple times to be quiet. My son was just having fun. You know little boys; they don't always hear what you want them to."

"Yes," Hannah said, her own anger beginning to rage. "I know people, *grown* people, who are the same way. What happened? Please."

"He went into the kitchen and picked up Ricky by the arms and slammed him to the floor."

Garcia was crying now. Keeping her eyes shut didn't block out what she said she'd seen that day. Instead of drawing sympathy, her tears irritated Hannah.

"I didn't know what to do," she said. "I mean, he wasn't dead or anything. Berto was so sorry. So sorry." The words stuck in her throat. "*Sorry* that his temper got away from him. We ran a cold bath and put Ricky in it. He was swelling up. We didn't want to call the ambulance. We didn't want somebody to tell us we were bad parents and take him away. I put two trays of ice cubes into the water to bring the swelling down. I even dumped packages of frozen corn in there. I . . ." Garcia stopped. Her convulsing sobs were audible from the nurses' station, and the big woman with the clipboard made her way toward the open doorway of Sunshine 4.

"He said that if we told them Ricky fell down, we'd be okay. We wouldn't get into trouble. Berto didn't mean for it to happen. I didn't think anyone would believe us. I prayed that they would. I did. An accident is an accident, right? No matter how it happens, right?"

Hannah had heard women like Joanne Garcia with their day-late, dollar-short fountains of sorrow spewing to the heavens, and she hated them. She also knew from years of working such cases, that sadly, not all children could be saved. The numbers of the littlest victims continued to grow. Despite all educational programs, the shrinks with their soliloquies on anger management, and the efforts of law enforcement, the number of battered, bruised, and even dead children grew by tragic leaps and bounds. For a second, Erik and Danny and their tiny charred Buster Brown shoes returned to her thoughts. How Hannah wished, as Joanne Garcia surely had, that time could be rolled back and things could be different.

"You ought to get a better lawyer," Hannah said, her anger building like a kettle on high heat. She pulled a sheet of paper from a file folder that Ripp had brought along.

"I'll see you go to prison for your son's murder. Further if I can find a DA willing to stick his neck out a little, you'll go down on a second murder-two charge."

Joanne's eyes were open wide in terror as Hannah sprang forward. "The baby girl in the basement morgue was close enough to term to survive if you hadn't done what you did . . . and if someone had bothered to find you in time. That makes you practically a serial killer in my mind. Women like you make me sick."

"What are you talking about?" Joanne croaked.

"Your husband was in county custody the day Enrique was injured." Hannah held out the report and pointed to the date. "He couldn't have killed the boy. You put your boy in the bathtub. *You* couldn't stand the noise!"

Ripp stepped forward and tugged at Hannah's shoulder, but she broke away and continued her rant. Garcia's terrified eyes gleamed like a couple of bullets.

"You make me sick," Hannah said, loud enough to reach the nurses station. "You women who snuff out your kids are the scum of this planet."

"Better go," Ripp said, grabbing Hannah and pulling her away from the hospital bed. In doing so, he accidentally popped Garcia's IV line. Garcia screamed in pain.

"You'll have to leave right now," said a cranberry-clad nurse with her practiced, authoritative intonation as she scrambled into the room. "This is too much. The patient needs rest now, not the third degree."

Hannah was stunned by her own rage. She was angry and embarrassed at the same time. She and Ripp walked to the stairway.

"What got into you back there?" he asked.

She shook her head in agitated disgust. "She killed her *son*. She killed him and tried to pull the battered, abused, cigarette-burned mother-of-the-year number on us. First she kills her boy, blames her daughter, and then poisons her body with pills and kills her unborn baby."

Several nurses and an orderly stood by with their mouths agape. Two in the horseshoe whispered loudly.

Hannah touched her face. Her cheeks were warm. Her heart was thumping.

"She is the worst kind of human being and I've met some—known some—of the worst."

"You lost it in there," Ripp said, not really listening to what Hannah was saying. "I thought you were going to slap her or something." He swung the door open, and the two started down the stairs. Hannah kept her mouth shut. She'd said enough.

"I guess this isn't a good time to bring this up," he said. "I told that writer Marcella Hoffman I'd talk to her at lunch today. I'd like a little recognition, too. She wants to talk to *me*. You know, not everything is about you."

Hannah felt her skin grow hotter. She'd have slapped Ted Ripperton if he weren't the son-in-law of the county attorney.

"Thanks for nothing," she said stiffly.

*   *   *

"Judge Paine! What are you doing here?"

A Spruce County Clerk's Office employee waved from across an ancient mahogany counter. Behind her was a warren of cubicles decorated with family photos and memos.

"That's me," Veronica Paine said warmly as she pulled up to the counter. "I've said it before, you just can't keep an old lawyer from the courthouse. Seems like home around here."

"We try." The woman from behind the counter smiled back. Next to her, an enormous bouquet of lilies and gardenias with a plastic pick held a card that read: "Lordy, Lordy! Look Who's 40!"

Veronica smiled. "Happy birthday."

"I'd be happier if my sister hadn't advertised my age!" She smiled back and both women laughed. "What can I do for you?"

"Just here to look at some old files in the vault. Some things niggling at me, after all these years."

"Can I get you some files? What's the case number?"

Paine shook her head. "No I can do it. I still know my way around here."

The woman behind the counter handed her a ring of keys with a tape-covered oversized tag emblazoned with: VAULT KEY DO NOT REMOVE FROM CLERK'S DEPT. The keys clattered together as Paine started down the stairs to the basement. A woman making photocopies nodded in her direction.

The basement was well lit with fluorescent tubes—not the least bit creepy. It was filled with gray metal shelves that went from the floor to the ceiling. On each shelf were the saddest stories ever told in the annals of Spruce

County's history. The two little girls who had gone miss-ing until their remains were found in the woods around Lake Joy. The farmer who had thought his wife had been cheating on him, so he took his life by throwing his body out in front of his neighbor's tractor. A high school track coach who had sexually molested at least three of his stu-dents. All real. Boxes were filled with the manila files of depositions, court filings, and whatever paperwork told the tale of Spruce County's most sordid chapters.

Veronica Paine walked to the southern corner of the basement, behind a partition of shelves used temporarily to store files that had been out for review. Behind the par-tition was a vault containing the most sensitive evidence held by the county. She turned the key, swung open the heavy door, and walked inside. It took only a moment to orient herself. She turned on the lights and walked over to a rack marked with the sequence of numbers where she knew she'd find the case she wanted to see.

It was Claire Logan's well-perused file. In the back of the file was a packet marked: "Sealed by the order of the Superior Court, County of Spruce, State of Oregon." There was a familiar signature on the outside of a grimy-with-time cover sheet—her own.

She took a seat, flipped on a library lamp, and sliced open the file. For a moment she felt the whoosh of air move through the room, and she looked up. The air con-ditioner rumbled, then another whoosh of air and the scent of the bouquet from the clerk's counter upstairs.

Good God, she thought, *those gardenias sure have staying power*.

CHAPTER THIRTY-TWO

"I think you should bring in Louise Wallace for a good grilling."

It was Bonnie Ingersol's voice over the Northern Lights rotary-dial telephone. Bauer tried to move the phone to the bed so he could make himself more comfortable, but it was bolted to the nightstand.

"What did you get?" he asked.

"Zip," she said. Bauer detected some excitement in his old partner's voice. "The woman doesn't exist. She's a complete nothing insofar as the computers are concerned. No Social Security number that we could trace."

"Which means she's never filed an income tax return."

"Right. And never held a job that we can tell. Unless she was paid with cash in some under-the-table deal."

"For her whole life? Not likely."

"No driver's license in any of forty-nine states. Still

waiting to hear back from Hawaii. You know Hawaii, they're not in the system yet."

"She drives," he said. "I've seen her car parked out front of her place. And she lives out in Bumfuck, Egypt, anyway. Need a car out here for sure. Hell, you need a four-wheeler to get around."

"It gets weirder, Jeff," Ingersol went on. "Unless you screwed up royally—or if the lab guys did something stupid—"

"Thanks for the vote of confidence," Bauer cut in.

"There aren't any good prints on the sample you sent down here. A preliminary examination came up with a single partial. *Yours*. Nothing else. And they ran the badge holder every which way but loose."

"Blank? I saw her hold it. I *gave* it to her."

Ingersol didn't know what to make of it. She didn't doubt Bauer, but it was very odd.

"Maybe she had gloves on?" she asked. "You know, those clear plastic surgicals?"

"Not possible. Her hands were dirty from working out in her flower garden. She examined my badge. Should have been some latents on it."

"Nada."

Bauer thought of the splendid buttery yellow house that jutted out and overlooked the icy waters of the Pacific. *How could Louise Wallace manage such a place?* Her fishing resort—which as far as he could tell was without guests during the summer season—couldn't be that successful. It couldn't, he thought, generate the income she needed to have such a place. Unless her husband had left her a bundle, she had to have the money on her own. If she was Claire Logan, Bauer knew where the money had come from.

"I'll contact the sheriff," he said, "and we'll bring her in for questioning. It can only be voluntary, of course."

"Get her on driving without a license or something."

"Just what I had in mind."

"With any luck, she'll be too messed up with worry to even think about the jurisdiction issue. Anyone with a badge is a cop, you know."

Ingersol laughed. "You're right about that one," she said.

"If this is Logan," Bauer said, "this is the closest we've ever come. This is different than the other times. I feel it."

Bauer dialed Kodiak sheriff Kim Stanton's office. He was glad that he'd made his courtesy call when he first arrived on the island. It was always much more difficult asking for assistance after bursting into someone else's jurisdiction and telling them what they needed to do. The deputy answered. Bauer told him he wanted to bring in Louise Wallace for questioning about some criminal activity many years ago.

"What exactly are we talking about here?" the deputy asked.

"Homicide and arson. The Claire Logan murders," Bauer said, not sure why he volunteered so much except he knew that he needed the locals on his side and not as advocates for Louise Wallace.

"Sheriff knows Louise, and you're barking up the wrong tree," the deputy said, unruffled, as though the woman had been accused of shoplifting or some other petty crime. It was obvious that he knew who Claire Logan was because he didn't ask any follow-ups about the case. "You Feds do things your own way. Long as you make it brief and get on your way, he'll back you."

"Look, I need your help. I need a marked car and someone to take her to your office for questioning."

"Done," he said. "She's a nice lady. She'll want to clear this up."

It was almost 4 p.m. in Louise Wallace's tidy kitchen, and Marge Morrison was slicing leeks and zucchini for a quiche she was making for dinner. A piecrust weighted down with navy beans was convecting in the oven. Moments before, Morrison had called Beth Tyson to ask her church friend to feed her cat. She said she was staying with Louise for a couple of days "to help sort out some misunderstanding." She followed that call with one to notify her employer at the public utility that she'd need a few days of vacation to take care of a sick friend. The leeks were turning translucent in the bubbling butter when the doorbell rang.

"Louise?" Morrison called out from the kitchen stove. "Can you get it?"

"Be right there," Louise answered from somewhere in back of the house.

Morrison went on stirring and enjoying the gorgeous view from the sparkling kitchen window. Scattered whitecaps mottled the blue of the water.

A few minutes later curiosity got the better of Morrison, and she called out again. "Louise? Who was it?"

This time no response came. Morrison turned the flame on low, set the big wooden spoon into a ceramic rest, and went to investigate. She watched her troubled friend talking with a man she didn't know and one of the deputies from the sheriff's department.

"What's going on here?" she asked.

Wallace turned around. Her face, lined from years of working outdoors, was a study in complete calm. Given the circumstances, Louise's calmness surprised Morrison. She'd have been jumping out of her skin with worry and agitation.

"It's fine," Louise said. She put her hand on Morrison's shoulder. "I'm going to town to talk to these men. I want to get this off of me."

"Are you sure you shouldn't speak to your lawyer first?" Morrison said, though she wished she hadn't. She didn't want the two men to think Louise had any reason to seek a lawyer's advice.

"I'll be fine. I'll be back in time for dinner. Quiche is always better served room temperature anyway, right?"

Morrison smiled and grabbed her windbreaker and offered it to Wallace. "In case the breeze kicks up."

And with that, Louise Wallace walked across the driveway to the police cruiser. Morrison's eyes stayed on her as she got into the car. She barely even noticed Bauer until after her friend disappeared behind the shut door.

"Are you the FBI agent?" she asked Bauer.

"Yes, I am." He identified himself.

Morrison looked at Bauer as if she had something to say. Finally, she spoke.

"Just wanted to get a good look at the man who made the biggest mistake in the history of the FBI, and no offense, really, but the FBI has had a few."

Bauer felt embarrassed. The sweet old lady who had given her old friend her blue-and-white windbreaker hated his guts. She telegraphed it so perfectly.

"I might be wrong. I've been wrong before, ma'am," he said. "Only time will tell."

"She's one of the most wonderful people I know. Lou would do anything for anyone. Believe you me, you'll be saying you're sorry."

"Maybe so."

Morrison turned around and returned to the house. Bauer was going to try to pin down Louise Wallace and determine who she was. She was going to get on the phone and call the First Methodist ladies and get their phone tree in action.

"Louise needs us," she told Beth Tyson. "She is being accused of an unspeakable crime."

Within twenty-five minutes all the ladies knew. And without exception, all stood squarely against the FBI and what it was doing to a beloved and trusted friend.

CHAPTER THIRTY-THREE

Kodiak sheriff Kim Stanton had known Louise Wallace since he was a teenager when she helped coordinate the search and rescue youth group of which he was a member. Stanton was almost never angry. His good nature formed the rock-solid foundation of a deserved reputation as a gentleman in a land that was sometimes short on such men. Even in his dealings with the underbelly of Kodiak, poachers and pot growers, he was considerate and fair. No one had ever seen him yell at a perp or toss one to the ground.

Stanton had been on a shopping trip to Kodiak's minuscule mall with his wife when the deputy agreed to assist in bringing Louise Wallace in for questioning.

"The Feds think Mrs. Wallace is *who*?" Stanton was not happy. His black hair bristled. "This isn't going to happen here. Mrs. Wallace? *Claire Logan?* I'd be laughing my ass off if I weren't so pissed off."

Louise Wallace, dressed in black slacks, a white cotton top, and tennis shoes, sat in a chair outside Stanton's office while S.A. Bauer finished briefing the local sheriff. Stanton shook his head in disbelief and shot a look of sympathy in Louise's direction. She was a considerate and sensitive old lady. It wasn't that she looked the part. She was.

Louise smiled at Stanton when their eyes met. She sat quietly, with the windbreaker folded on her lap. She refused a soda when one of the younger deputies offered it.

"I'm just talking to her," Bauer said to Stanton. "We're just going to have a conversation. She's agreed to it."

The two men talked a while longer, and Bauer emerged first.

"Do you want a lawyer?" he asked Louise. Stanton stood by and shrugged in embarrassment.

"No. Don't see that I need one. Or do I?"

"We're just going to talk," he said. "Sheriff Stanton will be with us every step of the way. All right?"

"I'm sorry, Mrs. Wallace," Stanton interjected. "This won't be long. Then you can go home."

Wallace nodded and smiled. "It's all right. I want to clear this up and get home. I have a houseguest."

The three went into a room next door to the employee break area. It was no larger than a storage closet and outfitted with a table and chairs. Over the next forty-five minutes, Louise Wallace told her tearful story of her sons who had died in the car accident. She told the men how she had come to Kodiak to start over.

"Look at me, Kim. You've known me for twenty

years, since you were a boy. I'm Louise. I'm not what he says I am, nor could I ever be." She glared at Bauer. "I lost everything and started over here. I didn't use my Social Security number because I didn't want any part of my life catching up with me."

"I don't blame you," Stanton said. "I had no idea about your boys. I'm sorry."

Wallace looked at him with gratitude. Bauer knew he was standing on thin ice. He was the outsider. She was tough and convincing.

"I just want to be left alone," she said.

Stanton felt guilty about making Wallace relive the past and apologized several times for the intrusion. He didn't see anything sinister about her or her story. She was the woman who had done so much good for so many on the island.

Bauer was less convinced. "We'll check out your story, of course," he said.

She nodded. "I expect you will."

"No family? No one who knew you before you came here?"

She shook her head. "Not anyone that I can recall. I really wanted a fresh start. I never looked back to the Lower Forty-eight after I came here."

She was unflinching as the kid-glove interrogation worked its way to a close. She seemed like the nice old lady next door, though Bauer reminded himself of a recent case that had made the Oregon news, a kindergarten teacher who killed her husband before going to teach a full day—as if nothing had happened.

Wallace explained it was true that she had no driver's license. She didn't get one for the longest time, because she wasn't driving much anyway.

"Then I started driving, you know, a little. Finally, a

lot. And before you knew it I was too embarrassed to admit I didn't have the license. Everyone knew me, so it never came up. As far as my I.D. was concerned."

Stanton didn't help matters much. He was hanging on her every word, nodding in agreement as if she were preaching and he was seeing the light. Bauer thought of the fingerprints, or the lack of them, on his I.D. badge.

"Can I see your hands?" he asked.

"Kind of a strange request," she said, staring him straight in the eye. "But all right." She put her hands on the table. She wore two rings; both were gold with channel-set diamonds.

"Could you turn them over? I'd like to see them face up, if you don't mind."

Her hesitation was brief. She rolled them over. All of the fingertips were a darker shade of pink than the rest of the flesh.

Bauer remained expressionless. "What happened to you?"

"Cannery accident," she said, her eyes riveted to Bauer's. "I was cleaning equipment with the sulfuric wash. I misread the proportions of the activator and . . . well before I knew it my gloves were eaten away at the tips."

"I think I remember hearing about that," Stanton said. "Dad worked at the cannery."

"Yes," she answered. "I believe he did. I think your father was one of the men who helped me."

When the interview was over, Bauer had little more than before he'd picked up Louise Wallace. He didn't let on what he'd found out about her Evergreen State Mental Hospital alibi. He knew that the institution had burned down. All records went up in flames.

A Kodiak reporter and photographer was already outside the sheriff's office, more a testament to the fact that word travels fast on an island than that the reporter was particularly resourceful. One other person had also arrived: Marge Morrison, who stood by the door of her pickup waving her arms. She called out Wallace's name.

"We're not going to let them do this to you," Morrison shouted across the oil-soaked parking lot. "We're getting you a good lawyer! Cover your face, dear, and get in my truck!"

CHAPTER THIRTY-FOUR

Marcella Hoffman waited like a steely-eyed statue in the lobby of San Louisa County Courthouse. She'd read the local paper twice, including the classifieds and a Target circular. Hannah saw her right away. The first thought that crossed her mind was that the years had not been kind to the reporter-turned-author-turned-has-been. Hoffman had the kind of pink shrink-wrapped face that indicated Retin-A and a nip-and-tuck. Now in her fifties, her hair was colored to a solid black helmet that made her look older, not younger. She smelled of cigarettes and lattes. An oversized Coach bag was slung over her shoulder, nearly tilting her to one side.

Hannah gulped back the bitter taste of her own anger at seeing Hoffman and proceeded to the white marble stairs leading down to the basement lab and offices.

"Hannah?" Hoffman called out. "Hannah *Griffin*?"

Hannah ignored the voice and continued down the stairs, but Hoffman clacked across the cavernous foyer after her.

"It's me! Marcella. Marcella Hoffman."

Hannah swung around and shot her a frozen stare. There was no point in denying who she was. After all, if Hoffman had tracked her this far, to this obscure location, then she was a better reporter and had better sources than Hannah gave her credit for.

"I know who you are," was all she could come up with.

Hoffman smiled. "Can we talk somewhere?"

"I have nothing to say to you. I never have."

"Look, I didn't come to make you angry. I didn't drive out here all the way from Los Angeles to cause trouble. That's not who I am or what I'm all about. You know that. I came for a story."

"You're wasting your time. There is no story here. Please go."

"But there is and you know it. The people have a right to know."

Hannah felt her face grow hot once more. Why was this woman coming into her life now? "We're not having this conversation. Please go, or I'll ask security to escort you from the building."

Hoffman shook her head. "I have a lunch date with your associate, Mr. Ripperton. Hate to miss the date. I'd have to explain to Mr. Ripperton why I was barred from the building."

A bailiff walked past the intense pair and offered his assistance.

"Everything okay?" the young man asked.

Hannah felt cornered, but nodded. "Fine. I just ran into an old friend. We're going downstairs to catch up."

Hoffman gave a fake warm smile, her big teeth reminding Hannah why she and Aunt Leanna had called the woman Dog Face.

"Old friends," Hoffman said. "I like that."

A couple minutes later the two women were behind the door of Hannah Griffin's office.

"Let's be direct. Okay? What in God's name do you want?" Hannah said. "What more can you take from me?"

"Such attitude," Marcella said, setting down her enormous bag. "I want to help you tell your side of the story. I'm a reporter."

Hannah wanted to lunge, but she held back. "A *reporter*? As though that gives you license to pop into someone's life anytime you see fit and wreak havoc. Please, don't give me that bullshit about being a reporter. What do you want?"

"Such hostility," Hoffman said, planting herself in one of the pair of visitors' chairs in front of Hannah's desk. "You have me all wrong. Didn't you read my book?"

"It made me ill."

"The truth can do that. You know that," she said looking around, "given your job here."

"I really don't want to talk to you. I have a family. I want to put this behind me. Can't you understand?"

"Yes. I talked to Ethan. Nice fellow. Amber sounds adorable. Wish I was going to be in town long enough to see her recital."

"Leave my family alone."

"I'm not after your family. I want to get the interview of a lifetime, that's all."

"I'm not interested."

"Don't flatter yourself. I want to talk to your mother."

Hannah wanted to reach across the desk and strangle Hoffman. Anything to wipe the smug look off her nip-and-tucked face.

"My mother is dead. Didn't you write the book on it? Or have you forgotten?"

Hannah noticed Ripperton walk past the windows next to her office door. He glanced in her direction and eyed her somewhat anxiously—not because he was concerned about what was being said—but because he didn't want to miss his chance for lunch with Hoffman.

"Liz thinks she's alive. So do I," Hoffman continued.

Hannah's face must have betrayed her feelings. She didn't know who Dog Face was talking about.

"Marcus's mother," Hoffman said. "Liz Wheaton. We've been friends for years. I'm friendly with a lot of the old gang from Rock Point."

"I'm sure you are. I don't know Mrs. Wheaton. Never met her."

"But you've just seen her son, haven't you?"

Hannah didn't say a word.

"Don't look so shocked," Hoffman went on, oblivious. "I have sources. Better than you can imagine. There's only one little thing I haven't been able to figure out. And it is a doozy. Where did your mother go after she left Rock Point that night?"

"Who says she left?" Hannah thought about the box of shoes that had been sent to her. She wondered if Marcella Hoffman had been the sender, but she didn't say anything about it.

"She was too smart. Too smart to let a house burn down around her and a piano fall on her." Hoffman walked over to the door. "Now, Mrs. Wheaton knew how to find you. And here I am. Are you going to help me find your mother?"

She twisted the knob on the door.

"Or am I going to tell everyone who you are?"

"You wouldn't. Even you couldn't do that."

"Watch me."

"If I knew, I'd tell you."

Hoffman was in her nasty mode. "I know you saw Marcus up at Cutter's Landing. Liz told me. I know that Jeff Bauer went with you. So tell me. Where is she?"

"I really don't know," Hannah said, wanting to kill Hoffman. She found herself planning it as they stood there. She would take the cord from the phone and wrap it around her turkey neck. She'd pick up the crystal paperweight that Ethan had given her for passing the bar and she'd smash the woman's skull. Everything she saw in her office could be a weapon used to end Dog Face's miserable excuse for a life.

Ripperton knocked on the door and stuck his head inside.

"Lunch still on, Miss Hoffman?" Ripp looked concerned.

The reporter nodded and flashed a warm, but Hannah was sure, phony smile. "Sure. Hannah and I are finished for now. We're getting together a bit later to continue our interview."

The air hung with hostility, but Ripperton, the investigator who was forever incompetent and clueless, stayed true to form. He didn't get wind of anything.

*　　*　　*

Twenty minutes after Ripp and Dog Face left for their "interview," Hannah had sufficiently pulled herself together to call Bauer at the Northern Lights in Kodiak. The front desk patched her through, but Bauer wasn't in and the call went to voice mail.

"Jeff, Hannah here. That bitch Marcella Hoffman paid me a visit just now. She said Marcus Wheaton's mother told her where to find me. How could that be? I've never even met Liz Wheaton. Call me. Hoffman says she's sure my mom is alive. Please call me. I need you."

For the next hour Hannah tried to put her mother, Wheaton, and Hoffman out of her thoughts as she attempted to refocus on the Garcia case. Her emotions had frayed, and she knew it. She was on the brink. A series of phone calls did little to provide the calming she needed. A phone call to Ethan at work was a zero; he was "up to his neck in alligators" and could only spare a moment.

"You don't have to talk to Hoffman at all," he said.

"It isn't that simple," she answered back, almost to herself. "I wish it were."

Ten minutes later, County Attorney Bill Gilliand came to the door of her office. He seldom stopped as he passed by, preferring to offer a nod of recognition while he kept on moving. Handsome and charismatic, Gilliand was all politics. He saved his personal interaction for when it mattered. Staff meetings, court, and fund-raisers. But this time, the morning she was coming undone, Bill Gilliand strode into her office for the first time.

"Hannah," he said with a concerned look in his eyes, "I heard that it didn't go well at the hospital with Garcia. Ripperton says you almost jumped on her."

I could kill him, Hannah thought.

"It wasn't that bad, but I guess I was a bit physical," she admitted to her boss.

"Yes, *physical*," he mused. "That's what we leave for the cops to do," he said, a veiled reference and a not-so-subtle dig against her husband. "I'd like you to take the rest of the day off."

She got up from her chair and walked around her desk, leaned back, and sat down on the corner of the desk. It didn't bring her to Gilliand's commanding height, but it didn't make her feel as small as a schoolgirl, either.

"I'm fine now," she said. "It was just . . ."

"I'm not asking. I'm *telling* you. I think it would be best. We don't want to get into a problem with Mrs. Garcia, or anyone else for that matter." He walked a couple of steps to the door and turned around. Then almost as an aside, he offered, "A hospital nurse called and complained. It wasn't just Ripperton. And actually, hard to believe as it might be, Ripp was concerned about you."

A few moments later, Hannah stood in the checkout line of Ralph's Grocery not far from the Griffins' place on Loma Linda Avenue. She bought a bottle of chardonnay and some Oreos. The cookies were for Amber and Ethan, who shared an incredible sweet tooth. She'd drink the wine. Considering what she'd been through, Hannah intended to drink a lot of it.

CHAPTER THIRTY-FIVE

The Griffin house on Loma Linda Avenue was so still, so hushed, that the omnipresent sputter of the air conditioner irritated Hannah. She wondered how it was that she had not made it a priority to have it repaired. The rumble noise coughed and hummed and rolled. Home early and alone, Hannah glanced over her shoulder as she stepped inside. A small figure ran toward her as she locked the door behind her. It was Amber's tabby. Hannah ran her hand over the cat's silky fur and cupped the animal's chin.

"Are you hungry?" she asked, not waiting for an answer. Even at five pounds overweight, the cat always seemed hungry. It padded after Hannah as she went to the kitchen with her small bag of groceries.

It was ten minutes before six. Amber was still at her

dance lesson, and Ethan was probably charming the other mothers as they waited in the parking lot of the studio. She emptied a box of brown-and-orange kibble into a dish set on a plastic place mat under the breakfast bar and poured fresh water into another bowl. A happy cat started to eat and purr. Hannah retrieved the bottle of the California chardonnay that she liked more for its label of a braided wreath of oak leaves than she did the taste of the wine, which she sometimes found too sweet and overly fruity. She poured herself a glass, a *big* glass. The globe of the stemware was almost grapefruit size. Hannah flipped through the mail and settled herself in a chair to watch the TV news before her husband and daughter interrupted her small moment of tranquility. Her mind raced. Her boss had sent her home and Marcella Hoffman was trying to snare an interview by sweet-talking Ripp. As a talk show ran its credits over the pockmarked faces of its guests and its sanctimonious host, she went over to the window to close the white plantation shutters. Coppery light reflected from the neighbor's windows, the beginning of the evening sun as it dipped slightly lower in the smog-smeared sky.

The cat snuggled next to Hannah's feet as she returned to her chair to watch the news. On the screen in front of her, helicopters careened in the air as images of the news-gathering process were paraded. A handsome man with a yellowish suntan and teeth too big for his mouth announced the lead story.

Wine splashed on Hannah's thigh. It was an involuntary response. She looked at her hand holding the chardonnay as the chilled liquid rounded the lip of the glass and dribbled down the stem. It was almost the feeling of an earthquake, deep and hidden. Hannah set down her wine and stared straight ahead, absentmindedly using her hand to wipe at the spill. Yet all the while, she could not take her eyes off the screen.

"*. . . speculation is running throughout the Northwest that an Alaskan woman named Louise Wallace is the notorious serial killer Claire Logan . . .*"

She set the glass hard on the coffee table. Hannah could feel her heart pump faster and the bile in her stomach rise through her esophagus. She grabbed her hands together and gripped tightly.

The image of an elderly woman flashed across the screen in slow motion. It was brief. Hannah leaned forward as though closer proximity could enhance her view. But it only made the picture appear as though it had been a painting by Seurat, tiny specks of color with soft edges blurring from one side of the screen to the other. Besides, the video was out of focus and the woman's head was turned in such a way that only the side of her head could be viewed, but not enough so that her profile could be made out. While the newscaster went on, more images filled the screen. A sign for the town of Kodiak. An old car. A dog barking in front of what appeared to be a fishing camp. In the last shot, the same woman held a blue-and-white windbreaker over her head in the fashion of felons who wish a semblance of anonymity, or anyone who has been caught on tape on a video-vérité cop show.

Her eyes fastened to the screen, Hannah's pulse raced as the anchor went on to another story. Fifteen minutes went by, but Hannah heard none of the other stories. Instead, she thought only of her mother. The ringing phone jolted her back to the moment. She grabbed at the receiver and pressed it to her ear.

"Hello?" she said.

"Hannah?" It was Bauer's gentle voice. "Are you all right?"

"A little shaky, I guess."

"You just saw her on the tube, didn't you?" He let out an audible sigh. "Damn it," he said, "I wanted to warn you before the news hit down there. Don't you ever listen to your phone messages?"

Hannah felt the warm and numbing effects of the chardonnay. She glanced at the answering machine. Its red eye mocked her with a steady wink.

"I hadn't played them yet."

"Jesus," he said. "I'm very sorry, Hannah. I wanted to—"

"Is it *her*?"

Bauer hesitated for a second. "Probably not. I mean, we really don't know yet. You know the media runs with a story like this faster than we do. They don't mind burying an apology in agate type in the classified section later or at the end of a newscast. We can't. We never say we're sorry, so we don't like to rush."

"Do *you* think it's her?"

"Could be," Bauer said. "I honestly don't know."

"What are the facts, Jeff?" Hannah reached for her glass and gulped more wine. She glanced at the clock. Their conversation would be cut short at any minute. A little dancer and her daddy would be coming through the front door.

"Sketchy. She's doesn't have a 'Sosh' number. No driver's license either. Needless to say, she's not talking. Not a peep. And get *this*—she has no fingerprints."

"You mean she hadn't left any prints at the scene?" Hannah asked, though after she said so, she knew fingerprints were of no real value. None had been left at the farm to compare with: the whole place was ashes and rubble.

"This lady's fingertips have been scarred over or something. Somehow erased. She either had some terrible accident at the cannery like she says or she erased them with a blowtorch or an acid dip. I don't know. But there isn't a damn thing there. They are completely smooth."

"I see. What does she look like? The TV shot was so quick, I could scarcely tell."

"Like an old lady. Kind of tall, graying hair, blue eyes."

"My mother had blue eyes. Has blue eyes."

"Are you going to be okay?"

"How tall is she?"

"Tall enough," he said. "Look, we don't know anything. So sit tight. Are you going to be all right?"

"I'll be fine. Ethan will be home soon."

"Good. Hey, got your message about Liz Wheaton. We're running her information now. I'll let you know as soon as I get anything of interest. Sit tight."

"Okay. Call me with anything at all. I mean it."

Hannah hung up. Her timing was good. She heard Ethan park the cruiser and she heard Amber's little feet run up the sidewalk to the front door. She did her best to shake the worry and concern, the coiled snakes of mixed emotions, from her face.

"Mommy!" Amber's exuberant voice called out. "We're home!"

CHAPTER THIRTY-SIX

Bauer removed the plastic sheathing from a motel-room glass and poured himself a couple shots of Wild Turkey as he contemplated his next move. After the interview with Louise Wallace, he and S.A. Ingersol conferred about some details she'd learned about Liz Wheaton through Social Security and Oregon Department of Motor Vehicles.

"No shit," he said when Ingersol told him that Marcus Wheaton's mother had transformed herself and was working at, of all places, the Spruce County Clerk's Office.

"She's packed on at least sixty pounds, stopped bleaching her hair," Ingersol said, excitedly, clearly enjoying the revelation. "And looking at the DMV photo in front of me, I'd say she probably had a little nip-and-tuck on her face, too."

"I vaguely remember her as a faded party gal who could have used some work. And that was twenty years ago."

"What's more," Ingersol went on, "she's been a microfilm copier technician for Spruce County for almost a decade. She calls herself Liza Milton—Milton being the name of one of her old tricks, some dope that actually married her."

Veronica Paine was stunned when Bauer called her cell from Kodiak with the revelation. Photos from the fire, torsos of dead men in uniform, and witness statements fanned out in front of her. She let out a sigh. She'd never noticed Marcus's mother in all her years as a judge, and admitted she felt more than a little foolish.

"How could I have been so blind?" she asked.

"Ingersol tells me that the DMV photo looks nothing like the shots taken during the trial. You wouldn't know it was the same woman," Bauer said.

Further, Paine had seen the news report, but had regarded it with about as much credibility as the other dozen or so Claire Logan sightings over the years.

"It's a guess, of course," Bauer said, "but I think Liz Wheaton—or whatever her name is—sent the shoes to Hannah Griffin."

Paine wasn't so quick to jump to conclusions—a holdover from her days on the bench when hearing all sides was a necessary element to critical decision making. She conceded it was a good bet, however.

"If Wheaton's mother worked in the Clerk's office, she'd easily have access to the exhibits, like the shoes. Even though we keep a tight rein on them, they are public records, you know."

"Right," Bauer said, sipping his Wild Turkey, "but why would she send them to Hannah? Why do that?"

"I don't know. I'm not a fortune-teller. But it seems to me that she must have wanted to elicit a reaction. Maybe to hurt Hannah or shock her into doing something—like go with you to see Marcus."

"I've thought about that. But why? Hannah was just a kid when the place burned down."

Paine let out a laugh. "Haven't you learned the key to investigations yet?"

Bauer was a little irritated by the question. Paine was enveloping her words in a kind of schoolmarm effect that he found a little condescending.

"What's that, Judge?" He did his best to remain polite.

"Not everything makes sense, Jeff. There isn't absolute meaning in everything these nut cases do. They'd like you to think so. The public would like it, too. But the fact is, sometimes people do crazy things."

Bauer finished his glass and eyed the bottle, contemplating another drink.

"Maybe so. Thanks, Judge."

"What's your number at the Northern Lights?" she asked.

He gave it to her, hung up, and started to pour.

Ethan Griffin got out of the shower, dried off his thick, black hair, wrapped a towel around his love handles, and planted himself on the edge of the bed. Hannah was sitting up, the newspaper on her lap. She was not reading.

"Where are you?" he asked for the second time as his wife stared across their bedroom, then back to her husband on the bed. She thought of Bauer, Kodiak Island, and the woman that might be her mother.

"I'm here," she lied.

"No. You're not. Maybe body only. But nothing more." He stared at her. He wanted to argue, and Hannah knew it.

Hannah could hear the toilet flushing, and she knew Amber had gotten up to go to the bathroom. It was after 11 p.m., and she was so tired. She turned away, looking through windows etched by misdirected sprinklers and smudged by her daughter's small fingers. She studied the outside world, illuminated by garden lights, as if out there was some great clue as to what was happening. And, above all, what she should do.

"Hannah, I'm worried," Ethan said, slumping beside her. "You're not yourself and we need you." He felt her slight recoil from his forced closeness and studied her profile. Her skin was ashen, her eyes sunken and underscored with faint smudges left from sleepless nights. She had lost weight, and her hair, though pinned back in a loose ponytail, was limp and dull. If Ethan Griffin had not known the reason why Hannah had begun to fall apart, he would have believed she was the victim of some grave illness. She was in need of *medical* attention. *God*, he thought, *it was her mind that was fucked up. No MD could fix that.* He wondered if any shrink could either.

Ethan offered her the afghan folded at the foot of the bed.

"You need to rest," he said.

"I can't rest," she said, pushing it away. "I can't sleep. I don't even want to try anymore."

When Ethan tried to put his hand on Hannah's shoulder, she turned away.

"Ethan . . ." her words fell off to a near whisper. "I'm so tired of all of this."

"We're *all* tired," he said. Not knowing how to comfort her, Ethan left the room.

At that moment, and at countless other instances strung like a necklace of razor blades around her neck, Claire Logan could not be excised from Hannah's thoughts—her true memories of what happened blended with the tales created and exhumed by the news media in search of a story. Marcella Hoffman had been the worst of the offenders. Seeing her at the courthouse had done nothing but push Hannah closer to the edge.

A car passed by on the street, its headlights filling the bedroom with a brightness that brought Hannah out of her thoughts. Then the car was gone. Hannah thought once more of Hoffman and wondered if she had been casing Loma Linda Avenue. A shiver went through her and she got up, pulling the afghan over her shoulders. She walked down the hall and nudged Ethan, now asleep on the sofa.

"I'm going to Kodiak," she said.

Ethan lifted his head from the sofa pillow. "Oh, Hannah," he said. "That's not a good idea. Nothing comes of these trips. It just tears you up."

"I can't help it. I have to know."

"What are we going to tell Amber this time?"

"I have business in Alaska."

"Not that. What are we going to say to our daughter if this woman is your mother, her grandmother? Or what if Marcella Hoffman decides to write an update about you and your life? What are we going to say to Amber?"

Hannah didn't have an explanation, though she'd considered the problem a million times.

"Scoot over and hold me," she said. She climbed on the sofa next to Ethan and he put his arms around her. There was barely enough room to hold the two of them on the narrow sofa cushions, but it didn't matter. With the world spinning out of control, Hannah Logan Griffin fell asleep.

The next morning, Hannah found herself in bed at 6 a.m. Ethan was already dressed.

"How?" she asked sleepily, remembering the night before.

"Carried you here. The two of us don't fit on the couch," he said, patting his stomach. "One of us needs to diet."

Ethan said nothing about what they had discussed the night before. He saw no point in it. He told Hannah that he and Amber would "single-dad" it again.

"Thanks," she said, sitting up and sliding her feet to the floor. "This will be the last time."

"I hope so, but I doubt it."

She had printed out online airline boarding passes that included a commuter flight from Santa Louisa's airport to LAX and a connection in Seattle that would put her in Anchorage late that night. Another flight would get her into Kodiak around midnight. It was the best she could do. It gave her a few hours in the office. Everything was planned to the minute. She'd call Bauer from Anchorage. From home, she changed her office voice mail to indicate she'd be out in the field all day, but to please leave a message as she checked them frequently.

Marcella Hoffman was waiting outside the main lab door. Wearing an ecru suit and jade blouse, Hoffman waved at Hannah.

"Morning," she said.

Hannah felt her stomach drop. "What are you doing here?"

"Had breakfast with Ted Ripperton and just hoping that I'd run into you. Saw the news last night. Think she's your mom?" Hannah ignored her question, and Hoffman followed her into her office.

"What exactly is your connection to Liz Wheaton?" Hannah asked, setting down and opening her briefcase, revealing her airplane tickets among file folders bearing the name *Garcia*.

"Friends, I told you yesterday. We became friendly when I did my ten-year-after update."

"Do you know where she worked?"

Hoffman made a face as she sat down. Her eyes lit on the plane tickets, and seeing that, Hannah closed her briefcase. "I'm supposed to ask the questions," Hoffman said. "Unless, of course, I'm on the witness stand."

"Consider it just that. I'm sure you know all of this, but play dumb for my benefit. I got a package not long ago. A package from Spruce County. Stolen evidence."

"I don't know what you're talking about." Hoffman shifted in the visitor's chair.

"I said to *play dumb*, not *moronic*. Look, I know that you and Liz Wheaton and the package were connected. You know what surprises me? That you could be so cruel. God, I feel like a fool."

"I had nothing to do with the shoes. All I wanted was your address. Liz provided me the information. Got it from her son's parole folder. Your address was there . . . you know to be contacted in the event Wheaton ever escaped from prison."

"What does Liz Wheaton want from me?"

"She never said."

"Get out of my office. Or I will call security."

"You wouldn't dare."

"Watch me." She picked up the phone and pushed zero. "I'll have your ass in jail for stealing criminal records. I never said the package contained any shoes."

Like a cockroach terrified of the saber-beam of a flashlight, Hoffman scuttled out the door. An hour later, Hannah was at the Santa Louisa airport headed toward the one and only gate served by Orange Leaf Air.

The gigantic stuffed polar bear at the Anchorage airport was startling at any time of day, but in the evening, after flying for hours and a couple of glasses of wine, the fourteen-foot taxidermist's dream looked like a monster. Preoccupied with a volatile mix of hope, anxiety, and fear, Hannah Griffin didn't notice the white monstrosity until she looked up while fiddling with the contents of her purse after the long flight from Seattle. She nearly dropped everything. It was 11:30 and the travel gods had smiled on her: the flight to Kodiak had been delayed thirty minutes.

She composed herself, found a phone booth, and dialed the number of the Northern Lights Motor Inn. It rang a dozen times before an obviously snoozing night clerk answered and took her reservation for a room for that night, before patching her over to Bauer's room.

"I'm coming to Kodiak," she announced with an exaggerated confidence that even she didn't buy, despite where she was.

Bauer attempted to shake off his sleepiness and the residual fogginess of one-too-many glasses of Wild Turkey. "Not a good idea," he said. "Nothing you can do here."

"I'll be there in an hour. I'm at the Anchorage airport now."

"Jesus Christ," he said. "Can't you let me do my job first?"

Hannah looked around the airport and spoke quietly. "I've waited a long time for this, too. If Louise Wallace is my mother, I have a right to see her before the circus—the media circus—comes to Alaska and takes over."

Bauer exhaled a loud sigh. "Like I told you earlier, we really don't know who Wallace is or isn't. Really, I understand your position and I wish I had done a better job of preempting the shock of the news story yesterday. I wish I had."

"Can we discuss this in the morning?" Hannah asked.

"Okay, it's late," he said, feeling a little relieved. "Where can I reach you?"

"In the room next to yours," she said. "I just made reservations."

Bauer's relief evaporated. "Just great," he muttered. "See you at seven."

Right on schedule an hour later, Hannah, her big purse, and a small carry-on bag waited for a taxi on the curb in front of Kodiak's small-fry airport. The air was surprisingly warm—not California balmy, of course, but warmer than she imagined Alaska would be. She thought of the Orlando trip she'd made in search of her mother. She hated Florida because of the experience and even turned down the opportunity to participate in a sex abuse conference held just outside Walt Disney World. Amber, she knew, would have loved Disney. Waiting, Hannah hoped that Alaska, at the opposite end of the country, would be different. She even prayed it would be. She hoped that the woman Bauer had seen was indeed her mother.

Over the years, Hannah had seen flashes of her mother's visage in the faces of so many women. She saw her mother's features in a woman sweeping up spilled popcorn at the mall. The middle-aged woman was hunched over, shoving the broom as though she intended to scrape the surface of its waxy sheen. Hannah even tapped the woman on the shoulder in order to get a better look. She had seen her mother in the gestures of a college professor, in the voice and laugh of a colleague at the crime lab. Once, though she never admitted it to anyone and never would, she had even seen a fleeting glimpse of her mother in her daughter's laugh.

Veronica Paine had done everything for the law because she loved it. She had never broken the rules. She just didn't have it in her. *Never had.* As she sat at her gleaming walnut dining table, warm brandy in hand, cigarette smoldering, she knew that following the law wasn't always fail-safe. It wasn't the best course in being a human being. Not really. In front of her was the file she'd stolen from the vault in the basement of Spruce County Courthouse.

She reached for her handheld phone and dialed Hannah Griffin's phone number in Santa Louisa. Her heart pounded. A man's voice answered.

"Mr. Griffin?" she asked.

"Yes, this is Ethan Griffin. Who's calling?"

"This is Veronica Paine. I'm calling for Hannah. Can she come to the phone?"

Ethan sighed. "I wish. She's not here. She's away for a couple of days."

"Oh, I see."

"I know who you are," he said, filling in an awkward silence. "And I know who my wife is. What do you want?"

Paine fiddled with her lighter, a habit so old and so bad she used to keep one out of view of the juries whenever she heard a case. The finger-fidgeting calmed her.

"I need to tell her something. It's important. Where is she?"

Ethan was quiet. "I guess it's okay for you to know," he said. "She's up in Alaska with that FBI agent friend of yours chasing her mother's ghost."

"Oh no," Paine said. "Has there been another Claire Logan sighting?"

"Not exactly." He glanced down the hall toward Amber's room, the door shut, the little girl asleep. "Marcus Wheaton said she was up there, living on Kodiak Island."

Paine gulped her brandy. "I'm sorry," she said. "I wish I had called sooner. I could have saved her the trip."

"Nothing would keep her from confronting her mother."

"That's just it," she said, taking a deep breath. "Claire *isn't* her mother."

When the conversation ended some half hour later, Ethan Griffin had to sit down. He was thankful that Amber was asleep and didn't see him just then. He felt his hands shake a little as his thoughts stayed riveted on Hannah. His eyes watered, but he didn't allow himself to cry. What Veronica Paine had told him had shaken him deeply, but Hannah would need him more than ever. His last words to the former prosecutor echoed in the air: *"Why didn't you tell her? This could have changed everything for her?"*

Veronica Paine hadn't been able to shake the unsettled feeling she'd had back in the basement of the Spruce County archives. *Had the whoosh of the air conditioner been a person lurking somewhere?* She'd felt like she'd been watched since then, so even in her own home when she thought she heard the back door creak, she turned with a start. She squinted over the bright light coming from her lamp, into the darkness.

"Abby? Is that you?" Paine asked, calling out her dog's name.

There was no answer, of course. And no dog came bounding through the house to the study for a treat.

A second later she saw a figure appear in the doorway, then a face.

"So it's you!" Paine said, turning to reach the top drawer of her desk. A Ruger Blackhawk her husband had given her for their twentieth anniversary lay next to a caddy holding rubber bands and paper clips.

"I remember you," Paine said, still reaching. A flash of light. The noise of gunfire. It happened so fast.

And then it was over.

CHAPTER THIRTY-SEVEN

Marge Morrison got up a little after midnight and put on the borrowed robe she had placed across the foot of the bed in Louise Wallace's comfortable guestroom. She didn't even have to look at her watch or at the alarm clock, so certain she was of the time. She liked to joke that her bladder was the size of a Ping-Pong ball, but it was hardly a laughing matter. Getting up every night had been a routine for years, but it was still bothersome and a little irritating. From a glass on the nightstand she fished out her dentures and put them inside her mouth and walked down the hallway toward the bathroom. When she went past Louise's bedroom she saw a sharp flood of light leak from under the doorway.

"Lou, are you okay?" Morrison asked after taking care of business and returning from the bathroom.

"Fine, dear. Just couldn't sleep," Wallace's familiar voice called out. "Going to try again."

The light snapped off, and she could hear what sounded like something sliding across the wooden floor, then a thud.

"Good night then," Morrison said, thinking little of the sliding noise, "and pleasant dreams." The friend from First Methodist tucked herself under a billowy eiderdown and fell back asleep.

The following morning, Hannah and Bauer stood in the office of the Northern Lights next to a rack of brochures promising good times on Kodiak Island. They were dressed in blue jeans and buttoned-up shirts, as though they were a pair of tourists contemplating a river-rafting trip or a bear-watching excursion.

"I almost said, just now, 'We've got to stop meeting like this,'" Bauer said, though he barely smiled. "Really. You shouldn't have come up here."

Hannah almost laughed. The idea of her not coming up to Alaska to find her mother never entered her mind. "I'm here because I have to be," she said. "Of all people, you should understand that."

"Look, I understand your interest. And I understand your obvious need for some closure." He winced at the word choice because, even to Bauer, it sounded cheesy. "God, I hate that word—*closure*."

Hannah stared hard at him, never taking her eyes from his. "So do I."

"Right," he said. "But the fact is you've had this thing hanging around you like a storm cloud, and whether Louise Wallace is your mother or not, you probably will still have some unresolved feelings. I mean, closure is only a concept, you know."

"Spoken like someone who doesn't need any," she said.

"Not fair," Bauer said, looking a little hurt. "You know better than that. I don't compare my part in any of this to what you have suffered, but it has been a big part of my life, too." He motioned through the window to the restaurant across the parking lot, and a moment later, they took a booth in the back and sat down. It was almost 8 a.m. Over strong, boiled-to-death coffee and a half-foot-high stack of pancakes speckled with mountain huckleberries, Bauer told Hannah she'd better eat up.

"You're getting thin," he said. "You have to eat something."

Hannah picked at the pancakes. "I'm not a kid anymore," she said, and they both laughed a little.

Early morning sunlight streamed into the windows; it was clear and unfettered, unlike the smog that veiled the mornings in Southern California. She knew no amount of makeup could conceal the exhaustion that had crept over her body and held her like a strangler. Even her brown eyes were dull. Bauer was worried about her and said so several times, but she told him to get on with what he knew about the woman who could be her mother. Bauer complied. He told her what they knew about Mrs. Wallace. How she ran a small fishing resort; how she had hurt her hands in a cannery accident; how she matched Claire Logan in general characteristics such as age and height; and how she was widowed a few years back.

"Widowed? Sounds like my mother," Hannah deadpanned.

Bauer shrugged. "Colon cancer. Doubt she could do that to anyone."

"I don't know," she said. "You don't know her."

It was the only bit of levity during their conversation, ghoulish though it might have seemed to any outsider listening in.

Bauer drank the last of his coffee and signaled to the waitress for a refill.

"I don't know if you'll see this as good or bad news," he said, but the caution in his voice indicated whatever he was about to tell her was, indeed, bad news.

"Talked to Warden Thomas yesterday afternoon. Wheaton's in the infirmary again. It looks bad for him. Doubtful that he's going to make it to his parole hearing after all."

"Oh no," she said, feeling puzzled by her empathy for Wheaton. "What is it?" In a weird way, she had wanted to find her mother for Wheaton as much as for herself. He'd been stupid and devoted to her, and that needed to stop. She felt a little shaky and put her hands on her lap to hide the slight tremor of her shattered nerves.

"He couldn't breathe on his own," Bauer went on. "His emphysema, you understand. He's a big guy. His lungs can't support what he's become, size-wise. They brought him back, but he's not going to get out of the clinic alive. At least the warden doesn't think so."

While Bauer waited for more information from S.A. Ingersol in Portland, Hannah spent most of the earliest part of the day finding out how much Louise Wallace was loved by members of the Kodiak community. If anyone had deserved a park statue for selflessness, it appeared it was Louise Wallace. She'd been on this and that committee. She donated to the homeless. She even worked once a week at a food bank. But if it was an act, atonement for sins too dark to be measured, all of her good works were suspect. Hannah knew she had to face Louise Wallace herself, and there was no time like the present.

Without telling Bauer of her plans, Hannah got directions to the Wallace address from the motel clerk, a man of about forty who shook his head at the mention of the old woman's name. With utter certainty, he said that Wallace was "getting a raw deal" and was being harassed by the Feds for "something she didn't do." Like half the island, it seemed, the motel clerk went to church with Wallace.

"I love that lady," he said. "We all do."

Hannah didn't want Bauer to know where she was going, though she knew once she was gone he'd probably figure it out. She rented the last car available from Island Rentals and it was a beaut, a pink sedan that once had been the conveyance of a top Mary Kay cosmetics sales representative. So much for traveling unnoticed, she thought, giving in to a brief smile. With all that was going on in Kodiak and at home in Santa Louisa, a smile felt welcome. Brief, but welcome.

The drive to Louise Wallace's home was one of the most beautiful Hannah had ever experienced; trees of the deepest, nearly black, green, marched along the side of the roadway. Ferns spilled down the hillside to the crackling white waters of rushing rivers. Every now and then a break in the wall of green revealed blue, icy waters and an occasional cabin or ragtag mobile home. It was a gorgeous day, and if her business hadn't been so grim, Hannah Griffin would have stopped to savor the moment.

Alaska, she thought, *is rugged, rough, but stunning at every turn*. She looked to the west and saw ridge tops covered in snow, and it chilled her. Her mind started down the path toward the lady with the coveralls and down vest, and she fought it. As if in answer to a prayer, her cell phone rang, interrupting her thoughts. She reached for it and looked at the display. It was Ethan. For a split second, she debated whether or not to answer. He was always worried. He'd tell her the same thing Bauer had—that she ought to go home. On the third ring, she gave in.

"Hi, honey," she answered. When Ethan didn't respond, she repeated herself, thinking the connection was bad. Kodiak had only three cell towers.

"Hannah, I have something very important to tell you." Ethan was using what she always thought of as his *cop voice*. His words were steady and calm.

The sound of his voice frightened Hannah. "Oh my God," she said. "Is it Amber? What happened? Did that woman come back?"

"God, no. She's fine," he said. "Amber's fine. This isn't about Amber. It is about *you*."

"You just about caused me to crash. Don't do that."

"Are you driving?"

"Uh-huh."

"Better pull over. This is important." Ethan was glad his wife couldn't see his face just then. Tears brimmed at his eyelids. In a moment, he knew, they would fall quietly down his cheeks. But she wouldn't see them.

Hannah found a clear spot on the shoulder, slowed down, and pulled in front of a wide dirt driveway flanked by an outcropping of mailboxes. She worried it was her uncle. Someone must have died, the way Ethan sounded.

"All right," she said. "I've parked. What is it? You're scaring me."

Ethan drew a deep breath. He had agonized over how he would tell her. He knew this was the kind of information one should give in person, but that wasn't happening, given where his wife was and what she was about to do.

"Veronica Paine called, honey," he began. "She told me something very upsetting." Ethan was running out of momentum, and he knew it. He didn't know how to couch what he had to say. He blurted it out:

"Claire wasn't your mother, Leanna was."

At first the words didn't compute. *How could they?* "What?" Hannah sat in her pink rental car, her mouth agape, her heart a jackhammer. A car passed by. "You don't know what you are saying."

Ethan told her what Veronica Paine had said, his tone bouncing from concern for his wife to anger toward those who'd held the secret about her. "Leanna had you when she was fourteen. Your mother and your father," he hesitated on those two words, unsure of amending them or going with what they'd always been to Hannah, "adopted you."

Hannah's jackhammer heart beat faster. "I don't think so," she said. She flashed on Aunt Leanna, her pretty eyes, full of love. The smell of citrus came to her. The gentleness of her hands as she brushed away tears from a nightmare. She was so gentle. So unlike her mother.

"I'm afraid so," he said. "It was a private adoption. The adoption papers were found in one of the bank deposit boxes. They were sealed by order of the court. Since Leanna was your only relative, and was coming to get you, those who knew figured *she'd* tell you one day."

"How could they—*she*—do this?"

"Hell, I don't know. Think about your aunt. She was just a kid when she got pregnant. It couldn't have been easy for her. Think of the times. Her older sister offered to take you . . ."

Another car whizzed by, snapping Hannah back to where she was and what she was about to do.

"Are you okay? Do you want me to come up there?"

"Don't worry about me," Hannah said. "I'm fine. I'll be fine."

She turned off the phone and stared at the road in front of her, and she cried.

CHAPTER THIRTY-EIGHT

The yellow house was aglow as morning sunlight poured over it like honey from the sky. Slowly pulling into the gravel driveway, Hannah could see a woman by the gazebo, setting a hose with an oscillating sprinkler among plantings of three- and four-foot spires of foxglove and delphinium. Her nerves sparked and adrenaline pumped. She tried to shake off the uneasiness. As the sprinkler swirled, the woman turned around and noticed the car. And for a minute Hannah stared and wondered why she had even bothered to search for her mother in the first place. *Why did she care? What had she wanted from a reunion?* All of that had been made all the more confusing with the extraordinary revelation that Ethan had just provided. Not only *where* was Claire Logan, just who *was* she? Was she her mother at all?

"Mrs. Wallace?" Hannah called out across the yard. Her voice was a little timid, and she cleared her throat. The sprinkler clacked and sprayed a ribbon of mist. When the woman didn't respond, though she looked right at Hannah, she called out once more.

"Hello?"

Marge Morrison looked over and smiled. She hadn't worn her glasses and she squinted at the visitor emerging from the pink Mary Kay car. Morrison might have been wary at the sight of a stranger, given the incident at the sheriff's office, but it wasn't her nature to be unfriendly or indifferent. "I didn't hear you, dear," she said, removing a straw garden hat and letting her silver ponytail swing freely. "Louise is inside. Are you a friend?"

"Yes," Hannah replied without thinking. She was more nervous than she'd ever been—and she knew she had good reason to be. Her breathing was rapid and shallow. She'd waited for this moment a long time.

"I'm not surprised," Morrison said. She dusted off her hands. "They've been coming in droves. Lou has more casseroles and salads than a supermarket deli."

Hannah forced a smile. "I didn't bring anything. I actually came to talk with Louise."

"That's all right," Morrison said, stepping over a little sprinkler-made stream running across the front of the flowerbed. "Let me turn the water down and I'll be right with you."

Two minutes later, they had their shoes off, borrowed slippers on, and were inside. Morrison led Hannah to the room with the floor-to-ceiling windows overlooking the icy-blue waters of the bay. Hannah searched the household bric-a-brac as if there would be a clue from Rock Point. A hint of the past. The place was beautifully ap-

pointed with matching furniture in striped and checked
fabrics, but strangely cold. Nothing hinted at the owner's
personal interests. It had that distinctly Pottery Barn am-
bience, matchy matchy, but completely soulless. *Nicely
done. Neatly done.* Baskets of pinecones and framed oil
paintings of lighthouses and the like, but nothing seemed
to be culled from someone's real life. Amid all of that
was an elderly woman. Hannah's eyes fixed on her.
Louise Wallace sat in the blue wingback chair. Her ashy
blond and gray hair was pulled back. *She was not the
woman who had accosted Amber back in Santa Louisa.
Her hair had been black. Good,* Hannah thought.

Her eyes were hidden behind the glare of eyeglasses. A
combination magnifying lens and light fixture swung
over her lap where she was working on a counted cross-
stitch pattern depicting a basket of red apples.

"Lou, someone . . ." Morrison looked a little embarrassed because she hadn't bothered to ask the younger
woman's name. "Someone's here to see you."

Hannah's heart was beating like a sparrow's. "My
name is Hannah Griffin." Perspiration rolled down her
side.

Louise Wallace looked up to meet Hannah's eyes and
offered a friendly smile. Hannah froze the image and ran
it through her mind like a computer in search of a matching file. *What about her face? What about her eyes? Her
teeth? Was there anything that matched?*

"Why, let me think," Wallace said, setting down her
cross-stitch. "I don't think we've met. Have we?"

Hannah's brain was still scanning. Nothing hit. Noth-
ing was saying to her that Wallace was anyone she knew.
Her mother, adoptive or otherwise. *Zero recognition.*
Hannah felt weak with relief. "Can I sit?"

"Certainly," Wallace said. "But you're not a reporter, are you?'

"No, not a reporter. I'm an investigator."

"An investigator? That sounds interesting." Wallace swung the magnifier to the side of the chair. Her movement was swift and a little startling. She smiled at Hannah and called to her friend.

"Marge, would you bring us some tea? More of that lovely chamomile we had earlier this morning?"

Her glasses on so she could get a good look at the visitor, Morrison nodded and disappeared into the kitchen.

"I've been sitting all morning," Wallace said, "but I've been through so much lately, there's not much more I feel I can do." She shifted her wiry frame in the wingback. "Are you—Hannah, is it?—from the law office? They said they'd be sending someone over here. I thought it was going to be someone I knew. I know everyone on Kodiak Island."

Hannah shook her head. "I'm an investigator, but I'm not involved in your case and I'm not from your lawyer's office. I'm here on my own. I'm looking for my mother."

Wallace barely glanced at Hannah. Instead she admired her cross-stitching; her scarred fingers smoothing the red of an apple. "I have no children."

"Now? Or never?"

Wallace gazed out the window, the bay a frosty blue line to the horizon.

"Look at me, please." Hannah moved closer. "Don't you know me?"

"I can see that you are troubled. I'm sorry, but I can't help you."

"There is something about you that—"

"—reminds you of someone? That's sweet. But I'm so sorry. You're not one of those children searching for their birth mothers? Are you?"

Hannah's face was red with anger, and she fought for composure. "No, thank God. If you are Claire Logan, then I *know* you're not my biological mother. And I thank God for that."

Wallace fiddled with her cross-stitch, the silver needle glinting in the stream of sun that had sent streaks across her lap. It was the first time her visitor—her pretty, young, and apparently *motherless* interrogator—had mentioned the Logan name.

"I haven't a clue what you're talking about," she said.

Hannah listened to each word as if each syllable could provide an answer. Morrison brought the tea in and set it down. Louise thanked her and said the two of them would be taking their tea out to the gazebo.

"This girl's searching for her mother. She thinks I might know her."

"*Be* her," Hannah corrected, only to see the reaction. But there was none.

"I see," Morrison said, uncomfortable with the obvious tension in the room. "I'll pick up in here; you two go on and enjoy the morning. I'm sure you'll sort things out just fine."

Balancing fine china cups and saucers, Hannah and Louise slipped on their shoes on the front steps, and Morrison went looking for the vacuum. When she couldn't find it anywhere, she poked her head into Louise's bedroom on the west side of the house. A grand four-poster bed with a damask canopy and a pair of matching chairs commanded the room. It was the bedroom of a queen, and Marge Morrison doubted any woman in all of Alaska had such a splendid boudoir. Morrison ran her hands over the silvery fabric. In doing so, she noticed a suitcase on the opposite side of the bed from the doorway. It was heavy with clothing and slid halfway under the platform of the bed, out of view. She gave it little regard and got the vacuum from the walk-in closet.

Out in the gazebo, Louise Wallace took a seat first and indicated Hannah should sit next to her in order to take in the view of the garden. A clematis vine climbed over a rail, and the heavy, earthy scent of marigolds wafted through the air.

"Now really, what do you want from me?" she asked, her genteel smile fading into a cold stare. "I assume you are here to 'get the story' like that awful Hoffman woman?"

Hannah could hardly believe her ears. The name caught her off guard. Dog Face was faster on her feet than she'd have ever guessed.

"Marcella has talked to you?"

"You *know* her?" Wallace let out an impatient sigh. "It figures. She phoned me last night, and I'll tell you what I told her, the damned FBI, and anyone else with half a brain. I am not Claire Logan. Never have been. Never will be." She sipped some tea and looked around her yard; a tapestry of flowers filled every bed. "A couple days ago my life was as peaceful as all of this. And now my world's being turned upside down by a bunch of outsiders."

"Maybe I'm not such an outsider." Hannah was tentative, but she pressed on. "Maybe, in some twisted way, I'm a part of you?"

Wallace kept facing forward, as if something very interesting was taking place among the flowers of her garden. Her expression was frozen. "Like I've said, I have no children, no family. My husband is dead. That's the only part of me that mattered."

"Look," Hannah said, "I need you to face me. I need to look into your eyes. What about Erik and Danny?"

Wallace turned toward Hannah, but her eyes were ice. "I don't know anyone by those names. And I'd really like you to go now."

By then, Hannah Griffin had wound herself up like a mechanical toy. There was no stopping her. It didn't matter what Wallace said.

"What about Aunt Leanna?" she asked. Leanna's name stuck in Hannah's throat, so tight with emotion. The woman who had been her savior, who had raised her after the murders in Rock Point, had been her mother all along. "What about her baby . . . about me?"

Wallace remained ice. "Honestly, you're completely unhinged, and I don't know anything about anyone you're talking about."

"Your sister . . . she gave me to you to raise as *your* daughter. You, a *mother*. What a sick joke that turned out to be."

This genteel, cookie-baking, Methodist do-gooder was unruffled. Hannah wanted to grab her right then and there, but somehow she held back. Wallace just sat, cool and dignified.

"That's disgusting," she said. She spat out her words, contempt in every bite. "What kind of a woman would give her baby to her sister? That sounds like trash to me."

You're trash, Hannah thought. *You're evil.* Instead, she defended her aunt.

"She was the nicest woman in the world. I loved her more than anything. More than I ever loved you, Claire Logan."

It felt good to say those words, as if Leanna was there, all lemony and sweet. It felt good to say Claire's name.

There was a flicker of interest on Wallace's face when Hannah's words indicated a past tense. Leanna, it was clear, was no longer living, and Wallace seemed a little interested. But as quickly as it came, the curiosity evaporated.

Finally she spoke. Her words were dismissive. "I don't know anything that will be helpful to you."

"I think you do," Hannah said. "Are you Claire Logan?"

Wallace wore a mask of willful, maybe even *practiced*, incredulity. She stood and faced her accuser. "I will not stand for this kind of harassment. Leave now or . . ." she stopped.

"Or you'll kill me?" Hannah asked, pressing harder. "Throw me in a ditch with quicklime? Tell your friend here that I deserved it? That I didn't matter? My life wasn't important? Remember you told me how much you loved a military uniform? And the security that came with one?"

Even though she had sounded defiant and confident, inside Hannah was anything but sure about anything she was saying. Louise Wallace could be Claire Logan or she could be the Brownie Troop leader she remembered from Rock Point. *She could be anyone*. Her features had been pinched and sanded to oblivion. Nothing about the woman seemed all that familiar, not in the sense that she could be sure she was or wasn't her mother from so long ago. She even took in a deep breath, knowing the power of the sense of smell to recall a memory.

"You *are*, aren't you?" Hannah said more as a statement than a question. "You *are* my mother."

Louise Wallace, or whoever she was, would have no more of it.

"I've reached my limit. Get out of here. Look for your mother somewhere else. Try Mexico . . . that's where I'd go if I was Logan. Someplace warm."

"I've looked for you for my whole life. Since you betrayed my father. Since you betrayed Marcus Wheaton."

Again, was there a flicker of recognition? Emotion in the cold blue of her eyes?

Wallace stood. "I want you to get off my property."

Hannah wasn't ready to go. She wanted answers. She grabbed the old woman's arm. It felt muscular and strong, not like some old lady who spent her days cross-stitching. This was the arm of a woman who chopped wood. Dug trenches. In that instant, feeling the pulse of the woman who could be Claire Logan, Hannah could feel herself losing control. She wanted to throttle Louise Wallace, just as she'd wanted to lunge at Joanne Garcia back in the hospital room in Santa Louisa. *What was with these women? These so-called mothers?*

"I hate you! I've hated you since the day you left me!"

"Stop! You're hurting me."

"You don't know what hurt is. Hurt is burying your dad. Your two brothers. Waiting for your fucking evil mother to come back and get you and hating yourself because you still loved her. No matter what she's done. That hurts."

"I don't know . . . what . . ."

"You *do*. I know you do."

"Please. Let me go! Marge! Call the sheriff!"

Wallace struggled to get away, but Hannah yanked hard and felt a pop. *God, I've done it now. I'll be arrested for assault. I'll lose Amber. Ethan will know I'm no better than Claire Logan, mother or not. Headlines would roll across the country. But I don't care. I don't care*, she thought.

The sprinkler spun and the two women wrestled for a moment in the gazebo, one trying to get away, the other trying to hang on as if she could squeeze the truth out of the other by wringing it out of her. In truth, it was all Hannah could do to keep from strangling her. The sound of a teacup shattering on the gazebo floor, pieces scattering like a mosaic under their feet. The noise, harsh and sudden, was like a gunshot. It brought Hannah out of her rage. *What am I doing? What in the world?*

"I'm sorry," she said, crying now, "I hurt you."

Wallace's eyes were full of terror by then. "Yes, you did! Look what *you* did. Those were my best Belleek. I think you broke my shoulder! Let go of me."

"I saw Marcus Wheaton in prison," Hannah blurted, not ready for their conversation, their *fight,* to end. "He told me where to find you. Marcus is the reason I'm here. He's the reason the FBI is here . . . why Marcella Hoffman is calling you. You really played him, you know. Twenty years later, he still loves you."

With a surprisingly powerful swipe, Wallace pulled Hannah's hand off of her, and she rushed down the path toward the house, never once looking back. "Go bother someone else. Better yet, get some help. I'm not who you think I am; who you apparently *want* me to be."

The crunching noise of breaking china under her feet

distracted her. For the first time, Hannah looked down at the shattered cup. A portion of a cup had fallen next to her purse. A half moon of winy, red lipstick frowned from the rim. She returned her stare back to Wallace. She refused to let the old lady get the last word.

"I don't know how you sleep at night," she called out as she hurried across the gravel driveway to the pink car.

Wallace was at the front door by then. "Nytol and a shot of brandy," she muttered, glancing back at Hannah, and hurrying inside without bothering to put on slippers. Hannah could see Marge Morrison looking busy wiping down one of the windows. Her friend had been listening to every word.

"I have never forgotten what you made me do. Never!" Hannah screamed and slumped behind the wheel and turned her car around for the Northern Lights, feeling sick to her stomach. Tears rained. *What have I done? What kind of daughter doesn't know her own mother?* Then she thought of Amber and wondered what kind of mother would leave her little girl at home while she chased ghosts that she had prayed didn't exist. She turned on the radio to distract her from her thoughts. When she thought she was lost halfway to the island's biggest town, she found she didn't care. She was on an island, for goodness' sake.

How lost can you get on an island? she thought.

But a second later, a news report jolted her like seeing a kid dart in front of a speeding car on rain-soaked pavement. *It couldn't be.* Hannah slammed on the brakes and pushed the volume control to its loudest setting. The reception on the remote island crackled. At first she thought she misheard it, but as the piece wrapped up, she knew her ears had not played tricks on her.

"Paine was best known for her role as the prosecutor in the infamous Claire Logan/Marcus Wheaton murder and arson case. Her assailant is still at large."

"Oh God . . ." she said, "not Mrs. Paine. . . . Not now."

CHAPTER THIRTY-NINE

If there was a god to thank, it was for the fact that no one recognized Hannah Griffin as the media began its swarm of Alaska's ruggedly gorgeous and now mysterious Kodiak Island. Two affiliates from Anchorage and one of the syndicated tabloid magazine shows had already begun their descent on the island, and it wasn't even a ratings period. Claire Logan was vintage, albeit sinister, Americana. She was the boogie woman. Even if she wasn't around. Or if she had died twenty years ago. The murder of the Oregon prosecutor who had put her away was the cherry on top of the sundae. And if Louise Wallace had made good on her threat to call the sheriff on Hannah, well so much the better for the reporters circling the island.

As she approached, Hannah saw Bauer talking to a woman in front of the motel office. She wore a hideous faux-leopard print that was more *Frederick's of*, than merely *Hollywood*. Even before she turned around, Hannah knew it was DF.

She barely acknowledged the author/reporter. "Isn't there some other motel on this island?" Hannah asked Bauer.

Bauer cracked a nervous smile. "I was thinking the same thing."

Hoffman snuffed out her menthol with a sharp twist of her calf-length boot. She didn't miss a beat. "Oh, hi, Hannah! Isn't this exciting?" she said. "We're all together. I haven't told anyone but my producer that you're here. I'll stay away," she said, making the motion across her collagen-soufflé lips, "for the exclusive."

"Fine, Marcella," Hannah said, though she had no intention of ever going on camera with DF or any other reporter.

"Doug!" Hoffman called out to a young man slumped over by his rusted-out van. He was weighted down with spools of wire and a camera the size of a microwave. Clearly annoyed, Doug Jackson nodded. Hoffman continued, "We're going up to First Methodist to see if we can shake loose some of Louise Wallace's old friends. *For balance.* My whole career has been built on balance."

Hannah barely glanced at Hoffman. "I forgot," she said.

"I thought we were getting along. I don't know why you have to be so harsh."

Bauer did his best to brush off Hoffman. "Well, sorry I can't talk. You'll have to go through Portland PR. But, of course, you'll be wasting your time until after the investigation concludes."

"Still so ethical," Hoffman said. "And so handsome. You've really grown into your skin since Rock Point."

Bauer turned a shade of pink that matched Hannah's rental car. "Good luck, Ms. Hoffman," he said, while wishing more than anything that the overburdened cameraman would drop the camera on Hoffman's head.

Bauer followed Hannah inside the office.

"I think she likes you," Hannah said.

"Like a cobra."

Hannah asked the front clerk for any messages. None from Ethan; two from Ripperton. She folded them and tucked them inside the front flap of her purse.

"There's something I want to talk to you about," she said as they walked toward the hallway.

"I know you went and saw her."

"Yes, but that's not it. That isn't really what's on my mind."

Bauer was puzzled. "What do you mean? You just went and saw Louise Wallace. And it isn't on your mind?"

Hannah kept a step ahead of Bauer as they walked the long dark hallway toward their rooms in the minuscule no-smoking section of the motel—just four rooms. Bauer put his hand on her shoulder and turned her around. Her eyes were weary.

"What do you think? About Louise?"

"I don't know. I feel incredibly foolish. I don't know if she's my mother or not. But that's not what's on my mind, Jeff. I want to talk about something I've never shared before. Not even with Ethan or my Aunt Leanna. No one."

They started walking again. "I guess I feel honored," he said.

"Reserve judgment. Once I tell you, you might not feel so inclined."

It was after 2 p.m., too late for lunch and too early for dinner. "Want to talk in your room?" he asked.

"You've got the honor bar."

He laughed. "Nope. No honor bar at the Northern Lights."

"I could smell it on you this morning."

Bauer stuck the key into the lock and turned the knob. "All right," he said. "I have a bottle in my room. Come on in." He poured them both a shot of Wild Turkey and took a seat on the sole chair in the room outfitted with a TV, a nightstand, and twin double beds. Hannah sat on the bed closest to the window. Light from outside cut through the split between the dark green curtains. Her eyes were puffy. And for a moment, Bauer was back in Rock Point, Oregon. He could see the frightened little girl who had grown into the beautiful and accomplished woman. He remembered how her hair had hung in her eyes, a shield from what was going on around her. He recalled how quiet she was at first, then how she talked in an endless stream without coming up for air.

Bauer had never forgotten what had happened. And the moments he had counted as the most meaningful of his life were those weeks before the Wheaton arson trial when he had comforted the young girl. Not chasing Claire Logan because she had killed twenty people, but because she had left behind a terrified and lonely little girl who would have no choice but to live with the sins of her mother for the rest of her life. He felt as though he had been her protector. He never could forget the little girl.

As she sipped her drink, she started to talk. Before she was finished, Hannah Logan Griffin had downed the rest of Bauer's booze and unleashed the Pandora's box of demons and nightmares that had haunted her for twenty years. Hannah wasn't like the girl who had been raped by a family friend and kept her mouth quiet so long that she suppressed what she knew to be true. The imprint on her brain was so indelible that Hannah just compartmentalized it. Stored it. Locked it up. It was always there ticking, reminding her like a slit wrist that never healed.

She remembered it was about half an hour before midnight when the noise outside and the chill of the December night awoke her. She remembered hearing her mother's and Marcus Wheaton's voices.

"I wasn't frightened when I went back to sleep," she told Bauer, sitting on the edge of the bed in his motel room. "But I'm frightened now." Bauer could see her trembling hands attempt to mimic steadiness as she rested the glass of liquor on her lap.

"What is it, Hannah?" he asked.

She held her fingers to her lips. She looked fragile, wan. She was a splinter, ready to break. Without warning, the motel room seemed to contract like the wheezing lungs of an old man. It was spinning and heaving. Hannah groped for something to steady herself. *To reach for Jeff Bauer.* Blood drained from her face. For a split second, she thought she might vomit. She was white.

"You okay?" Bauer held Hannah's hand, but it was limp and warm. *Unresponsive.* Her eyes were impassive, staring into something far away. He moved his hand to her shoulders and gently rocked her.

"Hannah, can you hear me?"

She shuddered. She was far away. *Long ago.*

It was a scene in black and white, first snow, then the dark of smoke. The triggers of the strobing images were the sweet smell of the Wild Turkey, her father's favorite drink. Hannah could hear ice cubes tinkle in cut glass tumblers. Icy. Clear. Feeling his presence just then brought a rush of emotion. *How she missed him. How Amber would have loved him.* Hannah gasped for air and the face of her father faded. Suddenly, her mother's image came into view. It was clear. It was *her.* Cold eyes, a tight, bitter mouth. Hannah tried to shake it away. Something else took her back to the farm to the night that changed everything; that ruined everything. *Teacups.* It was a set of Belleek, creamy white with a chain of shamrocks around the rim. They sat in a semicircle around a teapot, which was on the dining room sideboard. They had been her mother's prized possession, the first thing she'd bought when she'd made a little money off the farm. She had always loved fine things. She'd always told Hannah that exceptional belongings were the payoff for hard work and sacrifice. Her teacup collection was her first treasure, greater than the love of her children, her husband, even Marcus Wheaton. Sitting in the gazebo, wrestling for memories—for truth—the shattered cup of the same design and the way Louise Wallace's eyes flashed disappointment, not *fear.* It took her to a dark place.

"Hannah, can you hear me?"

It was Jeff Bauer's voice, bringing her back. *Slowly.* The room continued to spin. The Wild Turkey. The cup. The faces of her brothers, her mother, her father, Marcus Wheaton. All spun around her, mouths moving, explaining, crying, demanding.

Only one asked for forgiveness. It was Hannah's own voice.

The room came into focus. Jeff Bauer's penetrating eyes looked at her with even deeper compassion. "Are you sick?"

She shook her head and swallowed hard. The Wild Turkey. The shattered cup. The memory was no longer buried. Tears rolled, but she did not make the sounds that come with crying. She was too scared, too full of resolve.

"It wasn't the smoke that woke me up the second time," she said, the memories now crystallized. "Oh, Jeff, it was Marcus Wheaton who woke me." Her body shivered and her vocal cords constricted, but she didn't stop. The dam had been broken. "He stood over my bed and put his hand over my mouth. I didn't know what was happening. I thought he was going to hurt me."

Bauer touched her knee. Hannah didn't recoil, but allowed him to comfort her. "What did the son of a bitch do to you?"

She shook her head and steadied her drink. "It wasn't like that," she said. "Marcus told me to be quiet, very quiet."

"Dear God," Bauer said. He put his arm around her. "I'm sorry," he said *gently*.

"Jeff," she said, "that isn't it. That isn't it at all. Something happened today. Now I remember. I know she killed my brothers. I knew it, and I didn't do anything about it."

The words didn't compute. In twenty years Jeff Bauer hadn't imagined that Hannah had any real knowledge of what had really happened that night. She'd never said so. She'd held it together so damn well that everyone back in the Portland field office thought Claire Logan's daughter escaped the horror of Rock Point by not *seeing* anything at all. They all thought she was lucky. Some of the younger ones said she was better off. Clean slate. Living with really knowing would be too much for any of them.

"What are you saying?" He hated himself for pushing

her. Bauer hadn't pressed her hard enough when she was thirteen, and that thought also made him sick. She was just a girl, for crying out loud. How hard should he have pushed?

"Marcus led me out of the house. I didn't . . . I didn't get out of the house alone—I was with Marcus. I didn't call for my mom because he told me to be quiet. He said that I'd die if I said a word. There was flocking everywhere and he poured kerosene as we walked past Mom's and the boys' rooms."

Hannah brushed her dark blond hair from her eyes. Bauer could see that her brown eyes had welled with tears, but she had kept herself from crying.

"She flat out killed the boys with her bare hands," she said. "Marcus was supposed to handle me because I was a girl and . . . get this . . ."

Her voice trailed off, and she found herself back on the tree farm. The white of the snow. The sick smell of the kerosene. All was there. A tear fell, and she moved to wipe it away. She wouldn't allow her mother to get the best of her.

"What?" the FBI agent asked. "What?"

Hannah nodded. "It would be easier to suffocate me than Erik and Danny. But my mom, yeah, she could multi-task like nobody's business."

But there was something else.

"I'm sure she killed Didi, too. I saw her mother on one of those shows on cable. It was long after it happened. But I know that after my mother questioned me and my brothers about some jar of teeth she'd kept, and Didi took the blame."

"Teeth?"

"You heard me."

Hannah's eyes, dry by then, got huge.

"These were from the days before DNA was even really thought about. I think my mother bashed out her victims' teeth with a hammer. And she saved them like a ghoul. Like what she was."

"Those were Didi's teeth?"

Hannah sipped her drink and shook her head.

"No, I don't think so. I mean, no. It was after my mother confronted me with the jar that Didi disappeared. I heard my mother talking on the phone, and I knew she was lying when she said Didi had left the farm 'weeks ago.' She boxed up some of her things and gave them to Rock Point St. Vincent de Paul. She burned the rest. Didi's mom kept calling . . . she was sure my mom had done something to her. She just didn't know that Didi was one of many. I guess I knew. Marcus knew."

Hannah Griffin tightened like a potato bug, all into herself, on the edge of the bed. The light from the window slashed at her glistening face.

"I just sat there," she said. "I just fucking sat there while the house, the buildings burned up. I sat there until the firemen came. I just sat while everything was burning. I knew what was happening. I didn't know all of it. But I knew enough. I've known enough for my whole life."

Bauer's arms enveloped Hannah's shoulders and she closed her eyes. He could feel her shaking. And as he held her he thought of the shoes that had been introduced in court so long ago, and a question that no one had asked. There was no need for it. It wasn't a murder trial. Marcus Wheaton wasn't being charged with their murder, and Veronica Paine didn't see the relevance of two boys dressed at midnight on Christmas Eve. But Bauer had always wondered why the boys' little corpses had been found fully dressed all the way to their shoes.

Hannah provided the answer.

"The boys thought they were going somewhere. They thought they were going to go with Mom. But they didn't. They went to heaven."

Not wanting to move her, Bauer took the hideous orange and green bedspread from the other bed and covered her. She opened her eyes and looked into his.

"Don't," he said. "You need rest. Sleep here."

She closed her eyes. "Stay with me?"

"I'll be right here."

CHAPTER FORTY

Glacial water splashing over her head could not have awakened Hannah with more bracing impact than did Bauer's voice. He pressed his hand on her shoulder and was pushing it gently.

"Hannah, something terrible has happened," he said. "A fire. Louise Wallace's house is ablaze."

She kicked off the bedspread and found the floor with her feet. Though it was 10 p.m., it was still gauzy daylight outside. She saw she was still in Bauer's motel room. The television was on low, and Hannah could see that Bauer had kept some kind of vigil while she slept. He must have raided the vending machine a time or two, since peanut butter cups and Doritos wrappers curled next to his chair.

"What in the world?" she asked.

Bauer stepped back and stood in front of the green curtains. He was worried, and he could do little to hide it. "Marcella Hoffman called," he said. "She's already on her way out to Wallace's place. There's been a fire."

"Fire?" Hannah's mind sharpened, and she remembered how she had unburdened herself to Bauer. So intimate had been her disclosure, Hannah felt a flush of embarrassment.

"This isn't happening," she said, looking for her purse. "What does Marcella have to do with it?"

Bauer shook his head. "She just hired the kid with the camera to keep a watch out there. The kid didn't see anything. Not until he saw the smoke rising from the upper-floor door. Called the fire department, but by the time they got out there the place was half baked."

"I'm going," she said.

"There's nothing out there."

"My mother," she said. "My mother could be there."

"Get a coat," he said. "Gets cold even at a fire site."

"We can take my car."

Bauer didn't think so. "No, we can't."

"But it's right out front," she said.

"I've seen your car," Bauer shot back. "And we're not taking that pink thing anywhere. I'll drive my rental. Come on."

The Wallace house was remarkably unscathed by the fire, thanks in part to Marcella Hoffman's insatiable need—and greed—for the ever-lucrative Claire Logan story. She promised her cameraman, Jackson, an extra $300 if he'd cover the house throughout the night. He parked across from the fishing cabins, surprised that all were boarded up for the season—a month early. He brought a sleeping bag, four liters of Coke, and a bag of barbecue chips. He was relieving himself against a 200-

year-old cedar when Marge Morrison's pickup passed by, headed for the highway. Twenty minutes later, he smelled smoke. When he walked closer to the Wallace house, he could see a thin stream of black smoke funneling from one of the turrets. A call to the fire department and one to Hoffman's room at the Northern Lights brought immediate help and a surprising browbeating.

"I'm thinking of firing you right on the spot. If you called the fire department or the police before calling me, you don't know the first thing about being a journalist."

"I thought the women inside could use some help," Doug muttered.

Smoke rubbed against the buttery yellow of the turrets, but there was no flame. Not that anyone could see. A squad of volunteer firemen with a pump truck and pick-axes arrived within ten minutes of Jackson's call. It took only ten minutes to extinguish the fire. The staccato blue sheriff's lights filtered through the smoky air.

By the time Bauer and Hannah arrived, the place was already considered a crime scene. Bauer parked next to sheriff Kim Stanton's cruiser and surveyed the scene before he even reached for the door handle.

"This might be rough," he said.

"I can handle it," she said, getting out of the car.

"It started in the bedroom," a fireman said. "Smoking in bed would be my guess."

Hoffman and the other media types with their unblinking eyes and cans of Coke and glowing cigarettes had gathered by the gazebo, the closest point to the scene the firemen and sheriff's deputies would allow. If the sound could be turned off—the hissing of water against ash, the cracking of wood, and the shattering of glass—the scene would have been less ominous. A cloud of creamy white flowers had just unfurled in the garden. The air smelled of smoke and flowers. Hoffman was playing the part of queen bee, talking loudly and abrasively as always.

"Doug, get the shot!" Hoffman yelled at her beleaguered assistant. "The strobe of the fire truck lights makes good video!"

Bauer approached the sheriff, and a pair of firemen huddled halfway between the house and gazebo.

"One victim," a fireman said. He was a handsome man with big shoulders and a mop of dark hair. He wore the kind of expression that indicated no matter how many times he'd had to do it, it hurt to say the words.

"Who?" Bauer asked.

"Woman. Elderly. Louise Wallace, I'd say. Found her in bed. Looks like there was a propane leak from the kitchen cooktop. Coroner's taking her now."

"Mrs. Wallace never hurt a soul," Stanton said.

Three men carried a stretcher with a shroud-covered figure to the open jaws of an ambulance.

"Has she been identified?" Bauer asked.

"Not yet. Badly burned. Her face is in bad shape. We call her a 'crispy critter.' A visual identification won't be possible."

"Dental?" he asked.

"She apparently had china clippers, but they're gone."

Bauer's expression revealed that he was unfamiliar with the term.

The young fireman was only too glad to explain something to the FBI. "China clippers. False teeth."

Bauer nodded, and just as he did so, Hannah turned and grabbed his wrist. She put her fingers to her lips to indicate that he shouldn't say anything. Her eyes were glistening with tears, spilling down her cheeks. He obliged.

While Hoffman cackled on about how she was going to do this and that, Hannah and Bauer walked over to the car away from the ears of the media. Hannah's crying eyes held an intensity that Bauer hadn't seen since she was a child.

"What is it?" he asked.

"Call the airport," she said. Her voice was low, muffled by her own sobs. "Notify the harbormaster. We can't let Louise off this island. She's alive. I don't know who the woman that the coroner picked up is, though I suspect it is Mrs. Morrison."

Hannah was possessed by what she was certain was absolutely true. Bauer didn't get it, and his puzzlement annoyed her.

"What gives here?" he asked. "Pull yourself together. I knew you shouldn't have come out here tonight."

Bauer put his arms around her. He didn't care what Hoffman or any of the other vultures thought. Hannah was in quicksand.

"The moonflowers," Hannah sobbed into his shoulder. He held her, but she pushed away from his embrace and faced the garden. In the fading light of the day, the white of moonflowers floated above the greenery. "They were my mother's favorite. They used to be mine, too."

"You sure?"

"Jeff," she said, "Louise Wallace is my mother. I know it. *I feel it.* And I think that Marge Morrison is victim 21. I think my mother did what she did best. She killed again."

"This morning you didn't think Louise was her."

"I didn't know. I didn't really want to know. But I feel certain now."

Just then Marcella Hoffman walked up. She was wearing a Kodiak Island sweatshirt and jeans a size too small.

Her hair was floppy in the summer wind. It was clear she'd been in bed when her associate alerted her that Louise Wallace's house was spouting smoke and flames. She repeated an old nursery rhyme as she approached. Bauer's face was stone. Hannah had turned away when she saw her coming.

"Ladybug, ladybug, fly away home. Your house is on fire and your children . . ." Hoffman stopped herself when it was apparent that neither the FBI agent nor the CSI from California thought much of her cleverness. "Hope I'm not interrupting," she said, switching gears. "You look like the cat that swallowed the canary, Special Agent Bauer. What can you tell me?"

Bauer didn't want to respond to her at all. But experience with the woman had proven that Hoffman refused to be ignored. "Not a thing," he said. "Wish we did. I'd tell you just to get you off my back."

She let out an exaggerated laugh. "Very funny. Really, what's happening here? I knocked on Hannah's door first. No answer. Funny, isn't it?"

"Not as funny as you think," Hannah said. She glared at Hoffman, and Bauer defused the confrontation by pushing Hoffman aside.

"I'll say this once nicely," Bauer cut in. "Please leave her alone. Go find another story. Can't you dig up anything else to write about?"

"Nothing as good as this," Hoffman snipped, undaunted. She looked around the scene.

Sheriff's deputies and firemen went about their business as the steamy smell of burning materials drifted through the slowly blackening air.

Hoffman stood her ground and lit a cigarette. "Any of you seen Liza?"

Neither responded, but the look on their faces told her what she needed to know.

"*Liz* Wheaton. Marcus's mother," Hoffman repeated.

"What is *she* doing here?" Hannah asked.

Hoffman let out her skin-crawling laugh once more. "She's the reason we're all here."

It was Bauer's turn to jump on Hoffman. The veins in his neck pulsed. He could feel his hands tighten as though he were going to punch her. "What are you talking about?" he asked.

Hoffman stepped back. "This is no big deal, so don't get hostile with me." She sucked on her cigarette. The ember glowed like one of the devil's eyes. "Why not? Why shouldn't Liza be here? We wouldn't be here without her. I told you this was like some goddamn reunion! The Claire Logan Case Reunion. I like that. Maybe I'll lead with that on the show I'm doing for Fox."

Hannah flashed to Joanne Garcia at the hospital and how she had wanted to throttle her. The same feeling of rage pulsed through her now. She fought it while wondering if she did grab DF and snap her neck, whether Bauer would stop her. *Probably not*, she thought. *He hates her as much as I do.*

"You're one sick bitch," Hannah said, edging toward Hoffman.

Bauer stepped between the two. He was more interested in hearing what Hoffman could say about Liz Wheaton than refereeing a fight between the reporter and her big "Get."

"What do you mean, the *reason* we're here?"

"Didn't they teach you how to work your sources at the FBI academy?" she asked, crushing out her cigarette with the heel of her boot. "Liz or Liza or whatever she wants to be called and I became friends when I did my ten-years-after update. I told you that. She got a job at the court clerk's office in Spruce County. Small county. Not enough workers who can alphabetize or type, I guess."

A sheriff's deputy called for additional assistance from one of the volunteer firemen with a halogen light, wanting him to illuminate the inside of the house. The man ran over to the front door.

Hoffman kept her eyes on Bauer and Hannah, clearly enjoying her moment of revelation. She told them that when she and Liz/Liza became friends she pressed her to get her an interview with Marcus Wheaton. Wheaton had refused; he didn't like the way he looked.

"Camera shy. The pig," Hoffman muttered.

"He is very heavy," Bauer said. "He's quite ill, you know."

Hannah said nothing. She looked past Hoffman to the gazebo and the moonflowers, and fleetingly her childhood in Rock Point came to mind. The good times. The times before her father had died—had been murdered, she corrected herself. The times before Marcus Wheaton, Didi, and the men in uniform—the Silver Eagles, as her mother called them.

Hoffman paid Hannah no attention. As observant as she prided herself on being, she was no great student of human behavior and emotions. She couldn't see anguish or rage unless it was broadcast at her through a TV screen. She went on to say how Liz came up with the idea to track down Hannah.

"Believe you me, I had nothing to do with it. She did it on her own." Hoffman fixed her gaze on Hannah and continued. "She knew Marcus would see you. She convinced herself he'd tell you where to find your mother. Or at least where he *thought* she might be."

"How did she find me?" Hannah asked, her stomach once more churning.

"Through prison and parole records. Copies of victims' names are kept with the file for notification if someone is released, or escapes."

Hannah shook her head. "But my name's not on the list."

"I know," Hoffman answered. "I mean, that's what Liza told me. She said your uncle's and aunt's names were included in the file. It wasn't that hard to find you after that. I mean any pimply-faced kid from a collection agency could do it. Liz sent the shoes. Wanted to get your attention. I guess it worked."

Bauer's appearance had grown hot. He wanted to knock Hoffman across the face.

"Liz is going to prison," he said. "You might be getting that jailhouse interview yourself—on the inside."

Hoffman laughed. "What's the charge? She didn't break the law. And I certainly didn't."

"She stole government property. The boys' shoes were property of the state of Oregon. And Ms. Hoffman, if there's a way to tie you into it—any way at all—you're going down, too. I'll do whatever I can to see you pay."

"You should be thanking me—" Hoffman started to say.

"Hey!" the deputy with the halogen light called out. Everyone turned to the sound of his voice, ratcheted up with urgency and fear. "Got another one in here. Another body!"

* * *

Liz Wheaton had survived the Kodiak fire. It had been her body the deputy had discovered on the floor of Louise Wallace's kitchen. She was airlifted to a hospital in Anchorage where she was treated for smoke inhalation and burns on both hands and portions of her neck. Her recovery would not be swift, but she'd make it. She'd be well enough to face charges back home in Rock Point. Federal charges were also a possibility. What's more, among the things recovered from her purse was a list of names and phone numbers, including Bauer's room number at the Northern Lights, the Griffins' home and work numbers, and Veronica Paine's cell number. Everything smelled of White Shoulders perfume, heavy and sickeningly sweet. A bottle had broken and doused the contents of her purse. To those who had come to know Liz Wheaton, it had become the smell of fear and lingering hate. Testing would be needed to confirm it, of course, but gunshot residue appeared on the sleeve of a sweater she'd been wearing. If GSR was the only tie to a firearm—and to Judge Paine's murder—investigators expected a search of her place in Rock Point would turn up more.

"A mother's love can be deadly," Bauer deadpanned to agent Ingersol when they spoke on the phone.

"As devoted as she was to Wheaton, he'd never returned the favor. He'd never given up the one thing she wanted—the whereabouts of Claire Logan."

Bauer looked out the motel window. The "Vacancy" sign had been dimmed. The media was flocking to the island in numbers that had never been seen before.

"In a way it was a sick triangle." he said. "Maniac Killer, Crazed Mother, and Duped Lover."

*   *   *

As word of the fire and the secrets it seemed to reveal filtered through the island grapevine, the healing process of the ladies of the First Methodist would not come easily. They had been devastated by Louise Wallace's betrayal and heartbroken over the death of their beloved friend, Marge Morrison.

Unable to sleep, Hannah sat up in her room at the Northern Lights and tried to pack, certain that Claire Logan had escaped the island. After learning that a woman traveling alone and matching Louise Wallace's physical description was at the Anchorage airport for a red-eye to Seattle, Bauer took the first flight to Anchorage. He'd arranged for the plane to suffer a "mechanical failure" and endure a two-hour delay. Manufacturing such delays was a common tactic to slow down a felon's escape route while the Feds figured out what to do.

At 2:45 a.m., a bleary-eyed Bauer and two other agents from the Anchorage field office boarded Alaska Airlines Flight 21 with an eye on the passenger seated in 4E, first class. She was listed as Lucille Watson. The gate agent admitted that her passport photo was dark and a little on the fuzzy side; however, he was sure she was the woman in the First Methodist cookbook, Louise Wallace.

The first two agents boarded the plane and went to the woman, who was bent over reading the in-flight magazine. A Baileys Irish Cream sat on the console next to her. Bauer came up close behind them. He felt his gun in his waistband. Ready, should he need to draw it.

Just as he prepared to tell the woman she was under arrest, she looked up and smiled.

It wasn't *her*. Bauer knew that in an instant when his eyes met the woman's puzzled gaze. The wheels were in motion, and there was nothing he could do about it.

Headed for her daughter's in Tacoma, Washington, a retired teacher from Homer, Alaska, received the shock of her life as two other agents rushed back behind her.

"Oh, my God," she called out in complete horror, knocking over her Baileys. "One of them has a gun!"

A couple of passengers screamed, and one of the flight attendants accidentally triggered an inflatable life preserver to fill with air. Bauer and the other two pulled the terrified woman from the plane as fast as they could, but in the end she wasn't Claire Logan.

Not even close.

EPILOGUE

The crew of the *Katya*, a rusty, oil-leaking Russian trawler, was preparing to drop gill nets five miles off the Alaskan coast when a deckhand spotted a twenty-four-foot fiberglass Bayliner bobbing on the surface of an unusually tranquil Pacific. It was the first week in September. From fifty yards out, it appeared the outboard motor was off and the small boat was adrift. It rose and fell like a yo-yo. *Katya*'s captain, a short man with a sunburned pate, cut his engine and ordered two of his crew to tie up to the Bayliner and check it out. The fishermen assumed the small white boat had been a dinghy for a larger pleasure craft.

In the sputtering noise of a stopping engine, one of the men, a kid no more than seventeen, climbed into the boat and made a quick assessment that no one was aboard. In the corner, by the outboard, the boat's canvas covering was slumped. A couple of inches of water floated paper cups and a pair of life preservers. The flotsam and jetsam were tragic testimony that whoever had been on that boat was probably dead. And given that the boat was in decent shape, it hadn't been long since someone had been aboard. The next storm would smash the fiberglass to bits.

He shouted to the others that no one was there. But as he turned around to return to the *Katya*, something made him go over to the canvas covering. He bent over and kicked the corner of the heavy, seawater-soaked fabric. A foot emerged, then a leg. He lifted it completely open.

"Help!" he called out. *"Someone's here!"*

Under the sodden white canvas, he had discovered the nearly frozen figure of an elderly woman. She was crumpled into a ball and soaked to the skin. Her fingertips were skim-milk blue. The kid bent down, his knee soaking up the seawater and felt for a pulse. Slight, but steady.

On September 27, the *Redhook Telegram*, the daily paper for the "Outer Inland Empire" of British Columbia, ran a story about the Russian vessel's remarkable discovery and rescue. Facts were scarce because the ship had been in disputed waters. The less said the better.

MIRACLE AT SEA:
Trawler Rescues Elderly Woman

A 71-year-old grandmother was plucked from certain death when the crew of the Katya rescued her ten miles from Point Newton. Suffering from hypothermia, the woman, who asked that

her name be withheld pending notification of her daughter, was treated on the
trawler and admitted to Redhook Clinic
for observation.

She was released Monday, before
search and rescue investigations could
be completed. Her whereabouts are
unknown.

Special Agent Bauer drank his coffee as he read the
small news article in his Portland office. Another field
agent, who considered himself the ultimate newsreader,
had clipped and faxed it to him. After reading it, Bauer
crumpled it into a small ball and shot-putted it into the
trash can by the door. It was possible that the woman described in it wasn't her. It was hundreds of miles from
Kodiak, and survival would have been highly unlikely.
Claire Logan, *Louise Wallace*, whoever she was, was
gone, and gone was good enough. *Let her go*, he told
himself. *Let her go.*

When she returned from Alaska, Hannah went straight
to the basement lab in the Santa Louisa courthouse. From
the bottom of her purse, she retrieved the broken piece of
a china cup that she had picked up from the gazebo floor
when she had argued with the cold-eyed woman she had
once believed was her biological mother. *Had once believed.* The cup, creamy white and with a single green
shamrock intact, had been wrapped in the discarded plastic covering from one of the motel drinking glasses. Hannah knew the technique left plenty to be desired, but this
wasn't a court case. It was personal. She wiped the inside
of her own cheek with a cotton-tipped swab. She put the
cup shard and the cotton swab in separate envelopes and

took them to a lab across town that specialized in pater-
nity tests.

"Hi, Hannah," said the counter girl, Carla, from behind a glass cage that ensured integrity for all samples.
"Lab at County backed up again?"

Hannah shook her head and smiled. "No," she said,
"this is personal."

The girl looked interested, but had been well trained.
No questions were ever asked of any clients.

"Okay. Call with results?"

"Sooner the better."

"I'll rush this for you."

The next day the phone rang in the lab. It was Carla.

"Hi, Hannah. Prelim and confirmation just came in. I
don't know if this is good news or not," she said. "Both
samples good. These two people definitely *are* related."

Hannah caught her breath. "Mother, daughter?" She
could hear the sound of shuffling papers as Carla flipped
back pages and read.

"Nope. If you're looking for a familial tie, markers say
aunt/niece or cousins."

Hannah didn't need to hear any more. "Destroy the
samples, please, and thanks."

"No prob. Will do."

Hannah stared out the narrow window of her office
door. It was quiet in the lab. She felt empty, and a little
alone. Wheaton was right. She was nothing like her
mother. Nothing at all. And probably because of that, she
decided not to say anything to Ethan or Bauer or anyone.
If she wasn't her mother's daughter, then she wasn't
going to be a sister to Erik and Danny anymore. There
was, she thought, something wrong about leaving those
boys alone—a second time.

The night after she got the lab results, Hannah and Ethan Griffin made love. She held Ethan as tightly as she could and asked him to hold her with all of his strength. She had looked into the eyes of the woman she thought had given her life and she had seen nothing. No recognition whatsoever. No connection ran from one woman to the other. *Nothing.* But she was home, in the arms of the man she loved, while their daughter slept in the room next to theirs. Her life was her own. While Ethan held her, Hannah let go, too. Even if the rest of the world couldn't, it no longer mattered. She let go of that night so long ago.

ACKNOWLEDGMENTS

My thanks to fabulous agent Susan Raihofer of the David Black Literary Agency for saying, "You can do it"; to Kensington Publishing's editor extraordinaire, Michaela Hamilton ("You did it"); and to my wife, Claudia, and our daughters, Morgan and Marta. Thanks for all the sage advice, savvy comments, and kindly nagging. My gratitude also to Kathrine Beck, Tina Marie Brewer, Susan Higgins, Julie O'Donnell, and Phyllis Hatfield, for their much-appreciated support along the way.

Don't miss Gregg Olsen's gripping thriller

THE GIRL IN THE WOODS

Available from Kensington Publishing.

Keep reading to enjoy a sample excerpt . . .

CHAPTER ONE

Birdy Waterman went toward the ringing bell and an annoyingly insistent rat-tat-tat knock on the glass storm door of her home in Port Orchard, Washington. Her cell phone was pressed to her ear and her fingertips fumbled in her pocket for her car keys. She retrieved a tube of lip balm—with the lid off and the product making a mess of her pocket.

Great! Where are those keys?

"Hang on," she said into the phone, grabbing a tissue and wiping off her hand. "Everything happens at once. Someone's here. I'll be there in fifteen minutes."

She swung the door open. On her doorstep was a soaking wet teenaged boy.

"Make that twenty," she said, pulling the phone away from her ear.

It was her sister's son, Elan.

"Elan, what are you doing here?"

"Can I come in?" he asked.

"Hang on," she said back into the phone.

"Wait, did I get the date wrong?" she asked him.

The kid shook his head.

Birdy looked past Elan to see if he was alone. He was only sixteen. They had made plans for him to come over during spring break. He hadn't been getting along with his parents and Birdy offered to have him stay with her. She'd circled the date on the calendar on her desk at the Kitsap County coroner's office and on the one that hung in the kitchen next to the refrigerator. It couldn't have slipped her mind. She even made plans for activities that the two of them could do—most of which were in Seattle, a place the boy revered because it was the Northwest's largest city. To a teenager from the Makah Reservation, it held a lot of cachet.

"Where's your mom?" Birdy asked, looking past him, still clinging to her cell phone.

The boy, who looked so much like his mother—Birdy's sister, Summer—shook his head. "She's not here. And I don't care where she is."

"How'd you get here?"

"I caught a ride and I walked from the foot ferry. I hitched, but no one would pick me up."

"You shouldn't do that," Birdy said. "Not safe." She motioned him inside. She didn't tell him to take off his shoes, wet and muddy as they were. He was such a sight she nearly forgot that she had the phone in her hand. Elan, gangly, but now not so much, was almost a man. He had medium length dark hair, straight and coarse enough to mimic the tail of a mare. On his chin were the faintest of whiskers. He was trying to grow up.

She turned away from the teen and spoke back into her phone.

"I have an unexpected visitor," Birdy said. She paused and listened. "Everything is fine. I'll see you at the scene as soon as I can get there."

Elan removed his damp dark gray hoody and stood frozen in the small foyer. They looked at each other the way strangers sometimes do. Indeed they nearly were. Elan's mother had all but cut Birdy out of her life over the past few years. There were old reasons for it, and there seemed to be very little to be done about it. The sisters had been close and they'd grown apart. Birdy figured there would be reconciliation someday. Indeed, she hoped that her entertaining Elan for spring break would be the start of something good between her and Summer. Her heart was always heavy when she and her sister stopped speaking.

As the Kitsap County forensic pathologist, Dr. Birdy Waterman had seen what real family discord could do. She was grateful that hers was more of a war of words than weapons.

"You are going to catch a cold," she said. "And I have to leave right this minute."

Elan's hooded eyes sparkled. "If I caught a cold would you split me open and look at my guts?" he asked.

She half smiled at him and feigned exasperation. "If I had to, yes." She'd only seen him a half dozen times in the past three years at her sister's place on the reservation. He was a smart aleck then. And he still was. She liked him.

"I'll be gone awhile. You are going to get out of all of your wet clothes and put them in the dryer."

He looked at her with a blank stare. "What am I supposed to wear?" he asked. "You don't want a naked man running around, do you?"

She ignored his somewhat petulant sarcasm.

Man? That was a stretch.

She noticed Elan's muddy shoes, and the mess they were making of her buffed hardwood floors, but said nothing about that. Instead, she led him to her bedroom.

"Uninvited guests," she said, then pretended to edit herself. "*Surprise* guests get a surprise." She pulled a lilac terry robe from a wooden peg behind her bedroom door.

"This will have to do," she said, offering the garment.

Elan made an irritated face but accepted the robe. He obviously hated the idea of wearing his aunt's bathrobe—probably *any* woman's bathrobe. At least it didn't have a row of pink roses around the neckline like his mother's. Besides, no one, he was pretty sure, would see him holed up in his aunt's place.

"Aunt Birdy, are you going to a crime scene?" he asked. "I want to go."

"I am," she said, continuing to push the robe at him until he had no choice but to accept it. "But you're not coming. Stay here and chill. I'll be back soon enough. And when I get back you'll tell me why you're here so early. By the way, does your mom know you're here?"

He kept his eyes on the robe. "No. She doesn't. And I don't want her to."

That wasn't going to happen. The last thing she needed was another reason for her sister to be miffed at her.

"Your dad?" she asked.

Elan looked up and caught his aunt's direct gaze. His dark brown eyes flashed. "I hate him even more."

Birdy rolled her eyes upward. "That's perfect," she said. "We can sort out your drama when I get back."

"I'm—"

She put her hand up and cut him off. "Hungry? Frozen pizza is the best I've got. Didn't have time to bake you a cake."

She found her keys from the dish set atop a birdseye maple console by the door and went outside. It had just stopped raining. But in late March in the Pacific Northwest, a cease-fire on precipitation only meant the clouds were taking a coffee break. Jinx, the neighbor's cat, ran over the wet pavement for a scratch under her chin, but Birdy wasn't offering one right then. The cat, a tabby with a stomach that dragged on the lawn, skulked away. Birdy was in a hurry.

She dressed for the weather, which meant layers— dark dyed blue jeans, a sunflower yellow cotton sweater, a North Face black jacket. If it got halfway warm, she'd discard the North Face. That almost always made her too hot. She carried her purse, a raincoat, and a small black bag. Not a doctor's bag, really. But a bag that held a few of the tools of her trade—latex gloves, a flashlight, a voice recorder, evidence tags, a rule, and a camera. She wouldn't necessarily need any of that where she was going, but Dr. Waterman lived by the tried and oh-so-true adage: *Better safe than sorry.*

As she unlocked her car, a Seattle-bound ferry plowed the slate waters of Rich Passage on the other side of Beach Drive. A small assemblage of seagulls wrestled over a soggy, and very dead, opossum on the roadside.

Elan had arrived early. Not good.

Birdy pulled out of the driveway and turned on the jazz CD that had been on continuous rotation. The music

always calmed her. She was sure that Elan would consider it completely boring and hopelessly uncool, but she
probably wouldn't like his music either. She needed a little calming influence just then. Nothing was ever easy in
her family. Her nephew had basically run away—at least
as far as she could tell. Summer was going to blame her
for this, somehow. She always did. As Birdy drove up
Mile Hill Road and then the long stretch of Banner Road,
she wondered why the best intentions of the past were always a source of hurt in the present.

And yet the worst of it all was not her family, her
nephew, or her sister. The worst of it was what the dispatcher from the coroner's office had told her moments
just before Elan arrived.

A dismembered human foot had been found in Banner
Forest.

CHAPTER TWO

Tracy Montgomery had smelled the odor first. The twelve-year-old and the other members of Suzanne Hatfield's sixth grade Olalla Elementary School class had made their way through the twists and turns of a trail understandably called Tunnel Vision toward the sodden intersection of Croaking Frog, when she first got a whiff. It was so rank it made her pinch her nose like she did when jumping in the pool at the Y in nearby Gig Harbor.

"Ewww, stinks here," the girl said in a manner that indicated more of an announcement than a mere observation.

Tracy was a know-it-all who wore purple Ugg boots that were destined to be ruined by the muddy late March nature walk in Banner Forest, a Kitsap County park of 630-plus acres. She'd been warned that the boots were not appropriate for the sure-to-be-soggy trek inside the one-square-mile woods that was dank and drippy even on a sunny spring day. There was no doubt that Tracy's mother was going to survey the damage of those annoyingly bright boots and phone a complaint into the principal's office.

"That's why they call it skunk cabbage," said Ms. Hatfield, a veteran teacher who had seen the interest in anything that had to do with nature decline with increasing velocity in the last decade of her thirty-year teaching career. She could hardly wait until retirement, a mere forty-four school days away. Kids today were all but certain that lettuce grew in a cellophane bag and chickens were hatched shaped like nuggets.

Suzanne brightened a little as a thought came to mind. Her mental calculations hadn't been updated to take into account *this* day.

Technically, she only had forty-three days left on the job.

A squirrel darted across the shrouded entrance to Croaking Frog, turned left, then right, before zipping up a mostly dead Douglas fir.

"My dad shoots those in our yard," Davy Saunders said. The schoolboy's disclosure didn't surprise anyone. Davy's dad went to jail for confronting an intruder—a driver from the Mattress Ranch store in Gorst—with a loaded weapon. The driver's crime? The young man used the Saunders driveway to make a three-point turn.

"Want to hear something really gross?"

This time the voice belonged to Cameron Lee. He was packed into the middle of the mass of kids and two beleaguered moms clogging the trail. "My cousin sent me a video that showed some old guy cutting up a squirrel and cooking it. You know, like for food."

Ms. Hatfield considered using Cameron's comment as a learning moment about how some people forage for survival, but honestly, she was simply tired of competing with reality TV, the Internet, and the constant prattling of the digital generation. They knew less and less it seemed because they simply didn't have to really *know* anything.

Everything was always at their fingertips.

Ms. Hatfield knew the Latin name for the skunk cabbage that had so irritated Tracy's olfactory senses—*Lysichiton americanus*—but she didn't bother mentioning it to her students. Instead, she sighed and spouted off a few mundane facts about the enormous-leafed plant with bright yellow spires protruding from the muddy soil like lanterns in a dark night.

"It smells bad for a reason," she said. "Anyone know why?"

She looked around. Apparently, no one *did*. She glanced in the direction of Viola Mertz, but even *she* didn't offer up a reason. The teacher could scarcely recall a moment in the classroom when Viola didn't raise her hand.

If she'd lost Viola, there was no hope.

Ms. Hatfield gamely continued. "It smells bad to attract—"

"Smells like Ryan and he can't attract anyone," Cooper Wilson said, picking on scrawny Ryan Jonas whenever he could.

Ms. Hatfield ignored the remark. Cooper was a thug and she hoped that when puberty tapped Ryan on the shoulders, he'd bulk up and beat the crap out of his tormentor. But that would be later, long after she was gone from the classroom.

". . . to attract pollinators," she went on, wondering if

she should skip counting days left on the job and switch
to hours. "Bugs, bees, flies, whatever."

"I'm bored," Carrie Bowden said.

Ms. Hatfield wanted to say that she was bored too, but
of course she didn't. She looked over at one of the two
moms who'd come along on the nature hike—Carrie's
mom, a willowy brunette named Angie, had corked ear
buds into her ears for the bus ride from the school and hadn't
taken them out since. Cooper Wilson's mom, Mariah, must
have too. She flipped through her phone's email, cursing
the bad reception she was getting.

"It might smell bad," Ms. Hatfield said, trying to carry
on with her last field trip ever. "But believe it or not this
plant actually tastes good to bears. They love it like you
love a Subway sandwich."

Only Cooper Wilson brightened a little. He loved Subway.

"Indigenous people ate the plant's roots too," the teacher
went on. She flashed back to when she first started teaching
and how she'd first used the word *Indians*, then *Native
Americans*, then, and now, *indigenous people*.

Lots of changes in three decades.

"Skunk cabbage might smell bad," she said, "but it
had very important uses for our Chinook people. They
used the leaves to wrap around salmon when roasting it
on the hot coals of an alder wood fire."

"I went to a luau in Hawaii and they did that with a
pig," Carrie piped up, not so much because she wanted to
add to the conversation, but because she liked to remind
the others in the class that she'd been to Hawaii over
Christmas break. She brought it up at least once a week
since her sunburned and lei-wearing return in January.
"They wrapped it up in big green leaves before putting it

into the ground on some coals," she said. "That's what they did in Hawaii."

"Ms. Hatfield," Tracy said, her voice rising above the din of not-so-nature lovers. "I need to show you something."

Tracy always had something to say. And Ms. Hatfield knew it was always super important. Everything with Tracy was super important.

"Just a minute," the teacher said, a little too sharply. She tried to diffuse her obvious irritation with a quick smile. "Kids, about what Cameron said a moment ago," she continued. "I want you to know that a squirrel is probably a decent source of protein. When game was scarce, many pioneers survived on small rodents and birds."

"Ms. Hatfield! I'm seriously going to puke," Tracy called out. Her voice now had enough urgency to cut through the buzzing and complaining of the two dozen other kids on the field trip.

Tracy knew how to command attention. Her purple Uggs were proof of that.

Ms. Hatfield pushed past the others. Her weathered but delicate hands reached over to Tracy.

"Are you all right?" she asked.

The girl with big brown eyes that set the standard for just how much eye makeup a sixth grader could wear kept her steely gaze focused away from her teacher. She faced the trail, eyes cast downward.

Tracy could be a crier and Ms. Hatfield knew she had to neutralize the situation—whatever it was. And fast.

"Honey, I'm sorry if the squirrel story upset you."

The girl shook her head. "That wasn't it, Ms. Hatfield."

The teacher felt relief wash over her. *Good*. It wasn't something she *said*.

"What is it?"

Tracy looked up with wide, frightened, almost Manga eyes.

"Are you sick?" the teacher asked.

Tracy didn't say a word. She looked back down and with the tip of her purple boot lifted the feathery stalk of a sword fern.

At first, Ms. Hatfield wasn't sure what she was seeing. The combination of a stench—far worse than anything emitted by skunk cabbage—and the sight of a wriggling mass of maggots assaulted her senses.

Instinctively, she swept her arm toward Tracy to hold her back, as if the girl was lunging toward the disgusting sight, which she most certainly was not. It was like a mother reaching across a child's chest when she hit the brakes too hard and doubted the ability of the safety belt to protect her precious cargo.

All hell broke loose. Carrie started to scream and her voice was joined by a cacophony. It was a domino that included every kid in the group. Even bully Cooper screamed out in disgust and horror. Angie Bowden yanked out her ear buds like she was pulling the ripcord on a parachute.

No one had ever seen anything as awful as that.

Later, the kids in Ms. Hatfield's class would tell their friends that it was the best field trip ever.

CHAPTER THREE

Birdy Waterman parked her red Prius on Olalla Valley Road behind a row of marked and unmarked Kitsap County sheriff's vehicles. She pulled on her badly wrinkled raincoat, also red, from the passenger seat and called over to Deputy Gary Wilkins, who stood next to the main trailhead. At twenty-six, he was a young deputy and this kind of thing, a *dead* thing, was still new to him. He was a block of a man, with square shoulders and muscular thighs. He nodded in her direction and his gray eyes flashed recognition and anxiety at the same time.

"Your turn?" he asked, already knowing the answer.

Birdy shut the car door. It was *her* turn. The county had a PR nightmare on its hands the previous year when a coroner's assistant screwed up a homicide case. In an embarrassing and ultimately futile attempt to save himself, he put the blame on the sheriff's detectives and their evidence-gathering process. It was a colossal error that hadn't yet healed over when the coroner and the sheriff decided a "working together" rotation was the solution to all of their problems.

People in both offices could still recall the subject line of the email:

There's no "I" in "Team."

It was an eye-roller of the greatest magnitude.

Because of that memo, and the weeks of touchy-feely training that ensued, Birdy was standing in the muddy parking strip while the nephew she barely knew was probably burning down her house, making that sad frozen pizza she'd offered as his best bet for a hot meal. She almost never visited crime scenes, but she was in the rotation when Ms. Hatfield called 911.

"How's the family?" Birdy asked Gary, slipping on her coat as a seam in the sky tore just enough to send down another trickle of Pacific Northwest springtime weather. She picked her way across the little ridge that separated the forest entrance from Banner Road, a nine-mile thrill ride of a two-lane blacktop that hopped up and over the hills of the southernmost edge of the county. She wore street shoes instead of boots, because distracted by her nephew's sudden appearance on her doorstep, she hadn't considered she'd be traipsing through the woods until she was halfway there.

Banner Forest. Stupid me, she thought.

"Good. I mean, not really," Gary said. "Abby got a stubborn cold, which means I'm next," he went on, referring to his two-year-old. Birdy liked Gary and right then she especially liked that he didn't ask for advice on how to help his daughter get over her cold. She was a doctor, of course. She'd had the same training as an MD, but her patients had little need for calm bedside manner.

They were always dead.

"What happened here?" she asked.

"No one has really said anything to me. Other than, you know, the kids apparently found a dead body down the trail. They were pretty freaked out."

"I imagine they would be," Birdy said. She indicated the row of sheriff department cars.

"Kendall here?"

Gary tipped his head toward the dark, tree-shrouded funnel-like opening of the trail that led deep into Banner Forest.

"Yup," he said. "They're all down there by—and you'll love this—Croaking Frog."

Birdy arched a brow and looked down the pathway.

"What's that?" she asked.

"The name of the trail," he said. Gary had found something amusing in the worst of circumstances. He'd make a very good deputy.

"Croaking Frog?" she repeated, though she was pretty sure she heard him correctly.

"Welcome to South Kitsap County," he said. "You'll find Kendall and the others about a hundred yards down that way."

Birdy followed his fingertip toward the rutted trail into the woods.

Kendall Stark was a homicide detective Birdy liked working with more than the investigators in her unit in the sheriff's office. That wasn't to say that Birdy thought others in the Kitsap County Sheriff's Department were any less competent at what they did. They were skilled investigators, no doubt about that. It wasn't because Kendall was the only woman either. If that had been the reason, Birdy would never say so anyway. Saying so would surely invite more sensitivity training.

And yet, if she'd been completely honest with herself, the forensic pathologist did believe that Detective Stark had an ability to empathize with a victim's family to a greater degree than some of her male counterparts. It wasn't solely her gender—there were plenty of women in law enforcement who were so cerebral, so clinical, that emotions were sealed behind a fortress of their own making. Birdy had trained with several at the University of Washington who were all about CSI and crisp white lab coats and heels that thundered when they walked down corridors—an obnoxious drumbeat announcing their impending arrival.

Kendall was different from those women, Birdy thought, because she was a mother. And a good one. In Birdy's world, a good mother—and God knew she learned that little fact the hard way—had the ability to understand the loss and suffering of others and the hurt that becomes a festering wound. Those were the cases in which a child was murdered, the darkest, saddest, of any that came across either woman's desk. The obvious truth about any homicide was that no matter the victim's age, he or she had a mother.

Kendall was where she needed to be—at the scene or with witnesses. Birdy needed to be in the lab.

Or at home with her nephew.

Cross training, she thought, *was so irritating.*

She glanced at a trail map on a sheltered kiosk behind Gary, but it looked like a crudely executed rendering of a sack full of snakes. The forest was crisscrossed by a series of hiking and horseback-riding trails that had lately been taken over by dirt bikers. Several trails—including Tunnel Vision—featured earthen ramps that sent bikers soaring into the air. When the forest was saved from development, the vision of the committee that had fought for it had been to see it used as a nature preserve, a hiking and horseback-riding trail.

Not a speedway for dirt bikes.

From what Birdy had learned from the Comm Center's call and from the sketchy remarks of the young deputy, it appeared as though something had happened to one of the kids on a class field trip. And since she was called in for the major case rotation, she made the assumption that a child had been killed. Birdy knew that cougars had been spotted in Banner Forest, as well as the notorious case in which a black bear mauled a man when his dogs frightened the mother bear's cubs.

There were two lessons there. Never let a dog off its leash. And never, ever anger a mother bear.

Birdy followed the muddy trail to the intersection of Tunnel Vision and Croaking Frog. The ground was damp from the rain, but so compacted by the dirt bikes that it wasn't as gooey as it might have been. Tire treads laced the pathway.

Maybe that's what happened? A kid got hit by a biker? A terrible accident?

As Birdy passed a NO HUNTING sign nailed to an old growth cedar stump, another possibility ran through her head.

Maybe someone accidentally shot a child? Thought a small figure in the woods was a deer? Deer were thick in that part of the county. Even with NO HUNTING signs posted all over the place, there were plenty of rule breakers—

especially midweek when fewer people frequented the woods.

As she drew closer to Croaking Frog, she recognized the voices of the techs and Detective Stark.

Kendall looked up. Her short blond hair had grown out some and softened the angular features of her face. The spikiness was gone and the look flattered her. Even her deep blue eyes benefited from the change. "I wondered if it was your turn to be a team player," she said.

Birdy glanced past the detective.

A tech was hunched among the sword ferns.

"There's no *I* in *Team*," Birdy said, recalling the obnoxious training they'd all been forced to attend to ensure that mistakes would never happen again.

"You make an Ass out of U and Me when you assume something," Kendall said with a sigh. "Thank goodness the ass that got us all into this mess got fired."

Birdy was grateful for that too. "No kidding," she said. "What have we got here?"

"Not much," she said.

"No visible sign of cause?" she asked.

It wasn't Kendall's job to determine what happened to any victim, of course. But that didn't stop most detectives in most jurisdictions all over the country from announcing what they were "pretty sure" had occurred.

Kendall shook her head. "No, not that. What I mean is not much of anything." She pointed downward. "All we've got is a foot."

Birdy wedged herself into the mossy space next to a human foot painted with a writhing mass of maggots.

"I'm not eating dinner tonight," Kendall said.

Birdy had seen worse. There were far more hideous images etched onto the tissue of her brain than a mass of maggots on a dismembered foot. If she'd been asked to make a top five list of the worst things she'd ever seen, it would include the case in which a Silverdale mother held a toddler's face against the red hot coils of an electric stove, killing her. That haunted her every now and then. Also, a case in which a Bremerton woman poured battery acid over her sleeping husband and seared out his eyes. He survived for four agonizing months in a Seattle burn unit before mercifully succumbing to his devastating injuries.

But that wasn't the worst of them all.

The most revolting case of all was that of a Port Gamble man who killed his wife and literally put strips of her flesh to dry on a clothesline behind one of the historic homes in the darkly charming town at the very northern edge of the county she served as the forensic pathologist. He sold her remains as jerky at a store in nearby Kingston.

A maggot-infested foot? Piece of cake.

"I can't exactly say this is doing much for my appetite," Birdy said, though it really didn't bother her that much. Decay was a part of the cycle. It had its purpose. She saw the sense in how all things return to the earth. She knew, for example, that the trees all around them had been fed by the decomposed flesh of animals and human beings.

She moved closer. Lighting was intermittent. Saucers of illumination spotted the space from breaks in the canopy of cedars that rocketed skyward. She did a quick assessment, while the investigative team pulled back.

The foot was human.

Small.

And although it was hard to say for sure, it appeared that some of the toenails had been painted a lively shade of pink.

Birdy looked up at Sarah Dorman, one of the crime scene techs who still held anger over the blunder that not only bruised the entire department, but, more crucially, let a killer go free.

"I'm doing my job, Dr. Waterman."

"I know that, Sarah."

Sarah, with her long red hair and pale complexion, could never really hide her feelings. She looked back at the foot and scowled.

"I don't make mistakes," she said.

"Of course not. I'm not here to try to catch you making a mistake, Sarah. I'm here for the training protocol." Birdy took a short breath. She knew Sarah wasn't mad at her, but she'd been the first on the scene and no doubt had to put up with some boneheaded comment about the collection of evidence and who was responsible for what.

"Now, will you brief me on what's been done? And really, Sarah, can you at least fake a smile? Our work is hard enough."

The other deputies stepped back to give them some space—and more than likely to escape the stench. Birdy crouched closer. The wind blew and shifted the canopy. The foot under the fern glistened in the light.

"Upon my arrival deputies had already secured the scene," Sarah said. "Because of the wet trail and the likelihood that we'd lose any potential trace—probably lost any when the kids were here anyway—we've already photographed and searched the immediate area."

"How immediate?" Birdy asked.

Sarah kept her grim face. "Twenty-five yards."

"That's a big area," Birdy said with a tone that was more approving than questioning.

Sarah lightened a little. "Right, but we wanted to go wide because of the weather and the, well, you know, the possibility that there might be other body parts nearby."

"Good work. Find anything?" Birdy asked.

"Not really anything we think is connected to this. But we did pick up a Doublemint gum wrapper, a used condom, and a couple of beer cans."

"Somebody used this place for a make-out spot," Birdy said.

Sarah shrugged a little knowingly. "Yeah. I mean, I grew up here and well, yeah. Kids, probably."

Birdy scanned the trampled scene. "Any footprints collected?"

"Yes, a few," Sarah said. "But to be honest, things were pretty trashed by the time we got here. Lots of kids running around screaming and stuff. The teacher did her best to keep everyone away, but I have a feeling that a bunch of them got a good look at the foot."

Birdy understood. "I know I would have."

Sarah smiled for the first time. It was a genuine smile and not one offered up to soothe the feelings of those angry about the training session.

"Good work, Sarah," Birdy said.

Kendall, who'd been talking to another deputy, joined Birdy. When Birdy stooped down low, the detective followed her lead. Without saying a word, Birdy put on a pair of gloves. The two women held their breath and the forensic pathologist lifted a frond of the fern that had partially covered the ankle. It was too dark to see, so she crouched lower and took a small Maglite from her bag. She turned on the flashlight and sent a beam over the maggots. In response, the mass writhed like the crowd doing the "wave" at a Seahawks game.

"Can you tell how long the foot's been here?" Kendall asked.

Birdy leaned in—almost close enough to touch it—though she never would have done that.

"Hard to say if it is third or second molt," she said. "We'll have to look at them back at the lab. Since we're all hovering here, I'm presuming this is all you have for me."

"Search under way," Kendall said.

"Who found the foot?" Birdy asked.

"A girl named Tracy Montgomery. She's a sixth grader in Suzanne Hatfield's class at Olalla."

"Nature walk day," Birdy said, looking upward as the sun cracked through the sky, once more revealing the blue that reminded her of her father's faded chambray shirts, his practical uniform for the outdoor work he did in the summers. Birdy grew up on the Makah Reservation at the very tip of Western Washington. Nature was always around her family. The woods were a second home.

She turned to Kendall. "Did you talk to her?"

"Yes," Kendall said. "She says she didn't get near it. Didn't touch it. Her teacher confirmed her story."

"All right then," Birdy said. She looked over at the tech. "Sarah, when you collect the evidence I want the top six inches of soil. That sword fern too."

"What kind of square footage are we talking about?" Sarah said, knowing full well that the word *footage* was probably on the edge of inappropriate. She hadn't meant it; it just came out that way.

"Four feet all around," Birdy said, this time with a smile back at Sarah.

Sarah scrunched her brow and went to work with another tech. They finished taking photographs, carefully bagged the foot, and started on the soil samples. Each scoop of black loamy dirt was tagged with coordinates inside a four-foot grid that had been staked around the decomposing body part.

Birdy walked along the trail, scouring it for any sign of who might have left the foot—or the body that had been severed from it.

Kendall called over to her. "You think a bear mauled someone?"

A piece of pale pink fabric caught Birdy's eye and she motioned to Sarah to collect it.

"Don't know," she said.

"We had that mauling a few years ago," Kendall said.

"Right. Read about that." Birdy set a yellow collection marker by the fabric, a shred of nylon, probably an undergarment. "I don't think so," she went on. "I think an animal would have dragged that foot to its den or, even more likely, consumed it on the spot."

"If there were any footprints—animal or human— they've been obliterated by the rain and Ms. Hatfield's class," Kendall said.

Satisfied there was no role for her right then—and she'd followed the orders to be there—Birdy started down the trail toward her car. "Let me know how the search goes," she said. "I'm heading back now. I have unexpected company and a foot to examine."

"You seem less excited by your company than by the maggot-infested foot," Kendall said. "Who is it?"

Birdy turned around and looked at her friend. It was one of those looks that said far more than words. "My sister's son."

Kendall blinked back with surprise. "Your sister's?

That's interesting. You almost never mention her. In fact, I didn't really even know you had a sister for the first year you were here."

"Don't get me started." Birdy sighed. "You don't have enough time to hear my family story."

"Try me sometime," Kendall said.

Birdy unbuttoned her raincoat and walked toward the light coming from the roadway. She knew the detective meant it. Kendall was a real friend, but Birdy's family baggage was of such serious tonnage that she barely could carry it, let alone see a need to drop it on the shoulders of someone she admired.

Connect with Us

Visit us online at
KensingtonBooks.com
to read more from your favorite authors, see books
by series, view reading group guides, and more.

Join us on social media

for sneak peeks, chances to win books and prize packs,
and to share your thoughts with other readers.

**facebook.com/kensingtonpublishing
twitter.com/kensingtonbooks**

Tell us what you think!

To share your thoughts, submit a review,
or sign up for our eNewsletters, please visit:
KensingtonBooks.com/TellUs.